A
BURIAL FOR
FLOWERS

A BURIAL FOR FLOWERS

Pan Pan Fan

Pan Pan Fan was born in Beijing, China and moved to the United States at the age of four, where she currently lives. *A Burial for Flowers* is her first novel.

First Edition

ISBN-10: 0692704868
ISBN-13: 978-0-69-270486-8

To the Ding Family Women,
whose bravery lives
through generations

"The present is the only thing that has no end." – Erwin Schroedinger

Contents

Part IV

Part V

Acknowledgments

Part I

CHAPTER 1

The Story of the Monk and the Prophecy from the Land of Illusion

Somewhere far off in the land of Illusion, which had also been known by the little, lost village set against Wu Dang Mountain as the land of Memory, there was a monk who was traveling by foot to seek the advice of a rumored fairy, Nostalgia.

The monk, whose hometown was deep in the high mountains of the distant west, had wandered very far. On the third month of his journey, the monk's canteens ran dry of water, which had until then been plentiful from the snow melts and streams. His throat drying and cracking with thirst, the monk sat beneath a juniper tree and looked out at the mountains he had just traversed with their white peaks blurring along the horizon. He closed his eyes and let the beads of sweat roll down his forehead and wrinkled neck. The monk, a small man with sandals made of deer skin, breathed in the juniper berries and longed for a wind to cool him down. Suddenly, the monk thought he heard water, a light *drip drip drip* sound that played with his dry thirst. Thinking it was his mind deceiving him, he kept his eyes closed and breathed slowly, in and out, out and in, *drip drip drip*. The sound of the water changed from ringing bells to a harp running over rocks, slowly and then quickly, crescendoing and echoing off the surrounding mountains. The monk opened his eyes.

He gasped – out in front of him, out of thin air, was a large river, and where the vast valley of ground-hugging shrubbery had lain, a lush forest canopy shaded him from above. "I must be imagining this," the monk said to himself in disbelief.

Suddenly, a voice answered him, "You've discovered the land of Illusion, my dear friend. You are tired from your travels. Please, come forward."

The monk slowly rose, putting one hand against the juniper tree and advanced one step after another toward the river, his sandals damp from the now-wet ground. Suddenly, the water began to flow quickly, and the river levels overflowed the riverbank and onto the rocks and rising still, met the forest floor. The monk, terrified, put his hands over his face for fear of the flooding water, but to his surprise, the water immediately silenced. When he opened his eyes again, a figure, neither man nor woman, but the most terrifying and beautiful figure he had ever seen, emerged from the swiftly rising water.

"If what you're searching is in this land, then I'm afraid I cannot help you, but if what you search for is in the land of Memory, and therefore Story, since Story is Memory, and both inhabit the land of mankind, then I believe you have a few things to ask me," the fairy said. The image began to brighten. His eyes burning from the light, the monk forced himself to crouch and lifted a hand to shield his eyes as he hoped to catch a silhouette.

The monk hesitated. Finally, after weeks heaped upon weeks of travel, and after reaching the land of Illusion, he had forgotten all his questions. Panicked, he spoke his uncontrolled thought aloud: "Is this real or is this a dream?"

The fairy Nostalgia was silent for such a period that the monk feared he had asked the wrong thing. Then, the fairy replied, "Humankind understands so little about the nature of time. Can you not have many memories which lay upon each other running along the same stream of

14

the present? Can the water not flow from east to west and yet be in both places at once?"[1]

Confused, the monk pondered the fairy's words and then regaining his senses replied, "But fairy Nostalgia, the rock moves because I have pushed it, and the stream that flows from the east to the west is not the same stream just a moment ago."

This time, the fairy tossed its head and laughed, "Your mind is challenged by the reality you do not expect." Seeing the monk put his head down in shame for his reply, the fairy softened and said, "Tell me my dear visitor, how does love move? Does it move from north to south, and does it need the passing of time to exist, the change in time, or is it something that remains there beyond those things which move north to south and within the bounds of passing time?"

The monk thought very hard at this and then replied slowly, "No, Love -- Divine Love – moves as the still point while all things that surround it move and spin. Love does not move north to south, nor does it live in time. Tell me, can mankind know Divine Love?"

At this the fairy smiled sadly. "The mind moves while the body is still; the body moves as the mind is still; and all those things can be moving or be still relative to the other. There is an old story. It is a story told about two souls, who before they came to human form, one lived as an enchanted bird and the other, a beautiful flower from the mountainside. Every single day, the bird visited the flower and watered it with the dew from the mountain leaves so it could live, as the bird loved the flower. Slowly, the flower began to grow, and having been fed with a magical water, the flower began to grow into the form of a maiden, shedding its past form. Soon after the transformation, the maiden found that the bird was getting older and weaker, and one winter's day, the bird stopped visiting the maiden and bringing her dew from the mountain leaves.

---

[1] Parmenides, "On Nature"

Lonely and grateful for the bird, the maiden vowed to repay the bird in another lifetime. Day after day passed, and the sad maiden, devastated by her loss, asked the fates to allow them both to be born into the human world so that she could repay her debt with a lifetime of tears. The next morning, a young woman woke up with a dream about being a flower watered with the fresh dew born of the mountain leaves. As the dream fairies escape soon after humans wake, the young woman soon forgot everything about her dream. As she got out of bed, something sharp pierced her heart, and thus began the repayment of her debt."
2

The monk, his face still shielded by his hand replied to the fairy's story, tears in his eyes, "So Divine Love is a tragedy in human form."

The fairy comforted him, "Oh, my friend, you have already forgotten. The stream does not run east to west, and as the world turns, seek the still point, the axis. Move beyond the sad time which runs your mind. Divine Love is no tragedy in human form. It is the unmoving substance between the moving body and the moving mind." With this, the fairy turned, and the waters began to rise again, soon licking the forest floors violently until the monk was forced to retreat back into the woods for fear of drowning. The sound of the water beating against the rocks and spilling far into the trees frightened him, and suddenly while retreating, his foot caught on the tangled root of a juniper bush. With a small scream, he tumbled onto the ground and his eyes saw nothing but a seeping darkness around him, which stung his eyes and nose, and wiping the sweat from his brow, the monk slowly awoke. Finally opening his eyes, the monk saw that he was still sitting against the juniper tree with the smells of the berries stinging his nose. Before him, he saw nothing but the rocks and shrubs he had stumbled into in the heat and dryness. Rubbing his sore neck, he said, "I have had quite the dream." Suddenly, a small red flower fell onto his sandal from the cuff of his robe, a stowaway from the mountains he just crossed, and looking down, the monk saw that the sleeves of his robes were damp with wetness just as he realized he was no longer thirsty—

___

2 Cao Xue Qin, *The Story of the Stone*

* * * * *

"—So was the monk dreaming or did it all happen, and he walked into the land of Illusion?" the older man asked, interrupting and leaning in toward the younger man, kneading the sore webs between his fingers in anticipation of continuing the story.

"In the legend, it's unclear, though I like to interpret that perhaps it's a bit of both," the younger responded.

"And what about the maiden? Was her debt repaid?" The older man felt unsatisfied with the narration.

"It was a gamble, Father Turner," the younger said for the first time that evening. "The end was fixed the entire time, but no one knew how to make the first move... There was little memory of winter. The rain took it away, spreading the smells of car exhaust and dirt from the gardens outside the museum. It was like that in April here. If you dare..."

Earlier that day, Peter had walked into Father Turner's residential room and had closed the door tightly behind him, shutting out the cold air and frost from the glow of a small fire burning from an electric fireplace whose wood made a *pshh pshhh* sound. He had shaken his feet and slowly removed his outer coat, an old greyish brown thing repatched a few times, and kept it hung neatly on his arm. The young man had taken off his dark and worn leather shoes. He had not removed his scarf. He stood standing in the room and shifted his toes against the rug; cold, but they were still there. It had been an unusually long winter, and still at the end of March, the cold bit into the air and laid frost on the ground. It had snowed that morning.

"Peter," Father Turner began after the two settled down into brown easy-chairs. "I've been waiting to hear from you ever since they told me you were coming back from your trip earlier today. Can I get you a glass of

17

water?" The old man's presence was far larger than his small, curled frame set beneath his thin mop of white hair.

"Father Turner...I'm so happy to see you," Peter said. His round face filled with freckles and light brown eyes, set contrast to his deep, soft voice, while his clothes clung loosely on the bones of his tall frame: he had lost weight during his trip. The room was barren, with white walls except a small bed in the opposite corner of the fireplace and one painting, a small Crucifixion of St. Peter, whose image was made larger by the empty walls surrounding it. "I'm sorry you were waiting. The flight was delayed. Please, no, don't get up. Don't worry, I'm...I'm all set."

Peter walked over to Father Turner who stood glowing against the electric fireplace and embraced him, his face barely reaching Peter's shoulders, which hunched forward. "Peter, it's good to have you back."

Peter moved to the chair beside Father Turner and shifted his toes again. He searched for the words to begin but found his mouth suddenly dry and regretting his refusal of the water, he swallowed. The room had been and was silent except for the light sound of the firewood hissing against the dry air. Father Turner slowly sank into his chair and put his arms against the armrests and gazed toward the fire. Peter's mind raced as he searched for a place to begin, and slowly as he looked from the priest to the fire and down again at his red scarf and to his toes, he felt as if the air was slowly leaving the room.

"Father," Peter tried to begin again. "I have seen a great deal."

Father Turner turned to the young man and smiled, creasing his eyes so the crinkles revealed that even in this short time, the man had aged. "Yes," was all he said. Then they were quiet again.

"Peter, have I told you that while you were gone, I've amassed tremendous skills in the game of chess from the other patients I've been visiting, and I think I'm ready to play you in a game soon." The words

18

escaped slowly from him, and the older man looked closely at the younger, and all the while, the air had returned to the room, and the white walls had shrunk, and the sound of the fire had returned to its warm glow.

"I have seen a great deal of terrible things," Peter began again. "I have seen things that I feel I cannot relive again, or if I do, your ears will be the last to hear them. I have seen...I have seen things that are beyond horror and beauty. The most beautiful...the most beauty in the world has been presented in me, and I struggle to begin. The impossibility..." His words trailed off. With a trembling hand, he slowly removed his scarf and placed it on the ground beside him with his coat.

"Remember that story telling, your own narrative as you choose to say it, has no necessary linearity, Peter, just begin where you think you feel your memory serves you best, and the rest will follow in time," Father Turner reminded Peter.

"Alright then," Peter replied, "I'll begin with this fantastic story, which will fit into the larger picture. Somewhere far off in the land of Illusion, which had also been known by the little village set against Wu Dang Mountain as the land of Memory, there was a monk who was traveling by foot to seek the advice of a rumored fairy, Nostalgia..."

CHAPTER 2

How Henry Smith Began to Play with a Gun.

"There was little memory of winter...," he continued after a pause. The silence grew, and the white walls faded, except for Peter's voice, "The rain took it away, spreading the smells of car exhaust and dirt from the gardens outside the museum. It was like that in April here. If you dare...if you dare, you can take a run along the rivers early in the morning when it's raining and let the rain soak you through while you watch the brown river breathe in the cold morning and tumble itself westward. Then you can come back to your apartment to espresso and sit at the window to watch the people and the traffic snake through Saturday along the farmers' markets and the bistros serving coffee with their long lines, and the little window shops that manage to survive year after year. You can sit there all day if you like, in the warm, next to a furnace in the kitchen, watching the rain and the people and the traffic. You may want to make another espresso. You could read the paper, or the Sunday Magazine, the stories of lives living themselves out in a glass globe that I was peering in. It was, it felt as if all the world ran each story before me, and I was presented with the most magnificent and the most horrific experiences laid upon one another like a stack of cards, and each hand was dealt out with a mysterious and uncontrolled probability, and suddenly all the players were engaged in the most chaotic, the most beautiful, dance..."

* * * * *

...April 25, 2020 present day. Henry Smith found himself lying half-dressed in bed. He had gotten up, managed to put on a light blue shirt for work, and then slinked straight back into bed. He was lying on his back, and he was thinking about it all again, his eyes rolled to the back of his head behind a curtain of closed eyelids. So he got up and took the revolver from the drawer of his bed stand, so now it only contained a crumpled up piece of paper scribbled with, *"What is identity but the canvas of all our experiences?"*[3] In one swift movement, Henry Smith put the gun straight into his mouth. He relaxed his gaze and closed his eyes.

Eight mornings of this. Day eight of waking up to the same thing – that same feeling of absolute dread and stickiness, of both overwhelming exhaustion and anxiety, of all the ceilings lowering into his face, and there was just nowhere to go. Nowhere at all. How did it get like this? Henry, a man with dark hair that framed itself around a strong, angular face that set deep inside his skull a pair of equally dark eyes, found himself waking up to a nightmare every single day: that old man's body that didn't disappear. Last night he had dreamt that as he turned this old man's body over -- and while the rain was dripping into his eyes, and he could still taste the scotch in his mouth -- suddenly that old man's eyes burst open, and they were his father's eyes! His father, with the same recognizable distance in his gaze, looking at him from fifteen years ago, looking at him and he was laughing and crying at Henry. Just like that. His life was over.

With the Company's Board meeting coming up and this whole nightmare, Henry couldn't stop thinking of those words, "Take control of your life. Just do this. Come on, don't be stupid for god's sake!" The rain was in his eyes, and what could he feel other than wet and the numb, hot buzzing of knowing he just did something awful, and everything from that moment on would be reshaped, redone? His fingers slid across the cold wall. Henry had his eyes closed, the revolver still in his mouth. Could he do it? Did he actually ever have the resolve? That was the

---

[3] Erwin Schroedinger, "What is Life?", Lectures at Trinity College, Dublin, 1943.

entire problem, wasn't it? That Henry had, for the eighth day in a row, stuck that revolver in his mouth and tasted it and remembered tasting it and then remembered remembering tasting it. He could feel how it was cold at first, but he had kept it in his mouth long enough without doing anything so that even the metal became warm and tasted like dried blood, which was really the taste of iron, before he took the revolver out again. He exhaled, then inhaled, sharply, involuntarily, and he felt the oxygen seep into his body again, trembling. No, he couldn't do it. But what resolve he would have if he did! "Take control over your life." Those words echoed down to him like a quiet scream down an empty passageway smelling of rain and scotch and old tobacco.

Perhaps Henry only thought about doing it because it gave him a chance to feel that he had an option. He'd thought about it for some time. He wondered whether he would have enough self-control to actually do it, or whether he'd be pushed beyond the self so much that he'd have no other option but to pull the trigger. Whichever was the case – control or absolute lack of it – everyone once in a while, Henry just wanted to play with a gun.

Henry looked outside his window, and the morning invaded uncomfortably through the pane and reflected off his barren, white room, forcing him to squint for the second time that morning. The frenzy of the silent five lanes of traffic greeted him on the 38th floor, and it was as magnificent as screaming in a soundproof glass box, which gave Henry the following thought: what if he were displayed like that, in his apartment? Like some kind of exhibit in a glass, soundproof box, and suddenly he shot himself, and no one could hear the gun shot but suddenly his body just exploded, and blood sprayed the entire room very unexpectedly to the observers outside. And it would all be silent, and he, all over the glass walls and on the glass floors and ceilings in his soundproof glass box – all five million little splattered, wet and soon-to-be rotting pieces of him stuck to glass – would be saved from the screams echoing outside his little box.

He finished getting dressed, quickly put the revolver back into its drawer, grabbed his jacket, and slammed closed the door behind him as he left.

It worked like this: It wasn't just him. It was his entire generation who were all born with a set of axes that oriented their little internal directions, and sometimes, a series of things happened that tilted their axes, where no one noticed it at all since these little things happened over so much time, like a slow corrosion until one morning, they all woke up as someone with a different axis, and they felt absolutely the same, like the day before and the day before that. An entire generation of people unknowingly afflicted with the same tilt-of-axis disease. On some occasions, changes happened suddenly, and their axis was jolted from its pivot, and they went a little berserk because they had no idea why they're walking sideways or upside-down, or why their lives suddenly changed the way they did. It was like walking forward and backward every day for thirty years, and then suddenly, waking up to find the only way to move was to scuttle from left to right.

For Henry, it may have just as well been that he woke up one morning as a crustacean and found himself scuttling right to left with a frenzy he couldn't control. But if anyone else had seen his life, a vision outside his axis, they would have realized that the entire world was changing, and that Henry was trying to stay still, trying to hold onto his axis, dragging his nails into the ground to fight it all from pulling him away. He was playing hide-and-seek with everything else, and they were out there, dragging him from his hiding spot…

* * * * *

…*Nine Nights Ago, April 16, 2020.* Henry was sitting wide-eyed with the veins bursting from his head in agony. He was nearly drooling from the mouth in the driver's seat of a cranberry Rapide S., a Company Aston Martin taken out for the special occasion: a funeral and an inheritance. Howard sat in the passenger's seat, regretting that he had allowed Henry to continue drinking past midnight and wondering when they'd start moving on the road again as it was late, the hunt was over, and they were going home empty handed and soaking wet.

The evening earlier had been suits and ties, black and white, and filled with enough laughter, pauses and champagne. Henry could have been a tight-rope walker with a nervous gait. Henry and Howard had both been at a large Company gathering in an old art museum in the south-west corner of the city, which overlooked one of the city's two large, brown rivers and a sea of floating lights.

"Henry, it's best if we moved forward on the offer. It's the right time." Duane, a broad-shouldered man with perfectly parted, perfectly white and thinning hair turned his large back to face Henry. He'd drained his Highland Park single malt, and rattled the ice cubes about in the glass. "I want to wait until after next Thursday." They spoke in soft voices. They spoke with their heads turned toward one another. They spoke, both cradling their drinks, Henry shifting his from one hand to the other watching the light dance on the edges of the lead crystal.

"That's not...possible..." Henry muttered. Was it possible? It probably was; so many things were.

"But I think that's what we should do. I don't want to hold it off any longer. It's been long enough, and if we don't put in the offer, another company will." The young man looked at the old man briefly and put his head back down as to listen closely again, leaning his ear in closer to the old man's wrinkles.

"I know David's early death was a shock to you, and you're still processing, you're so young to lose a father...it's been difficult...for all of us." He paused. He sipped his drink. He, too, leaned in closer.

"My mother and my sister are flying in for the proposed time of the ceremony. They've been waiting for me to have this happen now. They'll arrive on the Tuesday." From far away, they looked like old friends. Duane smiled, and he rubbed the rim of his glass with his index finger, took a sip, looked down at the glass, and looked up at Henry. The taste evaporated through his sinuses and out his nostrils when he spoke again. His eyes fluttered at the warmth in his balding head.

"Henry, I can promise you, if we don't move to complete the acquisition now, someone else will…"

Henry responded as Duane inhaled for the next word, "And we can wait for that."

"It's a huge mistake. I know your father trusted your judgment on this, but I've had a lot more experience with these…Look, Henry, David Smith had been one of the first people I met when I arrived in the city. Neither of us had much money, and we were both working mindless jobs pushing excel sheets and making other people richer while looking for ways to make it big ourselves. We were too educated and too proud, but coming from being poor put a chip on our shoulder that lit a fire under us. I know David. If he were still here, I know he wouldn't want a delay in this." Duane extended an arm and placed his hand on Henry's shoulder.

Henry took a stiff step back, paused and then replied with a sigh, "I'm thankful for your experience. But this isn't a good time. Now, I need to go, but if you have any questions on the details of the wake, you can call Sam."

Henry walked away from Duane, and as he did, he took more of his scotch, quickly, and let his right hand shake as he held the drink to his mouth. That bastard! It was unbelievable how he had been manipulated the past two weeks! His mother and his sister were coming, and each time Henry thought about it, he couldn't help but contort his face a bit, and his dark eyebrows convulsed, and he found himself gripping his glass with both hands, wildly agitated. He thought about how he had let this go on for two weeks without a proper ceremony, and now the two would

26

be arriving on Tuesday, expecting a ceremony for his dead father. His mother, while she never married David, would never have let this happen. Thinking of her Chinese-American pragmatism and sense of duty, Henry found himself hot in the face. It was shame, the kind that is one shade deeper than embarrassment because it is mixed in with a staining, bitter guilt that brooded and festered and violently clashed against an artificial sense of "I should have." Henry put a stop on the thoughts, the catapulting intuitive anger and instead walked straight over to Howard, a young man with strawberry hair whose round face and boyish features lured a stranger into thinking he was perfectly naive, with all his cards out on the table for viewing, while his eyes said something different: this man was playing the game two steps ahead.

Howard stood entertaining his musings, his freckles dancing around his face as it smiled, speaking to two women in white cocktail dresses serving drinks who, themselves, could have just turned into little bottles of wine right there. They were so pretty, which led Howard to the following thought: The tragedy of a pretty thing was that the moment the switch flips on in that complicated tunnel where thoughts traveled that the immediate reaction to the woman is that she is pretty – whether this reaction happens within a woman or a man doesn't matter – but the woman, upon first impression, is only an object, like the wine bottle. Now, the wine bottle can eventually turn into a woman again, say, if the woman says something that triggers a flicker of interest or has some kind of sex appeal (and then she will turn from a pretty bottle into a sexual thing, or maybe for many people, the pretty bottle *is* the sexual thing, but that depends on preference). In any case, the moment a girl is just pretty from far away, she's already turned into an object. And so he mused even more and found himself quite clever at wondering why so many women cared about standard beauties when all they needed was a spark, some kind of imperfection, a birthmark placed on the right spot on an otherwise flawless plastic face, flashing eyes, or the odd raised eyebrow, to displace them from being merely an object to be had.

Their dresses reflected off his glass of scotch and danced with the light;

the chandeliers reflected off the walls inviting out the blue and green and red of the paintings. The new night air came in through a half-open window and flushed out the old.

"Ladies, so who are you accompanying to this Company event?" Howard smiled, thinking of the wine bottles. Henry approached them and turned to look at Howard and then the wine bottles and then Howard again.

"We're working the event," she said. She looked briefly from Howard to Henry, her face expressionless. Her gaze stopped at Henry's, and she was waiting for him to speak.

Henry gazed downward, turned his body from hers to block her view, and very quickly he whispered, "Howard. I just. I don't want to do this now."

"Henry, are you kidding me?" He smiled at Henry and extended a hand onto Henry's shoulder.

"I'm leaving soon, then. I need air." Henry said without looking up, his face even lighter than usual, with the sockets of his eyes sagging deeply into his face. The two women stood nearby looking at the wine glasses, quiet, and resigned. They blended in with the chandeliers and the large windows and all the other very glittery, very pretty things. "Howard, I just...I just spoke with Duane. I don't have control over this. " Henry heard the exaggeration as he said it, but he wanted to use anything to prevent the series of events that was about to happen, which he had known so well from precedence.

"Henry, you need to relax about this right now. This whole thing is a celebration for you so enjoy it. Relax. We'll worry about Duane later, along with the list of other things that'll need to be done when all of this fun goes away, but for now" and with his voice dropping, "Come say 'hi' to the girls; we don't have to do anything, but you need to take control

28

over the Company's affairs. Just, just not now. Think what's happening now."

"Fine," Henry resigned and took a slouching step forward.

"Ladies, let me introduce you to Henry Smith." Howard smiled, opened his arms wide and smiled even more, and he bent forwards to bow to them, theatrically. "He's the reason for the event. As you may know, Henry is now the new CEO of the Company. Youngest in history. Ladies, you may begin your applause." The girls smiled and glittered, reflected and shined off the walls and the bright ceiling and all the paintings in the room.

The rest all went very quickly. Henry resigned to speaking to the sparkling women, to more drinks, to the floor spinning, to the room spinning, the entire evening spinning until he spun into his car with Howard in the passenger's seat, and they flew out of the event two hours later with the entire road spinning them onwards. He drove on through the dimly lit park with blinking blue lights in all the trees until suddenly, a man fell -- no jumped -- from the tree above them and landed right in front of Henry's beautifully rented Company Rapide S Aston Martin, the cranberry coating just waxed, and he landed with a *thud!* so loud it could only be appropriately accompanied by the screeching of brakes of a very fast car.

The car stopped when Henry felt the weight of body hit the bottom of the car, and Howard immediately jolted awake, gripping the side of the seat. Henry backed up. He opened the car door. He stepped out. Howard was waiting inside, immobile but both his eyes locked onto the road in front of him. Dead! Dead! No, alive...he stirred. Then slowly, a back hunched up, and slowly, the back hunched itself into a squat, and suddenly, the man grabbed onto Henry's shoulder - there were scars on his hands - and leaned in with a dead whisper, his broken aged teeth hissing, "We are in an age of anxiety, Henry Smith. You do not belong here. Return and sympathize. Put the gun into your mouth and give back. Give yourself control again." With that, the man slowly slumped down again, lower and lower, until he was a pile of broken man and tattered clothes on the ground. Dead, definitely dead, a pool of blood spilling from his face and forming an oval puddle, seeping out from around him, thickening, slowly. Henry froze. He thought he could smell the blood, or at least feel it was warm. It seeped under his shoes, and he bent down to touch the man's face. It was cold.

When Henry turned to look at his friend, he saw that Howard was kneeling next to him, his face inches away. "Don't touch him. Get away from him right now. Henry, stop. Step away, Henry."

Between the frozen moment capturing the rotting smell of the man and Henry's own terror (had that man been dying in front of Henry?) and the next, Howard had gotten out of the car, and in a quick movement pushed Henry out of the way.

"What the hell do you think you're doing? If you touch him your fingerprints will be all over him."

The rain washed the close memory of the screeching car tires, the thud and the spit-filled rambling into silence. Henry continued to gaze at the slump on the ground, Howard's words falling off him like the rain which splashed all around, contaminating everything, "Drive away right now! You have too much to lose for this guy. You have too much to lose. Take control over your life. Just do this. Come on! Don't be stupid for God's sake!"

Shaking, Henry looked closer. This dying man looked straight at him with eyes that weren't his! Henry could see the mouth partially opened and the grey mustache that was covered in a light dew of rain and shock. Henry imagined the man opening his eyes wide and hissing again, in his whisper with broken teeth, "Your father, Henry! Take what's yours!" It was all spinning again, and then that's when the nausea came, and Henry found himself vomiting all over, onto his shoes and the wet pavement, splashing more vomit, and he could smell the alcohol in the rejected recipe his stomach had churned up. It smelled of old scotch and nausea. The old man was dead. The man with the coin eyes was dead.

"Henry, get in the car. I'm driving."

"Howard, I have to... We have to tell someone. We need to get him to the hospital. He just -- just spoke to me."

"Henry, you're shocked right now. He's dead. We can't stay here."

Henry was silent, and he wiped the dripping vomit off his chin.

"Henry, listen to me. This is the best advice I will ever give you: Walk away. Your life means so much more than this." The night welded itself onto his voice, and each word came out steel, forged in between the desperate breaths of both men, "You just inherited this Company – this Company your father set up and worked his life for…He's dead, dammit, Henry, and you have to do it now!... If you want to talk about guilt, think about what you can do with this Company. This man was dead long before this car ever touched him. You happened to be the person to end it, but he died long before you ever touched him. That's the reason. Now get in the car."

Henry got into the car, and they drove away, the sound of the wet splashes of the tires driving against the pavement echoing through the roads of the park. Everything was wet to Henry, his own sweat sticking to him, as impermeable as the thickness of the suffocating air…

CHAPTER 3

A Stunningly Beautiful, Perfectly Average Woman

Peter shifted in his chair and moved his toes. He paused for a moment, and then he began again, his voice growing louder and his speech quicker. "...We are slave to and because of memory, this act that binds the chains around our hands and the leash around our necks. It is memory that brings us back to that incident when we did that or said this – an incident that excites the blood to rush to our faces, where we feel, more than anything, a deep-pitted shame. We're itching to get rid of it, and if we can, somehow, forcibly toss the memory aside from our conscious, it festers in our unconscious and suddenly we might find ourselves screaming something like, "No! I don't want mushrooms with that omelette! I abhor mushrooms!" without even realizing why we hate mushrooms so much in the first place.

"But I can't seem to completely hate memory either. The entirety of my being rests on these little images of things that have happened years ago. Sometimes even a gallon of coffee can't get me to remember the details of that wondrous moment when I first remembered feeling that feeling. It's like I am sitting on a conveyer belt looking at the history of my life through pictures on the walls along the belt, and suddenly, zap! A memory is stolen from me, and where there should be a photograph is now a blank slide. All I have is some shadow of the thing, some residual feeling, some unknown resentment that I cannot understand, that my second-order self cannot even attach itself to – that higher order "I" which can evaluate the addiction that your immediate "I" is attached to so that you may say, "No, but I want to quit smoking, I just can't do it right now. But if I had the choice to be able to, I would."

"Did you find love out there?" Father Turner interrupted Peter's musings and folded his hands neatly across his lap.

"Love, well, love...where do I begin?" Peter asked. "Perhaps, yes, perhaps this is the only way to tell the story of love...I find it so ironic that we should hate all things that we don't have control over –those things that stray away from our organized lists, our plans, our goals – except we love Love. We love the surprise of love, the absolute rendering of some shock our system finds itself in, and we love that we are out of control with it. In the English language, so much of how we describe the realization of love is used in passive voice, "I was struck by love", "she captivated me", "I was tormented by…", and so on…I mean, even to say "I love" is not considered a serious enough phrasing for that all-consuming, phantom thing and instead, we say things like "I am in…". It is those words, *in love*. To *be in* is a passive act. It implies that you are being done *unto*, a mere spectator to the drowning of the self in the quicksand of someone else's shadow...I don't think you could disagree that love, being uncontrollable, being built by accidental idiosyncrasies, is some deep sacrifice of the ego. The "I" fights and pulls and tears away, but that succumbing – the drowning – is the distinction between the singular "I" and the plural "we" and is exactly love. It's passive, it's giving, it's the suicide of the self by drowning. It is death by absolution of the self, a baptism.

What is transcendental is beyond the self, and what is beyond the self cannot be called autonomy – a calculated, execution of self-control –but perhaps it can be called free, a thing moving without constraints but without a trajectory of choice.

34

I don't know. I don't know.

It's humbling, I know…it was April 17th..."

* * * * *

…*April 17, 2020.* She had abandoned the bed an hour earlier. Ariella was in the kitchen, sitting at the window and looking at the windows of the other apartments which displayed a few peculiar sights: a child watching Saturday morning cartoons and eating chocolate ice cream; half-peeled blue wallpaper in the window next to the child watching cartoons; a couple in the window next to that one looking over old housekeeping magazines. She couldn't remember when she last touched a physical magazine, it was so long ago when the digital age erased all the physical things she loved the musty smell of so much. Even the dead trees were gone.

She closed her dark brown eyes, and if he could hear what she was thinking at that moment, Ariella would have been whispering to Sam, "I'd really like you to leave now." She cracked open a hard-boiled egg, which she had prepared a day earlier. The smell of it surprised her, and suddenly, she remembered when her family decided to go on their first vacation, her father having saved up all his days until he could take them somewhere. They had gone camping. On their way, her mother had packed four large bags containing thirty hard boiled eggs, four kilograms of cooked beef, six wool blankets, half their closet of clothes, a crock pot, three kilograms of dried noodles, three large kitchen knives and a cutting board, and the rest of the vegetables from their refrigerator.

Ariella, sitting in her kitchen, the egg half-peeled in her hand, was absolutely beautiful – stunning, in fact – and a man couldn't forget her once he met her – once he spoke to her. On the other hand, she wasn't pretty, and if that same man ever saw her, he'd forget her, lose her easily in a crowd. She had an unremarkable face that was balanced by an unremarkable body, and was average in height – she was neither petite, nor was she lanky. But there were two distinct features about Ariella: messy, long brown hair and a smile. If that man ever spoke to Ariella and made her laugh, he'd remember her laugh -- the way her eyes brighten and her lips move. Before he knew it, he'd be trying to make her laugh again, and she probably would, and he'd think she was absolutely beautiful. Just like that. From unnoticeable to distinct to beautiful, and all in a few seconds.

That's why when a man looked at Ariella from a distance, she would be completely plain, non-descript, average. When that same man spoke to her, he'd find himself thinking about her naked, in bed with him, and suddenly, he'd find himself obsessed with the idea of what lay underneath her non-descript clothes and all that averageness, that plainness becoming a thing of great and infinite mystery.

Ariella would say she has never betrayed anyone in her life. She was always very honest, even in her diminutive and almost soft way, a manner she developed alongside a deep fear of consciously offending anything. Although, if she were asked whether she has ever had an affair, she would say, "Yes." And if anyone tried to accuse her of betrayal for her affair, she would say, "But I was never his to begin with." Just like that, it would be tossed away as an affair, an extra limb growing from a tree that ached toward the sky.

A few hours later on that Sunday afternoon, Ariella sat in her living room with Howard, who had come by to visit her as he often did during those days. She was sitting on her yellow sofa very lost in her thoughts, while Howard kept interrupting them to make conversation. Her thoughts wandered to why she had fallen so quickly out of interest with Sam, a mild-tempered man who worked in insurance and took the underground to work every day, liked to curl up in a ball next to her in bed with his arm on her side, and who abhorred hard boiled eggs so that she would have to eat them in secret, early in the mornings before he woke. What she could not articulate to Howard but felt with absolutely certainty was

36

that she missed nostalgia itself – the act of missing something deeply and the loneliness that came with it, the very conscience of every binding moment in the day: "You are here, present and conscious." She could only feel that way, that rootedness, when she was alone, on those hot summer nights when she walked home along the brightly lit streets of the city by herself with her blouse hugging her shoulders stuck to her from the sweat of the humidity, or along the water with the docked boats with her feet aching against the backs of her shoes, or during the solitary walks on a sunny afternoon along the stoned courtyards, her hands clutching the straps of her bag. The rootedness was the sense of being alone without distraction, alone and alive with the fears that shook the otherwise inane details of the everyday firmly in her grasp. It was the feeling of absoluteness, the pure recognition that it was just she, moving to her own will without disruption. Finding herself wanting to escape and feeling that Sam wouldn't let her – he held on too tightly at nights and during the days when his hands couldn't find her, he found ways of entering her mind without her permission – she found herself escaping to someone else's bed as a cowardly, final act of self-preservation. As they sat on her balcony, she with a cigarette, and Howard with black coffee, she finally said, "I hope this ends it."

Without looking at her, he responded, "Well, he'd be a pretty pathetic guy if not, no?"

She looked at the burning end, dusted it off on the edge of the table, and put it down. "It's not his problem. It's mine. It's always been mine." She inhaled, breathed, stared at it, and then said again, "I told him it was done this morning, for the final time. I told him it was over for me a long time before then, that really, it never really was. God, I cried to him when I said it! It was horrible. He'd been trying to get to my friends. I just--I can't take it when he's upset like that. I'm pathetic. I have no control when it comes to this."

Howard stood up and walked over to her, and as he rubbed her neck, "You are actually pretty...pathetic...when it comes to this. What's his name again – John, you said? Well, tell John I apologize, but that he needs to find some self-respect." He kissed her on the head and then, "I enjoyed it." He looked at his watch. "I should go." He put his hand on her shoulder, "I'll see you soon." Howard walked into her bedroom and put on his shirt, trousers, and sweater to cover the buttoned shirt and found his socks at the foot of the bed, curled and sleeping next to his shoes.

She got up from her seat and wiped out her cigarette, walking inside, "You're a good friend. You're a goddamn bastard but a good friend. Thanks for listening."

He stood, buttoning his sweater, looking down at each little grey button carefully. "Well, at least we've got each other. Feel free to return the favor any time." He looked into her mirror and fixed his hair. With that, he walked across the room to kiss her quickly and walked to the door.

* * * * *

What was love for Ariella? Love occupied a small space in Ariella's brain that encased the following: standard memories laid on top of one another with parts forgotten and others made up, so that each memory infused into the next one and added to the drama and beauty, an exaggerated emotion played by forgetfulness and good storytelling, with tensions, creativity, naivete, and a very abstract sense of reality which released her from her rootedness and tugged at her conscience into something muddled between what is and what had been.

> *...The moment when Ariella fell in love for the first time, they were both kneeling on the ground along a river they had grown up near in a smaller town in a different place. They were young, much younger than today, as she searched for the memory. It was early April, and the peach blossoms had bloomed early, but wind from an earlier storm had knocked off a few branches onto the wet grass. She looked at the stream, then at the blooming trees, and then at the flowers that had fallen beneath the trees. She fell to her*

knees. She began picking up the flowers, and she dug little graves for them with her hands and buried them. Those flowers, how they lived through a winter of snow and a spring of frost, and they bloomed still! Everyone thought they were so beautiful when they bloomed, but when they fell? Who looked at fallen flowers? They were forgotten, sitting there rotting, sticky brown with a memory of, "there were flowers in springtime". No one could smell them anymore; no one could see them on the trees. And their memory? Tossed. Done. Set for another year -- a purge of memory. Forgotten. Ariella dug and dug. He arrived twenty minutes later and saw her by the stream, kneeling at the ground, crying, her hands creating little graves for the flowers. He didn't know what to say. He got down next to her and helped her dig and bury, bury and dig. When she tired, she sat up and looked down at her hands, brown and raw from the burials. Without a word, she searched for him and let herself need him. She gave herself to him and collapsed, her arms around his waist and her soiled face somewhere buried inside his sweater. She's never left since then.

But the moment always ended, and Ariella was always left with a memory. It was these memories that guarded her from loving anyone else, and the key to unlocking the little details which slowly and surreptitiously escaped her could only be retained in an absolute moment of aloneness edging toward loneliness, without any other memory to be made. So if a man finds himself loving a woman who does not love him back, it is most likely that she has given herself to someone else, and as hard as he may try, until he can exchange those memories with ones of himself, he will always be knocking at the door of that chamber, never to be let in.

* * * * *

Years ago, Howard and Ariella had met through Henry Smith. The three remained friends since their early young adult days when Howard and Henry attended the same college preparatory schools. Over ten years later all three found themselves living in the same city, a big haze of gray and brown in Henry's view. It was Howard who had first noticed Ariella, one of Henry's disappointingly few female friends. "She's pretty cute,"

Howard said unexpectedly one day.

Cringing and shifting uncomfortably, Henry replied, "Howard, you weren't sober when you met her."

"Ya, makes it more honest, then, doesn't it?" They had been walking back from the sports fields, and the sun was hitting the late afternoon, reheating the dried sweat on their backs.

"Maybe the three of us can do dinner?"

"Henry, if I want to get with her, it's probably better if you weren't there. No offense. Just not how I do it." He winked at Henry.

"I don't think she'd go for it to be honest. I didn't know that you even went for girls like Ariella."

"What do you mean? What are girls like Ariella? Henry, Henry, Henry! Girls are girls, last time I checked anyways."

"Uh, the smart ones. I didn't think you liked the smart ones. She's also emotional." Henry's voice trailed off, deflated.

"Henry, you have obviously mistaken my taste in women: I am an equal opportunist. I like smart girls, not-smart girls, genius girls, girls who are like maybe on the border, as long as they're cute and it's legal, and they can hold up a conversation. Actually, the conversation is a luxury. Look, if you're ok with it, just give me Ari's number. I'll take it from there." Howard slung the pack over his back and smiled at Henry.

"Yea, ok, here's her number. Just, hey, just, uh do me a favor. Just don't tell me any details, please?" Then he added, "And, yea, can you just be respectful?" A part of him began to feel like he was selling her and slowly, he regretted telling Howard Ari's number.

Sometime after their introduction through Henry Smith, fresh into their first jobs (Ariella as a historian-in-training, and Howard and Henry as young henchmen for David Smith's company), Ariella and Howard had begun to visit one another regularly. They had never considered it a true romantic relationship, and they had never considered any future together. They were separate people whose lives had accidentally collided, and they found it more convenient to see one another than not.

There was only one evening when Ariella and Howard had tried to formalize these meetings; they had dinner, a full spread of silverware and wine glasses, ordering in food from one of Howard's favorite restaurants. Ariella had begun a serious discussion, as she was prone to do, when they got back to Howard's pool house, sitting with her legs crossed on his sofa. Really, he didn't want to get into it and instead was waiting to unbutton Ariella's purple button-down shirt, but she kept talking about something he didn't have the energy to discuss.

Finally irritated at his lack of interest in the discussion, she responded, "Have you ever worked a day in your life?" She frowned at him and crossed her arms.

"That's irrelevant, first of all. Second of all, it doesn't make me happier that I haven't. It's the way life is. I mean, there's just nothing wrong in being in your own head and doing stuff according to what's in there." He really believed what he said to her. Howard had little patience for what he took as Ariella's pointless, do-gooder, yet "what can one really do"-type-laments: the cost of transportation of food to people in desolate areas, the lack of resources in the world, the driving inequality of technology, as if of all the things she wanted to pour her energy into, she had chosen the things she could do the least about just so she could keep lamenting about *something*, just so she could use it to leverage herself onto some moral high ground for a better outlet of her judgment.

41

"That's not the *way life is*. People do things for other people all the time." She crossed her arms tighter and shifted. He imagined that she was preparing herself like a rooster in a cock fight, and then he imagined being the other rooster in the pen. Looking at her edging closer toward him, her arms crossed tighter, her lips pursed, he settled to thinking, *She'd win if only because I'd lose out of apathy.*

"God Ari, it's late. Can we not get into this. These conversations never go anywhere. You're arguing oranges, and I'm arguing apples. It's not a good time. That's it." *This wasn't going to be a good night for him*, Howard had told himself then.

"You're just really sheltered."

At this, Howard sighed. He wondered how long she could carry on with this if he didn't put an end to it. "You're dramatic. And unrealistic," he said in reply. "And you know, what? A little condescending."

That had been the word, "condescending". At that word, she had gotten up, and walked toward her little lump of things -- brown coat, umbrella, sack of old books, blue purse -- on the ground near the front door. She didn't respond to him; she felt like he had stabbed at something sensitive inside her, like a tweezer poking in on a sore cavity.

"Ari, just stay," he said. "You're being more dramatic by leaving. Why aren't we allowed to disagree on something?"

"We disagree on a lot of things, but I just, I don't know. I kind of want to go back."

She paused until Howard finally asked, "Ari, what are you thinking?"

The Dreaded Question defined by the phrase *what are you thinking?* For Ariella, these four little words had always been an invasion, an intrusion into privacy. "Raisin bread."

42

"What?"

"That's what I'm thinking, raisin bread."

"Uh, ok. Do you want raisin bread?"

"No. It's just what I thought, and you asked me what I thought." Ariella had gotten used to keeping a few white lies in her back pocket in case of emergencies, and sometimes when she was caught off guard, they flew out of her before she could even refine them...

CHAPTER 4

An Unexpected Guest

...*April 17, 2020.* It was the perfect day to hide indoors. There was nothing pleasant about the city in the rain, causing a big, wet, city grunge that swept into a dark and thick ocean to the drains. Ariella woke up from her unexpected afternoon sleep to a jarring, rabid knocking on her door. She wrapped an old, green knit shawl around herself and went to open the door. Before she could even turn the handle, the door burst open, nearly forced her against the wall, and knocked over the umbrella stand. Standing in front of her, and nearing stumbling on top of her, was a man dressed in a black suit, obviously from the night before, his tie loosely hung around his neck, his white shirt dirtied.

"Henry?" Henry looked at her, his eyes darting from the umbrella stand to her sofa to her again. "Henry?" she asked again. Her question chafed against him. He continued to stare at her before he collapsed into her arms, which was really his way of trying to embrace her, and in doing so he almost knocked her over again. If Henry had known how to cry then, he would have cried and cried all over her, standing there in her arms, sobbing, clinging, wiping his wet anger off himself.

Instead, Henry loosened Ariella from his embrace – it was a hard grasp, as if he were hanging onto the last bit of sanity by attaching himself to her in a final, paroxysm of self-preservation, his hands finding the natty and shredded tendrils of her shawl, his fingers digging into the bits of shoulder beneath it. When he finally regained motor control over his panicked spasm, he said very resolutely, "I'm hungover." With that, Henry crawled onto her sofa and immediately grabbed the throw blanket and covered his wet self with it and wished with all his remaining will to go back in time to his pre-natal days sloshing around in amniotic unconsciousness while nutrients were pumped into him without his knowing. Then he gasped and let himself fall into a very deep sleep.

In his deep sleep, time unhinged. Henry found himself in a cave, and everywhere around him were tall and very serious looking stalactites that hung from the shadowed ceilings. With each step he took, the ground immediately produced stalagmites under his feet. Henry began to run. He tried to find an exit, even though he wasn't sure why he wanted an exit; he had been so happy to find and enter the cave at first. But the entire time, the rock formation in the cave began to close in on him until it created a little net inside the cave. Then, like those dreams where things shift and move without reason or a reason for a reason, there was a deep lake in the cave where the crystals hadn't grown. So Henry stepped toward the lake, carefully, as he was afraid that any step would lead to a stalagmite ending his short cave life. He looked into the lake, and he realized he couldn't see anything in it. It was as if the water wasn't even water but some dark, black viscous thing that contained something far denser than liquid. It was an infinite. And he realized suddenly, he wanted that infinite. He reached to touch the liquid, and an urge drove him to plunge in into the infinite, dark thing, until suddenly, he realized he was drowning. Drowning, but slowly, since the thickness of the thing took its time to enclose his nostrils and mouth, his arms and head. He tried to thrash. He thrashed his arms and his legs, and he found the viscous thing becoming solid around him, crushing his limbs, and he thrashed himself awake and onto Ariella's floor.

It was dark outside two hours later. The days were beginning to

46

lengthen, but they were still short enough for it to be possible to sleep through the daytime. Henry sat opposite Ariella in a new change of clothes and after a very long shower – he wore the same trousers he had on the night before, but exchanged his wet shirt and suit jacket for an old, oversized grey sweatshirt of Ariella's, his wrists sticking out like a modern, urban scarecrow. He held a cup of coffee in his hands and noticing the evening moon, put the coffee down, "I don't need this," he said.

"Henry," she began, "You look awful. Are you going to tell me anything that happened, or at least how the event was?"

Silence.

She tried again, "Or, are we just going to sit here and look at each other. I mean, look, I can do both, really…"

"Yea, the event was good," he found himself saying.

"Well, I want to hear all about it! I've been reading a few things about some big secret party that was going to be at the art museum. They closed early for it to set up."

"It was at the museum… did it really happen at the museum?"

"Was it crowded?"

"Yea, there were people. It doesn't seem like it could have happened all together."

"What didn't?" She smiled. His eyes weren't focused on her.

"What day is it?"

"Wow, you're definitely hungover. What a party! It's April seventeenth.

It's a Sunday. Sound familiar now? Am I talking to anyone in there?"

"My head...my head is just throbbing." He put his hands on his head, closed his eyes, and then opened them, watching the little colored spots fade into nothing.

"And I'm assuming you must have stayed out pretty late, huh? It looks like you were running through the streets all night!" She turned her head upwards and laughed. She looked at him. His eyes peered at her, recognizing the laughter. He looked away.

The window in her living room was slightly opened and there was a pool of water forming on her sill. The drapes were damp. He could smell the tar outside mixed with mud and the pollen from the trees. How could he even begin to explain it to her? How could he even form the words with his mouth, "m-m-ur-der. M-M-UR-DER"? He couldn't look at her; she was such a string that tied him to a list of memories that were filed under a heading in block red letters "IMPORTANT", and his conscience served the duty of puppet. There was a breeze, and the breeze brought some of the water indoors. She turned her head upward toward the window and a second later, got up to close it. Suddenly, he felt sick again. It started in his head but moved right to his gut and he could feel it just hovering there, the sickness. He could smell the revolver. It was safe in his bed stand, but somehow, the revolver smell invaded Ariella's room. So he excused himself briefly. She sat there, puzzled, and watched him walk into the wrong room.

Minutes later, Henry walked out of Ariella's bedroom and found the toilet.

Minutes after that, he excused himself for leaving early and ran out from her steps with her clothes on. People who saw him on the street mistook him for being drunk...

CHAPTER 5

The Inheritance

"Peter, now, hold on a minute…What's with David Smith's company? I guess what did Henry actually inherit?" Father Turner asked.

"Well let's see," Peter replied. "I need to make sure I've got this right. So right after David Smith received his doctorate, he was absolutely lost. He wandered from random consulting job to random consulting job, determined to never return to the indentured servitude of graduate school. He made and saved a lot of his own money during that time. Finally, sick of working for other people and realizing that his current lifestyle was not so different than his graduate school days other than the income he never had any time to use, he founded his own company during a venture investment boom. David used his final research project at the University, which the University had never fully funded, and continued it in a makeshift lab at a biotechnology share-hub. David Smith got funding from the venture capitalists immediately once he explained his first idea. Within five years, his company had its first successful product. Two years later, it went public. The Company's Headquarters had been moved three times in the last twenty years to accommodate the rapidly expanding number of projects and personnel needed. David Smith himself had spent a great portion of his youth being trained as a biophysicist, but remained, as he would call it outside academic circles, "a wild card." After all, he had been primarily interested in making a profit, and so when the university lifestyle bored him, he had decided to take his labs outside its impenetrable walls and onto the streets. There, modestly, the first stage of life of the Company had been formed.

David Smith had an astoundingly talented team of scientists with him, some from his previous university research group and others poached from surrounding groups. He had selected only the best, in his opinion, and had made them offers they found difficult to refuse living inside the glass walls of the institution. He made sure they were taken care of extremely well financially, and he gave them autonomy. David was a mater of wooing financiers, marketers, and investors. By its 10-year mark, Company multiplied aggressively in size to over one-hundred thousand employees and projects that boasted the commercialization of unexplored, man-manipulated, biological phenomena. Of course, what the investors and the public failed to understand was the reinvestment of David Smith's wealth into private projects, spun off as private companies, which were no longer reported to the Board of Directors. In short, David Smith appeared to be a mercenary scientist with the charisma of a successful businessman. While in truth, he was an armchair philosopher who lacked all morals and possessed all means. After the Company established a successful cornering of the market with its IPO, David Smith let "his followers" run the public projects of the Company while he embarked secretly on his greatest adventure and what he would deem to be his greatest achievement, his Holy Grail."

"And what about Henry? Was he so eager to join his father's company?" Father Turner asked.

"Henry Smith," Peter replied, "had never worked for any other man or woman other than his father. David Smith, sympathetic toward Henry's shy nature hired Henry's childhood friend, Howard, in a high ranking position in marketing, much to the dismay of employees fifteen years Howard's senior. David had immediately taken a liking to the boy constantly making jokes with almost anyone that crossed his path the first time Henry had introduced them years earlier. David had hoped Howard's natural charisma would spill onto Henry. David Smith had always admired the easy confidence Howard displayed, which he saw lacking in his own excruciatingly shy son. Despite the exposures and lessons David had tried to instill upon Henry to open him up to others, Henry had remained closed, always waiting behind the door instead of walking in. David Smith then spent the next ten years disappointed that while other boys seemed to be influenced by their friends, Henry had remained a stone, unchanging from a boy to an adolescent to a young man and then finally, to the same grown man.

Henry's own windfall in life's lottery came from one very passionate, short-lasting affair his father, David Smith, had with a very practical small-framed and beautiful woman named Xiaoling who sported a pair of intimidatingly sharp eyes set on an otherwise warm face with a soft chin. She was a quick-thinking woman who had a gift of quick fingers and toes, never let her hair grow longer than her shoulders, and darted around finishing multiple tasks at once as if her internal clock moved twice as fast as anyone else around her. In another lifetime, she would have been a legendary surgeon, but in this lifetime, she saw herself as a glad servant to her family, about which she once said with a sigh, 'The day I found out I couldn't make a difference in the world was the saddest day of my life.'

'How am I going to take care of him?' she had asked David Smith once the doctor confirmed that a small child was, indeed, growing quickly inside her.

'Raise him as mine. I don't like my first one much and the second one doesn't like me. I still blame my ex for that. So maybe the third's the charm.' David Smith had smiled, towering over her small figure.

'It would be so difficult for him. He doesn't...he's going to be different...'

You can imagine she had barely finished before David Smith cut her off with a nonchalant wave of his hand. 'It's difficult for all my kids. Henry won't grow up any different,' he had consoled her. Xiaoling had seen no other choice. With barely any savings in her bank account and Erica going into elementary school, she had thought of the life her unborn child could possibly have hovering between two extremes of either wanting everything he could never have and having everything he didn't want, the affliction she saw in David Smith's other miserable children.'"

"What a complicated childhood, and what a fascinating company. Surely, Henry must have felt buried under the responsibility of his father throughout his life. And Xiaoling? Where was she from originally? Did he ever inherit his mother's heritage?" Father Turner asked.

"No, Xiaoling immigrated from China when she was in her late twenties. She had met her previous husband at Beida University, but she raised Henry under the culture of his father. Henry was often caught between the worlds of his very different parents, but his father's presence had the stronger pull. Of course, this would have severe consequences for him, which I'll explain more…"

* * * * *

…*April 29, 2020 at a very long Board Meeting.* The Board was anxious to meet again for the second time that month. Henry stood in the long, oval room in front of the projector screen. As the lights darkened, he thought of the various twists and turns along the road that was been paved for him to be here. He never imagined himself running his father's company, but looking back and seeing the various events that had played out like little stops on a Monopoly board, he realized it had been determined to happen far before he caught on.

Henry imagined his mother's expressions when she negotiated with David Smith about Henry's childhood: He imagined she crinkled her nose and the little corners of her eyes raised up every time David made a joke. She was very polite. As Henry tried to imagine her conversations with David Smith years earlier, the Board Meeting continued to drag on.

52

Henry watched the faces darken as Duane presented the first quarter earnings, and he crinkled his nose the way he imagined his mother would. Henry had helped with the presentation but with each click of the new slide, he found himself drifting away. The room was so dark, and it was so cold, and he could swear there were members with their eyelids drooping lower and lower…

When Henry was five, he was taken to his father's company for the first time. The Company had had its initial public offering three months earlier, and David Smith's office was knocked down, expanded, rebuilt and then furnished to look like a Manhattan penthouse. "Henry," David had said, "this was a lot of hard work. Do you see where hard work can get you?" He had made Henry walk around the new room twice and look out from the windows onto the bay. Looking down from the tower and onto the people below, Henry had suddenly felt sick. He had vertigo. The building had spun Henry around and around.

Henry opened his eyes. He was in the same room, looking out at the same streets, feeling the same sickness in his stomach, but now his father was gone.

"Let's have a break. You guys all look like you could use some coffee." Duane flicked the light on, ending his own drifting musing. The suits got up and ruffled themselves and filed out the door.

Henry watched as the last Board Member left the room and tripped on his own clumsy feet, nearly knocking into the woman in front of him. Henry noticed the emptiness of the room, and he thought of his father and the presence David would have had in the meeting. He felt even emptier.

"You having trouble running?" David Smith once yelled across the field when Henry was young. There had been a light drizzle, and the air was still sharp from March's melted frost. "No…No, I'm okay," Henry had tried to yell back, his lungs couldn't keep up with his sore legs. He had been done with this three hours ago, but on the occasions his father came to watch the games, Henry knew the mornings lasted into

53

afternoons, and if he were particularly clumsy, into the evenings. "I think you need to go and start working on your speed. You're slower than all the other boys! You won't catch up that way. You're losing the game before you begin. Let's end the day after you do an easy five miler." David Smith had pulled out his umbrella and hand warmers and watched as Henry ran around the field, lap after lap, gasping in the cold. Henry would always wonder, years later, what meetings and phone calls his father had missed so that he could stand in the wet cold with his son, who had little talent for sports.

The suits filed back in one by one and sat in their original seats. A man leaned back and clicked his pen, his long legs crossed. Duane stepped toward Henry and motioned for him to come close. "You're okay with the presentation you'll give?"

"Ya, I finished the slide deck earlier."

"Good boy," Duane replied. Henry stared back, and his throat tightened. He choked back tears and quickly looked down.

Good boy. That was something David Smith would have said with a loud pat on the back, a I'm in control kid kind of response which was a signature David Smith gesture of approval. When Henry was moving into his two-story apartment right next to the college campus, David Smith had examined the room and asked, "Do you have enough saved from your summer internship to get you through your first semester?" As if prompted before he finished, Henry replied, "Of course, and from the internship the summer before that."

Good boy. David Smith was as opaque during his life as he was in his death, but even in that room, with the lights shut and Henry standing at the attention of the dozen sets of eyes on him, David's presence permeated everything. Still. There were memories from when Henry was five until recently, each one of which answered to a "good boy" or "you'll fall behind". All those isolated events and conversations were a mystery to Henry until one day, he received a call from his father's estate lawyer who asked him and his mother, Xiaoling, to a meeting. "There's a few things to discuss, many of which will be of particular interest to you. I suggest you come see me in

54

person," the man had said slowly and quietly on the phone. This was when a reluctant Henry was presented with the inheritance: one-hundred percent ownership of the company and half of David Smith's other, non-property, financial assets.

As Duane's voice droned on, Henry relived how the financial luck was truly on his mother's side. In fact, she and David Smith had only spent one night together – a singular act which produced a seven-pound-five-ounce blotchy and difficult Henry, who then kept her up for many nights. It was his mother who ended it and a much older David Smith who never forgot it. She had still been in mourning over her last love, who left her pregnant and with a four-year-old girl Erica. She was two months pregnant when he went crashing through a windshield and straight into the highway meridian. Dead on the spot. She suffered such shock at the news, the fetus had no chance of surviving. In a state of desperation six months later, Henry imagined she must have rebelled against fairness and began an affair with a married man, to take something from someone else as it was done to her. But his mother always knew it was a mistake. With what Henry sensed as a deep sense of guilt and punishment, she raised him in a nearby house so that he and David could have some chance at a relationship. After David's divorce, Henry and his mother moved in while David Smith continued his own busy life, parallel to hers with his hand on Henry's future. In turn, she never asked anything more from David. How did his mother now take David's death?

"So, how will we face the rest of David's family? I had been hoping to encourage Henry to spend more time with my family in China, so he can understand more about his own heritage. Before, David had been so adamant about Henry working at his company...and now...I'm afraid Henry's stuck with something he doesn't even necessarily want, and he's so young and just lost his father. Scott and Helen should have a say in this, at least how the company is run. Maybe they'd want to be more involved?" Xiaoling asked Larry, a tall, balding and stiff lawyer with hunched shoulders and a dark mustache, during their only meeting in which Henry's inheritance was disclosed. Larry wore a black suit that day. Xiaoling clutched her purse tightly across the dark table in Larry's office the entire time. Henry sat silently at his mother's side and felt his stomach spiral from shock to dread. He had no idea where

to begin.

"These things are always difficult and can be awkward to deal with. In this case, you at least know that neither Scott nor Helen were contesting the position. They have enough property and money now..."

"Henry is really young—"

'—Well, he really isn't. I mean, not if you look at some of the greatest companies in history. Most great entrepreneurs and business folk make it big when they're young – straight out of college or even before then – far younger than Henry even! He'll be fine. He has enough advisors and senior members who have been doing this a long time. It's an age of opportunity."

"No, no, but Henry hasn't had other experience. He's only worked under David. His dad's been his only direct boss for the past nine years, and well, indirectly? David's always coached Henry to prepare him for working in the Company. And in that way, I think the Company was a huge shadow over all of our lives, and I'm not sure..."

Larry said firmly, "Xiaoling, how long are you going to keep sheltering the boy?"

Larry looked at Henry. Henry put a hand on his mother's arm and, noticing how small her arm was under his hand (those same arms that held him and nursed him in memories), opened his mouth to speak. Xiaoling and Larry became silent and fixed their eyes on him. Under his mother's sharp stare, Henry faltered. Larry felt the silent, dry seconds pass with unease and softened his tone, "I'm sorry, Henry, I don't seem to have heard you."

"I meant to say," Henry began, finding the floor beneath his feet, moving his toes back and forth against the hard shoes, "I'll be alright." That was it. "I'll be alright," he reaffirmed.
Xiaoling looked at Henry again, and as he stared back at her, he knew somehow his father had had the last word from the grave. I'll be alright.

56

"It'll be alright," Henry said. The suits looked up, and Duane paused from his presentation.

"What did you say, Henry?" One of them asked.

"Ah, just reiterating Duane's point. Duane, please go on." Henry was grateful for the dark room, which hid his blushing.

* * * * *

Two years before David's death, sometime in the summer of 2018, David took his estate lawyer, Larry out fishing on David's favorite boat, *Apollo*. "I love all my kids the same, but some I respect more than others," David Smith said to Larry. David took a long drink from his beer and looked out at the open waters, hoping the fishing gods would be good to them. During summers, the two men often held their business discussions on the *Apollo*, while navigating the cold choppy waters just past the harbor. "And when I think about what it means to carry the name on, you know, I can't imagine Scott's got anything to offer – he's a good egg, but he doesn't have much to offer – and Helen's smart enough, but she doesn't like the family affairs. Her last campaign in the household was for a dog, and she got it. But my youngest, Henry, I've always respected him. Once he's finally down on a path, he's got some kind of resolve. He's got grit. You know what I mean?" David Smith looked at Larry.

"Well, you were certainly hard on that kid." Larry replied, shaking his head. He never raised his gaze to meet David's.

"Henry has my respect."

"Coming from an old guy like you, yea, I see where getting on your good side takes the work of a Saint." Both men laughed. They stared at the clouds sitting on the horizon on an otherwise perfectly bright day.

David Smith stared at the skin on his hands, the wrinkles, the little brown spots that kept appearing every year, multiplying faster and said, "I was too busy when I had that kid, you know that as well as I do. I couldn't do the normal stuff...the usual shit dads do with their sons like I could with Scott. But I think I succeeded in making sure he knew what responsibility means...he knows that." His words began to drag, *Ree-SPON-si-bil-i-teee,* elongated with fifth-beer-induced slurring, and he started thinking about what he had left Henry.

"Well, he's about to get a good testing of it."

"If we're lucky, I go first, and you tell my grave how it goes, alright?"

"I think we better move on to scotch for the rest of this."

"That's the best idea you've had all night." The two men walked toward the boat cabin, in the sunlight, floating on the water with only the past to worry about, the future set on paper and signed with tremendous expectation thrust on the inheritors.

"Larry, there're a few ways men can live forever. I don't buy any other bullshit someone might tell you," David Smith said after the papers were signed.

"What do you mean, David?"

"Time is really a circular thing --"

"Okay, let's skip the Kant and go to what you really want to talk about, whether Henry, your socially anxious, shy kid is capable of running a Company."

"Philosophy not your thing these days? It was Kant who said in the First Critique, 'time and space do not exist in themselves...'"

"It hasn't been for some time now. I wake up in the mornings, I work, I have dinner with my wife, I sleep. So go on, what were you trying to get at?"

"Immortality."

"Oh, future generations. Of course, we look at some infinite horizon ahead of us, and it's just future generations, like bequests."

"Kind of like that, but I see you're really not in that mood...more of an economist than a philosopher are we? What if all of time was really just all the moments – space itself – layered on top of one another, disguised, and what if we could unlayer the layers...somehow with the one thing we know can encompass all moments in one? Spread them out like clothing on a line or shoes at a flea market?" Larry sighed. David Smith continued, "...but I guess if you could pick one of the three of my kids to live through, who would you pick?"

Larry paused. He wasn't sure whether or not it was a smart idea to entertain David Smith three scotches in. He was even less sure whether the philosophical musings were preferable to choosing a favorite child. In the end, he decided that as a lawyer, he should give his client some honest advice: "Henry's the only good one in the lot of them, sorry to say David."

"You want to be remembered as a good guy, you know?" David Smith's voice trembled, and Larry saw something in his client's eye he had never seen before: uncertainty. Suddenly Larry saw that the man who stood in front of him had grown very old from when they had first met.

"David, it hasn't been easy…you made those choices…"

"No, but it's not easy to change now."

"But Henry?"

"He's a hell of a lot deeper into things than he knows. I've dragged him into it. It's his future, his destiny, if you'd like to call it that."

"I don't want to know any more... Jesus Christ, David! Henry Smith is just a boy!"

"It's the only way I can reverse the thing..." David began slurring his words, and walked over to the mini bar to make another drink.

"Fucking hell, David, you didn't go that far. I didn't know you were talking about the Project!" Larry began yelling, the ice cubes in his glass clashing against the simultaneous jostling of the boat and Larry's extended gestures.

"You're the only person I trust, Larry, you've been good to your clients, extremely dedicated and very professional..."

"I've known the boy for too long, I can't."

"He'll be stuck in it forever..."

"I know the consequences!" Larry's face turned red. Henry Smith! Not even he, David's only loyal friend and advisor, could have seen it. But now he was left with the mess, just as he was left with the mess of so many clients before David Smith even approached him with a beer, a pocket full of money, and a big smile. "David, I swear to god I am going to retire after you."

"You'll tell him in person?"

"I will tell him about his inheritance. Nothing else is my business."

"That's all you need to do. Make sure you tie up the legal ends, that it's a smooth transition without too much publicity. Keep it from, *especially* from...the other executives."

"I understand. But only the inheritance, David."

"Yes."

The men were silent for the first time that day, and thus began David Smith's behemoth and simultaneous projects of trying to die and unwind his assets.

Before the afternoon on the boat, Larry was part of several major events in David Smith's life: the birth of his three children, his second and third marriages, and his mother's death at the age of eighty-nine. After the afternoon on the boat, Larry's job would continue: David Smith's funeral, the inheritances, and a few matters related to the Company, as he was heavily invested in both David Smith's technology and Henry's childhood.

* * * * *

April 29, 2020. It had been raining nine days in a row, and Henry Smith stepped from his desk and looked out the window. He saw the grey and black figures run across the street, sleek little shadows who held newspapers over their heads to avoid the splashes of rain. Looking down, he could barely tell if they were men, women, or children. The brightest colors outside were the neons of store lights and the flashes of taxis, and all of it was blurred by the quick movements of scurrying people and the filtered haze of rain.

"Wet week, isn't it?" Duane's voice came to him at his door.

Henry turned around, "How is it that people think they'll stay dry putting newspapers on their heads?"

"It's really not a bad solution for walking across the street…well, unless it's a downpour. Let's just be glad we're both inside."

"So how do you think the Board Meeting went?"

"I thought you did well. You're starting to grow into the role." Duane nodded.

Henry stayed standing and replied, "I'm glad you think so."

"I've been doing this a long time, son, and I'll just say that it just takes a lot of experience. Little things. Nuances. You'll get into it, but that's what we're here for. What I'm here for." His face suddenly hardened as he looked at Henry.

Henry felt his forehead become warm, "Well I'm glad my dad helped me so much."

"He wasn't so involved toward the end the same way a lot of the rest of us were." Duane responded immediately, quieter, poised and prepared.

"He still knew what was happening."

"It's hard to know what's happening when you're a founder and figurehead. And he was great at that, don't get me wrong. I'm not trying to get you on the defensive here, but I just want you to know I'm here to help you." Duane's last words came out slowly, as if he wanted Henry's brain to take its time to wrap around the concept – I am here to help you.

"I appreciate your thoughts. I should get back to preparing my statement now, and the mortuary is already having a hard time preserving everything given how long it's taken. You'll be at the funeral this weekend?" *Preserving everything,* Henry cringed at his own words and felt the dread of truth slamming itself into him. He realized in some instances, like when he first awoke in the morning, he would forget his father was gone. He spoke of the body as if it were someone else's, and he was half-expecting David to re-appear, as if from a horribly planned

62

joke.

"Of course...Henry, of course."

With that Duane walked out of Henry's room slowly and shut the door on his way out. The downpour continued, and when Henry looked out the window again, the streets were cleared except for the drowned newspapers that tugged at the grates of inundated storm drains...

CHAPTER 6

Memories of the Estates

...Henry Smith, both in his youth and early adulthood, did not see the need to spend as much time as his friends developing the skills of entertaining women. So instead, he spent most of his female-time with his sister, Erica, or Ariella, which simplified matters since he knew both so well, and in turn, they knew him so well that they allowed him plenty of room for error. It also helped that Ariella lived only two miles from his father's estate, and the long walks on the windy trail he took through the underbrush of the forest along one of the many now dried-up creeks provided some of his favorite childhood memories. They were escapes where he discovered an infinity of stories and day-time fantasies. The really good ones he'd play in his mind over and over again.

The memories of visiting the old estate and the adventures Henry had in the surrounding forest came and went after he moved to the city, though one memory always lived on the surface of his waking mind. It was springtime, it must have been May or earlier, and Henry had set out into the woods to walk along the path to spot different colored mosses and to sit under the trees to think. The path diverged and one direction led to a nearby park alongside a river that ran miles from east to west. The river passed through thirteen towns from the distant mountains before returning to the gaping mouth of the bay. Some time ago, the town had planted rows of peach trees, which blossomed vehemently before the hard rains wash them away. Henry had made his direction toward the park, and as he had stepped out of the trail and faced the river, he had seen his friend stooped down beneath a peach tree. He had arrived too late: the last night's storm must have knocked the blossoms from the trees, and a sweet stickiness permeated the air; there was a chill, the cleansing footprint of a spring rain.

He had made his way toward her as the brown river rolled onwards, set against a grey sky while the branches of the trees clutched against the thick billows of clouds. She had been bent over, hovering, and shaking little shakes that were quiet and terrifying to him all at once. He had seen her burying the flowers, the pink petals smeared by the water, scooping them up and putting them into the ground. Wordlessly he had approached her, and he put his hands onto the soft, wet ground, feeling the cool moisture extend into his fingers. Henry had begun scooping the flowers slowly and putting the forgiving ground on top of the petals, but as he had continued to scoop, lay and bury, he had found himself working in greater agitation and speed. Sitting along the riverbank in the park and looking down at his hands, he suddenly noticed that they were brown from dirt, a brown that mirrored the rolling river which he had so hoped would flush the memory from him as it washed the petals away into some deep, unknown distant place. Next to him, a young woman, a girl really, began silently to cry.

* * * * *

October 13 a few years earlier. Henry sat at the old wooden desk of one of his father's summer homes in Maine. There was a small island about three miles from the mainland, and it used to be occupied by a small tourist company that would rent out the rooms during the summer. David Smith had bought the island sixteen years prior and had kept the old house. Henry had come that summer for three weeks to keep his father company. David Smith had just discovered that he had pancreatic cancer. He had decided the moment the doctor with the elongated face looked down at him from his red-framed glasses and began with, "I am afraid I have some news…most men do get this, so I don't think you should be too concerned…" that he would keep it private. So instead, he took Henry with him without explaining much and told him that he needed, "someone to keep him entertained while he spent some down time in the middle of nowhere."

The house was a historic treasure ground, and its contents had survived all the renovations. The attic displayed old newspapers dating back to September 9, 1933. Henry loved the old house; it was his favorite of all his father's homes. It sang and creaked to him especially on windy days. The wood smelled of the 1950s. At one point the inhabitants were tourists, or perhaps just New Englanders searching for a weekend alone. Henry liked to read through the old writings in the notebooks that were jammed inside the desk, even the old Christian proverbs.

Looking through the notebooks of scratch proverbs and little notes was a distraction. It was right about then that Henry began to notice his own thoughts. It crept into his sleep first; he noticed he would wake up at odd hours and have trouble falling back asleep. Then, he felt it in his stomach, an exhausting, silently screeching feeling of nervousness, like he was always on the edge of something, walking on a tightrope whose destination was completely blocked from his view. In fact, he was blindfolded, and all he could tell was that he was on a tightrope and trying not to fall. The anxiety would dig into him slowly and exhaust every part of his brain until he was too wired to sleep. He would have periods of desperately wanting a distraction from his distraction.

When Henry was little, he would sit in the car and watch all the other cars fly by him like little streams of colors down the highway. He'd look out and wonder what the little people in the little cars thought: what they were doing; whom they went home to; what they were afraid of; what made them laugh. He could never really imagine it perfectly, but calmed him. As he looked down at the musty, yellow paper with the words scribbled, "The river's tent is broken: the last fingers of leaf clutch and sink into the wet bank"[4]. Late autumn nestling September's heat, he felt the same way as he had while he sat in the car watching streaking colors along the drive.

At the wooden desk, Henry looked out the small window onto the dark grey water. The sun was just rising, a red half-dot that smeared a rainbow between the water and the sky, and suddenly, the feeling came back: tightrope, nausea, knotted stomach followed immediately by Feeling of Airless Room which left him searching aimlessly for causes.

"Henry?" David Smith's voice and the following creak came to Henry.

Henry waited until he found his own voice again, "I'm up here. In the study."

"Good," The footsteps were closing in. The house was singing. "I wanted to show you an old newspaper I found in the attic you may like." The door to the study opened. David Smith looked at Henry from the doorway.

"Oh, wow, thanks. Yea, I'll come up in a bit." Henry didn't look up; he was still trying to find his feet.

"I can leave it on the table for you in the kitchen downstairs, or, you can come up with me now, and we can take a look at it." When David Smith heard the news, he first went to the office and looked at his conquest and thought of all the dead Captains he slew along the way – the failed enterprises of others, the efficiency of his own plans, and how he would be immortal through his work.

"Dad, if you, if you don't mind, I can take a look at it later." Henry's

---

[4] Eliot, T.S., The Fire Sermon, The Waste Land

voice was barely audible.

"Are you alright? – "
"—Ya, I, uh, am just tired."

"—are you sure? You're not looking normal, Henry. You should go outside for a little."

"—Ya, I think you're right. I'll just be outside. I'll take a look at the paper soon. That's exciting, though."

"—if there's anything else, if you just…need to talk…I mean, we can do that." This speech was un-chartered territory for the man, and he embarked on that journey of expression like he did with any of his goals: gusto, fervor, ambition.

"—Dad, did you ever…" Henry began. "Have you…" He tried again. "I feel nervous." It was all he could mention. It was an utter linguistic failure. Again, another miscommunication, another useless uttering of words that barely formed the idea he felt. It was frustrating, but beyond anything, Henry regretted opening his mouth. As he heard himself say those words, he blushed. Of all things to say! "Nervous?" What does that even mean? This was his chance to prove to his father he was half-intelligent and competent, and that he wasn't wasting his time, and "nervous" was all that he could muster?

"What are you nervous about? Is something going on?" David Smith was puzzled. "Is it a girl?" He walked into the study and pulled a chair next to Henry.

"No, no girls. Well, actually, I am dating *a* girl, but she's not the problem. Well, no, I mean, she was kind of an issue, but we talked. You know, we worked it out. It's fine now."

"Do you have a drug problem? It's ok if you do. I know a lot of respectable people who do blow every once in a while. Just don't do that at work, kid." David Smith tread carefully around the issue, hoping to avoid more serious discussions.

"No, no it's not that."

"OK, good, even better. Hate that stuff. You don't want to get into it. Bad for your nose."

"Ha. Yea. I imagine...I just..." Henry tried again, gesticulating carefully, "Sometimes, I feel nervous. Like, a knot in my stomach....but no, no nothing is wrong. I promise. It's just a feeling; I think it goes away. I bet it's worst in the morning." Better. This was better. He was still failing but at least this was closer to honest.

"You just feel nervous out of nowhere?" At this, David Smith was intrigued. He leaned in closer to Henry, as if inspecting his face.

"Yea...no I know that sounds stupid. I mean, I just, I just worry. I don't know. It's like, I've just had to be in school for most my life, and there's a lot more than just sitting and listening to people. I don't think I'm making sense." Henry drifted. Inwardly, he began thinking of February afternoons. On February afternoons, there was a calmness in the snowy woods, a feeling that all the sounds – the voices and the traffic – become absorbed by both the cold and the white, a very particular type of silence marked by absorption. On those afternoons, when Henry used to look outside his window in February, he'd turn off all the lights, and he would hear the sounds of birds and the snow falling from trees, the world awake and whispering and full of secrets to hide. He wanted to regain that calmness.

"Ah. Henry. I think that's normal. I probably felt that way at your age," David Smith lied. "Not sure what you want to do but too many options. Is that it?"

70

"Sort of—", Henry lied in return.

"You have a lot you can do, and it's all there, in front of you. It's a matter of figuring out what to do. Let me give you some advice: set your lands in order. If you take care of your business, it'll follow. It's simple. You don't need anything else." David Smith took the opportunity that opened in front of him to tell Henry exactly what he had meant to say all weekend. "No, business, well, it's not as easy as it sounds, Henry. I've been thinking about this and actually wanted to talk to you." David Smith had prepared exactly what he was going to say. He could recite it like he was speaking from note cards, "It's why I asked you to come here in the first place. May as well have the conversation now. Look, you just have a lot of options. The roads are hardest to pick when there's a lot of them. Take care of your job; that comes first. It's really like taking care of yourself. Nothing else will give you as much sense of self-satisfaction as that thing you create. There're two philosophies of living that I have faced, and it comes out every day in the work place. One is to nurture ideas, and the other is to nurture people. If you have to choose between the two, choose ideas. People bend to ideas. Those are the invariants. Those are the real things. People rarely stand still through time, but ideas, if they are good ideas, will last generations. Sounds pretty simple and maybe almost too simple with all this other mumbo-jumbo people like to spew out these days, but it's the best advice I have for you."

"No, that's great. Yea, it's great. It's good. I get it."

"Well, you should be nervous. I'm glad, actually. You've got great years ahead of you." David Smith smiled at Henry. Henry Smith smiled back. With one-hundred-and-twenty-one words or so, David Smith had set the next eight years in motion.

In the small, wood-floored and wood-walled study, the pine salt air came in through the window. Outside, along the grey painted deck, the old sea rose hips were reaching a full red and bobbed up and down to the Atlantic sails in the distance. David Smith retired to his attic search with

Henry by his side, the two men looking at old records of long passed stories in newspapers far into the night.

Part II

PRELUDE

Alms for Preta

Preta. Preda. *ègui.* The ancient storytellers of the east whispered their names. *Preta.* According to Buddhist folklore, those who roamed the town whistled through their throats and left the hillside and the gorges at nightfall, knocking on every house. They wrestled through doorways and begged with their thin outreached hands extended, the knuckles wrinkled and dried, or with one hand outstretched and the other as a fist covering a needle throat; their stomachs bloated unhappily and dragging on the ground. No one knew where the hungry ghosts had come from, but some had guessed that the villagers had forgotten the alms, while others thought it the demon form of the hunched deltas of the great Huang He, seeking refuge from a long travel. "I bring you to the edge of the river, the open gap of teeth, rotting, waiting, sucking air from the dry clouds. The soiled water you cannot drink, and the mountain is dry," Prophesies foretold. "You can see the violet rip through the air. See, there, rainless thunder again."

The candles were not lit. The lanterns remained dark, and all along the great river at night, the bobbing sounds of moving water rushed through the dead air.

The emaciated swarms marched through the fields. The river crashed into the cliff sides whose sediment stripes carved the land's story along the rock. The backs of men and women rose and fell, like waves on the sea, their shiny spines like the glitter of the sun.

While the mountain was quiet, there was no peace. The dry air crackled, echoing partial thoughts of spoken conversations. There were rocks everywhere, and the mossy surfaces gleamed on the edge of the brown water.

It was the sounds of yearning that drove the ghosts to the towns. They felt they were coming home. They grasped at their necks, as if a bullet hole had long dried out the blood which had once danced through their bodies, and all that was left which they could feel was a great thirst and a very large, insatiable stomach that drooped and craved, wanted and screamed. They were chained in their minds by want - desire, hot-feeding, body-fueling - digging into every part of their consciousness, until they roamed desperately with their faces clinging onto a jaw, a nose, and two bulging eyes which carried a strange grey color. If someone could shine a light on them, the hungry ghosts would display old sallow, yellowed skin that turned translucent, apparitions between the earth and death.

Another day, another new day, another day ending.

CHAPTER 1

Wei An Jing

At this point, Peter turned to Father Turner: "But before I can explain the Buddhist folklore, there's something else that I should say at this point. During my research, I sifted through numerous papers, books, and historical magazines. I found one that intrigued me, and as I begin this next story about a young man in 1960s Henan, China named Wei An Jing, I can't help but remember this one photo which terrified me, shaking me awake with exhilaration in seeing the tremendous cruelty and creativity of humiliation and suffering. In 1913, a millionaire banker traveled to Mongolia on an exotic adventure and took a very peculiar photograph. In 1922 it was published in the forty-first issue of *National Geographic*, wedged between two articles – one on the Gansu Earthquake and another on Canoeing in England. The photo, it keeps me awake at night, Father – is of a woman. The woman has the face of my mother but she does not look like my mother, and her hair is short and wild. She is chained and locked in what looks like a large suitcase at first. There are small bowls of water next to the suitcase, but she cannot reach them. Soon, I realized I was not looking at a suitcase but of a coffin, a real coffin that this woman was alive in and condemned to die in, condemned to die by starvation. There is a cutout in the side of the coffin for her face and one arm to reach out, and in the photograph, she is reaching toward the chain. It is a futile move. She knows she cannot unchain the coffin, but she reaches out, and it is at that moment when I realize she cannot move the chain but is still reaching for it – as if to do something; to try – that I realize the little bowls of water are to keep her alive to prolong her suffering. Then I realize, in this order, that the coffin is portable. The tribe was nomadic. They wanted to keep her with them to taunt her for her adultery so that she could always know that at any moment, they could free her, but inside, deep inside, she knows she will not be freed, but they want to keep that hope in her to make her suffer even more since not all suffering is equal...

"...But Father! The man behind the lens of this photograph! How he stood there photographing it, sending it to the west for a magazine! And then we see this photograph and soon enough we read about Canoeing in Oxford as if all humanity is categorized between the civilized and the savage: here's two buckets, put yourself in one of them. That there is some kind of line which distinguishes us, behind the lens, on the other side of the paper looking at the photograph, that this savage thing we read about is mythological, Shakespearian, a horror story, is only to cover up what we really know – it is we in the photo. It had been us all along. This treatment of a single person, the world inherits. Somewhere deep into its history, this world's identity, it exists beneath a surface only to resurface. We will inherit it. I will say it again..."

* * * * *

...*Henan, China 1960.* There was only rock, nothing but rock -- and where there was no rock, there was only dust. A heavy dust that filled the air and kicked itself from the ground and settled on every breathing thing. The horizon was red; the wind was warm. The warm wind brushed against Wei An Jing's bristled and sun-tanned arms. He stood tall, his dark hair illuminated by the sun while his bones displayed eagerly from his body. His day began early, minutes before the sun rose, when An Jing's stomach had growled loudly. Somewhere nearby a child began crying. "See, you woke up little Ling Ling with your loud stomach," An

Jing's sister, Lu, had said to him in the dark, both lying on straw mats. Her voice was barely a whisper. An Jing rolled over onto his side, his ribs pressed against the hard wooden plank. His daily labor in the fields was increased while his rations were kept the same.. He opened his eyes, which were a color that remained a mystery to the entire village from the day he was born, a strikingly dark grey, they looked nearly blue and nearly brown but not quite either. It was as if the boy had never lost his baby eyes.

"I may as well just get up now," An Jing had replied to his sister. Slowly, he rose and walked toward the darkened door. He opened it and breathed in the stale morning air: still no rain, but the sounds of the other farmers. He and others like him had been tied to the land by the very skin on their necks from nine thousand years back and up to this day, their backs toiled in the same heat as their ancestors and those ancestors before them. Still even, years later after the revolution and the open doors, the others like him would still be tied to the land by housing registration, and years even from when that is relaxed, they would be tied by an invisible chain which chewed some across the world with the same anguish: being born, mysteriously and inexplicably, into the wrong body.

An Jing was up early with the tills to tend to the millet fields, and the soft movement of others pierced his ears. Both wars were over, and after eleven years of peacetime, there was excitement and celebration and revolution but there was no rain and only made-up promises which made Wei An Jing sick to his bowels; the revolution marched on, and they must have missed the band leader's cue, straggling behind with their hands in their pockets and their stomachs empty. They had sung their praises to the salvation, the sun, which had brought them a new heightened awareness of what the people could do, hand in hand, singing, their plows tilling the land, celebrating the new tractors which were brought in a year earlier, melting their pots together to industrialize a nation. But there was still no rain; there was little to plow, and the toils of the new equipment broke against the sweltering backs of the starving. In short, Wei An Jing was hungry. He was hungry the day before and the day before that. He was hungry as long as he could remember, though he knew that only two years earlier, they had celebrated his tenth birthday with great zeal and excitement, and as a present, his mother had boiled an egg from the family chicken. Wei An Jing looked into the future with an irresistible excitement.

It's been two years since that birthday. The day after, the village had established a communal kitchen with three other villages, and suddenly the meals were free. An Jing's family had given up their chickens, while his neighbors had given up their ox, and his other neighbors their pigs, and the sacrifices and gifts were enumerated in a long list. It had all been for the commune. "Don't horde from the people," they were told. "We've given all our hogs and chickens. We are great daughters and sons of the revolution. We celebrate the Sun as it rises in the East and sets in the West," it began. The animals have long been slaughtered since then. Not even the bones remained from which the children could suck the marrow; the fields and trash have been thoroughly searched and hunted. "Where has all the extra food gone? Perhaps over winter, we will see the great planning emerge," they told themselves. At first the children had made a game of it, roaming in packs through old fields that may contain treasures, but as their hunger became more prevalent, even the children sank into a constant worry over the uncertainty. "Why are we still searching for old, rotted vegetables if there's plenty of food left in the kitchens like the cadres keep saying?" one child asked. "Stop being stupid," his older sister answered, "if they hear you, things will be worse for us. Just keep looking and keep quiet."

The food had come on enormous ladles for the first three months since the new law, but slowly, the meats and vegetables disappeared, and then the grain began to disappear. During one particularly difficult month, there was no food for three days. The children stayed home and cried, waiting for their parents to come home from the kitchens, only to find nothing on the dinner table except some boiled water. "Drink some water so you don't go to bed hungry," mothers would say. The children cried in their sleep.

An Jing's mother's condition had begun to worsen. "I'm fine, son," she would say to An Jing whenever he asked.

"Let me take your place in the fields, then," he had said to her. Meanwhile, her arms and legs inflated themselves like a freckled, flesh colored balloon, and that day as Wei An Jing stepped outside and felt the warm, humid wind brush his arms, he thought about lying down on the ground, covering himself with dust so that he could rest. "No," he said to himself. His mother was unwell, and he would send another unheard letter to the province capital in hopes it would reach someone along the ladders of influence who could do something, send someone to feed them all, or do nothing but at least let them know they were left for dead so they could stop worshipping the sun every single morning. One hundred and forty two letters. At one hundred and forty three, he was giving up not by choice but by the softening of his legs which tug at him like weights strapped onto his ankles, tying him to the ground. He tried to get up again, and the exhaustion put a deep hesitation in him that let his fingers uncurl from the letter which rested in his palm.

The letter floated from his grasp. "Ahh!" Wei An Jing shouted in frustration, and he watched the wind carry the letter several feet from him. He feared someone would find the letter and so he slowly moved toward it and grabbed it from the base of a small pomegranate tree. The tree had not flowered for the past two years, and its bark from the limbs down to the roots were stripped for a poor evening's meal that lasted as even worse indigestion days later. The tree bark would be boiled, and it would stick to the inside lining of stomachs and refuse to leave. Wei An Jing groaned and moved slowly toward the post office with its red painted roof, an old building that had been at one point a central monument in the village, an intersection between the crossings of the cities and the village. Next to the post office was a large rock, upon which his neighbor's four-year-old son lay sprawling, too exhausted to move.

Outside, the bodies moved languidly, slowly, softly, and lightly, as if they were all tied down to the very earth that had sprung them, violently, years earlier. Inside, every organ screamed and moaned, contorted and rebelled, the very nexus of something terrible gathered together and left brittle fingernails, weathered skin and shrinking bones. They were light and heavy all at once, their stomachs tying them to the ground, and the lightness of their skin ready to blow away at any moment.

* * * * *

Unable to think of anything better to do and too young to plow the fields for the family ration points, An Jing had a habit of going trash dump to trash dump with his older sister, searching for any thawed signs of last year's food.

"Have you checked the old abandoned field across old Peng's house? Peng died last month, and I don't think anyone has visited those fields," Lu said. The grey button-down shirt and trousers hung from her limbs. Just two years ago, she had nearly outgrown those clothes, but An Jing could swear that she was shrinking, slowly disappearing and hiding behind the patched and repatched clothes she wore day-after-day, washed once a week and never changed. She washed diligently, her hands rubbed raw from the board, scraping off mud and street grime. Lu had never used soap, but she had heard that even in the cities it was scarce, and so she used her dirtied water, wondering what soap felt like.

"Do you think his body is still in the house?" An Jing asked. The last thing he wanted to encounter would be the flies that hung around the dead. It was as if there was a cloud of flies which surrounded the entire village, waiting to feast and lay eggs on the bodies which were dumped on the sides of all the roads except those which left the village. Those roads were kept clean and clear. The family members were too exhausted to bury the bodies, so they had built a fortress of the dead that surrounded the living, an enclosure that creeped in week after week.

"Don't be afraid, An Jing," Lu replied. "Here, I'll go look, and you can stay behind if you want."

"No, I want to come with you," An Jing said. "It'll be easier with two. One can serve as a look-out." She concealed her fears from him, but he watched her more carefully, and he knew she was afraid.

The two walked toward old Peng's house, and as they trekked down the dusty road, An Jing realized the hole at the bottom of his right shoe had become even larger. He felt the little stabs of rocks hitting the thick sole of his skin. Soon, he'll be shoeless. "It doesn't matter," he muttered to himself.

"Did you say something?" Lu asked.

"No, just talking to myself again," An Jing replied. His sister was two years older than he, and yet she took care of him as if she were twice her own age. Their mother and father woke as the sun rose and worked in the fields with the other three thousand commune members, and they came home with empty eyes, carrying what they could muster from the communal kitchens back to the house, which was placed in one large pot, boiled with more water from the town well, and then served as lunch and dinner for the entire family past sundown. Breakfast was air. No one slept through the night.

"Okay, is anyone looking? Let's go into the field and see what we can find," Lu replied. She had heard rumors of villagers being beaten for searching for food in old fields that were abandoned. They had heard the rumors of labor camps, far away places in the west where enemies were sent and no one returned. "Right-leaning tendencies," the cadres had said, "will be severely punished." These words were written on scrolls, which were hung from buildings and schools. In the end, between the fear and the hunger, the hunger was always more convincing.

An Jing looked around and saw the street around them was abandoned.

"Let's go quickly," he muttered and grabbed Lu's hand as the two climbed up and over the stone wall. His arms and legs tired from hauling his body up, and An Jing was amazed he and his sister had the strength to stand afterward.

Lu carried a small bag with her, and as they began walking through the old abandoned field, her hands clutched the straps of the bag tightly. "Start digging through the ground. Sometimes, the winter's frost keeps the turnip ends frozen and edible for the next year."

An Jing knelt down and begin to sift through the earth. His fingernails soon filled with dark brown dirt. "The earth is rich," he said, "so why are we starving?"

"Stop saying things like that out loud. Don't bring any trouble right now. Did you hear how old Peng died? He was accused of being a right deviationist...having this plot of land and using it, and they doused him with cold water and left him out overnight in the winter. He was blue and stiff the next day." Lu retorted. Then she knelt down and began searching through the earth. "Oh, look! This land is full of stuff!" Lu smiled. An Jing looked at her. He had forgotten what her face looked like when she smiled. It was odd, her skin was sallow, and her mouth stretched across her face from one angular corner of her cheek to another. Her teeth were tiny. Yet, her smile lightened him. Three years ago, she had been beautiful.

An Jing would keep the image of that smile in his mind for a long time. Long after his sister died, he would still remember the smile she gave him in old Peng's abandoned plot as they dug up old rotten turnips that had thawed from the winter but kept cool deep in the ground. She would die one month later, the old turnips causing her indigestion, or maybe it was because she had given him more food at her own expense. In any case, he wouldn't be there for her death. He would be gone by then, and he would hear about it much later, when he returned to the village and realized it was abandoned. For a moment, An Jing would believe everyone moved and left without his knowing, but he would later accept that they had all returned to the earth that he was dishelving in old Peng's yard. Standing there, hearing about her death, An Jing would think of the possibilities that Lu may have had, had her life not chosen the path it did: He would imagine that when the college entrance examinations came, she would have taken them with everyone else, having studied little since she cared for the family at home. Perhaps she would have passed, but most likely, she would have failed. She would have remained her father's guard all her life, caring for him and doing his chores. Perhaps would work as a local town officer, perhaps even at the mail office. But perhaps her diligence in caring would extend to the questions on the paper in the grand examination, and perhaps her absolute giving nature would have been rewarded - in some alternate possibility - and perhaps Lu would have been a great party member in a big city. Wei An Jing would sigh, thinking of all the many routes that his sister's life did not take.

An Jing and Lu spent three hours in old Peng's plot, digging up the old harvests which had been left in the ground to spoil from a previous year. Her bag full, Lu tucked it beneath her shirt, hiding the finds. They walked to the gate slowly. An Jing climbed over first and said, "There's no one around." He grabbed the bag from his sister, who climbed up the stone wall after him. He held his hands to catch her as she jumped down, and she flopped into his arms. Then, he placed the bag of turnip ends under his shirt, and they walked toward the other side of town. Along their route down the west side of the village, they saw that half a dozen new bodies were piled at the street corner that led to their home.

"Don't look at them," Lu began. "It'll upset you if you know anyone there." She put her hand to her face to shield herself from the pile of legs and arms, outstretched and folded. The legs and arms looked peaceful, like they were no longer hungry. An Jing followed her and looked down at his feet. The soles of his shoes were destroyed, and his skin rubbed against the hard, hot ground beneath him.

While An Jing and Lu never spoke of it, a hunger ghost visited each

85

family after dinner, reminding them of past traditions they had now long forgotten. "We should have done something for these ghosts," the villagers had first said. "But what?" another would ask. At first, the villagers had thought they were hallucinating, but as soon as the peasants began to talk to one another secretly behind the backs of officials about the hovering specters who demanded more and whistled when they spoke, they realized that the ghosts were real. Either the dead were visiting or the dead were living amongst them or the dead was leading them to the next day. No one was sure. No one knew what to do about it, so they lived amongst the ghosts harmoniously, sharing the dry air of the evenings and the cold pale sunlight of the morning...

CHAPTER 2

Wei An Jing's Fantasies

...The old rats ran through the alleyways and across the rooftops, clever creatures avoiding capture for rat stew. They scuttled around old bones, rattling them, finding meat to gnaw. The bones were chewed clean, licked and sucked for marrow. Old Peng was glossy and smooth, his skull resting underneath the pomegranate tree. After the beating and the dousing, he had wandered the town all night humiliated and confused, and had stumbled into his own yard which he had abandoned and had overgrown with weeds. He had broken down shivering until he was weeping, his cold grey lips cracked. Old Peng had wept and wept like a child. No one was left. His wife had been buried two weeks earlier, and walking over to her grave, the site of a pomegranate tree that had been planted after the birth of his first son, he had knelt down and pressed his chest onto the soil. "Had I known it would be your last day," he had cried, the tears streaming down his face, leaving a snail trail through the mud and dirt on his cheeks and down the corners of his nose and onto his chin, "had I known...why didn't I come home earlier? I had rushed to the kitchens but they were closed early. I came home with nothing. Nothing! And had I had something, would you be here with me? Your last day, if I had known it, I would have stayed in bed and held your hand just a little longer and left this earth with you. I would have touched each finger, and held them so that your transition to the next world would not be lonesome."

He had pulled at his shirt, then at his collar, and then at his hair. He had twisted his hands together until they were raw and chewed his own teeth until he could feel the grinding hit a nerve, his sobs coming in fits of silence across a gaping mouth missing three teeth. Then old Peng had stopped weeping and stared at the branches of the forlorn tree. Suddenly, he had begun digging with his bare hands. He had dug until his nails were torn and his fingers raw, and he had not remembered how long he had dug. Upon finding the corpse of his wife, he had pulled it out until a decaying hand emerged from the earth. Holding it, like it was some old treasure, old Peng had laid down and died.

That night, three hungry ghosts came to visit Old Peng and his wife, sitting beneath the tree, their hands outstretched on Old Peng's body, their voices whistling in the dark as the rats found their suppers and scurried in the night with thin hairless tails trailing against the earth. The rats feasted on the corpses that laid above the ground, unburied, rotting underneath the pomegranate tree, feeding it. And the hungry ghosts looked onward with pleading eyes, "water, water..." they whispered.

Old Peng's wife, Mei Hua, had been a beauty. Her reputation had stretched across the province, so when she had married a shy man of moderate wealth and modest stature before the revolution, her neighbors were shocked. "The money the family could have made, marrying that one off!" they whispered. But Mei Hua, whose mother and father had died years earlier, gave no heed and lived in a happy home with young Peng, raising chickens and fruit trees, through the wars, the revolution, the three children...but neither she nor her glowing beauty saw past 1961 -- like their neighbors two houses down, or the neighbors a street away, or Mei Hua's two aunts, four cousins, and daughter.

* * * * *

Three weeks later, one evening, An Jing and Lu sat on their straw beds waiting for dinner while their mother and father stood near the stove.

The communal kitchens had run out of food and had closed, so they were allowed modest cooking in their own homes again. Lu had a made a soup with the unearthed treasures from old Peng's yard. The smell of the soup was indistinct with all the left over pieces of things they could possibly digest thrown into one large pot with three times as much water as needed, a thin brownish fluid brought to a boil and salted so they could drink more water to fill their stomachs after the soup were gone.

Watching his mother give him and his sister the thickest portions of the soup, waiting for them to eat first before she had a drink of the leftover broth, An Jing felt sick to his stomach. Her arms looked worse, puffier. At first, they had marveled at the bloat, and even laughed. Lu and he had played games with one another, poking each other's arms and watching the indent of the finger remain on the skin for long after. They had poked and poked, until each looked spotted. But now, neither had the energy to entertain the other. The edema was not going away, no matter how much boiled wheat husk broth she drank, and one evening, An Jing had watch his mother cut herself with a dull knife, and he had sworn that instead of blood, a pink ooze flowed and bubbled out of her: she had confirmed his worst fears that she was thinning, possibly disappearing, even from within.

Afraid of vomiting and wasting the precious bits of nutrients, An Jing offered the contents from his bowl to his sister, who looked at him in confusion, "Brother --," she began. Before anyone could say anything further, he got up, walked out the door and into the night without a word, angrily wishing to disappear.

It had been a long time since he cried, but An Jing sat against the rock underneath a brightly lit night sky, crying and hiccupping, much like the way old Peng had done when he came back to find his wife dead, her hand grasping a ladle. It was the kind of crying that lost all shame, dizzied and drunk in its own sadness. In the darkness, An Jing felt safe with his interrupted hiccups and tears.

Sixty years ago, his great grandfather had owned some land, marrying two women. It was the turn of the century when the opium trade was blooming and hungrily sucking up the wealth, and Wei An Jing's great grandfather gambled away the last of the money. From his grandfather onward, the family was poor, wandering from street to street to sell labor for food, always staying close to the land which gave birth to them: Wei An Jing had in his genetics the ability to till the land and sense when the millets would harvest most prosperously, when the rains would nourish and when they would wash away the nutrients. They were the people who lived on the banks of the Huang He, and whose lives existed because of it or taken in its wrath, the water and bodies spilling onto the banks during angry flooding. Over two thousand years, ceremonies and sacrifices were held on the very soil in which dozens of young girls were thrown into the river as a gift to the Heavens to appease the fickle river. Emperors on Earth wanted to elicit the pity of the Emperors in the Heavens, and temples were constructed. Even two thousand years ago, human bodies had been found at the mouths of the altars, immobile and vacant, having died mid-prayer. Two thousand years later, in poorness had been how his grandparents had met, both begging, one slightly wealthier than the other. On a train ride selling yams, Wei An Jing's great-grandmother had offered his grandmother -- then eighteen to a young -- to a strong farmer whose slow smile warmed a room with crooked teeth. Seeing an opportunity in their future, the dowry had been settled carefully in an old kitchen next to the hearth, and Wei An Jing's destiny to exist was predicted over forty years before his birth...before he came to the earth blotched and crying, hugging at his mother's umbilical cord, reluctant to leave the warm, safe womb.

Suddenly, An Jing saw the figure of a shadow moving toward him. Upward, the sky danced, the Milky Way swooning under the weight of the hanging stars, unmoving in their positions from An Jing's rock. Soon under the moonlight, he saw it was Jian Qui Hui, his classmate and a young girl who caught the eyes of a few other older classmates. Embarrassed, Wei An Jing turned from her so that he could wipe the tears from his face. Though had he seen his own reflection, he would have noticed the brown streaks that smeared his face.

"Are you talking to yourself?" she asked. The words rolled out of her carefully and slowly to ease his embarrassment. Her voice was soft and her face was calm. The clouds covering the moonlight did not permit him to see that something rustled and threatened to disturb the peacefulness deep inside her. It was her eyes, which were endlessly pleading.

"It's my favorite activity these days in this village. Better than working in the field or pretending to learn in school," he replied, hoping he could frighten her off and discourage more conversation. Feeling bold by his cruelty toward the quietly suffering thing, he continued, "They've left us here to die. They've just forgotten. Like we're nowhere on the map. Even you, with your good marks in school. They've forgotten all of us."

"Who?" she asked. She moved no closer to him and stood there, watching his back, ten feet away from the rock. Still fearing to embarrass him, she planted herself there, below him and far enough that he could escape her questioning if he needed.

"The Idols, the Gods, all of them, man or supernatural." Hearing his voice say this, he suddenly wished he could take it back. What if she didn't understand and became frightened? What if she reported him? Suddenly, he was furious with himself, and he felt his face reddening in frustration which turned into fear with each passing second of her silence.

"What do you wish for?" she finally said, her muted figure now growing with the words she threw at him.

He hesitated a moment, and then he turned around, his eyes beginning to tear again, "I wish to die."

With these words, she too began to cry. The evening light illuminated her face, which glowed starkly white, and he saw what the two years had done to her as well: her shoulders jutted underneath her cotton shirt in sharp angles, and he could see the stitches that brought her waistband closer together. Suddenly, he imagined her as a rag doll who followed him into the darkness and listened to him cry. Upon this, he was deeply ashamed at how carelessly he threw his words out. He had been selfish.

"Qiu Hui," he began, "I didn't mean it…"

"Little Ling Ling died this morning," she managed to say quietly. "They're planning to cremate the body tomorrow, but after losing their only son just a few months ago, I don't know how that family is going to carry on. Don't say things like that please. Think of your mother."

He imagined his mother was at home, laying awake in bed so hungry her thoughts began to gnaw and eat away at her own mind, knowing just how many days she had left in the month to feed the family without the commissioner giving them a bigger ration than what he gave them the previous month, living moment by moment while her body mutinied and began to coalesce, the organs sticking to themselves in revolt, all to keep him and his sister alive another miserable day. Another miserable and hungry day. Time sprawled out in his memory, which slowly moved from when the hunger began to a month, to six months, to a year, and now reaching two years, he saw the infinite horizon upon whose doorstep he stood, begging for history and time to reverse, knocking at a door which remained closed and locked to him.

When he regained where he was again, he saw that Qiu Hui had moved onto the rock next to him and lay down. She was looking at the sky and counting the stars, one by one. "Does that make you feel better?" he asked her suddenly, hoping to put his own weaknesses out of both their memories.

"Sometimes," she replied starkly, then slowly and more hopefully, "It's truly fascinating how many stars are out there, how the sky is just littered with them, and with each one, I wonder whether there's another me, living far away in a different life, happy and full. Maybe there's another you, too."

"Maybe I'm a leader in this other world."

"You could be!"

"And I could make sure my mom, dad and sister all have enough food to last them the rest of their lifetimes, and my sister would go to school, no, she'd even go to college, and me too." Had he said those things? Had he dared to even dream these things? When did these things seep into his mind and poison his thoughts? Those dreams, those wishes, they sat above his head like a little cloud. During the day, he swatted them away, "Focus!" he would command his desires, "You need to be strong enough to take care of your family." But at night, as the sun set, it was as if the curtain to his life closed with the waning sun and the next curtain - the curtain to his wishes - began to lift, and he was on stage living the grandest desires that robbed him of sleep.

The clouds moved, and the stars shined unblocked. They stood fixed at first, and then they began to move as he stared at them, and one by one, the longer he stared, the more they vibrated, until suddenly the fixed positions of the stars began to shift, and one by one, they flowed and fell...the entire milky Way was dancing like it always had. It was he - An Jing realized - who had assumed they stayed still, but truly, the stars moved as the earth he was standing on moved, and both the sky and the earth moved so that it was hard to tell how one movement changed the other, how one thing created another. It had always been and it would always be, yet somehow - in that moment of lightness - he had seen something.

Suddenly, as if an arrow pierced his thought, An Jing realized he had stormed out of this house earlier without telling anyone where he was going. Scared his mother would still be up waiting for him, he quickly apologized to Qiu Hui and headed back toward his home, passing the

93

empty, barren fields that mocked them pitilessly. When An Jing's mother had given birth to her second child, her first son, she marveled at how pink and messy he was, crying out of the womb as if she had perturbed him from a great and wonderful sleep. He had refused to sleep for the next three weeks, and as she fed the crying little thing that sucked on her and clutched at her, she felt a tremendous love for the little thing whose life depended on her own. "I must live," she had told herself softly in the dark of the night as his mouth reached around to her nipple, "I must live," she had repeated in the dark as a consolation to her own promise. From that day, she had become a shell of being which fed its children and lived through the fibers of their growth, through the newness of the world explained by their grasp of the air around them, placing form and edges onto *things* to make them objects, placing abstractions onto the objects, making connections and leaps between the ideas, and taking on an entire life which was independent of her and yet still, forever, part of her.

As An Jing entered their small house built of red clay, he saw that his mother had left him a bowl of soup, knowing he would return. He took the soup outside so he could eat it without disturbing anyone and after finishing it, felt eerily hungrier than before, a big hole of guilt rumbling in his stomach...

CHAPTER 3

Wei An Jing Begins a Very Strange Journey

…Wei An Jing's mother died on a cold November morning one month later. That same morning, Lu lost her hair and stopped speaking, and city officials from the Province's capital received guests from Beijing on a very private First Class Train, eating pickled vegetables, sauteed pork and scallion steamed buns. Old Peng's house had been ransacked, and soon after, the house and all entrances to the yard were boarded up by officials to prevent entry from villagers, or deviants of the revolution: stealing was outlawed even for the hungry. The village was silent; there were no crying babies, and the young children no longer played outdoors but stayed inside lying in beds or remaining close to the warmth of the stove, their callow skin shivering tightly against their shrunken bones. There was a silence that pervaded the air as the days became shorter and the nights colder. An Jing's mother was cold within a day, the warmth escaped first, and then her lips seemed to drag against the weight of dead muscles. Those cold little children born before the year the great famine began would never make it through that winter, their bodies would be dumped alongside a ditch. The ditch would be shallow, no more than three feet deep. There would be no burials for the dead. One mother would go insane, wandering the streets days after her two young daughters' deaths, clutching their old clothes and talking to the air, as if the clouds themselves were enshrined with the faces of her little lost ones. As for the others: they'd already forgotten how to mourn. What was left of those who had stayed behind clung to this world with their shortened breath in silence and fistfuls of lost hair. There was no shortage of hair; it was everywhere -- hair that fell onto the ground next to straw beds, hair that blew through the air and clung against the corners of houses both outside and in, and hair that fell in heaps in the fields. Each bowl was as empty as the day before, and the hair clumped into big piles.

And there was still silence.

There was little left of the town except for a few half memories, a feeble history that rose in the darkness from the timeless moments, laughter, brightness, hope, liberation and rain. There had been no production quota then, and they had had small plots to farm on. Yet even those things seemed far away -- what was before the great hunger was war and before war a different hunger, but perhaps far away, perhaps distant enough in the past and the memory; there were better times which each lineage had inherited from mouths to ears, story after story. It was the only thing that reminded An Jing he was still human.

An Jing's humanness knocked on his door in the evenings, when he tended to his sister and father, ladle in hand, scooping up the mix of wheat flour congee, the humanness spilling over outside and around his bowl. Sweet potato was a blessing, and having run out of that two months earlier, he had turned to corn husks, the dry things sticking in his teeth, keeping him awake late at night. The more he hungered, the more his humanness visited, his thoughts sticking to his mortality and running over the memories he kept close to him. Lu sat at the table, her hands busy with the corn husks, rolling and kneading, as if she were making a bread. An Jing told her stories in the evening. He told her about when they would walk along the great river in the summers and thinking of where the waters had come from - the far away lands, and they would tell stories of what the water had seen.

"The water had seen a great warrior," he might say.

"A great warrior from another land trying to invade our homeland," he imagined her replying to him in her mind.

"The great warrior had magical powers," and so these conversations would go.

He retold these stories, picking the best ones, and sat next to her, holding her hand. Some nights, he would take out her comb and slowly comb her hair, watching the clumps fall out, keeping note when her hair loss accelerated and feeling desperate, wondering if somehow he could put the hair back on her head, strand by strand, she would live.

Sitting inside his house soaking in the warmth of the stove, An Jing looked out the window at the deserted town, and thought:
"There is nothing left here except my memories of something that does not belong here anymore. Those memories have escaped, but we shall have to search for them somewhere far. In another year, this town will no longer have a living soul in it, and the lying fools have erased our entire history and existence with it. As far as they care, we were never here."

He felt his humanness leaving him. He got up, opened the door to the streets, spat angrily onto the ground and watched as the sand curled up along the wet spit. The wind hurled itself at his face, and he closed the door immediately, afraid he would let the cold inside to sweep away the remaining life. The coals in the stove burned, and he inhaled the smell of the smoke, thinking of food in the ashes.

But leaving the village to find work was a difficult proposition for Wei An Jing; he had a sister to care for whom he was convinced would never recover from her mother's death. Will their father tend for her if he can barely tend for himself? An Jing was one of the few who remained in the town who could read and write well enough to leave in the current state to look for work in the city - the others from his school had either left earlier or had stopped their schooling to spend the days at home or in the fields, making up for family members who were too weak to work.

What about his humanness? Humanness dripped down from the heavens and chained him to the earth, so that his own flesh burned with want and desire for the sickened land beneath his feet and between his fingers. The land starved him; it chained him to his own coffin, and it would cover him with the very dirt he could not eat and only his own delusions kept him free each day, making decisions as if his will were at the helm of the boat that went from side to side. It was the same humanness that crept into his conscience and self-consciousness, chaining him to fear and silence. The result was that An Jing's mind was chaotic: he wanted to leave, yet he could not, beyond even the safety concerns of his father and sister. In fact, he had become inconceivably intertwined with another inexplicable and complicated matter. Wei An Jing was in love, in love before he even knew it was love, before he even knew the word for love for he had only used the thought, the feeling, the attachment without words...

* * * * *

Peter sighed and broke from telling the story. After a rested pause, he continued, "And so when I tell this story of Wei An Jing, I am reminded, shocked into remembering, this photograph. They had been punished in the same way as this unnamed woman in the photograph, to starve slowly but to be allowed the delusion of life. But their stories, that of An Jing and his family and his village, is lost as sand on the dunes of a vast history which has largely been forgotten...But we will inherit it."

"Peter, would you like to continue, then, on An Jing's story?" Father Turner asked.

"Yes, because here, and I interjected since the story does take a turn here, something unexpected happens to An Jing...

CHAPTER 4

Mysterious Arrival of Grain

...After their first night star gazing and sharing their fears and secret dreams and their fears of their secret dreams, Qiu Hui had begun to follow An Jing around, longing for his company. If she was busy tending to chores or searching for food along the bank of the river, he'd come by just to talk to her, distracting and slowing her, giving her body of bones and skin weight. He knew that night weeks ago on the rock as he rushed home that she was inexplicably attached to him. During the entire time that he ran through his mind the lofty idea of leaving, it was she who soothed his anxieties into calmness and harnessed his confidence so that the mere idea of leaving was a possibility. After that night on the rock, they had begun meeting every single day. Some days, they were wordless, and others, they searched the earth together.

"Do you think the snail can breathe under that big shell?"

"Of course it can. It's like all living things. It has to be able to breathe."

Qiu Hui herself could not understand how she felt this first attachment springing up from within, but it was characterized by a fluttering in her stomach and sweaty palms. She was even quieter around him than otherwise, but her quietness rested in comfort. When they did speak, they philosophized. She challenged him, pushed him to the edges of thinking, and quietly, she gave him hope.

Before her, his words had been escaping him, threatening to fly off as he focused on breathing - in and out and out and in - his lungs moving upward and downward and fighting off the cough which threatened to explode from him.

Without Qiu Hui, he would never have had the idea of leaving. "Why do you need to stay here if you can leave and bring help?" she had asked.

With her, because of her, the thought of leaving her behind tormented him for she was immobile, tending to two younger siblings and a sick father. "You can come with me. We could go together. Two is better than one anyway. We could try to reach the city and tell them what's happening," he had suggested one winter evening while they were out looking for food in the neighboring villages. The mourning for his mother had turned to a desperation that fueled action, and he spent the past seven days searching for food in old composts from years past, like in Old Peng's yard, hoping still the frost had kept old turnip ends and leaves from decomposing.

"No, I can't leave. It's impossible...there'll be no one at home," her voice had drifted, and he knew that she was turning the options in her mind, and that the wheels would keep turning themselves revolution after revolution and she would become lost her own thoughts.

"I understand." In that instant he saw a possibility, a life with one road, a drifting chain of cause and effect slowly beginning to slide in place before him, and he knew that his life would be far away from hers and yet running parallel at the same time, like a train that switches tracks mid-platform.

So it was a rather curious matter when, several days after An Jing insinuated a future for himself and Qiu Hui, he received a notice, a letter stamped with red ink on thick paper, asking him for his services in the provincial capital immediately. The capital was one hundred and fifty kilometers away, and that he would need to arrange his own travels for one-third of the initial journey. Fifty kilometers away, he would come across a small village where a car, a real car, would be waiting for him at old Ning's abandoned tea shop. With the notice came a mysterious, large shipment of grain with specific instruction for allocation amongst the villagers and for An Jing's travels, which caused some panic and excitement. No one knew where the grain came from, nor was anyone clear on what exactly An Jing's new position would be. All they knew was that suddenly, there would be something to eat that night and the night after.

Incidentally, this mysterious event made An Jing quite a hero in the village, and he was decorated with old red banners of celebration and calligraphy and dressed in what the town could muster from old scraps of clothing hidden away in corners of dusty rooms, for those old things could not be eaten. "You must be a chosen son of the Party. Our town has been selected for our duties. You're going to make us proud and bring us luck. We knew it all along," his neighbors rejoiced. Then for those days leading up to his departure, he was brought babies to touch and bless, was visited constantly by fathers proudly bringing their daughters, and his family was raised to the status of local celebrities. "An Jing, you have good luck. Hold my child."

The only person who seemed withdrawn at the new luck for the village was Qiu Hui. She had become quiet during his final days. In fact, he was convinced she was avoiding him; every time he stopped by her house, her sister would come out to say that she was sick that day and ran a high fever.

Qiu Hui was, in fact, quite ill. That same instance when An Jing asked her to accompany him and she toiled with the thoughts of a life with him and the thoughts of the decay her own family would endure, she felt something inside of her -- some fiber which made the inner linings of her very muscles -- begin to tear slowly, and then suddenly (as the linings tore themselves) something dislodged itself inside her and crumbled apart. She was spinning, and something was falling out of her, day after day. It fell

101

from all sides of her. She was losing pieces of herself, like a porcelain doll chipping away as she spun faster and faster, on her axis which she could not change. Where she was lost she knew she could find herself again but find herself in an impossible place, which was of course nowhere else but beside him. In that very instance when An Jing saw the events of his life unfold with hers running along a different set of tracks, Qiu Hui saw the same images, flashing out in front of her one by one, but all the while, she saw that she no longer ran the rail on its tracks.

Was love a delusion or an illusion, an axis on which she spun but had no control over the speed or start and stop, or did she make it up, hold onto it as her crutch, spinning with it until she lost all other elements of herself? Qiu Hui would not have been able to answer it. Her decisions were always hers to seek out the next step: visit An Jing, show him something she had discovered, walk with him along the river, or lay next to him - exhausted - on the rock. But the trajectory that she fell onto was completely beyond her, transcendental, something which pulled beneath and within, without boundary or confirmation, loose and free, yet out of control all at once.

* * * * *

The day of his departure, An Jing woke up with great sadness and said goodbye to his father and sister in the early morning. His sister was silent, but he whispered to her as she lay in the straw bed with her eyes open: "I promise I'll return. Things will be okay until then. I promise. We've got enough to get on for a few months, and the new season will come before then. This year will be a better year, and I'll report back often and bring gifts. I'll bring you so many gifts." The air was cold even inside the house. His words were accompanied by the steam of his own breath. He touched her hand, and he felt her hand tighten and a warmness come across her face. She closed her eyes and slowly let go, finger by finger, slowly, as if trying to memorize the texture of his hand.

An Jing's father followed him to the edge of the village, wrapped his cold hands around his arm and said slowly, "Whatever it is you'll be doing, just remember to come home safe, son." With that An Jing wiped a tear secretly from his eye and turned to walk along the dirt road, hoping to hitchhike a ride to the province capital. From afar, both men looked similar in stature, wrapped up in layer after layer of clothing, like little cotton wads.

An Jing walked no more than five hundred feet when he came across a small stooped figure sitting on the road. It was Qiu Hui. Early in the morning, she must have left her house and walked, in the bitter cold, to edges of the town where she would expect him to exit to say goodbye peacefully.

"I brought you my coat. It's warmer than yours. Take it, you'll be tired." She put her head down and stared at the ground, her hand extended with the large coat hanging from it.

In that moment An Jing felt a deep resentment for Qiu Hui. This was her only coat. He had seen her wear it day and night, and it was an old worn thing that made her twice the size she really was. By handing it to him, she was committing herself to freezing, and all the while as he wore it, he would feel his guilt wrapped up around him to keep himself alive.

"Qiu Hui, just come with me!" he cried out suddenly, his voice choking with emotion. "This has become unbearable." He said it. He felt no reason to hold anything in. He would leave, after all. If she refused him, humiliating him again by refusing to come with him, he could turn away and walk from her. He could forget her. An Jing turned his own gaze onto the ground.

As a child, An Jing had been terrified of stepping into cold water. He would put one toe in, feel the water and the temperature of his toe reach an equilibrium before he put the next toe in. And this is how he had entered the rest of his body, limb by limb, slowly. One day, Lu had challenged him to jump in without hesitation, and fearing losing the

103

challenge to his sister, An Jing had jumped in, eyes closed, mouth puckered, ready to feel the cold envelop him. But once after the first time jumping in with his eyes closed expecting something unexpected, An Jing knew he could never be anything other than fully submerged. Love, for An Jing - in youth and even later as he aged - was like this.

So that morning, upon meeting An Jing on the road, Qiu Hui said nothing, but instead, she started at her neck and soon her shoulders, hips, knees began to crumple down, bringing her slowly to the earth. As she slowly slid downwards, she dragged An Jing's conscience with her. How could he have contemplated forgetting her? He needed her, longed for her company, another person to share the day with, those endless days when he woke up in the early morning cold and shivering, remembering that he still lived in this life, this minute, and living itself was the greatest defiance and the greatest victory against all the nature around them, and only she knew it so long as she had a breath in her. She understood him, and whatever foreign lands he reached, it only be she, who listened to his weakest moments and lived minute by minute with him through it. There were no other words - there could be no other words that would connect him to another human in the same way.

An Jing reached down to pull her up, and suddenly, touching her cold, damp skin, he felt something travel between them that jolted him suddenly. All at once, he saw the images flash like a dozen light bulbs in his eyes: a woman with dark hair and glittering eyes smiling and running to him; another woman, with hair as yellow as the sun looking at herself in a darkened mirror; and two young men laughing together, friends, all in places he had never imagined or seen or dreamed of before. And in that same instance, An Jing saw himself with Qiu Hui in an intimate embrace, their lives intertwined by an unseen fabric which tied itself across space and time. They held one another for a long time, they held one another for the first time, they held one another for the last time.

An Jing blinked. When he cleared his eyes, he realized Qiu Hui was gone.

104

That evening, An Jing's father had a very wakeful dream. In it, he was walking along a large road, the largest road he had ever seen, and it was loud with cars the likes of which he had never seen before. His eyes were wild with color, and when he looked up, he saw buildings alongside this large, busy road that made him gasp. Ai ya! It was as if the sky and the rooftops met; the towers were metal mountains against clouds, the heavens and ground were connected. An Jing's father suddenly saw, in the window of one of the large mountain-like towers, the face of a young man peering out. The young man, suddenly An Jing's father realized, was his own son but not his son, in a body similar but not quite An Jing's. The young man did not see him, but as An Jing's father looked closer, he saw this familiar young man suddenly put a gun to his mouth. No! An Jing's father tried to shout. He closed his eyes and put his hands to his face, and suddenly, he was awake in the darkness, in his own straw bed in his familiar home.

Three small alleyways away and earlier that day when the sun was still high and the heat warmed their backs, Qiu Hui lay in her bed with her door closed. She heard the knocking and ignored it, and when the minutes passed into a half hour passed into an hour and the knocking stopped, she felt a great emptiness inside her. Suddenly, she couldn't think of talking to a single person. The silence began to echo in her head, and then along the walls of her house until the entire thing filled with silence so unbearable that she wanted to shout, "I'm here! Please someone save me!" It was then that she began, slowly at first but then more quickly, to shed her tears, until there were small streams washing down her face and onto her quivering body. With each tear she shed, she felt an edge of levity, as if when she cried all her tears, she'd become a little cloud that would float to rejoin with the heavens...

CHAPTER 5

The Sibyl of Cumae and the Monk

…The Sybil of Cumae had no memory of being young. Through the years, she had seen the rise and fall of vast empires, spanning horizons and reaching edges of the earth that the old fashioned explorers had never dreamed before they set out on the seas, until the seas were no longer infinite but contained on the smallness of a globe which competed for sea and land. The world shrunk as time moved forward. Empires were shorter, expanding and tumbling faster until they tumbled at a dizzying telescopic rate of which the Sybil could no longer keep track. *Spiraling, spinning, tilting, and all the while she moved forward.* Meanwhile, she had lost count of her years; she had wished the grains of sand in her hand, but she had forgotten that while history was cyclical, her body punished her by keeping beat to a linear time. Her memory search forward and backward along with the rising and falling of history in the same pattern as the rise of the moon and setting of the sun; she had remembered the young boys, they had asked her, "Sybil, Sybil what do you wish?" and sitting in her cave, the lonely thing had said, "I wish to die." Yes, she remembered that afternoon when the boys came to her and taunted her, taunted her for her small frame and hawk eyes, for nearly disappearing but still sitting in her cage, counting history in grains of sand while her body disappeared.

On one peculiar day, the Sibyl of Cumae sat in her cage and had a dream, while the oak leaves blew circles on the floor of the dark atrium.

"Is my...is he...is he alive?" he asked in her dream. She remained silent. In her dream, she had wanted to say, "No, he really died," but when she opened her mouth to say it, nothing came out.

"What am I going to do?" He then asked. "Am I a murderer?"

She replied again in silence, "The truth will come out."

He kept asking her more questions, "Should I search my father's death? How do I do this right?"

With each question, she had tried to reply, but her replies only voiced in her head. Then finally, he asked, "What is my future?" She surprised herself by her own voice, which echoed through the caves, and came back in waves.

She replied by reciting a poem by Xie Ling-yun:

"As for my
Homes perched north and south,
Inaccessible except across water:

Gaze deep into wind and cloud
And you know this realm utterly."

Then she added a question directed at him, "Our bodies know the direction of time, but do our minds?"

She said nothing else and pointed him the way out. He thanked her and made sure to step over the leaves at the mouth of the cave. When she awoke, she set out to find the man whose face she had already forgotten and deliver him the message.

* * * * *

Even in the dryness, the desert, while the infertile lands gave birth to things that wilted in the sun by noon, cracked and died by nightfall, An Jing felt a freedom – a hollowed freedom as he thought of her name, running it through his memory as if he were afraid of forgetting. With the dead accumulating around him and the skin of the men withering and wrapping –twice, three times – closer to the bones, he was marching toward an end that had purpose.   Yet as he marched, An Jing found himself missing the things he had never noticed: the moisture that gathered around Qiu Hui's eyes, the warmth of his sister's hands even on the coldest days, his father's slow ambling weight which thudded against the dirt floors, reminding An Jing that he was yet still connected to that land.   All these things, and more, began to approach An Jing like little omens which followed his memory and surprised him – as if they had been hiding all along beneath the surface of the banal and only resurfaced as he could no longer reach them.   Sighing, only half a day's walk away from the village, he found himself struck by a deep sadness and understanding that when he returned to the village (and if he should return to the village), it would never be as it had been.

An Jing walked no more than half a day when, sometime in the late afternoon as the sun began to lean westward, he caught the figure of another far ahead along the dusty road.   He was feeling thirsty and had re-filled his water bag once already when he had stopped to eat some rice, which his father cooked the night before.   Chewing on the soft, fluffy clumps of cold rice, An Jing's felt a flutter of anxiety inside him: his home was now nowhere in sight.   His father's arthritis was bothering him, and at times, the aging man struggled to stand.   His father never spoke of it, but An Jing had seen it in the way he moved and held his breath.   Yet every morning, An Jing's rather rose out of bed to work, forcing his creaking bones to plow and till.   Now, with a mouth full of rice, An Jing imagined his father creaking around the kitchen, trying to make food. The communal kitchens were closed; "Better off for it," An Jing murmured.   Soon, though, he imagined his father stumbling around, dropping pans, bowls and ladles, now taking over a job from his wife which he hadn't done in years.

It was his father who had taught An Jing how to fish. They had stood on a large rock not far from the riverbank, lines dropped in the water. His father had told him stories to pass the time. He had learned how to read on his own, through an early apprenticeship in a dentistry, begging the literate to teach him words, and later once he had words to read, he consumed the Classics. "There is this famous story about two aristocratic houses sometime in the middle of the Qing Dynasty," his father had told him one time, "One of the houses, the Jia house, had a boy named Baoyu who was born with a magical piece of jade in his mouth…" and the story would carry on until their fishing lines tugged with reward. The rice stuck itself between his teeth, and An Jing realized that in thinking of his father and the long stories, he had begun to shed salty tears that leaked into his mouth. Ashamed at his own weakness, An Jing swallowed hard and wiped his face.

The figure in the distance became larger and larger, and An Jing squinted as he walked along the road, hoping the edges around the bobbing lump would smooth and level, giving him an idea of who was approaching, if anyone at all.

Minutes later, An Jing could see that the moving thing was a man, a small man at first who became a hunched man, who then became a man in a brick red robe. It was a curious figure. Soon, An Jing came across the monk, whose bald head hovered just around An Jing's shoulder. The monk stared and smiled at him with a set of curious, dark green eyes, a color An Jing had never seen before on a person. "Ah! An Jing my friend, I have long heard about you! How are you faring on your travels? Is life treating you as well as you had hoped outside the village?"

An Jing stepped back in surprise. How did the old monk know him? His dialect was strange, and An Jing, who had never traveled outside his province before, mused: was it Southern? Northern? Western? Something different altogether? Before his mind could allow him to compose a suitable answer, he blurted, to his embarrassment, "Who are you? How do you know about me?"

The old monk smiled. He walked up to An Jing and looked him up and down, spending quite a bit of time on the holes in An Jing's twice re-sewed cloth shoes and smiled. "That coat is not yours. The young lady you left behind, have you stopped thinking of her in the ten-thousand steps you've taken today?"

Unable to find a response to the monk's question and with his jaw agape, his eyes wide with shock, An Jing looked down at his own shoes and at the monk's thick sandals in disbelief. Finally, he managed to say, "I'll return to her and return her coat."

"Tch! You young men! You never know the right words to say! I have never pursued a woman, and I wouldn't have responded like a wooden plank." The monk shook his head and waved his hands furiously.

An Jing stood unsure of what he was more surprised by, the presence of the monk, the monk's presumptuous attitude about An Jing's life (which was none of his business, anyway), or the monk's reprimand at An Jing's dealings with women. Before he could begin asking the first question in his list of many, the monk began again. "Having a heart of suppleness is not your strong point, nor is it your destiny. I see your dilemma. I've traveled a long way to meet you, Wei An Jing. I've heard a lot about you. The mountains high in the west have buried my footprints on my journey, and my dreams have told me what you are doing." He smiled again.

"For heaven's sake who are you? How have you heard of me?!" An Jing screamed. His stomach grumbled, and he realized the rice from noontime had found its way into the muscles of his body, which begged for more. He wasn't sure what the monk heard better, his voice or his stomach.

The monk scratched his head aggressively and walked closer to An Jing, peering into his eyes and replied, "Of course, you don't know. By the way, are you hungry? I have a few steamed buns." The monk took from his knapsack three fresh steamed buns which appeared, in An Jing's hungry opinion, out of thin air. The monk handed them over to An Jing, whose hands barely reached to catch the buns.

"I come from the mountain Song where monasteries were built hundreds of years before your time. I'd been living there a long time when one night, I had a strange dream. I dreamed I had traveled across the largest mountains in the far west in search of the land of Illusion. I was very tired from my travels and having entered a desert land with no water, I sat beneath a juniper tree to rest and sleep off my fatigue. When my eyes opened, I saw that a riverbed had emerged in front of me. As my weariness and sleep wore off, the river began to rise. From it emerged a being - this man or woman whose presence was illuminating - I knew at once this fairy or celestial saint was not from this world. The fairy told me a curious story. I seemed to understand the story, though I do not remember any of it now. When I reached the height of clarity, as if this entire time in all the years I remember being alive I was living in a dense fog of unrealness, I awoke. There I was sitting beneath the same juniper tree, except my thirst was quenched, and my robes were wet, as if I had actually stepped onto a river. And somehow, my robe had in it a very small red flower. I reached a different kind of clarity, a lesser one, one where I could not see through the fog of unrealness, but I was aware of its existence. I jolted awake. I got up, in the night, and looked at the moon. I forgot I had woken from a dream. It was unusually bright that night, and the moon lit the grassy floors around the monastery and, ai ya!, I saw that beneath the moonlight was a sudden bed of little red flowers. Just like that, the dream and the dream in the dream came back to me in a flash."

The monk smiled at An Jing again as if this strange story of his dreams gave reason to his understanding of An Jing's life. Unnerved, An Jing found his voice again, "But how did the dream lead you here?"

The monk looked around him and saw a dried pomegranate tree and replied, "Let's sit beneath that dead tree for a bit. It's not much shade, but somehow it seems more civilized than standing here in the middle of the road, holding steamed buns. I might even have some pickled vegetables left. Let's share them together." An Jing complied, and the two walked to the pomegranate tree whose branches showed evidence of wear, the trunks torn and shredded to make a disappointing dinner. "Ah, much better," the monk said as they sat down.

"Before we go any further, what's your name?" An Jing interrupted politely.

"My name is fairly unimportant, but if you'd like to refer to me as something, if it makes you feel more comfortable in conversation, you can call me Mei Ming." The monk coyly replied.

"Well, suit yourself monk Mei Ming. But go on with your story. It seems nearly impossible and fantastical, and I've never heard anything like it...the land of Illusion...fairies that appear to be both man and woman....but go on. I've always liked stories." It would often be hours before the fishing pole ever felt a tug, and each new time they went to the river, An Jing would ask his father to try to finish the story but begin once again as he had always begun, about two households.

"So of course, when the red flowers appeared by the moonlight, I realized the dream was more than just a normal dream," the monk carried on at An Jing's suggestion. "I decided to consult a few colleagues on this, and the meaning of course took much discussion and debate. You don't need to know all the details of this. There are many rules. Young people never have much patience for it. But one curious thing is that, well, the red flower we found is a native to your village and, yes, well, to your village alone. Have you seen it before?" The monk rummaged through his pack and took out a book whose words An Jing did not recognize, and inside the book lay flat a pressed red flower whose five petals were creased.

113

An Jing's felt his stomach sick with nostalgia. Of course, yes, of course he'd seen this flower before. He had gone out to the fields to play with the village ox, and the field was littered with little red flowers just like this. At that time, his mother had long, black hair, which his sister Lu had inherited. Her hair shone hot under the sun. As she smiled, her hair would flutter around her in the wind, black and strong. The women often used the flower petals as dye to color their lips in the older days when they celebrated the passing of each birth year and the new year, when he heard laughter and the running of children in the village, the days when he, yes even he, ran naked and smiling, wide-toothed, down the streets screaming with happiness, kicking up dust onto his legs and all over his clothes. He remembered once when he was small, he and his mother were picking berries during the summertime in a fertile strip of land close to the river. He had clung onto his mother, as he often did when he was young, terrified of animals or strangers hiding behind the brambles. She had laughed then as she often did, "There's nothing that wants to eat you, An Jing! You're just a bean pole." At this memory, he felt sick. "Yes, yes of course. Yes, you're right. It belongs to us. It belongs to us." He heard himself speak. The steamed buns remained untouched before them. Displeased, An Jing's stomach rumbled again.

The monk put his head down and bowed. Then he replied, "My grievances to what this nonsense has brought to you and everyone else around you. My deepest sadness, and I will not be spared. But you do carry the flower on you. That's how I knew I found the right person, even though I wasn't sure before meeting you how I'd find you." The monk pointed at something pinned to An Jing's coat collar. Before then, An Jing had never noticed anything on the coat as he just took it from Qiu Hui in a blur of morning. But now, as the monk pointed to him, he looked down and from the corner of his eye saw the fabric of a pin, a small pin made carefully with small, careful hands, the fabric a bright red in the shape of a flower.

"So what am I to you? Are you coming to the village to help people? They need it, yes, please," An Jing's voice began in haste, "they're starving. We've been starving."

The monk's gaze became downcast and he said, his voice dropping, "I know the situation out here in the countryside. I have traveled very far to get here, and your village is one of many. It's an absolute despair. The human corpses pile as high as the sky. Where are the sounds of babies crying? The sounds of children running through the streets? Even the bickering of old ladies is missing. There is no humanity, no dignity...but we are leaving our monastery for those very reasons. Things are beginning to spread far. I was sent to deliver a message, but I do not have the ability to change the monster which has been turned on." An Jing's ears pricked and he listened carefully to the monk's words. "I had forgotten much of my dream that night and by early morning, I had not slept at all. In fact, I felt more energized and awake than I can remember, and in the morning, I began to remember pieces of the message. *'You must return. No matter what sacrifice, or the impossibility presented to you, you cannot stay in another world that is not your own longer than the time you're allotted. Humankind cannot bear much reality. You must come back to your village, no matter how far and long your journey is.'*"

When he finished his message, the monk seemed quite exhausted. An Jing looked into his face and he saw the age in the old man with perspiration clinging to his forehead.

"Monk Mei Ming, are you okay? You look unwell." An Jing was concerned.

"Yes, you need to carry on now. I will be just fine. It's time...it's time to meditate. Clear the mind. These days, the junk fills up so quickly that even greater moments of meditation are needed to wash it away from the precious memory space we are given." He smiled and held out his worn, coarse hands to wrap around An Jing's. Then he began again, "I once saw the execution of a peasant man who stole from a very rich landowner. He was beaten, then forced to kneel on rocks for hours in the public square, and finally, he was tied to a stake and his head cut off.

115

As they were tying him down, he was crying, screaming, negotiating the last of his life as if there was still a chance the verdict could be reversed. That something will fall from the heavens; that someone will make a mistake, and he will live. He was screaming so loudly that his screams echoed across the courtyard and into the houses, as if the sound itself would unleash some kind of miracle that could save him from what was about to happen and what was always about to happen, and the louder he screamed and cried, the sorrier he felt for himself. I looked into his reddened eyes then, just as I looked into his eyes when the blade hit his neck, and An Jing, let me tell you what I saw. What I saw was in his eyes. Suddenly, I felt that I understood him, I could feel him. The moment before a man dies, time becomes tangled. Those last units of time which add to a conscious moment expand. During the execution – the knife cutting into the neck, the poison coursing through the veins – that final moment is a coup de grace. The acceptance of that coup de grace is when the initial anxiety of 'could this still happen' or 'there is hope' disappears. What comes in its place is a certainty of answer and so shortly after, a peace. It has happened." The monk sighed and closed his eyes. He shivered, his hands holding An Jing's. Then, jolting into alertness again the old monk packed the uneaten steamed buns, now cold, into a cloth bag and handed them to An Jing, "Please take it. Your journey will be far longer than mine. Don't let yourself become too hungry before you eat. It's not good for digestion."...

CHAPTER 6

Prophesy Returned

…The next morning came with an anxiety that woke An Jing up from a restless slumber. "Some hitch-hike," he muttered to himself as he prepared his rucksack. "There hasn't been a car in sight yet." An Jing dusted himself off and took a drink of water from his water bag, which by morning tasted stale with residue, and looked up at the sky. The clouds were unusually low, as if they were hovering to consume him slowly.

After eating half a steamed bun, An Jing began on the road once again, hoping to see a car along the dusty road. "The clouds must be really falling apart," An Jing spoke to himself. He looked up at the grey which dropped in front of and around him and squinted at the distance, smelling the wetness of rain. An Jing could swear that somehow down the road, he could see the clouds swirling and dancing. "I must be hungry still," he said to himself again.

At this, a voice spoke back, "What you're seeing is real, Wei An Jing."

An Jing jumped up and looked around him, suddenly clutching his brown rucksack tightly. He didn't know if he had even enough rice and steamed rolls to get to the nearest town where a driver should be waiting for him. Losing his belongings this early in the trip would be devastating; he could only imagine his shame in returning to his father, empty-handed.

He swung around defensively, looking for the voice. Unexpectedly, he tripped on a tree branch in the fog and reached out to fall, landing on soft dirt. Lying on the dirt, the fog became denser until An Jing could see nothing in front of him, not even his own hands, which clutched desperately at his bag, which became cold and damp.

"Wei An Jing, you have nothing to worry about. Why are you so afraid?" the voice asked, husked and low. At first, he couldn't tell what kind of voice spoke to him, man or woman, child or adult. "If you stand up, you can probably see me better." This time, he decided the voice was definitely a woman's, but it was unlike any woman he had ever heard before. It was soft and rough at the same time, as if the owner who spoke was beyond years he could have imagined.

An Jing slowly pushed himself off the ground and strained his eyes into the distance. There, standing in the middle of the fog and what looked like clouds, was a being, a woman, but she was hardly a human. She wore a white cloak, which he had mistaken for a cloud until he saw a flashing pair of eyes. The woman on clouds moved toward him, and he could see that her eyes were a dark sea blue, which darted around, alive with activity, nearly frantic and frightening. As she neared him, he realized that her face wore what looked like ten thousand wrinkles across it, set in front of grey hair which streamed back and up and all around her as if she were charged with a magnetic force invisible to him. When she appeared, her entire body was enveloped with the clouds except for a small, tear dropped face.

"This is not the first unusual thing that has happened today," An Jing muttered to himself in disbelief. Then, looking up at the mysterious woman, he said, "I'm sorry if I've come across a road I shouldn't have, or if I have offended you in any way, I'll be on my way soon...but, how, how do you know my name?"

"I was called upon to do your reading. Did you not call me for that?" Her voice sounded irritable, as if she felt he was wasting her time. "Are you An Jing?"

An Jing arched his neck forward to get a better look. The figure that looked back at him was small and wispy, like an olive branch. "Yes, I go by An Jing, but perhaps you're looking for someone different." He avoided her eyes.

She paused, observing him, from his tattered cloth shoes to his wool jacket, where her eyes rested, and then to the rest of him and all the way up to his unkempt, unwashed black hair. "No, it must be you...it can't be anyone else. You asked me to tell your fortune, but you may not remember it, and, well, now that I think about it I can see how you wouldn't remember it."

"No, I...fortune? Did I hear you right?"

"Wei An Jing, I'm not here to waste your time. I'll give you what you've requested. Step closer," she commanded, and then, suddenly, a flurry of wind brought in front of him oak leaves, though he saw no oak tree on his path.

"Who are you?" he managed to get out, his throat scratching with a tingle of fear and disbelief.

"I'm the Sibyl of Cumae," she waved her hand, and the oak leaves danced under the direction of her wave. "There's not much time, and there's a chance your memory will fail you, but you are here afterall. So it's begun."

"What's begun?"

"Wei An Jing, you are a special man," the Sibyl continued like she heard nothing at all. "I will give you three prophesies. The first one, you have fallen in love with a woman who does not belong here. In this place or the next place, for this woman will appear twice, and you will not return her love, though she will give you everything because for her, she has owed you everything. There is no other way. Second, you will die, but you will not die at the hands of man. Third, and most importantly, entropy always increases in a system. Do not forget this."

"What are you saying," An Jing asked once more, his face contorting in confusion. The Sibyl's stare was as profoundly cold as her voice, and at his last question, she began to fade. The clouds gathered around her, and soon, she was nothing but a pair of eyes, looking through the changing grey, until suddenly, all he saw was the mist in front of him until he saw nothing at all. And then the world shut itself from him, and he saw blackness.

An Jing was unsure how long the blackness lasted, and soon, in the darkness, he was unable to discern whether his eyes were opened or closed, or whether he was awake or falling asleep. He moved his toes, slowly at first, the big toe wiggling against the sole of his shoe until the rest of his toes regained feeling again. Soon, the blackness faded into a light color, which brightened and spread to more colors, until the colors blended and danced in front of him, and he snapped his eyes open. He stood unmoved, but his heart fluttered itself against his ribs, and he could barely contain his surprise and unexpected elation, "Ah! How did I get here?" All around him was a city with streets filled with city noises and city people, people playing cards outside their homes, animals plucking their way around the dirt sidewalks and inside and outside of homes, a thousand bicycles filling the open road.

In front of him, Wei An Jing saw something he had never seen before, something he had only heard rumors and stories about, a distant fact learned in a textbook. A man he never imagined he would speak to, with dusty blonde hair, tall and square shoulders, began walking toward him. The man looked just like what An Jing imagined foreigners to look like, built without the refinery of his own features and rough with big noses. An Jing stood motionless, unsure whether he should move for the white stranger or stand still, watching. The man stopped in front of An Jing,

120

stuck out a large hand, the fingers coarse and the arm that came with it covered in dark hair. To An Jing's surprise, the man spoke, and he understood. "Are you Wei An Jing?" the man asked. An Jing nodded in disbelief. He suddenly realized the man did not speak his own native tongue, but that somehow, he inexplicably understood. "An Jing, my name is Jared, and I'm here to make sure you can make the next transition of the process."

And that was all he remembered...

Part III

CHAPTER 1

Apostles on the Wall

"Father, you must've seen many sons burying their fathers," Peter said. "While David Smith was certainly not a perfect father, Henry knew nothing else. Henry had barely connected with the heritage of his mother, though she secretly yearned that he would express more interest in the darkness of his hair and the angles of his face which were, as you can expect, different yet similar to David's.

But for Henry, the desire to become his father – especially as he entered adulthood – was stronger than trying to understand some distant past he never saw other than through the reflection in a mirror. David was Henry's North Star, and losing him exposed Henry to the vastness of a universe that he had always known was there but acutely terrified of."

* * * * *

...*May 1, 2020.* It felt very dry; the air cracked. Dry was like the ceilings and the walls, the silence of dryness vibrating around the dome, which hit him with thirst. Henry looked out at the blank faces in front of him. He looked down at the words scribbled on index cards and took another drink from his water canister. His sinuses tingled at the smell of the vodka mix. His throat was constantly dry, and there in front of him must have been hundreds (hundreds!) of viewers, all sitting in black and its variations. Henry could hear the coughs and mutters echo across the hall.

The funeral mass was held in a large stone church that had stood indomitably for over two-hundred years when the first stone was laid in the young city, the stained-glass windows telling the last stories of Christ's moments in the garden of Gethsemane: next, the crucifixion and finally, the resurrection.

"What my father accomplished in one lifetime," Henry continued. What did his father accomplish in a lifetime? How was he to express this in five minutes or fewer to people whom he had never once met before? How could he describe growing up around and with David Smith, both man and boy learning about childhood simultaneously? Faces looked. Faces were painted, the eyes fixated on Henry. Each face contorted itself: all the art, every single face in the story that began in Gethsemane and ended in the resurrection sighed a deep and exhausted sigh except one: the Virgin Mary, who stood beaming in the corner with a Baby Jesus in her arms, a non-conformity to the story itself: a birth before the final birth.

"What he accomplished…" Henry repeated, choking on the words slowly. *It will be okay,* Henry thought. *Take your time with the words. Like you practiced.* "He did, in one lifetime, what would take others multiple generations to accomplish. My father made sure the future would reap the rewards of his hard work. He did not…did not believe that life had to be what was in front of him, and he built something our century never thought possible. He lived as we continue to strive to live…". *Simon-whom-he-gave-the-name-Peter and James son of Zebedee swoons in the nightly air of the garden, the olive trees intoxicating.* With another deep drink from his canister, Henry felt himself becoming engaged with the blank faces in a way he had never before been engaged during presentations or speeches, and as he continued with his speech, he became so warm with affection that he was surprised and a little crestfallen when he reached the end of his index

126

cards. That was it. How could that be it? *Philip and Bartholomew are wearing blue.* After weeks of preparation, the entire thing was done in under five minutes. Henry wiped the perspiration from his forehead with his closing line, "...and to what my father built both in his lifetime and as his legacy, I hold not a day of mourning, but a toast." He looked up. The crowd, confused as to the proper response of those words, stood up and clapped. *And there's Andrew and John, Thomas and Matthew, James-son-of-Alphaeus, Thaddaeus and Simon-the-Cananean.* The clapping continued until it roared through the church and down the aisles and all along the pews. *And Judas, where is Judas?*

Earlier that morning. Henry had sat watching the fly struggle between the netting and the window glass. It had been bright outside. Day two of the fly. The thing had mysteriously gotten itself caught in the window through a crack that Henry had managed to open one night when he felt the air was getting unbearably stuffy in his apartment. "Well, you and I both," he had said. He had looked at the fly and listened to its violent buzzing, had thought about how its little mouth spit and regurgitated onto everything it landed on. It had disgusted him. Suddenly, he had felt a sickeningly overwhelming pity for the thing: its desperate buzzing, the frenzy in which the little body shook the screen as if it could break the netting, the way the little thing would stop and rest before crashing itself onto the netting again, its imminent death by being roasted by sunlight stuck between a window and screen. He had thought, "What must it be like to die a death like that? Crashing your body into netting and glass over and over again...wondering why all of a sudden you feel hot. Realizing you're stuck to moving only up, down, left and right but not forwards." It would not occur to Henry until much later that at that very time he had mirrored the life of the fly, that they had been in parallel: Henry and fly, and fly and Henry, streaming along and connected by a logic and causality that Henry was blind to at 8:30 am that morning.

* * * * *

May 2nd, 2020. "Henry!" Erica ran over to him and held him with long arms, their mother right behind her. Erica and Henry had no mutual resemblance. Unlike Henry's clouded grey-brown eyes – constantly looking as if he was gazing at something miles away – and dark unruly hair, Erica had light brown eyes and straight, monochromatically light hair which she often colored to several shades darker and even more shades lighter. While Henry constantly looked as if he were on the edge to speak but could say nothing at all, words fired themselves out of Erica while her face barely moved to support the thin lips broadcasting thoughts before she had reviewed them.

"Oh, Henry, you look like you haven't slept in far too long," his mother said. Xiaoling was wearing a light coral suit, and her black hair was tied back in a tight bun. The three stepped into a sunny café Henry had reserved on the river.

"I've just, well, I've just been busy at work. And on top of it all, this funeral. It's been a lot. I've been doing a lot." Henry managed to squeeze out.

"You *still* have to sleep." Xiaoling's voice pinched itself an octave higher. She embraced her son. The air was light, and the three walked into the Cafe Verona, a popular breakfast and lunch place, with a mixed cocktail menu that expanded far beyond its food menu. The sun was bright and happily lighting the docked boats, which floated and bobbed.

Finally, over poached eggs and tomato sandwiches and in between coffee with milk and sugar and "how-have-you-been-since-I-saw-you-yesterday" and other such requests for updates, no one mentioning the word they had stopped speaking about months earlier – *cancer.* Xiaoling asked, "Henry, the past few days, I've just been thinking, you know, seeing you here and everything. Have you been able to meet any new people?" She danced around her words stiffly. She kneaded her hands, which had turned a clammy red, and she sat with her legs crossed at the ankles and leaning forward to the edge of the table. Even her voice shook. Xiaoling never mentioned to Henry any grieving. He would not have seen the way

128

her voice shook, or how she darted from topic to topic, careful of avoiding any mention of death, David Smith and her own conflicted feelings of the past.

"What do you mean? I meet new people all the time. Everyday. I'm sick of new people. I miss the old ones." Henry joked. He knew his mother was dancing around the things she found unspeakable, and so he avoided them aggressively, afraid of treading onto an avalanche he knew existed since childhood. Instead, he laughed at himself, and looking at the two serious and unblinking set of eyes in front of him, stopped abruptly.

"I just worry that you're alone too much, and at this age, your friends start to become less available. I think you should find some time to work on your personal life. You know, just work on meeting people. Nice people –", Xiaoling wasn't giving up. She continued as if he hadn't spoken. Prompted by the closeness of death and mortality, she had every intention of using the opportunity of sitting in front of him – her hands inches away from his arm – to bring up the "when will I have grandchildren" conversation, and Henry had every intention – his body twenty feet away from the door - of squashing it before it began. He opened his eyes wide, staring at her with disbelief: of all the opportunities she could choose, it was during David Smith's funeral that she brought up his barren love life to express her own mourning.

But before she could finish, Erica interrupted abruptly with the full authority of an older sister: "We think you should get a girlfriend. You're getting old, Henry." She reached over and took a forkful of his untouched potatoes and spoke and chewed at the same time. Henry marveled at her multitasking, the potatoes mashing between her perfectly white teeth while she said nonchalantly, "Well, not like old old, but mom and I think that unless we stage an intervention," she said before swallowing the potato and then continuing, "You're just going to amble on like this until you're too old to take care of yourself. Your father's funeral was a wake-up call for us." She had grown up with him, living in the shadow of Xiaoling's decision to stay close to her son's father. But

129

having been the creation of love, Erica had resolved to move on beyond living in a stranger's home, under a stranger's wealth, and benefiting from a stranger's opportunities. She was four years older than Henry, exacting and shrewd, but never bitter.

"Have you guys been talking about this a lot behind my back? I'm pretty young." Henry smiled, eager to engage them again in joking.

"Yes, we have. And no, you're not young Henry," Erica said, irritated and speaking faster. "You haven't dated anyone since you were about nineteen, and that barely counts. It's not that you need to *find* someone immediately, it's just that you need to actually show some interest in this department of your life."

"The department of…" Henry sighed. Another failed attempt at a joke. He wiped his hand on his napkin.

"—Relationship. Commitment of some kind. Family. Hanging out with someone other than Howard. You have no idea even how to do your laundry. Neither of you do for that matter." Erica reached over for more coffee and filled her cup. She held the mug to her face and inhaled.

"Henry, your sister and I aren't trying to get into your personal life here. I'm just wondering. Also, you know me, I just want to make sure you have people who you're close with here. Especially now that you've gotten so much attention from work. You need family. Things are stressful, and that just means you shouldn't go through it alone. It almost seems like you've been going through all of *this* alone. We haven't been able to reach you in the weeks before the funeral! We're worried. This isn't an easy thing to go through, and you're just all by yourself. Too much of the time." Xiaoling kneaded at her hands. The food on her plate remained mostly ignored.

Henry knew this conversation was going to happen. He could hear it bubble up in her voice during the rare occasions he did speak to her, which decreased steadily after his roles became increasingly more difficult at the Company. "I'm not looking for anything right now. Things have been really busy, which is fine. It always is in the beginning. I can't really get my head around anything else..."

"—Henry," Erica interrupted, "you'll always be busy. We're not going to keep nagging you. Stop making that face. Here. I have a friend here in the city. She's wonderful. She's young, she's professional, and you should just go on a date with her."

"If I do, will you stop talking about this?"

"Yes."

"And will you not talk about this again?"

She replied, "We'll probably talk about it again, but we'll give it a rest for a little while at least."

He sighed. He knew she was lying, skirting around with her words, but the conversation had no foreseeable end until: "Alright. I'll do it. What's her name?"

"Dana. She lives here in the city."

"Well, now that we have this done, Henry, do you think plaid goes well with khaki? I'm trying to think of what to wear tomorrow for a day hike! Erica and I are taking the train out along the river and just spending the day outdoors."

"No mom, wear jeans."

"What's wrong with khaki's? I don't like the way the jeans fit. They just don't move as easily."

"- have nothing to add to this conversation, once again." Henry said. He was relieved and leaned back against his chair. He picked up his fork and then dropped it again on his plate.

"Henry, tell us what's happening at work…" his mother turned to smile at him.

He tried to focus on her, but when he conjured up what he could possibly tell her about his job, all he felt was the cold rain and he could hear Duane in his head, and he didn't know what to say other than, "Actually, I may need to leave soon, in the next half-hour or so. Sorry. Work is alright. Going on alright." He motioned to the waiter, "Can I have more water please? And the check?" Then he continued, "Things just never really take a break. But it's just taking time for that to settle."

"Do you think it will be like this for a long time?" Xiaoling asked.

"At least for the first year or so. The transition isn't easy." He exhaled, bored of the words that he heard from his own mouth. He wondered if his fear of speaking was really just a fear of boredom: even he couldn't stand listening to his own talking. With those words, the check came, and he put down a credit card to pay without another word…

CHAPTER 2

Becoming Animated

...After his family brunch and back at his apartment, Henry turned his phone on silent, closed the blinds, and crawled into bed. Minutes later and feeling uneasy, he got up, walked to the window in his bedroom and looked at the screen. The fly was dead. It was lying on its side at the bottom of the window. Henry went back to bed. Usually, he would have felt guilty for lying to his mother and sister about how he felt about the Company, but he couldn't sit there any longer. He found it difficult to be around them. Every word he said felt like it was coming from another, far away person.

His eyes shut, Henry tried to think of something bland. It was then, eyes closed, thinking of bland things, that the cold came suddenly. Within seconds, he felt the room temperature drop; his hands were frozen, and he felt his face tingle. The hairs along his body bristled uncomfortably against the bedding, the fabric chafing against him. He was sweating, and he was cold. He let his mind wander through colors, "light green, grey, blue-grey, stone-grey, sleep-grey", and slowly, his body relaxed, and he slept to escape his daytime...light green, grey, blue-grey, stone-grey, sleep-grey...grey...

...so he dreamed, and as he dreamed, the rules slid away: the sky fell into pieces of cloud, and beyond the cloud was a space which moved, a world of stars: the Milky Way which dreamed and danced, swayed and flowed...and he was free, he was sitting on a rock, looking at the broken sky into a space of stars, he was the Pacific, the Atlantic, the Baltic...

...In his dream, Henry found himself at the edge of a river that had a door mysteriously placed right in the middle of the air, hovering above the water and at the edge of the dock. The door had a gold handle, and the handle was warm. He noticed the sun was dancing with the clouds, and so for a minute, it would be sunny, and the next, it would be overcast and he could feel rain falling on the water, and the grass illuminated in different shades of green to match the moving clouds. It looked like fish breathing. "This is interesting," he said aloud. He looked at the door handle; the handle looked at him. He touched it again, and suddenly, the door flew open and magnified (or he shrunk). Looking through the door, Henry could see the other side ... It was a farmland, a vast stretch of grass and hillside, and the grass was stubborn, short and rough, and there were red flowers everywhere. It was windy on the other side. He could almost see the wind's color by the way it tossed the grass from one direction to the next. Henry shrugged. He stepped in the door. He fell onto the grass, and the door to the river disappeared...

Henry walked along a hilly, pebbled road that wound through the grassland and into the mountain gaps. He could see little oxen labeled all along the way, and they had words written on them, which he did not understand. So he kept walking, and the sun kept dancing with the clouds, and the wind was turning all kinds of colors, and suddenly, he saw a girl on the road ahead of him who was looking out at the pastures. As he passed her, he turned to look at her. It was Ariella. Well, not real Ariella, but the dream version of Ariella as he saw her: an Ariella that was not the thing he saw awake, but it was her, and the dream version of Henry found the dream version of Ariella to be absolutely stunning, and so he opened his mouth to speak to her. "DKRieeeskeirh". What came out was absolutely inhuman. She turned to see who or what had just yelled and gurgled at her...

"Hi, who are you?" she asked.

"FJDIekrellsioooo", he responded.

"Hahaha, you must not be from here. Are you lost?"

134

"dkriiiiieeessoo", he tried again. He knew exactly what he wanted to say, which was, "Ari, it's me! Surprise seeing you here."

"Aw, you need to be in the grass, and not on the road!" So she picked him up gently (and he looked at her with pleading eyes and a dripping nose and a drooling mouth to try to get her to see that it was him!), and plopped him onto the grass. It was then that Henry realized that somehow he had four little hooves and that he was quite little. He was a calf, full of a brown, mossy fur on the top of his head. Suddenly he noticed that he could hear the other calves talking, "Oh, look at that guy, he totally went to the road and tried to chase the human, what an idiot". To his surprise, he noticed Ariella was hugely tall, and then that was when it finally came to him that he had turned into a baby ox.

"Ari! It's me!" He tried to yell and began chasing after her again.

She turned to see what was shuffling quickly behind her, and laughed when Henry came running to her heels and looked up at her with brown eyes. "You again?! Alright buddy, I don't know what you want, but I'm going back to the house. You can follow me until I turn off, alright?"

"Ari, I have so much to tell you." Before he knew it, he was confessing everything to her. "Look, I'm not who you think I am. I committed this awful, heinous thing…and at the time, well, I thought it was alright to do. That it was the best thing to walk away. But now I don't know, and it's just been terrible. Weird things are happening at the Company as well. I just don't know what I should be doing – trying to fend off Duane or deal with this accident. Can we talk sometime about it? I just, I need to talk to someone. Someone. I need to know I'm not making everything up. Duane. My father. I just. Sometimes I think I am misreading everything, but I can't tell anyone about it at all. Ari, I trust you." The words flowed out of him, unhinged and unblocked, easily, as if the dam which had been built was ruptured full of language, and language -- all of it -- escaped out of him and into the air.

"Wow, little buddy, you've got a lot of talking in you! Maybe you're hungry." She stepped off the road and onto the pasture, grabbing a handful of forbs and knelt down,

135

holding it to Henry's face.

Henry waddled his way over to her impatiently, "Ari, I'm not hungry. I want to confess this thing to you. What's been on my mind. Oh that smells good. Let me try that, Oh, wow, that is good! Oh, man, Ari, where did you find that?" He couldn't stop eating it, and he found himself sticking his face right into her open hand, delighted and ashamed all at once, forgetting about the words.

She was petting him the whole time, and as she ruffled his little ears, he wanted to get closer to her, to be held by her, to keep her warmth with his round little body. She smiled at him and said, "Alright. This was our deal. I have to go into the house now, and you have to stay out here. You're the first one who has walked me home." She patted him again and stood up and opened the gate at the end of the road, and how she smelled! She smelled different, distinctly human, and he felt desperately alone as she turned around and began to walk to the house, closing the fence behind her. He wedged himself as close to it as possible and stood there, four little legs, looking at her walk away, four little legs standing there for a long time. He felt a strong longing for her to turn around and recognize him, to spend more time with him, and so he pined and pined, soft little moo-ing sounds. He forgot his words...

As it got dark, he grew afraid. He kept staring at the little house with little orange and yellow lights coming from the windows, and once in a while, he would hear her laugh. He would moo and pine, and no matter how many times he moo'ed, coo'd, eewww'd, she never came out. So he knelt down and lay at the foot of the gate, his gaze fixed on the house, waiting for her to come out in the morning. He closed his big eyes...

Something was stirring. Something was moving quickly. He could hear it. He was terrified. He tried to get up and move and run. He tried to shout, but he couldn't make enough of a noise. The thing was fast. It smelled horrible. He knew it; he didn't know how he did, but he did, it was bad. He needed to hide, to get away, but he wasn't fast enough. The thing was here! It was here! It was going to get him. He tried to run as fast as he could. Why couldn't he run faster? Oh, he could hear it, he could smell it, he could feel it was behind him. He shouted again, his words coming to him in a flash: "Ariella! Help me! Please, someone help me!" And suddenly, he felt

136

it on him, on his neck. The pain that erupted through him came and went, and before he knew it, he was a spectator to his own dream. He was human again...

And yet he was still the calf. It was a wolf, a wild animal he had never seen before his dream. The fence was a wooden one just to keep the animals within grazing parameters, but Henry had not gone with the others and instead had strayed near the house. Ariella and her father came running out of the house, and he could see the wolf had just hovered over him and was about to drag him away. "Damn wolves," her father shouted.

"Oh, Dad, it got one. Come here, can we save him?" She knelt down next to Henry-four-legs, "Oh, shit, Dad, this was my fault. Oh no. This one was my fault. I forgot to lead him back or put him in the barn tonight. He followed me back. Oh God, I feel awful. Baba he's still alive."

"Ari, he's really torn up." He knelt down next to Henry-four-legs, who was still looking at Ariella, waiting for her to pick him up.

"Dad, let's just take him into town. I think he can be ok." ("Yes, please let him be OK", Henry-the-Dreamer thought). She patted him on his head, and he realized how upset she was (and how guilty she felt) when he saw she was crying. Henry-four-legs still looked at her with his eyes, and he just wanted to say, "I'm sorry. I'm really sorry for everything. I've been horrible." He roared instead.

"Ari, the animal is going to die slowly. I think we should put him out." Ari's father patted Henry-four-legs, told Ari to move aside (she turned away, crying), and he quickly brought the sharpened knife down on Henry-four-legs. The Henry-the-Dreamer watched himself, Henry-four-legs, with dread and fear...

Henry woke suddenly. He felt something clenching in him, like there was a hot air balloon inside his body. It was a soreness of having had and lost something he couldn't describe. He looked at his clock – 8:32 pm. It was dark outside. He had the evening off from work. So, Henry put on some clothes and ran over to Ariella's...

CHAPTER 3

The Still Point

…"Henry, you've been making a few surprise visits lately. I mean, I don't mind, but are you ok?" Ariella was sitting on an orange striped rug, stretching her calves, and looking at him lying on the sofa with his eyes closed.

"Yea, I've been really stressed." He spoke with his eyes closed. "Stressed" was a vague word, and yet it was all he could come up with to describe what he was feeling. Stressed: not being prepared for a meeting, having an overwhelming amount of work, feeling isolated in the presence of his family. In other words, to describe the inadequate one word, a band-aid.

"A lot has happened these past few weeks," she responded. She looked at his shut eyes and saw his face had thinned tremendously in the past month.

"I had a dream," he continued, "I don't remember it, but I woke up in a sweat and just feeling terrible." As he said those words, he realized he sounded childish. But there they were, out there, and he would have to wait for her to reply.

"Oh. I think we'd call that a nightmare."

The kind yet teasing tone of her voice softened him. "Yea, it was pretty unpleasant. I felt it too, you know, the physical pain of whatever happened...It was really vivid, but I can't remember a thing. My dreams have all been like that lately." He didn't want to look at her.

"Vivid or horrible?" She walked over to him on the sofa and knelt down next to him, stretching her quads.

"Both." His voice cracked, or he thought he heard it crack. The sounds of the room came to him as he lay there: her breathing, the small rustles she made on the rug, the distant hum of the refrigerator, and the off-beat cracks of the room.

"I just think this is all a reaction to what's been happening the last few weeks."

"Maybe dreams are real. Or maybe they really reflect how someone feels. Do you read into them?"

She sat up immediately in half stretch: "Well, I tend to read into a lot. But I think dreams are definitely a reflection of incomplete thoughts or floating ones at least. Real or not, I'm not sure. But I think they're part of us. Like all thoughts." She bit her lip; her hair was tied up and wet. He no longer noticed the distance sounds of the apartment, but her voice focused closer to him, the hum no longer disturbing his thoughts.

"I don't like that I feel my life is a nightmare and my dreams are too." Henry opened his eyes and looked at her. Her expression was curious: her eyebrows were furrowed, and she looked as if she had been waiting to speak. "Ari – I just...I don't know what to do sometimes." He wondered what his expression was. He wondered if his eyebrows revealed as much to her, or whether had he seen himself in the mirror, he would have understood what to do next.

"Henry, what's going on? You haven't been yourself lately. I've been worried. I don't know what to say." More eyebrows furrowing, her lips barely parted, dry, breathing dry air, making his throat crack.

"I never know what to say." He stared at her. Closing his eyes, he found the words slowly, "Ari, do you ever feel like you had no choice? That you were born without your own choice?" Yes, that was it. That was the tracks which had no known destination and no known origin, but he saw the movement right in front of him, veering right, left, right, right and straight on, full steam ahead!

"Oh, Henry. I don't know if this is something for a discussion now..."

"I have everything. It makes it harder. To understand at least. To understand why I feel so empty sometimes. And guilty. I feel guilty a lot because I have more. So I think I have to do more, and I'm just riding along everything that's moving past me so fast. I can't seem to hold onto anything. Sometimes I think I've been walking dead for a long time." It was strange. The beginnings of conversations were always forced out, words walked themselves cautious and shrewd from his lips, as if his mouth had been holding them captive. Now, as his eyes were closed, and as he forgot that she was sitting so close to him but just heard the voice echoing his fears, he felt comfortable continuing even if it were one toddling step at a time.

"Just give it some time. You've been through a lot lately. It's shaken things up." The tones of her voice were steady. Did she even understand him? Did it matter?

"No, Ari, I mean, I just...I have nothing."

"Henry, no. That's not true. You have the world." You have the world. The vague spaces between each of those four words stretched to his imagination, and in seconds, he thought of the various things she could mean. The oceans, the forests, the vast lands of wild flower, the desert, the sky, the birds flying high...

"—But if I were born to someone else. If the same me were born with a different life, different starting points, I would never be anything. It's just circumstances. I think being successful that way just means you were one in a billion, which means that you could have been anyone in a billion and there's no you to you. Who knows who's doing what anymore. Who knows. I don't." He spoke with his mouth wide as if doing so would let the words out as quickly as possible to escape into the air.

"I think most people feel that way at some point, and if they don't, well they're made of something divine. We think that our lives have to be measured somehow, to know we're not wasting it. All that means, Henry, is that you want to live. To really live. It doesn't mean you're wasting anything. Where's this all coming from?"

"A deep fear. A fear. Ari, I am so afraid." He heard himself speak; *not bad, not bad at all.* He felt some air in his chest. He opened his eyes.

"You've, well, you've never mentioned this before."

"I was too focused on easy distractions to realize it."

"If this helps...I always wonder whether what I spend eight to twelve hours a day doing is worth anything at all. Like, whether I've let myself become so addicted to some one-dimensional thing – like working or my own life or whatever – that I forget other things." She smiled at him, unable to escape the gaze and yet, something stirred inside her which he did not notice, and she felt her stomach move without her permission. "Recently, I've just tried to find things that bring me outside myself. It's the only type of freedom I know. Otherwise, I think I'm just a slave to my own boundaries and issues and other random stuff that's going on in my head..."

"I don't know what I want," he shared.

142

She looked away from him, uncomfortable that the flushing on her face and sudden warmth to her hands may have betrayed her.

"Well, I think that's the first problem right there." Her voice became a whisper, and she moved closer toward the couch on which he lay, feeling her palms tighten against the floor.

Suddenly, he looked away from her and said, "But how do you know what you want if you were never given the choice from the beginning? Sometimes I feel like I'm drifting, unsure what time I'm in or where the time is going...like I'm constantly overwhelmed in this very easy life I have handed to me. I don't know if I belong here."

Frozen and feeling warm at the same time, she replied, "No one knows where that feeling of drifting comes from. I think that's where it all is, we need some constant wanderlust, or some message that isn't coming from the outside that says, 'this is what you want'. Henry, you know...you know I play a lot of music."

"Yea, too much music. You don't spend enough time with me." With this, he gave her one of his rare smiles. The smile hung on him so uncomfortably, she couldn't help but smile back and think to herself, *well I guess you never do this because you do look goofy, don't you?*

Instead, she replied coyly, "Haha, plenty of time. Too much time in my opinion. Anyway, to go back to what I was trying to say, so you have a piece of music. It's bland. It's been played about a million times by probably a million people, especially if it's a good piece of music. This thing has been heard by billions of people if you count all the people in all history who's heard it. So, for instance, take Vivaldi's Concerto Number 4 in F minor. Played and heard a billion times. Can you imagine how many musicians must practice that piece? And I'm not talking about practicing once or twice. But practicing for years. Trying to be a specialist in it, trying to get everything right, to have the position they want in the orchestra. So this piece, in total, is being played like a trillion

143

times multiplied by a billion. But when I play it, by myself in my room practicing so I can keep my seat in my little local orchestra for one more goddamn season, damnit, Henry it *feels* like I'm the only one who has ever played it. Like I am the only one who has ever listened to it. I put on the tape for the orchestra, and I play my part, and god Henry, let me tell you. It's like something new. Something being born. When I have those days, I feel like time is just something outside the music. The music plays and becomes something new, something alive. It's only like that because I put a part of myself into it. I make it my own. It's a thing that's been around forever and played over again and heard over again, but it's mine because I can do something to bring it to life. And you know what's the toughest to play? The slower pieces, the pieces with long notes, because you have to make each note sound alive and move even in its stillness. The thing lingers. In the lingering, there has to be some life to it. I don't think existence is any different. How many people have lived before us or will live after us…it doesn't matter. Your life is this sheet of music. Even if the notes were put in place, like your initial conditions or whatever, that's not the musician. There's something else behind it."

"You really believe that?" He shifted and looked straight at her, his smile gone from his face.

"Yes. I do. I didn't always. But I do. I live by it. I don't know how else to live."

"Well, Ari, on my music sheet, I see lots of notes, but I have no idea what instrument I am or how to make it come to life." He laughed at her.

At this, she laughed too. He knew then that he had come over to her apartment late at night, selfishly, for her laughter. It was like everything else she meant to him, packaged into a single moment of laughter which lingered in him for many moments after.

"Ari, sorry to just spit this out at you like this tonight. It's so late. I've been having a really hard time lately. I need you," he sighed, "I need you to be patient with me," he said at last. To Henry, Ariella was a thing that could do no wrong, a thing of sacredness from a book, and everything else he could imagine as being immaculate. He had no idea how to articulate or understand how she reached that role in his brain, but there she was, the "immaculate thing herself" occupying its own space in his brain.

"Whatever you need. I'm here." With that, she knew he had opened that small window which made her completely his.

"Can I just stay on your couch tonight?" The couch had already begun to sink to fit him, and Henry could imagine himself sinking deeper into the sleep that had for days eluded him.

"Sure, do you need a towel for a shower?"

"Why, do I smell?" His voice rose, he got closer to the edge of the sofa, and stretched his arms out in mock embrace.

"Kind of. Like a, hmm, furry animal." She laughed again. He got up and grabbed her from the floor and pulled her onto the sofa with him. They lay there for a long time until she got up to get ready for bed.

* * * * *

Father Turner leaned in and asked Peter, "So what do you think these dreams mean to Henry? Especially the one where he's the animal that's being attacked on Ariella's farm?"

Peter shook his head, and his red hair bobbed up and down against his round face. "The word "soulmate" is not what it is without reason. The soul is something made of space. I think it's one of those things you would expect would be able to fly away if it could. Like, if you tried to hold it too tightly, it would slip from your hands or just disappear, become nothing. Lust, on the other hand, is deeply earthly, it's like the blood that moves through you. Desire gives us form. It gives us body.

145

Soul gives us breath. Desire and urge is spontaneous and willing at the same time. It is rooted. It has feet. It's something that can be felt: a tingle, a loss of breath, a sudden feeling of absolute and uncontrollable elation and yearning and excitement. Soul, though, is something that has no space. It has no roots, and it fills slowly, like a basin of some infinite substance through its mass-less-ness. A "soulmate" is not a physical thing but a spiritual one. It had nothing to do with love. It had nothing to do with desire."

CHAPTER 4

Jared Sober and Henry Gives Himself a Pep Talk

...*May 2nd, 2020.* Jared sat on his uncovered mattress and blinked. The neon ceiling lights flickered. His eyes were crusted over by the night's sleep, and squinting hurt. The drug's effect had slowly disappeared, and Jared sat with a reused plastic bottle filled with 10% juice orange-aid. On the corner of the table there was a slice of two-day-old pepperoni pizza that had two bites taken out, the powdery white of the flour still stuck to the bottom of the box. Jared had no memory of eating the pizza, but there was no one else in the apartment. He looked around again, just in case. The shades were drawn, and he was too tired to walk over to open them, to look outside for the first time in three days. In his hole, he had lost track of time. He heard the drip of the faucet. At the sound of the water, the night before began to come back to him. He remembered he had stuck his head under the faucet to drink water because he had either eaten or inhaled something that made his throat feel unbearably scratchy. The burning had gone from his throat to his lungs, and he had felt as if his entire body were being consumed one fiber at a time. So he had stuck his entire head under the open faucet and drank heavily until he was unable to breathe.

The only way to wake up was to make coffee. He poured the rest of the stale coffee he had left into the filter and made about 10 cups. When it was ready, he poured the tart and burnt liquid into a large bowl and watched the kitchen light reflect from its surface. He waited a while.

Then he drank standing. It was 13:14.

Jared's phone rang at 14:02.

"Jared Conel?"

"Speaking." Jared's throat was dry, the air whistling between two missing teeth. He reached for the 10% orange-aid. He had the sour taste of the coffee still in his mouth.

"I have a job for you."

He recognized the voice, and the words slurred themselves quietly like a snail across the receiver.
"Yea?" Jared asked with a feeling of dread.

* * * * *

...Henry was standing on a cliff, looking down at the ravine. The sun shone brightly — it was brilliant and smelled like lotuses. He looked up. He looked down. He was dizzy. Then suddenly, he was flying. Flying and free.

The wind was in Henry's face, and a warm, billowing breeze lifted him up and then down again. He was a bird. He was flapping and flying and silent all at once. There were no other sounds. Even the wind, which carried him North and East and South and West, and every combination, was silent. The air felt like lotuses.

The winds carried Henry to a town, and when he looked down, he saw ditches weaving their way through the town center. Flying closer and closer, he felt himself compelled to a sweet, sticky scent he could not place. His stomach rumbled; he was hungry. As he descended into the ditch, scouring it for the sweet sticky scent, he saw that the ditches were filled with rotting bodies, some whose skulls had already been emptied by scavengers like himself. Inside his own head, he screamed. Outside, Henry's body flew closer and closer to the masses of bodies, until he could feels his claws descending on the

148

hunched back of a corpse, which is when he began tearing with his hooked claws and sharp beak, and tearing, and tearing…

Henry Smith was screaming and sweating through his bundled and knotted sheets when Ariella ran in from the room nearby. She shook him, trying to wake him. He felt her arms and couldn't place where he was or who she was.

Ariella was speaking quickly. "Henry. Henry, it's me. Henry, it's Ariella. Are you awake? It's ok. It was a bad dream. You're here. We're in my apartment." She didn't know what else to say. "Henry, Henry can you hear me? Wake up."

"What day is it?!" He screamed out.

"It's May 3rd. It's a Friday, but you were going to take the day off." Ariella's voice came to him slowly.

That morning, lying on Ariella's couch too afraid to go to sleep, Henry realized he had broken the pattern of trying to shoot himself in the face. Could it really have been eighteen days since the accident? He wondered how the days had passed so effortlessly when he lined them up for review and yet the day-to-day crawled inching along and thinking of the slowness, he then sank himself deeper into the couch, curling himself up and dosed into a dreamless sleep.

* * * * *

Later that afternoon, well after Ariella had left her apartment to work in the museum archives, Henry decided to go to his office anyway. He needed the presence of other people. Ariella lived on the east side of the city, which was a thirty-minute walk from the Company.

Shortly after arriving at the building and passing security, Henry decided to visit Howard's office on the 17th floor. "Hey, it's me," Henry said, tapping on Howard's office door.

"Oh come in!" The voice behind the door said. Henry walked in and saw Howard playing darts, the room filled with various games and distractions. Leaning in to throw one of the darts onto the board, Howard said without looking at Henry, "Did you get my message?"

"Yea, I did. Thanks a lot. I really appreciate it."

"No problem. How're you doing? How was the family yesterday?" Howard threw another dart and groaned as it missed the board completely and bounced off the wall. Without look at Henry, he grabbed another dart.

"Ugh, they're themselves. I mean, really themselves. Still. Even yesterday. After the funeral, my mom tried to set me up. They've left now though." Henry closed the door. "I want to talk about some things," he continued. He paused for a moment and wrote on a piece of index card, "CAR".

Having cast his last throw, Howard turned around and laughed. "Whoa! What are you wearing? You look like a clown! Let's stop and talk about that!" Then, spying the paper in Henry's hand, Howard followed with, "I was hoping you wouldn't bring that up again. In fact, I was hoping you'd talk more about your family. In particular, your sister. You've barely mentioned her. Let's just grab a drink near my place after work tonight. I should probably try to do something resembling work today, boss."

"Okay," Henry nodded, scrunched up the index card and stuffed it into his pocket.

"Great, I'll hear your pretty voice then." Howard smiled as Henry turned to walk out the office, relieved that he'd successfully deflected the conversation.

Later that evening, Henry met Howard at a nearby bar, a cavernous looking place set in the basement of a brownstone building next to a block of high rises. The bar, *Dillon's Ole Ale House*, had been around for as long as Henry could remember.

"Where do you think all these people live?" Howard asked while he and Henry sat at a two-person table in the corner. While Henry found the dark, cool cellar to be a comforting, quiet spot for a solo drink, he often had to work hard to convince Howard to go there since, as Howard once described, "the people who come here are weird and unattractive." This evening was no different, and while Henry relished in the anonymity of the odd crowd, some laughing raucously at the bar while others sat hushed in conversation and barely a soul in there with a suit, Howard looked distinctly bored.

"What do you mean? Probably in this city," Henry replied over a brown ale.

"Oh come on, like you've seen any of these people out on the streets here? Look at that guy! He's practically wearing a cape! This is like where all the freaks come out to meet. That guy in the cape probably thinks he's a vampire or a superhero…," Howard turned to a man in the corner, who was indeed wearing a cape and winked at him. The man winked back. "I swear, I think these people must come from other areas outside the city and just congregate here because they know they'd fit in."

"Yea, well, that's why I like this place. I probably fit in. I think I'm going crazy. In the bad kind of way." He took three long drinks from the amber and looked into the cup, avoiding Howard's gaze.

"Yea, you're not looking so good these past few days. I was going to try to call you after the funeral, but I just assumed you had family stuff. I prolly shoulda called anyway. You keeping it together though?"

Howard's response surprised Henry. Henry, despite having known Howard since school days, had never understood how Howard would respond to certain "serious" conversations. Oftentimes, Henry's attempts were met with fierce resistance in the form of humor, but on some occasions, Howard offered the straightforward and logical advice that Henry craved. Still, Henry had yet to distill an algorithm in Howard's moods.

"Yea...mostly," Henry responded. He sifted through his choice in wording, as if any wrong trigger would set off a landmine of distracting jokes. "It's work, but it's not just work. Half the time, I don't know what I should be doing with myself, and I just sit there watching the screen. But yea, lately, the other half of the time, I just have a bad feeling. I just keep having bad feelings about the whole car accident thing." He returned to his drink and focused on the amber colors, awaiting the response.

"Don't think about it." Howard stared at him, unmoving.

It would be an evening of landmines then.

"What? You're serious? How can I not? How do you not think about it? Have you seriously not thought about it at all the past few weeks?" Henry refused to believe that he was the only one who was deeply bothered by the entire incident. He had assumed that Howard's lack of response to him about this during the past few weeks was because they were both busy trying to forget about it. Had he seen something that Howard had missed? Or did he not really understand his friend, was Howard not who he thought? "How is it not a big deal? You're kidding me. You're joking, right?"

152

"It's not a big deal, man," Howard stated matter-of-factly. "No one's gonna know what happened to the car. It was an accident. People get in accidents all the time. *All* the time. Relax."

"Howard, I can't stop thinking about it. I drove away... I just drove away." Henry's voice drifted, and once again, he saw the man with the coin eyes. He could still feel the warm stench of the man's breath...the breath which carried the dying whispers given to him like an ill-received prophecy, "You do not belong here."

"Henry, you have to stop thinking about what if, what if, maybe maybe...etc. It's bullshit, and it's not going to get you anywhere. And at the end of the day, you fucked up an expensive car - and ya, it was your dad's favorite, but well, sorry to put it, but no one's gonna get you in trouble for that now, are they? Oh, and plus, insurance already covered for it. I checked the other day since I figured you were tied up with the funeral. By the way, I'm really hungry. Do you think they'd sell any food here? Like, human food not stuff for vampires or zombies. Did you take a look at that guy who just walked in?"

Henry stared at Howard in disbelief. Were they even talking about the same thing? He tried to wrap his head around what Howard was saying, but it was so distant, irrelevant. Somehow, Howard was completely unbothered by the murder, the killing, the hit and run, the very thing that had nearly killed Henry in his sleeping nights. Could he even trust Howard if he couldn't understand this lack of emotion, guilt, responsibility...? Why didn't Howard worry about it the same way he did? Could it be that Howard was lacking in insight or conscience, or perhaps the alternative, that he knew something Henry didn't?

Instead, Henry replied, "I know. I just can't seem to be alright with it. It's not settling. It's wrong."

"You're still thinking about it too much."

"Yea."

"It's useless to think about it. It'll make it worse. Nothing can be changed now, and you just have to focus on what'll make the future better."

"Yea."

"Henry, are you listening to me?"

"Yea."

"So, what are you thinking now?"

Just as Henry was ready to open his mouth to answer his friend, a curious thing happened: A man standing nearby fell over their table head first with a large pitcher of beer in his hands. The beer spilled onto Howard, splashing his shirt and pants, and the man landed on his stomach on their table, his hands spread out in front of him as if he were flying.

"What the...?!" Howard yelled, and he began furiously trying to accumulate napkins to dry himself off, looking down at his destroyed slacks and shirt.

The unknown man rolled to his side on the table and looked at Henry Smith. His gaze stayed on Henry's, then he opened his mouth to display a number of crooked teeth and two spots of gaping gums where teeth had been and said, "Well, whaddya know...".

Henry Smith jerked back. The coin eyes. The beard, the teeth, the crooked nose, the voice of the man who had bled all over him, whose blood Henry had spent two nights trying to wash off before dumping his ruined clothes in a neighbor's dumpster down the street. There he was, lying on their table, practically smiling at Henry. Their gaze rested for a second. As if in a duel, both men jumped up. Henry leapt from his chair,

154

grabbed his coat, and ran out the back door of the bar and into the street. Coin Eyes rolled off the table and on top of Howard who was still trying to dry himself, got up, and also ran out of the bar but through the front door. By the time Howard calmed himself down enough from the assault, both his friend and the man were gone.

* * * * *

Into the light-littered night, Henry ran until he noticed he had run straight back to his apartment. Walking through the emptied lobby, he barely looked at the doorman as he headed straight to the elevators, breathing heavily. Slamming the door shut, Henry slid down to the floor against it, his hands rummaging through his hair, pulling at it. He sat there, pulling at his hair for some time, until he could hear his own breathing slowing. Then, Henry slowly got up and walked to the bathroom.

Looking in the mirror over his sink, he ran over what had just happened: his inability to communicate with Howard, the random man falling on their table, the way that man had looked so much like the one Henry had run over, so much like the man he had killed.

When he was sick of thinking about the entire car incident, he decided he would practice his conversation with Howard again, bothered now by how distant he had felt, by the suddenness of the past few weeks' events, which put up a wall between him and one of his closest friends, his ally.

"No Howard, no I don't think you really understand," he began quietly at first, feeling odd about talking to himself in front of a mirror. Looking around him again and realizing there was no one there to hear him, he continued, "I have killed a man, wiped out his life, boom, just like that. He's done. Gone. Whatever his memories were, none of them are relevant now. I erased his entire history, and by driving away, I'll never know. I took away his existence. How do I prove it, you ask? Well that's a very good question. I don't know if I actually ran him over on purpose or if he jumped out at me. I can't remember. I have no memory of it at all. I can't incriminate myself, and I can't exonerate myself either. I feel like a fraud, living in the middle. Yes, that's right. I'm a fraud. I think you are too. You're a fraud. I didn't... none of this is mine, this life." He smiled. The figure in the mirror smiled back. It didn't interrupt him to say that no one needs to know, there were no consequences. So he continued.

"It doesn't matter. It's not Duane's Company either. Somehow you, yes you! I'm talking to you! You in the mirror, stand by. You have some problem, some inability to accept, that you have to constantly be re-optimizing, but you don't remember. You don't remember...I don't remember. But why do I need to feel guilt for something I don't have control over anyway? You frustrate the hell out of me!" His own reflection looked back at him. When he moved an eyebrow, the reflection moved an eyebrow. He blinked. The reflection followed.

"It's just how do you live with yourself?" The reflection was motionless.

"Oh, come on, don't ask me this now." The reflection moved, and Henry pushed his face closer to the mirror. He could almost suddenly see the person who stared back was another, someone else from a different time and a different place. He blinked. There it was, the figure again, the figure which now looked at him in the mirror with the same eyes, the same nose, the same high cheek bones. Henry closed his eyes, and he imagined his own reflection in the mirror. With his eyes closed, he sensed in the room with him the presence of another. He opened his eyes, his ears pricking at the idea. Looking around, he saw no one. So he continued with his practice conversation. "How do you feel you're worth anything?"

"Because the past doesn't matter. It's already happened, so who cares what it is or what road took you here or what you did to get you to point B. The whole fucking conclusion is that you're at point B. This is what matters. If you stood there counting injustices and histories, you'd be standing there for a long time and doing shit. At least I get shit done regardless of how I fucking do it. Hell doesn't exist Henry. Just dead people."

"Hell's right now for me. I'm in Hell, and I can't get out of it. I'm in it every time I close my eyes, and when I wake up, I am so tired, I can't even feel alive. Maybe that's the answer. Maybe that's it."

"You need to see someone."

"And tell them what? What am I going to say? Who am I going to tell about this? Whom can I trust to tell?"

He was silent for a long time and watched himself breathe in and out in the mirror. He imagined what would happen if he stopped breathing, if somehow the artery that ran along his neck to his brain were cut. The up and down of his chest would stop, and he would be gone. So quickly, maybe even without a noise.

"It started getting worse with my dad's death. Then the car accident, it just...I lost control that night. But I've been feeling this way for a long time now. I can't explain it. Just this unbearable loneliness and emptiness and exhaustion. I'm afraid to sleep. But I can't get out of bed..."

"It's just that you don't know what you are or what you're worth when you think that had you not been born where you were born...had something years ago slightly changed, that you were born into something just slightly different, that this would all change. It makes me feel like I've lost everything I think I have..."

"...But how am I supposed to be responsible? I'm supposed to just accept a passed-down story or memory from someone else? Someone else's history? Who's claiming it? I had no choice in these things in history. It's making me sick. I don't know it at all. I don't know

157

anything at all. What am I supposed to be doing with it? Some stupid purpose of history..."

He stopped and examined himself closely, and saw that he had without realizing it gotten his first white hair. It stood there, proudly, against its dark counterparts. He sighed. His throat was sore from speaking so loudly to himself, and realizing he had spent his evening talking to the mirror, turned away from himself and walked to his bed. There, he saw through the panoramic windows, the most magnificent view of the city. The lights illuminated across the avenue and the streets, through the small alleyways and all along the rivers like it was on fire...

CHAPTER 5

21ˢᵗ Century Painting

May 9, 2020. One week later and much to his annoyance, Henry received a call from Erica just as he was about to leave the office. "Henry," she said after briefly asking him how he was doing and while crinkling her nose on the camera, "I just want you to meet my friend who lives in the city. The one I told you about when we visited. She's single, and she'd like to meet people. It's hard as a single working woman in this city, and you seem like you could use some female companionship."

Henry groaned. The idea of sitting with another person, trying to force conversation with a stranger who wasn't a complete stranger because of the relationship through Erica was intolerable: His imagination had always stopped short just past the obligation step. He found conversation with the local barista to be difficult, and those barely lasted half a minute.

"Erica, I'm in mourning."

Undeterred, she pressed on, "I know it must be hard, Henry. It's almost hard on me, and I'm not even his daughter! But truth be told, this won't kill you. You need a little distraction anyway."

"I think it's the opposite. I don't need a distraction. I need to figure out how to keep focused. I'm always distracted." Henry sighed. He was already behind in answering his messages that day, and the next few weeks loomed up menacingly. He shook his head and hardened, "Erica, I really don't have the energy for this."

"Alright, how about this. I'll send you her contact information, and if, one night you randomly decide you're bored or want to give her a call, you can. I won't mention it to her."

"You've already told her you'd do this didn't you?"

"Damnit Henry. Yes, I told her I'd ask you."

"So I've met her?"

"Oh, yea, of course. Ages ago. I think it was at one of my birthday dinners. Or maybe graduation. I can't remember, but yea, you've met. She's always asked about you. Oh man, she'd kill me if she knew I told you this." Erica trailed off.

"Okay, fine. I'll go to one dinner." Henry reasoned it would just be one evening, and he would make his point to Erica that he tried, and it would be another few months of solitude before he would be asked the same questions again. And of course, he was curious which friend of Erica's had noticed him for so long.

"You will? This is great Henry!" she exclaimed, "I'll give you my friend Dana's details soon. She's a little older than you but has been living in the city for over ten years. She moved there for work. I think she does wealth portfolio management or something of that sort. We don't really talk about it. We went to school together."

"I'm sure I'll get to ask her all about it," Henry said half to his sister and half to himself, hoping his sarcasm was subtle.

* * * * *

160

May 12th, 2020. Three days later, Henry sat across from Dana at his favorite French restaurant near his apartment. The restaurant was famous for pot-au-feu and ratatouille, sparkling up traditional "peasant food" to create an "authentic" dining experience for those who could afford it. It was the place Henry had once taken Ariella, and what she described as "the rich's way of having a sense of irony". Most importantly, the restaurant was conveniently close to Henry's apartment in case he needed an easy exit.

To Henry's surprise, from the moment they introduced themselves outside of the restaurant, she was visually magnificent. In every way, Henry found Dana unusually proportional. Each of the shapes outlining her angular features combined in a way that modern scientists could prove was objectively "beautiful" to the naked, human eye across time, culture, and gender. She was beyond sociology and anthropology; she was full of perfected biology. What she lacked in sex appeal, she gained in perfectly positioned eyes, nose and mouth. Unfortunately, that was the problem: Dana looked like a 21st century Madonna painted by a 21st century Raphael, and she had about as much fluidity and life to her as a stiff, inanimate painting.

While Henry found Dana attractive, attraction to her was more complex. Attraction was one of those inexplicable urges involving a number of things that happened in Henry's brain without his knowing. He never understood those urges, and in particular why they were never practical for him. He could name characters in novels with whom he could easily see himself having an affair, and yet, he never found himself attracted to the women closest to him, the most physically real to him.

This is why when Dana immediately began introducing herself with great physical affection, wrapping her arms around his waist, brushing her hand against his shoulder, he realized she was feeling otherwise.

Dana's red-blonde hair reflected the low lighting of the ceiling and

161

bounced off the softness of her open back and then off the beaded sequence of her black dress. Her eyes were open wide, and Henry was convinced that she had the most vibrantly violet set of eyes he had ever seen. "Erica tells me you've just spent all your days in the office recently. How are you enjoying work?" She asked, breaking his stare.

"It's good. I'm enjoying it." Henry had trouble deciding whether there was anything else appropriate to say to her on their first meeting.

"Oh, that's so good to hear. Most people I know these days hate their jobs, and they're on their second ones. Or third. It's easy to change careers these days. Well, if you have the resources, but you know, we do, and we're lucky for it, thank god, but yea, I mean what you're doing is just amazing. I read about it in the papers, and obviously, Erica has told me all about it. I'm just so impressed." Dana straightened her shoulders and sat up, leaning closer to the table. She stared at Henry, eagerly waiting for him to ask her about herself.

"Uh, thanks," was all he mustered. Then, looking at her and realizing he needed to respond with something else, he asked, "Are you enjoying your work?" He sighed, unsure of whether he had asked her what she wanted to hear. To his relief, Dana replied with even greater fervor than she began.

"Oh, that? It's great. Actually it's fantastic. I love my job. Well, I don't *love* my job, but I don't hate it either. I mean, it's a job, and I make the right amount of money, and I am definitely on track to make partner in the next seven years or so. Well, I don't know that for sure, but I don't think there's anyone else who is getting as much attention with the bigger clients. Not that that's the only important thing. Work I mean. There's a lot of other things that are important."

She said it all in one breath. Henry nodded furiously and wondered when it was appropriate to take another bite of his dinner or whether he needed to ask her another question so that it would buy him some time to chew and swallow. He decided against it and instead took a small bite of scalloped potato, "Yea. I agree."

"What do you think is important?" He was surprised by her question. He hadn't expected her to turn the questioning toward him again so quickly; he was hungry.

"Uh, sorry, um..." Henry hesitated.

"Like, other than work, you know?"

"Uh, well, my family means a lot to me. I also like sports," he said chewing furiously, hoping she would share something about herself before asking him another question.

"Yes! Me too. I absolutely love family," she began, much to his relief. He took the opportunity to scoop more potato into his mouth, as she went on, "I mean, I just really think it's so important to be close with a group of people. And I'm an avid runner. I run every day. Six miles. I've been running every day for four years now. Never missed a day."

"Oh that's great." He wasn't sure what else to add. He searched for questions that may be interesting. She looked poised, her hands held a knife and fork neatly and gently, but she was leaning forward, and she finished every sentence with a smile, which jumped at the next word he uttered. He marveled at how she was doing it, how she could eat, talk and think of things to say at the same time.

The waiter stood nearby watching their conversation and whispered something to his colleague who smiled and interrupted the date by asking, "Sir, Madam, would you like some water?"

* * * * *

A few hours later, after finishing two bottles of wine and racing through

163

discussions about David Smith's estate and Dana's family (all things he could no longer remember the names or histories of), Henry found himself unlocking his apartment door with Dana at his side. If asked later, Henry would not have been able to explain why he brought Dana home that evening. Something in him felt deeply ashamed about it, but he was resolved to invite her to his apartment for another drink. In his head, he short-handedly blamed it on a moment's loneliness. He was, in fact, in the blurs of that moment craving human interaction, something physical and real, a softness and warmth his fingertips could brush against. She stood in front of him, glittering under the light, ready for touching. As they stood on his balcony, she came over to him and lightly rubbed his arm.

It was she who made the first gesture for romance. He went with the gesture and before he knew it, she was wrapped in his sheets in his bed asleep and he found himself panicked and terrified of what mutual expectations would follow. At once he felt wrong and he had no idea how to reverse the circumstances, but part of him felt the idea of a continued human interaction appealing. He longed to continue to be held. He longed to continue to hold someone else, some breathing, living thing that kissed and touched him. Lying there, with this dark bundle of warmth breathing, her chest slowly moving up and down, Henry felt an affirmation of the anxiety that he was in that moment...

CHAPTER 6

Stale Morning

...It was in the early, dark hours of the next morning, Henry began to think about his father for the first time that day. He reasoned that the dead man, staring at him accusingly with his father's eyes, must have somehow visited him in his sleep at night. Dana stirred next to him, and Henry stiffened, *Is she awake? What do I say to her?* Petrified, he lay very still until he could hear her breathing resign to its unconscious pattern of inhaling and exhaling, inhaling and exhaling. He slowly got out of the bed, his toes curling against the cold hardwood floor, put on a robe, and walked to his private mail slot near the front door of his apartment.

The mail slot was jammed full. He didn't remember seeing mail the night before. Henry had stopped receiving hard copy mail years ago, so when the decorative slit on the bottom of his front door was stuffed with papers, he looked at it in amusement. Henry crouched down and examined it, like trying to discover the crack in a leaky pipe. "Huh," he said to himself, and began to tug at the stuck papers. One envelope dropped on his foot, a large 8x11inch packet that had been folded to fit through the slot. Across it read: CONFIDENTIAL MEDICAL FILES. He tore the cover of the packet open and left the rest of the mail – all advertisements – on the floor.

The packet contained old medical files for David Smith that dated back thirty years. Thumbing through the pages, Henry saw lists of blood tests he had never known existed: CBC, BMP, BUN, CK, CK-MB, troponin, levels of LDL, HDL, and of course, complete profile genetics testing. He brought the files to the kitchen table and stood staring at them, reading through the various numbers, cell counts, missing cell counts, enzyme levels. Suddenly, as he thumbed through the test results a second time, Henry realized the test results were missing the section on chemotherapy. There were the radiology screens, biopsies, and yet what he had known for a great portion of the last few years of his father's life was always the lingering specter of the cancer.

In the last year, his father had allowed very few people to see him, handling all communications virtually. Even Henry's allowed once-a-month visits were carefully planned through his father's personal assistant, who moved away as soon as David Smith had died. Yet, there the hospital records were, indicating the length of stay, the treatments, the various visits, and no mention of the cancer whatsoever.

Henry began from the beginning and read through it again. He looked at the clock. Forty-five minutes of looking through the file. Those forty-five minutes, gone, and he has gotten nowhere closer to understanding what was going on.

Henry swallowed air; the morning was still an hour from rising. There was something deeply confusing about this: who had mailed these records to him anyway? Who had given the hospital the right to give Henry these hard-copy records? Why hadn't he received any notice that electronic records were available? Was someone trying to tell him something? He grabbed a glass from the kitchen counter, unwashed from the night before, filled it with water and, while standing at the sink, drank deeply. Wiping the water from his mouth, he began looking through the files again for the third time.

Henry weighed the records in front of him, the pages sprawled out across his counter, and thought of incongruities surrounding the past year as his

166

father lay dying, with "cancer" they had told him, but no sign of cancer anywhere on him, not a single record of it except for the last memory of the man. It had been morning when he had gotten call to rush to the hospital. And once there, he remembered the haze through which he saw his father's body, the dread of seeing the chest no longer move and pulse.

With the newly delivered information about his father's death, Henry realized that morning that he had spent his time wasting away at the guilty thoughts of a car accident, if he could even call it that!

A month ago, he had accidentally bumped into Coin Eyes, and thinking back on all of it – including the anxiety and panic that suffocated him – it was unclear whether any of it was his fault in the first place. Would Coin Eyes have died in the middle of the night if Henry had not hit him? Did Henry actually hit him or did Coin Eyes jump out of the car? Was Coin Eyes still alive given what had happened at the bar the other night? But also, was he, Henry, inheritor of his father's Company, in danger as well?

Who sent him these files, and how do they think they'll remain anonymous? Were they trying to save him by saying, "No, son! You don't need to go down that path. This was a set-up!"? Someone was lying to him. Maybe the entire incident with his father's death and the car accident with Coin Eyes was a set-up. It could have been someone in the Company. Surely, it was someone who had access to his personal address and calendar.

Manslaughter and murder were two different things, Henry thought. So, Henry decided he needed to refocus. He had been doing it wrong. This entire time he had been wasting his thoughts on one fear when that fear was about something else. It wasn't about the dead man! No, no, it was toward the man, or the men, who must still be alive, lurking and most likely wanting Henry to incriminate himself, putting ideas into his head and driving him to insanity. It would have been so easy for these types had Henry pulled the trigger. Yes, of course. His adversaries would have been thrilled if Henry stood in his own apartment and finished himself off with a lunatic's clean death and left them with everything. It was just that easy. Once the father is gone the son will have no head.

It was time to forget about the car accident; it was just that, an accident; he had no proof that the man was alive or dead before his body was hit. No one screamed out. No one else saw. In fact, Henry didn't even realize he hit something until he had completely driven over it. They had no idea. Howard was probably right the entire time. And this past month of hell? Useless. How useless! He had a business to manage and a plot to uncover. He was going to move on. He had to move on. He put all other ideas out of his mind and chose to follow, closely, on the ties of what those medical files revealed.

Henry eagerly swept up the files and jammed them back into the large envelope and walked to his shoe closet, where deep inside sitting next to three dozen pairs of various handmade, patent leather shoes in brown and black, was a safe. He opened the safe within fifteen seconds and threw the medical files in, locking it up again.

Next, Henry walked to his bed, quietly opened the drawer to his nightstand, took out the loaded gun and wrapped it in a pillow case, and put it on top of his safe. He then crawled back into bed with Dana, reclining against the pillow. She stirred and moved her hand to put his onto her warm body. He curled up and wrapped his arms around her, indifferent to who she could have been at that moment as long as she was a breathing and living thing.

* * * * *

May 10, 2020. Jared laid in bed that night unable to sleep again. When he looked into his closed eyelids, he thought he saw the entire darkness in the room spinning, spinning along, and when he let himself breathe deeply enough – inhale, exhale, inhale – he saw that he was no longer where he thought he had lain himself to sleep, but somewhere different. *It was dry there. The hot winds brushed against him, and the air smelled of a staleness that he recognized yet knew was far away. He was searching for something, someone, yes, someone was supposed to meet him at the village edge in this hot, abandoned place. He had been waiting for this young man disguised as a boy for a very long time. Suddenly, he longed for rain.*

Dreaming of the rain, Jared's inner mind through closed eyes sought out the image of his son. His son was sitting on a cloud. He shook awake. As he thought about his four-year-old child, Jared was stabbed from his thoughts and transitioned, without his permission, to his feelings. He felt so guilty. He wanted to end this whole thing. But he couldn't think of how he could go home without any cash; he had left so long ago to bring back money, and he couldn't return with his hands and pockets empty. He was too ashamed and too guilty. To have done all the things he had done, and to come home with nothing! Was his son old enough to feel shame?

In the darkness, Jared longed to go to the other place to feel the stale winds again. There – in that place – he was a stranger, a foreigner in space and time, and someone who could act without admonition or judgment. Or if that judgment came, he could escape. In every mission he was given, he escaped and came back. Came back to here. Here – in this world – there would always be another morning. And as the sun rose to a new day filled with the ideas and activities of things he could do but never actually managed to do, he felt a sense of dread. The early morning always brought a bitter taste of hopelessness to him.

Jared stared at the wall. He opened the nightstand drawer and found the King James version of the Bible. Like the night before, and the night before that, he opened it to a random page and began reading…

CHAPTER 7

A Little Cloud

About two weeks later, around May 23rd- 24th . "Henry! You're finally here," Howard said after he opened the door to his large 37th floor apartment. He was wearing a bright, red polo shirt and khaki shorts.

"You don't wear glasses, and your shirt clashes with your ginger hair" Henry remarked, looking at Howard's black, wide-rimmed glasses set out on his round face set under neatly combed hair.

"No, I don't wear. I stole them off a girl here at the party. Glad you could stop by and grace me, us, even as you insult my fashion taste," he continued, opening his arms wide to include the guests who filled his apartment, "with your presence. And who may this unlucky woman be to accompany you?"

Howard extended his hand to Dana, who smiled back and replied, "I'm Dana, Henry's date." Dana shook the extended hand, admiring her own polished nails and feeling satisfied she visited the salon earlier.

"Henry's date, huh? Well, I'm sure you're more than just that. Are you a...massage therapist? Musician? Model?..." He smiled at her again and then said, "I know, you're the Looks, and Henry is the...the...hey, Henry, what do you think you're good at?"

Dana exhaled and laughed with a high pitched frequency that sounded like it came somewhere from her sinuses, and she replied, "Well you're charming! Henry, why didn't you tell me about Howard earlier? Well, I am just so happy, so *so* happy, you invited us here. This is exciting and ...wow, look at that apartment, wow."

Her eyes gazed into the apartment, and she could see a scattering of colors on people whose mouths opened to laugh and whose eyes glittered with excitement. Dana suddenly felt that she had entered into an enchanted world, exclusive and opaque, one of which she had always walked the edges of but never entered. Here, with Henry, she felt crowned.

Howard saw Dana looking through the door and insisted, "Why don't you go inside and have a drink. There's plenty...everywhere in fact. Henry and I will take your coat and we'll come find you in a moment."

Howard took Dana's coat from her arm and put his hand on Henry's back, leading him to the coatroom. "So you actually date?" he asked Henry.

"Well, it was set up...," he searched for ways to explain the arrangement but settled for, "she's a friend of my sister's, and we've only known each other for two weeks. It's easy. It's low...well, it's low stress."

"Is this the first time you're taking Dana out as a date...I mean, are you publicly "dating" her?"

Henry, surprised by Howard's genuine curiosity and recognizing Howard's perplexity about the development as similar to his own, explained, "Well ya, this is the first time I'm introducing myself as dating Dana to my friends, if that's what you mean. I don't see why that's a big deal at all...is it?" Henry looked to Howard for guidance. In the past, Henry was never astute about these matters, and it was Howard who patiently explained the details that Henry always seemed to excel at

172

missing.

"It's not a big deal at all," Howard replied. "No. I just...well, I wasn't expecting it. You've just, wow man, you've just seemed edgy and kinda weird lately. I assumed things were bad with the funeral...but if you're out there, doing your thing, that's great. I support it. I think there'll be a few people who will be surprised, that's all. Not that you're doing anything wrong. Just not, well, not what they're expecting..." Seeing the hesitation on Henry's face, Howard said, "Come on, why don't you go find Dana, and I'll check your coat here...in my own apartment with the help of this gentleman." Henry nodded and walked out the door.

Standing in a nearby room at the party, Ariella, in the way that hearts have that intuition that they're in danger, sensed something the moment Howard pulled Henry into the coatroom. She had missed the conversation between Howard and the new woman and ended her own lukewarm additions to the conversation with a group of unknown investors. She was afraid to approach Henry for she had felt the threat immediately when she saw the immaculately dressed, stunningly beautiful woman walking toward the cocktail bar. So her heart, telling itself that the magnificent stranger was Howard's, engaged in self-preservation by watching Henry enter the coatroom while pretending to plug into another rather mundane conversation. From the corner of her eye, she saw Henry walk out of the room, alone, and instead of heading toward her, he moved toward the magnificent woman. With each step he took toward the new woman, Ariella's heart turned inward on itself, and the nerves of her body crept along her fingertips and into her temples, where they sat, transfixed in anxiety.

Instead of walking over to Henry, she began milling around other pockets of people, hoping for an entry into their conversations, a distraction from what she feared would become inevitable. Meanwhile, her nerves tickled with agitation, like an itchy muscle, making her unable even to focus on a singular person's voice, until "Hey, Ariella." It was said softly, and she recognized the roundness around the consonants indicating the soft beginnings of a person trying to speak.

She turned to Henry and replied, smiling hesitantly, "Hi Henry," and waited for him to continue.

"Uh...so, I'd like you to meet Dana. Dana, this is my good friend, Ariella. I've known her for years." Henry smiled and put his arm on Dana's back.

"Ariella, I'm so happy I can meet you. Henry's mentioned you before, and I've just wanted to meet you ever since." Dana extended a hand out to Ariella.

Ariella, ears red and buzzing, extended her hand to Dana's and shook it, "It's nice to meet you too. How long have you two known one another?" she managed to ask.

"Two weeks now. We've met earlier, and you know, I've always thought Henry was someone I'd like to get to know...and ya, it's worked out. This is a great apartment. I'm guessing you must know the host, Howard?" Dana looked at Ariella intently and then surveyed the apartment until her eyes rested once again on Ariella, who blinked back furiously at her, trying to keep her insides in.

"Yes, I do. I mean, I do know the host. You know what, I'm sorry guys, I just realize I uh...I...I left my previous conversation quite abruptly. I'm afraid I might be rude, but I should just...give me one minute, please. I'll be right back." She hesitated and turned to look at the ground, avoiding Henry, who stood there, motionless, unable to say a word at the unexpected exchange that occurred.

Then quickly, Ariella left the two and headed toward an empty corridor, where she breathed in and out and tried to process the thoughts of what had just happened. Was it all real? Standing there, she looked down and saw that she was wearing her new heels, and she resented them. She had gotten them for this party. Her heart, which in the shoe store was riding along in the clouds while her mind weighed the price of the heels, was now hiding somewhere. She had wanted a different role in Henry life, and now that Dana had arrived, she realized that her position was once again cast to the place she had been desperately trying to leave. Ariella no longer wanted to remain his friend. Yet after all these years, here she was again, each time realizing this was no less painful than the time before.

When she composed herself, Ariella returned to the party, where she spoke to a few more people, avoided Henry, even avoided Howard by association, and just fifteen minutes later, sent a text to Howard and Henry:

Thank you for the invitation. I realize I'm not feeling well tonight and need to head back soon. I'll see you both in no time. Ariella.

As she stood in the elevator, going downward, Ariella counted the floors as they passed, *38, 37, 36...3, 2...*until finally the bell rang, the elevator opened, and she could feel a gust of warm air coming from the vestibule door. Feeling trapped, she walked over to the door swiftly and walked home, breathing in as much of the new summer air as she could. It was a strange thing, this release. Her fingertips were numb, and yet she felt that the reality of everything she had tried to hide was coming loose at the ends, unraveling slowly at first but quickly, more quickly now, now so quickly that she felt under threat of losing the fabric of herself in it, her insides coming out now at the seams. And here was the old problem of perception being as deceiving as reality, her Cartesian nightmare bursting and awakening her to what she had intuited and feared. In her new awareness, she felt cheated. What illusion had her mind convinced her of?

Five minutes from her apartment, Ariella realized her feet had become blistered. Looking down at the shoes, she no longer wanted to wear them. No matter how she looked at them again, the shoes would always remind her of her own foolishness. She ripped them off her feet and left them on the sidewalk. Once inside her own apartment door inside her brownstone walk-up, Ariella crouched down, slid onto the ground with her back to the closed door and began to cry.

She cried and cried, and when those small things which were tightly carried inside her no longer felt painful and instead became a blur, she looked out her window and imagined what Henry was doing. And then she began to cry more, until she was thoroughly done, exhausted, defeated, puffy and red in the face and numb in the cheeks. Sometime early that morning, Ariella fell asleep and had no dreams. In losing all her tears and crying herself to sleep, she had somehow – with her perception turned inward and looking inside again – transformed into a rock, which neither cried nor woke.

* * * * *

Looking around his apartment as he walked from room to room, Howard decided to call a cleaner to come in. In the meantime, he would go visit Ariella. It was nearly noon. He imagined that she had left early last night after seeing Henry and Dana together, and the night along with early morning allowed enough buffer for her to have gotten over her crying, which he found particularly irritating. Howard figured that in this moment of reality, finally, she may be able to stop the daydreaming. Opportunity seeking was his forte – a talent which he'd boast on his resume if he could – despite having known Ariella for years now. She remained a particularly entertaining puzzle for him: emotionally uncontrolled with her unusual sensibilities and yet unpredictably strong, the most mysterious combination for a great game.

Howard was thinking of ways to take the edge off. The edge had crept up onto him the last few weeks. It woke him up in the middle of the night and kept him from sleeping again in the mornings. He felt it when he was in meetings, and it made him clutch his coffee even while everything else raged on around him: the parties, dinners, entertainment. Somewhere wedged in those thoughts and ways to chase the edge away,

176

he looked again at the soft, round people around him, waddling to whatever tasks they had planned. He felt no allegiance to any of them. What if he had to kill one of them, to save others, as an initiation, or to save the Company...who would he pick? Those soft, meaningless faces that carried the fat of childhood rubbed into his mind. Howard shook his head. "These are crazy thoughts. You need sleep," he muttered to himself.

As he walked in the shadows of the buildings, Howard swerved left and right, trying to weave through the crowd. No one seemed to look straight at him. Their heads stared down reading the gum-encrusted sidewalks. In that warm morning, Howard wondered if he could harm one of those silent, idling strangers, snuff one of them out, if he had to. Perhaps if his life depended on it, he could do it. Or perhaps for someone else. Or perhaps for a group of people, an ideology, a history, or just know he could, that he had the absolute strength and will to. He imagined his hands wrapped around the man's neck, squeezing and crushing, until the hoarse sounds disappeared, the chest stopped moving, and the arms went limp. It was so easy. It would be so easy to destroy something, wipe it from the earth, and forget about it. Then it would have been as if it had never happened.

That last breath, though. He couldn't stop thinking of hearing the last breath of life exhaled from a warm body, which would cool, slowly at first, and then be cold permanently, perhaps blue or discolored, an off yellow. So easy, and how hard it was to evolve, to spring out of those first combinations of elements and chemicals, the placements of protons and electrons, the energy binding all those tiny things together, was weak. It was pathetically weak, loosely bound to one another in chaos or nothingness, a small pattern tying it together. "But I shot a man in Reno just to watch him die. When I hear that whistle blowin', I hang my head and cry," he whistled softly to himself.

The edge followed Howard throughout his day and into his night, and as his mind turned to it again, he realized he had arrived at Ariella's apartment. Outside her building, Howard found a small, grey-brown pebble and threw it at her window. It missed, so he found another one, a little more jagged, and threw it again. *Click.* It hit her living room window, which faced the street, and he could see her silhouette appearing. Ariella opened the window, looked down, and saw Howard beaming up at her. She was wearing a light short-sleeved shirt, her long hair hanging teasingly against her shoulders.

"I thought you'd appreciate a visit today!" he shouted from below.

"No, I'm all set, thank you!" She said back, closing the window jokingly, and then reopening it said, "Fine, I'll let you in. But make your reasons quick."

"Running up now, once you buzz me in, my princess!" He walked over to the door, and when the buzzer announced his entry, he gallantly walked up the steps and knocked on her second floor apartment door. She opened it, this time having put on a light sweater to cover herself. "Ariella," he began, "you left early last night. I was disappointed you couldn't stay later."

"Why don't you come in," she said, raising a dark eyebrow. Her long, black eyelashes still had the remnants of the previous night's mascara smeared on them. Howard walked through the door, and wrapped his arms around Ariella, hugging her tightly. "Howard, I can't breathe. Please let me go," she managed to say.

"We're a bit touch and go this morning, huh?"

"I'm tired. It was a long night."

"Why was that?"

"Hard time sleeping," she paused and then said, "the usual issue."

"Well, he didn't tell any of us he'd be bringing a date," Howard ventured into the sensitive topic, treading carefully with his words to see what reaction she'd bring. "I was shocked, and I felt for you…"

"You know, I just, I'm sorry, I don't really feel like talking about it now. I've talked it to death. I'm just trying to focus…to focus on other things. Sorry, not sorry to sound defensive." She looked him in the eye and held the gaze, and for a second, her bottom lip quivered.

"I understand. I just wanted to check in." He smiled back at her, pleased that her armor was easy to poke through.

"Ya, thanks," she said to him. He waited patiently until she began again, "Okay, you're right. It was a hard night. I didn't expect it at all. So you really didn't know either?"

"No, no clue," he whispered and tried to put his arm around her.

"Howard, take your hand off my waist," she stated matter-of-factly back.

Disappointed, he decided he had moved too soon and said instead, "Well, I give it two weeks before he decides he's bored or vice versa."

"That's not really a comfort." she stated squarely and stepped away from him, walking instead to her kitchen and sitting at the breakfast table, "Anyway, how are things?"

With her distance, Howard knew he would fail to get what he had come to her for, and instead, followed her into her kitchen and took the chair across from her and lied, "Things couldn't be better. I'm living in the best of times. How about I come in and make you a cup of coffee? Let's see if I still know how."

Outside, the sun was high in the middle of the sky, reflecting off a million glass windows, lighting up a crystal palace…

CHAPTER 8

Plurality

May 25th, 2020. Duane reached the security desk at 23:07 and flashed his key card. Two men came and led him through a series of four sealed, titanium doors with KEEP OUT and PRIVATE signs across them and into a glass room where a small team of people were sitting around an oval table.

"Hello Duane. I'm glad you could make it. My name is Doctor Reynolds. I don't think we've met in person yet." The project lead scientist, a short but distinguished looking man with a hooked nose and bushy dark eyebrows, stood up and shook Duane's hand.

"Yes, Doctor Reynolds...you have some cold hands there, but let's forget the formalities here. Great to finally meet the brains behind all this. Thank you for getting together at this time. Have you re-tested the samples?"

"Yes, we have."

"And what's the news?"

"All results are positive. We were…quite surprised, to say the least, but it looks like the entire system had been tampered with and that well...quite frankly it's on. It's been on. For how many loops now, well that's what's got everyone confused. I'm not sure. None of us are sure. I lost command over that key a long time ago."

"Goddamnit. So what subjects did you use? We weren't able to catch the end of that on the call."

"We had used a few samples of cancerous cells about two years ago, and those results came back so surprisingly positive that we tested on lab animals – rats – and those results were also positive. We had gotten permission from human subjects after things went well with the rates and are in the process of clearing this with Legal and the S.H.T.S…uh, sorry, that stands for Scientific Human Testing Systems. It looks like we are the first company that has the advanced technology to do this."

"How did you know the loop has begun? I guess it doesn't matter if it was a test run. A test run's a test run, but there are policies for those things and we follow them. The rest isn't our problem. I wanted to move forward on this immediately and have the plant in India since it's the only place to synthesize the basics of the technology, but as you know, Henry was adamant about having that funeral then. Were you able to attend?"

"No, I was in China, at the Beijing Genomics Institute, dealing with this project actually. Yes, I have heard about that funeral. Quite a showing huh? Well, have you told Henry about this development? Although I suspect David Smith has already told Henry about it. In fact, I wouldn't be surprised if Henry and David were the only people to know what actually happened with the human test subjects. In fact, it may be the last test David left for us." Doctor Reynolds rubbed his thick black eyebrow with his left hand, thinking.

"No. I haven't said anything to him." Duane's voice softened, as if suddenly afraid they'd be overheard.

Doctor Reynolds responded by lowering his voice to a whisper. "Henry seems fairly capable. He's been working with David for a long time. Interested in the science. He's come in many times before down here, learning the nitty gritty, real science nearly since the project began. Since about six months ago, though, he seems like he's been a little distant from it, perhaps his dad's illness having something to do with it. I'm curious to know why David never thought about using himself as a test subject."

"Maybe he did," Duane whispered back. The room felt cold. It reflected a sterility that made it seem impossible that what was being tested in those very rooms that were sealed off, protected, heavily secured and monitored was the very essence of life: the thing that life used to repeat itself, carry on, an immortality of information. Duane inhaled the stale refrigerated air. Life, life, life in a refrigerator, life as information, life which was cold.

"Are you suggesting Henry?" At Duane's nod, Doctor Reynolds continued, "Well, I mean, no one can deny the kid is able to pull his weight. It's just this project has been highly confidential from the beginning. It hasn't even gotten full approval from the Board. The only other people on our side are China right now, and we haven't even told the guys in Brazil or Russia. Now I find out that Henry probably knows about it, but I can't ask him directly. Those are headaches I'll deal with. So for now, can I sit down with the team, and you explain exactly how this works...step by step?"

"Yes, of course. We have all the materials ready to present to you." Doctor Reynolds walked over to his team of four who sat at a table in the middle of a large room filled with books in casings or decorations.

"Great. Well, let's get started." Duane exhaled. It was going to be a very long night. David Smith's words weighed on him. "And as a final word, this is all done with the understanding that this meeting is confidential, correct?"

"Absolutely," Doctor Reynolds replied. He shut off the lights and turned

183

on the projector to a simple presentation. "So, Duane, I'm not sure if you know anything about physics and the laws of thermodynamics, in particular, the systems of entropy. Let me share with you a quote I find particularly inspiring for this project. In his seminar to Trinity College in 1943, Erwin Schroedinger had begun with the following statement which happens to sum up our work, nearly a century later:

'Today, thanks to the ingenious work of biologists, mainly of geneticists, during the last thirty or forty years, enough is known about the actual material structure of organisms and about their functioning to state that, and to tell precisely why present-day physics and chemistry could not possibly account for what happens in space and time within a living organism.'

I have always memorized that. Ever since I read the lectures."

"You'll have to be slow with this stuff." Duane said wryly, remembering why he always avoided getting involved with these people.

"Okay, so, basically, entropy is a measure of the amount of chaos in a system – which shows up as energy in our reality. As far as nature is concerned – in the way we observe it – it is directional, which means that it either remains constant or increases in a particular system. This system can include the human body or a small machine, any system we can measure units of energy in.

Basically, entropy moves in the direction of time. As time goes by, entropy increases as a whole. So if we decrease energy in a system like a calorimeter or whatnot, it'll increase outside that system in some form of wasted heat or energy or disorder.

In recent years, we've shown that some systems can hold entropy constant, and some systems – when we *mess* around with things a little – can show negative entropy without a noticeable energy increase in other places. Of course, we don't know for sure where or how the directional violation of entropy is being compensated. We believe that the universe works in parallel and balanced ways, so the concept of a directional thing

184

always seemed artificial, or at least unaccounted for by our limited view of a three dimensional reality that moved through one dimensional time in one direction.

For a while, we've believed that as we increased entropy when times moves in one direction, entropy must decrease simultaneously in a reality where time moved in the opposite direction, either in pockets of time or continuous time. You and I will not know how those pockets are chosen. But we now know we can access them. At first, we began working with small particles and their anti-particles to test this, and we found that this was indeed the case. Then we began getting creative: could this work with biological entities? Basically, our question was, 'could we reverse aging' without causing a massive destructive entropy blow-up outside the system...or, can man be immortal? Doctor Sparrow has a few slides she's going to show you now..."

Duane held his breath and listened. This was everything David had told him about. Everything made sense now: The conversation in the hospital room; the conversations leading up to it; what David had asked. The hairs on his arm stood and froze. It had already been done, and no one had told him. All those times he was in rooms with David, no one said a word to him, to include him, to give him credit for what he had done.

Now David was gone, and who knows in what form, all that clarity of the trust between them had left him.

* * * * *

It was the early hours of the morning. Most the team of Division III Sector 5 Group 9 had gone to sleep before coming back within a few hours. Duane had left the meeting feeling astounded and shocked and headed back to his apartment for two restless hours of sleeplessness. Two people were left speaking quietly in the white corridors, out of security's visual and auditory reach.

185

"Doctor Reynolds, I don't know why I haven't brought this up earlier…I guess I just had my doubts, but have you ever thought…that perhaps what we're doing, it's ethically…well, ethically *challengeable*? Well, especially because those test subjects were chosen by David Smith, and well, no one's allowed to know who they are. Not even Duane. We just lied to a superior based on a dead man's word." Nancy had left the building still wearing her lab coat, her dark black hair tied in a bun.

"Nancy, I think about it all the time."

"What do you tell yourself? Even these test subjects; well, they won't know they're in the loop at all. What they experience, we'll never know until they come back."

"Well, the Process has to get approved by the Board first before we reproduce it in any kind of meaningful way. And after it gets approved by the Board, it's going to go through the government, which has taken an interest since 2010, let's not forget…and then go through the International Collaboration, and god knows what other hoops. By the time it gets to the end of that, I think all the moral implications would have been squashed out. Or at least, it's really not our place right now to say anything. We've been funded for too long a time now. If we had issues, we should have said them earlier…and as for whoever is in it now? Nobody expected David to go so suddenly."

Nancy paced back and forth and pushed back, "But we're the ones pushing to make this a reality. I mean, what if…what if it falls through one of these check-points? Aren't you ever terrified of the consequences? I mean, I'm a scientist, I do this for the sake of knowledge…I haven't even dared to think about what it could mean because no one has given me the whole picture, but maybe that's the wrong way to do it. Maybe we should be demanding the whole picture."

Exasperated, Doctor Reynolds sighed and replied, looking around at the building, "God, Nancy. Yes, I've thought about it a lot…when David

Smith first said he'd fund the entire project after the Federal Government's budget for anything theoretical unrelated to defense busted, I wasn't sure whether it was something I could trust in the hands of one guy...and his, of all people's. But I do find myself attached to the science. It's an important thing to know whether man can make the Project happen, but I wonder if we weren't meant to know this or discover it, we wouldn't. Should that edge of curiosity be self-controlled? I don't know. But you're right Nancy, have we chosen sides already? And what those sides are, I'm not sure. Are they even relevant? Or is this just reality now?"

She looked over to him. She lowered her voice and scanned quickly for audit cameras, "Do you trust the executive team who will have the ultimate power over this?"

"I trust David."

"Did he...ever wonder...or, ask about the consequences?" Nancy asked.

"No," Doctor Reynolds replied, "He actually kept himself in check in the same way we do. He only knew one piece of the coding to start the system. The thing is, those individuals are linked now, and the system stops its loop once they all exit. It's how the causality works. You and I are just outsiders to it, bystanders to the players who are now, somewhere...in some time, deciding. Or maybe not deciding. Maybe they have no idea. But Duane? David Smith told Duane and only Duane about the structure of the project and who to talk to about it. If he trusts him enough to do that, I trust Duane. I've known David for a long time."

"And Henry?" Nancy kept pushing.

"Henry is harmless. I still see him as a child. I remember watching Henry grow up when David and I would have long talks at his estate. He really...of all his kids...he really loved Henry. It's easy to see why, the

187

kid's so smart and responsible but he's timid and kind. Not the brat you'd expect at all. God, it's a huge responsibility he inherited."

"Oh god, yes. Well, I'm sure Duane was disappointed—"

"—Can you imagine?" Doctor Reynolds interrupted. "Being second-in-command and to have the entire thing go over to a kid? Well, David surprised us even from the grave. That's for sure. But you've got to hand it to Henry. He's not doing too badly. There is no one up in that executive chain who has his back. No one likes him. Not a single bit."

She shook her head softly. Doctors Sparrow and Reynolds looked at one another and began walking down the long corridor, their footsteps echoing down the hallway and off the walls.

They passed through five security clearances and in the parking lot, Doctor Reynolds turned to his colleague, "Alright, Nancy. Get some rest. We're coming to the end of something that's taken up a lot of our lives...we're near the end."

"Well, I'm not so sure about that. But you get some rest too." Nancy opened her vehicle door, and she sat at the driver's seat for a long time filled with unease.

* * * * *

That afternoon, Duane sat in his office chair near the window when Henry knocked on his door.

"Come in!" Duane said to the knocks.

"Hey, you set up a meeting with me earlier?" Henry opened the door and walked in.

"Oh, yes, of course. Nothing important...just wondering how you were doing."

"I'm all right. A little tired as usual but managing. How are you doing?" Duane sat at his desk and looked up, resting his hands peacefully on the desktop.

"Not too badly." Henry stared and blinked at Duane.
"You're sure?" Duane leaned back on his chair and folded his hands behind his head.

He was convinced, in that moment, that there was a touch of sarcasm. In that second, he could swear – he could swear it! – that Duane knew about the accident and was trying to persuade him to slip up, to make a mistake. Henry could see it in the twitch of his eyebrow, the left one, and Duane looked glued to that chair. As if in fact, Duane had been following Henry in the days following the accident and had been questioning everything Henry was doing related to the Company. Henry felt he knew – he knew Duane was onto something. "Yea, I mean, busy just as you must be, but other than that...I'm fine."

"Not to put any pressure on you, but you've just looked really preoccupied lately. I mean, it's none of my business, but is the family all ok?"

Yea, you bastard, it's none of your business. "Yea, I've been trying to spend some time with my mom and Erica. They left recently actually," and he decided to add, "and I've been seeing someone. So maybe that's what you've been picking up on."

Duane smiled and chucked, "I see! Well, good on you Henry. I just, I don't mean to pry, but your dad and I were good friends, and I care about how you've been doing. So don't be too shy or feel you have to be so *professional* you can't walk in and talk. We go through the same worries, you and me."

189

There was something stilted and cardboard about his voice. Duane may have even noticed it himself because he cleared his throat and waited for Henry to speak.

Henry didn't speak. He just stood there and looked at him, as if he were waiting to be dismissed. The room was silent, but Henry was determined to stand there and be as uncomfortable as he could as the two men stared at one another.

Then the phone rang, and Duane said, "Oh, my wife. I should probably get this. We'll talk again soon, Henry."

With that, Henry turned around and nearly stormed out the door and had to remember to not slam it hard. He rushed through the building corridors and nearly crashed into a few unsuspecting people. Those who saw him may have even claimed that he was talking to himself, but they kept that to themselves.

That evening when Henry came back to his apartment, he received a message from Ariella, "Can I come by tonight?" He wasn't sure how to reply. He had planned to spend the evening with Dana, and he was late already. So instead he stared at the message like it was an impossible task, and stowed it away from his view, hoping that he could ignore it until the next day...

CHAPTER 9

Sybil Meets Scientist

"I believe," Peter continued, "it was also Schroedinger who famously said, 'Consciousness is a singular of which the plural is unknown; that there is only one thing and that what seems to be a plurality is merely a series of different aspects of this one thing…'

During the height of the Process or Project development, no one slept well. The people who were excited about the project on the team saw their names on prize lists with forever tenure and equally promising funding. Those who were against the project saw it as some dangerous, ill-fated unknown. Not even the philosophers were equipped to handle the actuality of it: eternal recurrence through an exploitation of the second law of thermodynamics."

But it was those same people who were too terrified to walk away; they had invested their entire lives in its development, fabrication and test, and it was that same curiosity that plagued them and controlled them, fed them and drove them, that made them want see what would happen. After all, none of those people were the finalists who pulled the trigger. Meanwhile, as the morality of it rested on the shooter, the final nay or "yes, do it, goddamnit", the rest watched as the results inched closer and closer, protected by one degree of separation…"

May 26, 2020. Doctor Nancy Sparrow sat in her chair facing the window. Her book lay open on her lap, ignored and unread. She reached over to have a sip of apple tea. She drew it in slowly and listened to the silence. Nancy was a middle-aged woman and lived alone. She had been married before, and the divorce ended amicably. There was nothing obviously unpleasant about the entire affair, but after several attempts at compromising, she never felt she could fully be alive while her needs and obligations were interwoven with that of another person's. When Nancy came to accept this, she saw it simply: she exchanged a life companion for a controlled peaceful stillness and its counterpart, freedom.

Nancy usually read for two hours before bed. Her reading the night before had brought tears to her eyes, but tonight, a new book lay on her lap. She just couldn't get into it. After each paragraph, she'd put the book down, take a drink of tea, and look out her window and start thinking about the Project.

Nancy was responsible. The outside lens staring into her world would see her as slightly difficult, overly honest, and some may even say a bit too aloof from the world, but she was responsible.

Nancy had been a serious and well-respected scientist at a National Laboratory in biophysics and organic chemistry, and when David Smith approached her about setting up a team of people with partially funded federal grants along with funds from the private sector (almost completely from David who then owned a great portion of the resulting intellectual property and know-how) she was in no position to refuse. It was the opportunity to advance her team, who had fought for grants and establishment before even she joined. She was responsible. She was responsible when David first approached her and then throughout her career, actively working away in his shadow. And even before joining the National Labs and turning her group into David's private project, Nancy

192

was the kind of professor who would not accept graduate students unless she could guarantee them a job after. It was this same sense of honesty and seriousness with which she approached the current problem.

That night, as Nancy sat in her armchair unable to read, she kept thinking about the implications of the lab results: She was just there to calibrate the system, a specialty of hers. She was the expert on the equipment, but she had no idea then what the *underlying philosophical goal* in it would be until the testing began. In fact, it wasn't even the idea of the testing that got to her, it was the company that wanted it done: the source of the funding, the intentions of it all, *that* was what disturbed her. That was what kept her up and thinking, restless and tossing.

Nancy's thoughts drifted from one thing to another. Her gaze lifted from the photographs she had along her walls of vastly different lands. She looked at the pictures closely, at the eyes of the smiling people, in the mountains, in the homes. Her gaze stopped at a photo of a young child and a goat outside an asbestos house. In the background, the grey clouds loomed closer, and the grass in the picture showed that there was a wind from behind. The child smiled with beaded eyes.

Nancy thought about her own life: she thought about the fundamental choices she had every day —to get out of bed, to remain in bed, to go to the lab, to move far away. In essence, every day was a choice to be alive or not. All those choices were hers, but its very greatness, its mystery was all tied to the idea that one day, it would all disappear just as quickly as it came. She had no choice over the day she was born, and she had no choice over the day she died...until now.

Nancy Sparrow sighed and closed her book. She walked over to her window and stood there thinking for a very long time. She was troubled by nightmares. They followed her to bed like some incurable insomnia, knocking at the door of sleep, "What's behind here - when you close your eyes?" So in that way Nancy hung onto her reality. Her past defined her, and memories created the decisions Nancy would make today and tomorrow: She looked back on her decisions yesterday with a spirit of determinism and freedom. Nancy felt ownership over her choices but she could not have done otherwise, and she accepted her life - the mistakes, the sorrow, the inexplicable, the ugly - as everything she could accept or reject in the story of herself.

Nancy had grown up in a small town. Her father had worked at a cereal manufacturing company and her mother took care of the children. Nancy was a child prodigy. A results-driven, highly ambitious young woman, Nancy conquered one challenge after another only to be seriously disappointed at the plateau of each of her victories. During the worst times, her past sprawled out like some glorious mountain of achievement which she secretly noted were irretrievable costs of her own commitment to her family and other personal matters. But Nancy was forward looking, so when she was one of the only girls in her town who went to a top-rated university and then again to the best graduate program and then achieved again and again and again: she never noted the actual feeling of victory but more so that she didn't let her own past down. Yes, Nancy was constantly running from her past while accepting it all at once. Running to somewhere higher and more admirable. She knew it, and as she found herself sitting alone in her bedroom at the age of forty-five, she felt that it was the only way she could have done it. There was no otherwise. The otherwise had been stolen from her the moment her elementary school teachers told her that she was the best student they'd ever had, a gifted child. She wiped away a strand of salted, thick black hair and looked at her dark complexion reflected from the window, the years showing around the corners of her sharp brown eyes.

But somehow this victory, the one the Company offered, terrified her. David had originally wanted the project to be a collaboration of the governments of nations, to power-check one another. But as the founder of the technology and the forerunning supporter of it, he had pulled the plug on those initial plans and made it confidential to the national government only, and then suddenly, even they had limitations. Nancy watched all this and wondered to herself: how is it that the people who understand the science behind this, and therefore the exact and acute implications, can be the ones who are left the most silent, without any real power at all? She was fiercely attached to the project like it was some unborn child of hers, but she feared it because it was a child to be reared by others out of her control. She wished this last opus of success were gone, but she didn't know if she had the resources to end it.

Nancy sat with her window open, feeling the June winds come in. They were cool at night and rubbed against her forehead and brushed the hair from her face; they spiraled throughout her room and touched her bookcase and the light drapes that hung from her windows. What was this little moment? It was a brief feeling of immortality, a moment that could have happened twenty years ago, ten years, yesterday, tomorrow. It was a feeling she could only recognize knowing that she would one day die, that the seconds that passed with each breath she took were finite. All the beauty in the world rushed into her during that moment she conceived of the absolute power of finiteness – the power of the meaninglessness of the shine of stars; the nostalgia of crisp, clean air; and the reason behind why Nancy would feel like a little girl every time she squinted at traffic lights, so all the colors would mesh into the night like a big fireworks show.

* * * * *

The Sibyl of Cumae sat in her cave, drinking an old mix of chrysanthemums and honey, and listening to people nearing. She was hunched over and looked at the bottom of the glass as she drained it. She sighed and looked up to see the coming of ships, their white flags boldly declaring their arrival in the light sky. She peered again into her cup, and when she looked up, there were no longer ships on the horizon. She was no longer in her cave, but suddenly appeared in that woman's room, the woman who had visited the Sibyl in her dreams. Now, the Sibyl was not sitting in her cave but on a coffee table.

"Hello Nancy," the Sibyl said. She blinked several times and stared, fixed, at Nancy who remained immobile with her back to the Sibyl and still facing the window.

Nancy looked up from her window and turned around. She rubbed her eyes. She opened them, closed them, and opened them again. The woman – a small, fragile, wispy woman who looked so tiny and forlorn she was almost invisible – blinked at Nancy again. Nancy could barely make out the blink; it was a quick and airy movement, but yes, yes, that person, that thing was alive.

"Hello," Nancy said, her voice barely above a whisper. She wasn't sure what she was responding to or what was happening nor who was the wispy figure in front of her, an apparition with bright eyes. Nancy wondered if she'd wake up, whether her own voice in a dream would wake her conscious mind. But the Sibyl did not disappear and Nancy was still sitting upright in her chair, a book in her lap.

This time, the Sybil spoke with authority. Her voice grew as her small figure seemed to sway with each passing breeze through the window. "Nancy, you will have to tell the truth, but you'll need to search for him when you remember that you have to tell him. And when he finds out, it will all be over because it was built for that moment. There is nothing to prepare. Be at peace. Sleep now."

With that, the Sibyl of Cumae found herself back in her cave, the chrysanthemum petals making patterns in her glass. She waited for the ships to come closer, knowing what they would ask her when they arrived.

* * * * *

Nancy blinked again, and she woke. She had fallen asleep on her armchair, the book sliding off her lap and her apple tea cold. She stood up and walked to her bedroom and closed the door. A breeze was still blowing at her window, a warm gust of air that somehow, oddly enough,

196

left her with goosebumps on her arms. As she looked out behind the curtain, she wasn't sure whether she was seeing something there, hidden, small and wispy, or whether she was still dreaming...

CHAPTER 10

Beaches along the River

The river's Huang He's embankment was rising, the yellow waters rolling menacingly. Henry was a small boy, a childhood self, which he could view at the same time, somehow consciously removed but still connected. Henry sat on wet sand. He tried hard to uncover a mysterious silver vessel that had been buried halfway by the beach sand. He saw his past through another set of eyes and was not sure why this younger self was so interested in uncovering this vessel. Each time boy Henry dug with his small hands, the river waves, which looked like an ocean, would come up and pile the wet sand back onto the vessel. Young Henry was frustrated, but as he became frustrated he noticed there were two other people, a small girl and another small boy, on the beach, and he desperately wanted them to help him with his digging.

As Young Henry ran toward the small girl, he suddenly noticed that it was the child form of Ariella, whom he'd never met before but recognized given his older cognition. He shouted, "Ariella! Ariella! Help me, please!" But as soon as he opened his mouth to shout, his voice was drowned by the rolling yellow waters and the winds, which knocked the air from his lungs and filled them at the same time. t was as if he had no voice. His chest rose twice as fast to breathe twice as hard. Ariella turned to him, her curls bouncing on her wet back and laughed. He could hear her laugh, but he couldn't make a sound. He screamed. It was a silent scream, which contorted his face into all kinds of expressions, his lips gaping open with wide eyes. She continued to chase the birds on the sand, spinning herself in circle after circle, laughing, happy, leaving him despondent. He wasn't sure what to do. So he decided to leave her for a minute and run over to the other boy he saw on the beach.

The other boy was crouched near the water with his feet in the wet sand that was lapped by the small waves. Henry noticed he recognized the boy, and, in a fleeting feeling of joy, realized it was the child form of Howard. Henry ran over to Howard, but suddenly, he realized that no matter how close he got, Howard didn't notice him. Henry inched toward Howard's face, waving his arms frenetically and shouted, "Hey! Hey! It's me!" Suddenly, Henry noticed that Howard was trying to drink a salty, contaminated water. It was then that Henry realized Howard was not really the Howard he knew, but a Howard that had become emaciated and shrunken and tired, his limbs hanging from him like dying branches, ready to be cut so that something stronger and sturdier would grow back in its place. And it was then that Henry realized Howard was starving and leaning into the water to quench his thirst. But the water, the plentiful, rolling, menacing water was a sandy water, a salty undrinkable thing. So Howard was stuck kneeling, trying to drink a water that would never quench him. Henry cried out. He looked at Howard with such pity and sadness that his own sadness woke his sleeping mind.

Henry remembered this dream vividly as if it were some kind of nighttime movie that he saw in the middle of the night. As he rolled the scenes over in his head he realized with horror, "I'm...I'm somewhere stuck in between the others...I'm just stuck, and no one can hear me." He said the words aloud as if trying to confirm the validity and strength of his own voice. It was a comfort to hear it. He was awake.

He turned to see a sleeping Dana beside him, her chest moved up and down slowly to her breath, her hand curled along the pillow with her palm up. At that moment, he was surprised to see her there. Henry wondered what she was doing sleeping next to him, and he looked at her in disbelief. Then he remembered who she was and why she was there, and he would later describe the feeling that flowed into and out of him at that moment as an irascible guilt.

* * * * *

By the end of the following week, Henry was undecided over whether he should be avoiding Duane or following him. Henry noticed, that of late, Duane was barely in his office. In fact, during that one week, Duane had missed two meetings, claiming that he had, "other matters" to deal with. Usually, Henry ran into Duane at least twice a day and right up to the funeral, Duane had been irritatingly close to every single one of Henry's projects. Where could he be this week? Duane was heading the IFO project in India and presenting at an academic conference in China, and he was supposed to travel to Germany this week to present the KCX drug but had canceled that trip at the last minute. No explanation – just that he had "other matters". Henry paced around his room. He stared out his window at the milling activity below and sighed. The last encounter he had with Duane had been after a meeting about IFO, when Duane had cornered him or maybe it was he who had cornered Duane. Regardless, Duane had been standing near the exit as Henry had been too close to the large man-size windows behind the dark mahogany meeting room table, and as everyone else had left.

"How's it going, Henry?" he had asked.

Henry looked around and realized no one else was in the room and responded, "Busy. How are you?"

"Running around here. Running around at home. It never changes, does it?" Duane replied.

"I suppose not." Henry glanced at Duane and down at the street. There was little to watch beyond the usual constant motion of things and people.

"Today, for instance," Duane had carried on, "we're getting the alarm system re-installed. Been a lot of robberies and small crimes lately. People getting killed. Not anyone important of course, but just little things. Manslaughter. You hear about that?"

Suddenly at this, Henry's ears had pricked, and he could still feel the heat that had risen in his face and caused him to color. He chose his words carefully. "What do you mean?"

"Oh, nothing huge. Just robberies in supposedly safe neighborhoods. There was a shooting downtown, but they think that was gang related, and it wasn't in the greatest area. May have been a hit and run also. Cindy just wants the alarm system on extra-alert, you know, in case our neighborhood is affected."

He knew. At that moment, Henry had been sure of it. He had been sure he had caught a glimpse of Duane pausing at the, "hit and run" words and had felt the seconds were drawn out like a large, balloon being inflated. The sun blasted in uncomfortably, frying him when Duane had planted those words. He had been hinting for weeks now, and he was doing it to terrify Henry, to signify that he knew.

But what Duane didn't know about were the medical files. Yes, now, while Duane may be antagonizing Henry, Henry had a piece of information, delivered straight to his doorstep and shoved into his own apartment. This could be the key piece of information, the hard evidence of all his ill-feeling...which he could use...which he in fact had been searching for not even knowing what its form would be. It had always been about his father and it had begun — not ended — with his death. Now, someone with inside information had delivered it straight to Henry, undeniable proof, that he held against his only suspect, the man with the motive actually to do harm.

Of course at the time, Henry had responded, "I haven't read or heard anything." Then he had continued, "Good luck with that. I have to run to another meeting now."

Henry paced restlessly in his office. Outside, looking from his large glass window, Henry looked down. It was a beehive, the people running into and out of buildings, scrambling for the bright yellow taxicabs, the bright flowers, alive with activity and purpose. "Enough philosophy for today!" he suddenly shouted, smiling to himself. Hearing his own voice, Henry realized it comforted him and allowed him the clarity of working through his other thoughts. He wanted to speak aloud, but being cautious, he mouthed his questions inaudibly to the houseplants that were placed neatly near his chair and desk. Did he imagine Duane's smug expression? Was he reading into those words, or did they seem out of place and context? The moment had passed so quickly, but at that time, he had felt so terrified that he didn't even look Duane in the face. He didn't really catch the full expression long enough. Did Duane's eyebrows twitch? Did he blink? All liars blinked, but he had made a mistake already by missing the expression, and of course he did. He bungled these things, as he always had. Why was he, Henry Smith, CEO and discoverer of foul play and cold blooded murders, just so frightened and immediately defended himself by becoming a huge, terrified, coward? What was wrong with him? He could have used that moment! And even if Duane suspected something – or worse, even if he plotted something – he had nothing to convict Henry with – and shouldn't Henry be on guard in case Duane was involved with anything? He shouldn't have walked away! Goddamnit he missed an opportunity. That was it. Should he go back into the room? See if Duane is still there? He should do that and so he did.

As Henry walked toward the Board Room, and as he neared the large glass doors that sealed the large, rectangular room, he saw that Duane was standing silently near the large windows on the other side of the table, his hand cupping his chin, deep within himself. Henry hesitated, forgetting what he had wanted to say. As Henry stood outside the room looking in, Duane turned. Henry moved three steps back until he was facing the corridor perpendicular to the room, several feet beside the glass doors. Duane opened the doors and as he pushed the handle said into his phone, "I'll be there."

In that second, Henry stood immobilized and frozen. A panic rose into him: he wasn't sure what he'd say or how he'd act, and now he felt like a fool for rushing back the way he did. His hands wet, and his forehead throbed, Henry noticed the perspiration that seemed to overcome him. It sent him into another panic. In the next second, Duane turned the corridor and stood staring at Henry, who was brushed his palms against his shirt. At that very moment, Henry felt the floor melt beneath him, and he was falling all over again, falling somewhere he didn't know. His feet no longer had traction, his hair was standing straight, grabbing onto the only thing that anchored it, his throbbing skull. The air was thick. It was so thick that it swallowed but cushioned him at the same time, balancing his free fall. He could smell something. It was a faint smell of burning rubber and the sounds of a bustling city. The smell choked him, and he could swear there were the jingles of bicycle bells and shouts of a language he felt was familiar but did not understand. He coughed as he descended into the thick air. He couldn't breathe, and the air became thicker. Time was stretched. He fell and he fell, slower and slower, until he stopped dead mid-air, suspended in the fluid…

In the following second, Duane opened his mouth to speak, but he was interrupted by Henry who said, staring, "Assured Home Security System Installation. It's a great security system. Is that what you use?"

Duane stood open mouthed, the words he had formed hanging from his dry lips in partial form – words that almost jumped but hung instead by some invisible string. He closed his mouth and found the word, "Thanks," swallowing before becoming silent again. Duane looked at Henry, and Henry looked at Duane. They stood there for the following second, neither sure of what to say next. Duane blinked. He opened his mouth, and the empty words, a short silence, hung there again by that same invisible string that seemed to pull all sound back into him. He closed his mouth and turned around to walk away.

* * * * *

Nancy walked into the main building and took the elevator up to the Executive Floor. The security guard at the front desk recognized her and asked if she needed help. She declined. "No, I'm fine, thanks," she said. She was juggling three large bags of presentation materials and regretted declining help as she struggled off the elevator several floors up. As she swore at herself, a young man stepped in front of her.

"Do you need help?"

Nancy stared at him. His messy dark brown, nearly black hair, looked like it needed a washing. "Actually, yes, could you please help me carry this to Executive Board Room 2? It's a walk through these halls."

"Of course. I know where that is," the young man replied.

"Great, thanks. You can carry these bags, and I'll carry that one." She shuffled around and handed him two large bags. She peered at him from behind her green-rimmed spectacles. Her otherwise curly hair was tied back tightly, and she recognized him immediately.

"Do you need help setting anything up?" The young man asked again.

"No, I'll be fine with the rest of it." She replied. He opened the door and waited for her to step in. He placed the bags onto the large oak table and stood, waiting, to see if she needed anything else. She looked at him, and for a moment, Nancy Sparrow and Henry Smith stared at one another without anything to say. "Well, thank you very much for your help. What's your name?"

"Henry. Uh, Henry Smith." Henry replied and stuck out a hand.

Nancy stood motionless while the room around her flickered out, and the temperature in the air changed, dropping as the walls darkened. She looked around and noticed that the dark walls had become a darkening sky, covered by thick clouds. She could see herself looking down onto a boisterous ocean which gave way to a dark and large island. She saw the cave overlooking the rocky shore and heard the feeble voice of the wispy woman, the one who looked as if she was disappearing, who called out to her, "I wish. I wish...I wish to die." The voice echoed. It was soft. As Nancy blinked again, she was back where she started and facing Henry. She stuck out her arm and shook Henry's extended hand, then fixed her crooked glasses onto her face again.

"I'm Nancy Sparrow. It's nice to finally meet you." She managed to say...

CHAPTER 11

Departure

May 30th, 2020. Ariella sat at her desk ready to open her mail, but she was distracted and nearly cut her finger trying to open the envelope. He had not called her back since she had last reached out to him. She tried again a day later, but having received no response, she sat looking at her window and evaluated the stinging feeling in her, a fresh thing that grew with time. She was offended, insulted – even Howard picked up on it – angrier as the sting sunk in. In the end, Ariella refused to be jealous of Dana-the-woman. Instead, she reasoned she was terrified of what Dana represented, and the entire fear materialized after Dana did, creeping out of the corners of her imagination which she had tightly locked.

Ariella sighed and pushed herself forward, looking at her mail and was surprised to see a letter from the National History Foundation. She read the words slowly, forming the sentences aloud. She read it again and again:

> *We are pleased to announce that you have been selected for the two-year grant in the amount of 120,000 USD to pursue your work in Henan, China for publication in…*

She got it! The grant was hers. She'd be traveling again soon in just a few weeks if all her organization went along as planned. It would be such a challenge and the fear of the challenge filled her with excitement. With tears brimming on the edges of her eyes she smiled.

* * * * *

Half an hour later, Ariella and her friends from her research group, Kyle and Em, were sitting down in Ariella's kitchen at the little yellow table that leaned against the window, eating a plate of cucumber and goat cheese sandwiches that Ariella had prepared. The sun filtered through the half-drawn shades and against the light curtains patterned by transparent, green leaves. Ariella's herbs – mint, coriander, basil, and oregano – sat proudly along the white sill.

"So, you're going to leave us? Is it for good or just a little while?" Kyle asked. Kyle had been a friend of Ariella and Em's for years since they've lived in the city. He had met Em as he was doing his graduate degree in sociology at the city university, working at a bookshop. The two had become friends instantaneously, and soon two friendships were three.

"Well, no, not for a very long time, but I will be traveling back and forth a lot." Ariella replied. "I think my first trip to Henan will only be for a short period of time, and I'll come back here to do some writing, and maybe travel there again...so the grant is for the two years of research, and I have a lot of flexibility in between."

"It's an amazing opportunity. How long has it been since you were last there?" Em reached over for a sandwich. A dozen silver and gold beaded bracelets dangled from her arm.

"Just three years." Ariella smiled and took a sip of her coffee.

"Do you know anyone? You've never mentioned having friends there...or knowing anyone in fact—" Kyle began.

"—which is why I'm going!" Ariella interrupted, "It's rare that happens these days. Anyway, I'm going to visit the site next week..."

208

"What? Already?" Kyle and Em stared at her.

"Oh, no, I mean it's just a short visit! Really, guys, I'm not leaving forever. It's a short trip this time, and then I can work out when I'd make the longer trip to actually do the research, which is the real stuff, which might take the entire year or more. But who knows…" Ariella sighed.

"This is the *real stuff.* I'm happy for you, Ariella." Em beamed.

"It's the farthest trip I've taken in a while, and, honestly, I haven't thought so much about it. If I do I'll be scared. I know it. But maybe it's not so bad to be scared."

"You're doing it the right way. It'll be an amazing experience. It's too easy to just get into the rhythm of things here and never want to leave," Kyle said.

"Enough about me, so have you had any more luck with the new dating program?" Ariella asked.

"Ugh," Kyle replied, "Not at all. This is the one thing that is really annoying in my life right now. I have a relaxing job – like today I could get the afternoon off, but I want to meet someone new. I can't. There's no one new. And I'm in the social sciences! There should be plenty of women, but somehow, I can't find a single one."

"Well," Em said, "it's because people like to be treated poorly, and you're nice. Up-front nice. No one likes that. Get with it. It makes you less valuable right away."

"I still don't get your theory on this," Kyle beamed, unshaken. He stood up to pour himself another cup of coffee which Ariella had brewed just minutes earlier.

"Yea, I noticed." Em said, looking up at him. "In my opinion most people like to think that they have to work for something. So if you're open and normal and nice right up front, when you first meet them, it confuses the hell out of them. They think you're trying too hard, you're desperate, you're lonely, la la la. I mean, really, you could just be a nice person. No one gets that. People want you to entice and attract them through your wit, your charisma, your hard-to-get-ness since you've got the whole population to pick from. And nice? That's just boring. That's actually an indicator that there's something severely wrong with you – like some secret you don't tell people – and so the only thing you have in you to be able to get people interested in you is niceness, which by the way, is the worst compliment you could ever give someone. That they're just nice. No one wants to be just nice. So ya, you put yourself out there at first. You're open, and you know what, nobody cares! It's like asking to be forgotten. You're better off being a funny asshole. At least you'd be memorable."

"I don't like funny assholes," Ariella said.

"Um, of course you do!" Em objected, "Look at that guy Howard you hang out with all the time, Henry's best friend. I can't be in the same room with the guy without feeling I'm dying of asphyxiation from the lack of air in the room due to his ever-expanding, huge ego."

"Okay, he can seem difficult. I agree. But he's just that...difficult. He's really not a bad person. I'd go so far in saying he's actually fairly interesting, and oddly kind if there is such a thing--"

"In that egotistical, megalomaniacal kind of way. It's disturbing. The guy wants to see poor people die in the streets and would call it survival of the fittest if he had to put a defense on it, and he's barely more articulate than a used car salesman." Em smiled.

Ariella broke out into laughter. Then looking back at Kyle replied, "But

210

no, Kyle, I don't think Em is totally right with her theory. I think you just work in a field that makes it difficult, as you were saying, to meet people! But I think it's really all a game of patience."

"And luck, and timing," Em finished.

"Hummmh," Kyle sighed, "Will either of you date me?"

"Absolutely not." Both replied simultaneously and immediately.

* * * * *

Ever since she was young, she had tried to capture the present. Sometimes, it was in the form of photography. Sometimes she painted. Even as a young girl, she had kept a diary, which she had maintained meticulously, scrambling to scribble every single detail of her day. It had been worse. She used to write in it every hour, trying to remember all the forms of events and conversations in present time. Now of course, Ariella wrote down thoughts when she feared she'd forget them, but she let the smaller moments, the laughter and smiles, slide away without memorializing them.

Tonight, she focused on her photos. She had an exhibit to prepare for in her usual arts space and finished writing the article on her freelance piece, *"The Disappearing American Small Towns"*. As she sat at her open photo-editor, looking at the images: an old, dilapidated clock tower; an abandoned brass mill; an old man playing the bagpipes on a historic but unused flight runway. Oh yes, she thought as she looked at the old man's cheeks, red against the clouded sky, "I remember that now," she said aloud. It had been a rainy day, and she had asked Henry to accompany her on one of her photo adventures, climbing over fences until they discovered a shortcut to the runway. It was an abandoned airport, and the deep cracks along the cemented roads had been bursting with light, green grass. The rain had drizzled on them as Ariella used Henry's kindly offered sweatshirt to protect her camera. The image stung her.

211

She decided that she would phone Henry again to see if he was free. She heard the silence on the other line, and suddenly, "Hello?" It was a woman's voice, which startled Ariella who was now strongly wishing she could hang up, except for the immediate recognizable voice of Henry who could be heard asking, "Can I have that, please?"

"Hello?" he asked.

"I'm sorry. Is this a bad time?" She breathed into the line, and immediately, she felt herself choking.

"No, not at all. It's late. Are you ok?" He spoke quietly to her.

"I...just...I haven't heard from you in a while. I wanted to say hi." She was honest. After all, she wasn't prepared to say anything else.

"Actually, I'd like to come over. I've been a bad friend. Let me tell Dana. I'll be there in a little bit."

"Are you sure? No, I mean, you two are spending time together. Don't worry about it. Honestly. I'm fine. I just suddenly wanted to see how you were doing and I didn't hear from you so I just got worried or just insecure or I don't know. I'm sorry. It's late." Immediately, she felt guilty for her interruption. She felt guilty for the other woman, and in that instance, he reaffirmed her claim over him. It was all she needed.

"I've been meaning to come by. Really. See you in a bit." He hung up.

Exactly thirty-seven minutes later, he showed up at her door with three distinct knocks, and as she opened it nervously, he rushed in and wrapped his arms around her. It was desperate and brief, and after untangling he immediately moved onto her sofa-couch next to the window in her room, which he was so used to. She could smell Dana's perfume on him, but she knew that tonight, she had achieved what her most shameful desires had wanted.

"Is Dana ok with this?" Ariella asked, and in that instant, felt slightly guilty.

"I told her it was important I saw you. But you know, you guys haven't really spent any time together. You two should really meet and actually talk or get to know one another better."

"How did you meet her?" Ariella sat down across from him, holding her tea.

"My sister. It was just supposed to be casual. It is…casual, I guess, but it's just constant. I'm not really used to answering to anyone or feeling responsible for a person's feelings so much." He looked past her. "I've been feeling unlike myself, and I needed something more unlike me to make things balanced. I just feel odd, lately. Sorry. Maybe I'm working too much and just spinning my wheels and never feel like I'm getting anywhere."

"Well, what's work been like?" She asked. And so they shared light-hearted stories about their days for hours: she about her research ideas, and he about the various frustrations of sitting in meetings eight hours a day, and then trying to catch up with his email the next three to four. He kept everything else from her – the hallucinations, the suspicions he had about being set up, the medical files… "I'll be gone for a year," she finally said.

"Oh…" he replied with a feeling that a rock had settled into his stomach and unsure of how else to respond without sounding selfish: he didn't want her to leave.

But, she spared him of his silence with, "I admit," she looked down at her finger nails and frustrated with her own inaction, looked up again at him and met his eyes, "recently, I've missed you." The words came out of her without her control. His phone went off before she could finish. He tried to ignore it, but it kept buzzing, and when he looked down, he noticed it was Howard and that it was edging into the early morning:

> *The company vehicle has gone missing. Tried to take it out tonight. It's gone. Records do not show where it is. Let's talk soon.*

"I need to go," he said to Ariella. As they both got up, he clasped onto both of her hands and held them to him. It was a moment that surprised both of them and as he embraced her goodbye, moving from her hands to her waist, he found himself clasping her to him and desiring her more than any person he could remember desiring. The feeling came as a shock to him. His heart began to race, and he would explain it to himself later as a the second sudden feeling of freedom. And just as quickly, he realized he couldn't possibly have her. In his mind, the Dana and Ariella were two separate worlds, like the past and present to him. One was gravitation, the other was levity; Ariella pulled him into his guilt and mania, while Dana made him feel normal. Around Ariella, Henry felt like a constant liar.

They breathed into one another, and as she held onto him, an odd and darkening worry grew inside her that this was the change of something...*Prema.* The word stuck to her mind, and she couldn't dislodge it. It was a dry fire, and they were two innocent children on a pilgrimage unsure of what they were doing. *Prem. Is this what Bhakti is?* She knew something was different, and suddenly, she felt as if she had not known him truly well at all. In that instant, she felt like she was facing someone different altogether. Then, just as it began, it was over. With that, he let go of her and opened the door to leave without a word.

Henry ran into the night along the river, broken, in pieces, fragmented by the crevices that had held him together until now. He hummed a song as he ran along the rushing brown waters in the night, the rats scattering around him and onto the riverbanks at the sound of his pounding feet against the pavement.

* * * * *

Howard and Henry met as the sun was fighting the dense fog of dawn that surrounded the river. They met on the north bank of the river about three blocks south of the Company's main building. Howard was smoking a cigarette as he waited for Henry to walk over, and when the two men met, they stood with their backs to the sidewalk, looking at the brown water.

"So, what's happened with the car," Henry asked. He had his hands in his pockets, and his grey scarf hung on him, lopsided. He shivered slightly in the early morning brown air, the dampness clinging to him until the sun began to light up the little cobbled alleyways, filling him with hope.

"I went to the Company garage. I wanted to find the car to make sure no one had taken it to a mechanic, you know, since we didn't check it after that night. I had the model and license plate, and they double-checked the date we used it. The serviceman said it was gone. Taken to repairs. No idea why it needed repairs. He couldn't give me any answers. He basically said he didn't know. Anyway, I had almost forgotten about that whole incident, but it got me a little nervous he didn't know why the car had been taken in." Howard put out his cigarette and spoke without looking at Henry. His voice seemed muffled by the air around him. Henry strained toward Howard to catch the words. He became irritated at Howard's calmness.

"Jesus Christ," Henry said. He leaned against the rail that held the riverbank hostage from the road. "This was exactly what I was afraid of. Do you think…"

"No, Henry. It's been nearly seven weeks now. We messed up a car. It's just that the car is missing. And well, a car is replaceable, but I left a few documents in there I shouldn't have. Goddamnit. Oh well. What'll

215

come out about my private affairs will come out. I've never been afraid of the Tabloids and neither should you." The early air from his breath hovered over his lips and disappeared. It was a dry day for early-summer.

"There's a huge chance they just took it in for inventory or maybe someone else had taken it, and it needed repairs." Henry tried again.

"Maybe. But you know what, I asked the guy if anyone had taken it since we last did that night, and he said no. But suddenly, they wanted to look at it. Fucking hell, Henry, it's really not a big deal. I had a few receipts in there that were embarrassing and private, but the publicists will deal with it if it ever gets out. It's no big deal. Not right now. You're all worked up. You're just, just making a mountain out of molehill, and I keep entertaining it."

"Let's not think about it right now. It's not important. There's nothing we can do. But let me tell you this. Duane has been fucking distracted or away far too much, and I've made a schedule to try to follow him this week. I'm going to do it. I have the entire plan figured out already. I just need some time. But for now, let's drop the car issue." Henry was settled.

"What the hell are you talking about, man?" Howard threw the cigarette butt onto the ground and stamped the embers out with his foot. He hated the taste of it, but he hated it less the more he smoked, so he kept on with it and reasoned it was a temporary icon for his ennui.

"He's so guilty, I can just smell it on him," Henry said again.

"Dude, lighten up. What are you talking about? You're rambling on like a crazy person." Howard shook his head and waved his hand at Henry.

"Of course he's involved in this like he's involved in the other thing." Henry smiled.

"Henry, man, seriously.   Get   a   grip!   What   the   hell are...you...talking...about?" Howard leaned forward.

"We got it handled.   Don't worry."   Henry reached out and patted Howard on the back.

"Henry, go get some rest.   You're haggard and rambling," Howard responded.   "I'm going back to bed."   With that, Howard turned and walked along the river toward his parked car...

Part IV

CHAPTER 1

Inertia

...June 15, 2020. Henry and Dana were coming over for an afternoon coffee, and Ariella was finishing her preparations by arranging white and pink carnations on her kitchen table near the window. She moved the pink and white flowers until they looked neatly spread, and thought of how she'd be leaving her comfortable little home soon. Originally, Henry had proposed visiting her, but he had called earlier that morning with a casual: "Dana would like to meet you formally". Ariella immediately called Em for support.

At 14:17, Ariella's doorbell rang. Ariella tightened the hair band that kept her hair pinned up and walked over to the door. When she opened it, she nearly laughed aloud at the odd couple that stood in front of her: Henry was half dressed, a button down shirt untucked and wearing sporting mesh shorts while Dana stood next to him in heels and a coral summer dress with dark pearls. The pastel outfit looked out of place and she was oddly smiling, her teeth and gums waxy. She, smelling of a department store perfume counter, had light make-up on, and her hair was pinned neatly half-way up, looking darker and redder than it had the night Ariella saw her. Em came from the kitchen and at the sight of the two, burst out with a laughter that ricocheted off of Henry who took an immediate step back.

Undeterred by the sudden noises, Dana stepped forward, "Hi, you must be Ariella! It's so lovely to meet you finally. I'm Dana, and I've heard so much about you." She held up a bottle of prosecco.

Ariella shook off her surprise and replied, "It's...It's nice, nice to meet you also. Please come in." She found herself staring right back at Dana, straightening her back, smoothing her hair, and also unable to move her gaze from the doll-like woman who just stepped into her living room. She wasn't sure whether what she felt was surprise or disappointment or a combination of the two. Henry and Em stood horrified, and glanced at one another. Henry shrugged. Em scowled.

Ariella directed her guests to the small dining area in her kitchen at the breakfast table. Immediately, Ariella began making espresso and handed a cappuccino to Dana first. Dana took a short sip of her cappuccino and asked, "So Ariella...what is it exactly that you do? Are you a sociologist or historian? I didn't really know."

"Oh, a bit of a mix of both—" Ariella began.

"—But Ari's pretty much the best in the field," Henry interrupted, "I mean, she's actually been published and works for a number of journals."

"Henry, are you trying to get her a job?" Em piped in. Henry looked at her without saying anything, and then he smiled.

"Dana, what do you do?" Ariella quickly deflected, noticing Dana's uncomfortable shifting.

"I'm in marketing. The firm I work for has seven global offices, and I was hired to work in North America, and before meeting Henry, I was hoping to travel to Europe...you know, really extend myself to that part of the world since I just loved traveling there. I love challenges like that.

Greece, Spain, Italy, Germany, it's always been so interesting to do business there. I also really want to make director, although, you know thinking about it again... I'd like to also have a family." She paused and put her hand on Henry's knee. Henry winced slightly and glanced at Em, who stared straight back at him as if saying, *I didn't say that! She did!* "Henry's work is just so busy, lately..." Dana plowed through Em's interruption, "it's even a miracle that we could come by today. He's just been living at work it seems. Right, Henry?" And before he could even so much as nod, she continued again, "So I just wonder whether it's possible to be a modern member of society – to work like a *real* person, you know, like as a lawyer or doctor or in business – *and* have a family. I mean, I suppose if you were part-time, which no one with a decent income can do these days, you could have it all...but we modern women need nannies! Employ some more of the less fortunate, I say. Sorry, I just met you guys, and I'm rambling on about all my worries!" She giggled at that. Em blinked at her.

"Are you joking? Henry is she—" Em asked.

"—Oh, well," Ariella interrupted, "I think we should have some snacks. Em and I made a few coconut bars this morning knowing you guys were coming. Henry likes those a lot." Ariella stood up, rushing to the stovetop, where a plate of coconut bars were sitting, the chocolate melting through the coconut flakes from the invading sunlight through the small window.

"Henry what's your plans for the next week? I may actually have a get-together at my place, mainly to get rid of the food stock piled in my kitchen. You're invited as long as you eat left overs, and by the look of you," she looked him up and down with an expression of uneasiness, "you need some food in you."

"Actually," he replied, "I'm about to go on a business trip for a week or so. We're just meeting up with a manufacturing company. Shouldn't be too much work, and it'll be nice to get out of here for a while—"

"—When are you leaving? You didn't tell me this," Dana said, turning toward him.

"I'm leaving late tonight, actually. I just found out early this morning." He was unapologetic. At this, Em smiled at him and gave him a nod of confidence. For all the years Ariella had known Em, she was aware that Em had never once approved of his expanding space in Ariella's life; instead, Em had used Henry as a pincushion for her growing sarcasm. As a result, Henry had to plead for Ariella never to let the two be alone in the same room. Oddly, though, during this one meeting they were laughing at one another and joking, gesturing wildly, and now, the nod. "It's not a long trip, and I may even be back by next weekend, but you never know with these things." As he spoke, he looked at Ariella, and though he had no notice of his glance, all three women in the room looked at him.

* * * * *

Two hours later, after the guests had gone and the silence inflated into her apartment, Ariella sat alone in her kitchen, next to the window. She began to hear the chirps of goldfinches outside and looked to see two small birds sitting on her sill at the flower pots, where she had planted a small feeder along with the geraniums. The birds hopped along the flowers, and soon, after weaving in between the orange blossoms, settled next to one another, their feathers expanding together so that two small birds soon looked like one. Before she knew it, Ariella felt her nose tickle, then her eyes, and then her throat tightened as she bit back tears. He was there for one minute, and then in the next he was gone. It had happened so quickly. It was same elastic that bound them and when pulled, pulled in different directions would snap them together with a strength equal and opposite to that which pulled them apart, never letting them settle next to one another peacefully. She felt no rest with him.

Ariella stepped up from the table, took the leftover coconut bars and set them on the counter next to her shiny red espresso machine. She walked into her bathroom and stood in front of the full-length mirror. Then she slowly took off all her clothes until she stood naked, looking at the shapes in front of her. They were the same shapes. Nothing had changed since she last looked, or the time before then. Her chin still stood the way it was, soft, and her face was still that same oval that tightened into her chin. Her dark, uncontrolled hair had grown longer, and it now reached well past her shoulders. Her eyes, warm and brown, so brown they were velvet, stared straight into her. Was she beautiful? She didn't know. As far as she knew, she was just a mismatch of shapes that some found beautiful and others did not. Did she want to be beautiful? Of course. Ariella would justify herself with believing that every woman wanted to be beautiful to someone, if only to herself.

Did Henry find her beautiful? She pondered this often. She often wondered that if she were the most beautiful woman on Earth whether that would change how he felt, or whether there was some innate polarization that kept their distance, when every single other part of her was being pulled, her to him and him to her. She wondered this more than she cared to admit, and it was this question that made her realize the absolute randomness of it all, and beyond that, that every single convoluted question ended up covering the same patterns of emotions: sadness, confusion, happiness, fear, attachment. These emotions were hidden in waves that undulated in the rhythms of the present and reassessed in moments of reflection on the past.

Watching the goldfinches, she realized it was ten years ago when she had returned from a two-month trip to Iran. Looking back at where she was ten years ago, she felt her memory allude to a younger self – brashly thinking she was full of maturity back then. As the goldfinches hopped from branch to branch, whe felt a twinge of embarrassment. In Iran, Ariella had gone with a small team of archaeologists working for National Geographic and helped film and write about the team's forty-day excavation. She was exhausted when she returned late at the airport upon her return, and Henry had waited four hours to pick her up, taking a day off from work and remembering to bring her sandwiches and tea for when she arrived. He drove her home that afternoon and helped her unpack, and while she lain in bed watching television and too tired to move, he made her a late lunch and sat on the ground at the foot of her bed. It was November. Outside, the air was dark and grey with a dry cold that signaled the coming of snow, a clear silence except for the stirring of a few remaining browned leaves that clung to branches and smelled of old apples. When she woke up, he had fallen asleep on her couch, a small down blanket resting on top of him, barely covering him. His feet dangled off the edges, and it looked like her couch just shrunk underneath him. He was wearing an off-white collared shirt with thin yellow-and-blue stripes with two buttons unbuttoned, and as he slept on her couch, she felt closer to him than she had ever felt. She knelt down to cover him with the blanket more, and as she did that, he opened his eyes and smiled at her slightly. Ariella reached over to Henry to pull the white-and-yellow knit blanket up more, and he grabbed her hand suddenly and held it for a second. She remembered standing there for two, maybe three seconds like that – he, lying on the couch holding her hand, and she, standing beside him with her down blanket wrapped around her still, holding his hand. It was an unusual gesture, but after the seconds were over, he had let her go and closed his eyes again, falling asleep. They slept apart for hours, and when they both awoke while the world around them had darkened, she had left her bed and sat against the couch while he remained sprawled across it. And while they both watched an easy-to-watch film she would forget years later, she suddenly felt herself spread thin around the world – pieces of her attached to various friends she had made during her fieldwork, impossible friendships that she'd have to leave every time she left the country – and sitting there with her memories, Ariella realized that she only felt truly at home when Henry was there. Every other time, she felt an indescribable nostalgia and restlessness that followed her from place to place, smelling of coming snow...

* * * * *

226

"…Examining Henry and Ariella closely," Peter continued to his friend and mentor, "inertia was their greatest vice." He leaned back and looked at the white ceiling for a moment, as if contemplating something he couldn't articulate. Deep into his story, Peter felt warm and realized that his palms had been sweating without his noticing. Peter wiped them on his knees. Father Turner rolled his neck gently, as if also waking from the story.

Then, Peter began again, "What about language? Those words: attachment, love, memory, soul? Henry never understood the word 'love'. He just never associated love with his own experience, but he was bombarded with the stereotypes of what love *should be.* And so when he had feelings or thoughts that were his own, he couldn't quite place what they were. He wasn't sure whether he felt love, lust, interest, attachment, or some combination of it. And because he couldn't associate a word with it, he wasn't sure how he should act. His normative was connected to his understanding of the language of how he categorized things, but until he could categorize those things in tangible, empirical ways, they remained enigmatic. Ariella was the other side of the same coin. Although she understood her own linguistic connection to the word *love* in particular, given her chance encounters and naturally more expressive personality, she was quite bogged by other words like, *commitment* and *impossible.* Together, they made the perfect mesh of ambiguity, with one part in language, another part in inertia, some bits in chance and the rest in fear."

CHAPTER 2

Inertia Part Two

...On that same day June 15, 2020. "So your task – and please speak up anytime you don't understand – your task is to fly the aircraft over the Reservation we spoke about earlier. Latitude and longitude are flexible as long as you know where it is. We will have a transponder for you. It will, uh, make you reachable even in the Reservation. You are asked to exterminate the individual in the aircraft with you with two – that's *two* – gunshots to the head. You are then asked to dispose of the body by burning. Burn the aircraft as well. You will be marked as missing and identified as someone else. You will then need to travel away from the site of the crash and release the emergency satellite signal. You will then be picked up by a black and unmarked helicopter and dispatched back here. You will then receive the rest of your payment through a direct deposit. Is that understood?" The voice said.

Jared looked at his computer and replied to the mechanical voice, "Yes. Understood. When is the project going to be launched, and will I be given the identification of the individual?"

"The project will be launched immediately. You will not be given any information about the individual prior to the flight. Anything else?"

"No. That's all."

"We'll be in touch   soon." The voice went offline.

Jared blinked at the computer. He set it on the table and went back into bed.

*****

That same morning, Henry was driving Dana to her parents' who lived in a nearby town outside of the city. They were silent for the entire drive until Dana turned to him and said, "You two have been close friends for a while, haven't you?"

"What?" He hadn't been thinking about Dana. In fact, he almost forgot she was there except he was following the directions for driving her to her parents'.

"You and Ariella, I mean." She responded dryly.

"Yea, since high school." He glanced at the time: 19:04. It would be another twenty minutes before he would arrive at her parents' place.

"So...do you guys have history? It just seems like your face changed when you were talking to her. You lit up. You need her approval." Dana looked at him. Her right hand grasped onto the car door handle tightly. "You've never looked at me that way before."

"We're really close. We never dated. We don't have history."

"Why not?"

"That's private. But really, I just never thought of it. I never thought of us like that. Ariella and me, I mean."

"But why not?"

"Why does it matter to you?" He was starting to feel irritable. Why did she care so much? He was respectful to her. They hadn't spent years together – it had been a few weeks, if that. Actually, if he wanted to be accurate, he could express that he has seen Dana a total of twelve times in the past few weeks, which totaled 86 hours, including hours that were unconscious; only 26 hours of conscious time. By these standards, he felt more attached to his doorman whom he has seen every day, almost twice a day for about a minute for the past seven years.

"It does. You changed when you were with her. You've just…you've never looked at me that way before." She sat frozen in her seat. Her shoulders were straight and menacing.

"I'm sorry. I don't know what you want me to say." He turned to look at her in an attempt to understand how their conversation had changed so quickly without warning.

"Why are you taking me to my parents'?" She managed to ask after a few seconds.

Startled, and afraid of giving the wrong answer, he was honest: "Because you asked me to. You had a lot of luggage. You didn't want to take the train."

"No." She paused, then said carefully, "No, what are you planning after this trip? When you come back?"

"I plan on going to work."

"You have no intention of meeting my parents, then."

There was no way Henry could answer this question correctly. "No."

"You have no intention of seeing me after you get back."

There was a pause, and then after a mild hesitation, he replied, "I wasn't looking at this as something ongoing. Well, I wasn't sure if it would. I'm still not sure..." His voice trailed off, and he despised how his own indecision made him feel like a coward.

"I see."

"I have a lot...a lot happening right now with work. I wish I could explain it better, but I can't."

"So what was I? Convenience to you?" Her chin wobbled.

He wasn't sure how to respond. The real answer would have been, *yes*, but that it was the real answer disturbed him about himself. It was as if he knew this all along, but somehow he had convinced himself that he had no responsibility over her. As he sat next to a person who was silently crying, he realized that he had developed the responsibility without noticing it. What could he do? Could he still see her again after this trip and placate her, give this another chance or at least some more time? It wouldn't have changed his life very much. There would be no difference to him between ending this now or extending it until after the trip and ending it in a way that made her feel less used. He wondered whether it would be more effort not to see her at this point. She was pleasant to be around, but that was all for now and the future felt like something   both   unimaginable   and   indescribable.

"I'm sorry," he managed with his lips moving softly and his voice quiet. He stared straight ahead at the road noticing the curvature of the yellow line winding itself along the river parallel to them.

"Are you in love with her?"

That question struck him between the ribs. He had no idea what she was talking about. "What?" He jolted his head quickly and glanced at Dana.

Dana stared straight at him, one hand clutching the side of her passenger seat and her body turned slightly toward him. "Ariella. Are you in love with her? Is that why you follow her around and visit her, even when I'm around?" She spoke without blinking and stared at him until he replied.

"No, Dana, this isn't about Ariella. I'm not in love with her. We don't have history. We're not secretly together. I don't understand why you keep bringing up Ariella." Henry sighed and shook his head again, his eyebrows furrowed as he pretended to concentrate more on the road.

"You really don't get it, do you?" Her body slumped, and she turned to look out the window while fighting back the pinching feeling of frustration in her nose.

"Can you explain it to me? I just...I feel like everything is coming as a surprise to me. I don't know what you mean. I thought we were talking about you and me, and now you're bringing up my friend."

"What are we Henry? I want a label," she turned toward him again and barked bitterly. "I want a committed contract on your end. I want something I can call this, so that I can play by the rules that people have made for centuries now on this sort of thing. It's been sociologically approved and stamped and done, and I want to do that." She spoke quickly. She sounded like she was becoming irritated at a business offer with a deal she was failing to close.

"Would that make you happier?" He didn't know what else to say. He wasn't sure what the implications of this new contract would be, or where it would go, but he wasn't ready to deal with it now, not with the fourteen minutes that were left in the ride.

"Yes, it would." She closed her argument matter-of-factly and pursed her lips in anger.

He realized he could have appealed to her – in that moment – and quieted her before dropping her off and giving himself time to evaluate everything she had just said. Instead, he replied, "I don't think this is the right time. Let's talk about this when we both get back. I just want you to know that I want to respect you and make you feel respected. But to be honest, this isn't the venue for this conversation, and I just want to warn you that I have a lot going on right now."

Fourteen minutes later, he pulled into the driveway of a short cul-de-sac, where her parent's large colonial style house sat at the end of a little half circle of maple trees. He got out and helped her with her luggage. Her parents were out of the house at the moment, but he didn't stay long. Soon after Dana was settled, Henry sped away, driving faster and faster down the interstate until he cleared his head of the entire conversation.

* * * * *

After Henry had sped away from Dana, he drove three hours to the Research and Development office which was located downtown about four miles from the Executive Office building where he worked. The Company cars were located in a garage a block south, and it made sense to double-check that *the vehicle* was certainly gone. Plus, before his trip, he wanted to make sure everything was running according to the newly approved Board schedule.

The helicopter that would fly him to the airfield was located on a pad nearby. 19:45, he pulled into the parking lot of the downtown R&D office after clearing security. It was mostly cleared out except for a few littered cars. Henry's stomach dropped at the next sight. As he was pulling into a tight parking spot, he recognized from the rearview mirror Duane's car sitting by itself along the skyline. Immediately, he froze. What was Duane doing here? And Duane was walking out of the building with a woman he recognized but couldn't remember. Who was that? Whom did she remind him of? Then he remembered: the woman he helped from the elevators. What was her name? Nancy Sparrow, of course! The name and face jumped to him.

Henry watched Duane as he stood standing opposite Nancy Sparrow. They stood about two feet apart. Her arms were crossed, and she was shaking her head. Duane was gesturing with his arms open wide, forcing his grey suit jacket to flail every time he expanded his arms. Henry couldn't see much of their faces. They stood there talking for over ten minutes, and Henry remained secretly parked, watching them closely. It could have been an affair. Nancy, wearing faded jeans and a long sleeve blue t-shirt, had her arms crossed the entire time, and she spoke looking down at the ground. Duane pulled out a cigarette. After the arm flailing, his tie hung crookedly against the outside of his suit jacket, clearly shifting without his notice. Henry found this entertaining and let out a laugh; he had never seen Duane so disheveled, nor has he ever seen Duane smoke before. Then, as Duane was still speaking and gesturing something Henry could not hear, Nancy Sparrow turned her back and walked away. Henry's jaw dropped. No one has ever walked away from Duane that way before!

But the meeting still nagged at Henry: Nancy was a research scientist, and so why, why would they be meeting off hours? Henry had never even met her before the elevator incident. He had met the head of the departments and various key scientists in the R&D department, but until that day Nancy ran into him in the Executive Building, he had never seen her at any Company events or meetings. If only he could hear them! As he thought this, Duane stepped into his vehicle and drove away a minute later.

Henry watched as Nancy Sparrow stood in the parking lot for a long time. She was a curious figure, standing there alone in her casual clothes, her lips moving as she talked to herself. She leaned against the car stroking a piece of curly hair that nestled hear her ear. Then, just as

Henry wished he could hear what she was saying to herself, Nancy opened her car door and sat inside for a long time before she started up the vehicle and drove away. Henry sat in the car and waited a few minutes after Nancy left the lot. Then he drove himself to the helicopter pad, forgetting why he wanted to check in at the R&D Building in the first place...

CHAPTER 3

Two Men the Same

"Well certainly things are beginning to become stranger and stranger for Henry, aren't they? I suppose Nancy was a critical part of the Project, then?" Father Turner asked.

"Most certainly, but Nancy's role in the Project was that of a chief architect. She did not participate in it herself, and she never wanted to." Peter said. "Nancy, from my understanding, was always a very respectable person. Unlike others who became easily blinded by achievement, Nancy was questioning the morals behind everything she did, and what I see as the things that bothered Nancy are things that still bother me."

"Well, what are they?" Father Turner asked.

"How do I explain this?" Peter paused for a few moments before continuing, biting his lower lip. With this fingertips on the bridge of his nose he said, "It's easy to read into history as explaining some genetic constant that exists in everyone across all time. Everywhere I traveled, it was like the basic thread of *humanness* was all the same, like every little child wanted to hold onto someone's hand. And all humans have, deep inside them, some well so deep that even they have never traversed to the very bottom. Those things that live in the depths of the well, those experiences which bring us to shame and rob us of words, those things that shed hot tears onto my cheeks, they live there in those dark, murky places that have clouds of forgetfulness to protect our daily thoughts from them. Imagine if we fell into such a well? Imagine if we were to live amongst those forgotten, hidden and put away, those things we are too ashamed to acknowledge in daylight or in darkness, blocked out a long time ago so that we would not live walking with our heads down, and our eyes downcast? But if you do manage to dive into the depths of your being, and you are able to love life from the bottom of a well, then you have learned love at its greatest moment – an eternal moment. See, the darkest, most hidden, most forgotten parts of the well hide the brightest, the lightest, the most ethereal things…

…So in this spirit, the dream of a nation – the amnesic dream – was born out of a desire to be rid of history. Let's forget about the past and move to a new place – erase all the deeds and determinism that history represents: the psychological, sociological, anthropological, political and philosophical. Your property is yours, and you can keep your prosperity too. This place has been un-owned and uninhabited, and you are the king of the wilderness! But where is the real autonomy? Where is the real history?"

"Peter, I must interrupt you. I apologize here, I'm lost. Are you still talking about Nancy? I'm just trying to piece together everything you've just said." Father Turner looked closely at Peter, leaning in sweat beginning to glisten on his forehead with the warmth of the room.

"Oh, yes, sure...I guess I got ahead of myself. Sometimes I wander. But let's try to do this linearly. So back to what I was saying about Henry's trip, and why he got in trouble with Dana, and that whole miscommunication...right, so...well…"

* * * * *

238

June 15, 2020. The wind kicked the warm air as the helicopter began its flight. Henry Smith sat next to the silent pilot. After a minute, he turned and shouted, "Hi, I'm Henry! I'm sorry, I didn't catch your name."

The pilot turned to him for a second and yelled above the noise, "Hi! Jared!" He didn't say anything else but turned away to look at the controls.

Henry was paralyzed for a moment as he caught a sight of the man's face – Jared's eyes – just barely as Jared turned quickly to him and back again to the controls. Henry let out a low groan, unheard over the noise. *It couldn't be!* he thought. *There's no way! And yet, yes, those were the eyes, those coin eyes, that beard, the sallow cheeks. It was the man, but he was supposed to be dead! Run over that night, so many nights ago. Could this be a mistake? It must be. It must be!* –Henry thought, his stomach revolting against itself. The helicopter churned its way through the thick air.

* * * * *

Thirty minutes passed in the helicopter, and Henry couldn't get himself to say a word to Coin Eyes miraculously alive from the dead (or perhaps who never died? Had he imagined it all?). Breaking his train of thoughts, a gust of wind shook the body of the helicopter. Why they hadn't arrived at the airport where his jet was yet? He was supposed to take a jet to his meeting, but the helicopter seemed to be making no movements toward landing.

"Hey, are we landing soon?" Henry managed, shouting above the noise.

"Change of plans. Was told from administration to deliver you directly," the man replied.

"But isn't this a lot slower? I didn't think helicopters had that range." Henry was confused. He had been told the meeting was an emergency, something he had to attend in person.

"Sorry, plans from above. I was just told to get you directly there," the man repeated. They were then silent and Henry, staring straight ahead of him, tried his best to avoid looking at the man seated next to him.

A little over an hour into the ride, Henry began dosing off, the rumbling of the machine drowning and lulling him toward sleep. Something heavy set inside him, and his entire face was sore with exhaustion. It was an effort to keep his eyelids open, and with all the insomnia behind him up in the sky thousands of feet above ground and water, he sat comfortably suspended in between the worlds and acquiesced to the heaviness of sleep.

It was a slam to the head that jolted Henry awake. He realized the entire air was quiet, except for a buzzing in his head, and as the buzzing increased he realized he tasted blood. It was warm, and he realized that his eyes were closed, and that the warm, wet feeling was his own blood. Before Henry could react to the pain, something hit him again on the back of the head, which launched him face forward onto a hard surface, and the world spiraled into a dark, dark, black.

Jared pulled Henry's body out from the cockpit and threw it onto the ground. Then he pulled out a pistol. Henry stirred and suddenly opened his eyes as blood covered his forehead and seeped down his face and onto the ground. Henry mumbled, and the man hesitated. Henry mumbled again, and put his hand on Jared's hard boot. Then suddenly, Henry began to laugh, an eruption that came out of a crumpled, darkened mouth filled with blood. As he laughed, he spattered blood onto the boot. Henry sputtered some more until he sputtered himself into a cough.

Then Henry began again, clearly this time, "Ironic, huh? But you'll hate yourself for this. I don't even care so much because now I feel like it's all even, man, sorry for running you over, maybe I'm already dead. You certainly should be. You're not, but I feel for you." Then he began

240

laughing again. His laughter was light, and all the little birds sitting in the trees, watching the event happening below chirped in response.

* * * * *

They were both victims. It was in that instance that Jared felt himself freeze. He couldn't do it. He had never felt this before. He had a clean track record with this. He was dependable, but in that instance, the laughing, bloody man in front of him reflected an image of himself that Jared had not expected. He wanted nothing to do with Henry Smith. He wanted Henry Smith out of his mind. Jared wanted his life void of this entanglement. He wanted to be alive again, and he wanted to die. So Jared brought Henry to the base of a large rock, left him some water, stripped him of his wallet and searched for any other remaining identification. Jared then dragged an unconscious Henry by the leg to the nearest pile of underbrush at the edge of the forest. He lit a match on the dead, dry leaves and took off again. The task was done, and Jared ran to the helicopter and took off immediately. The dying forest was dry as a desert. As far as anyone was concerned, the task was done.

* * * * *

Some minutes later, Henry began to stir, wakened by the heat around him. Peeling his eyes open, he recognized nothing. In the smoke-filled air, Henry gasped for breath, and instead his lungs found burning ash. He still couldn't see anything, but he managed to prop himself up and stumble through the deadened trees around him. Henry grabbed at branches, clutched onto them as he limped forward and wondered, briefly, whether he was at the edges of hell.

Henry laughed. He'd been there before, and here again, a part of him was almost excited now that his whole life was resting on the next few moments. It had only been the few moments before that had led him here, and the connection between all the events confused him in his scurry along the underbrush. He kept limping and crawling forward, the

241

blood dripping down his head, into his eyes and blurring his sight. Henry tried to wipe his face, but just touching it stung him more. He clutched at the branches and leaves and fell to all fours until suddenly his body gave out underneath, and everything fell dark. He felt himself falling until his head hit something again, and he was suddenly submerged in water. In newfound panic, he grabbed onto the nearest thing his fingers could find and pulled himself up onto some soft, wet surface. Then, he lost consciousness again…

CHAPTER 4

Experience

June 15, 2020…Ariella stood in her shower and felt the water rushing over her head and arms and back. She would often stand in the shower when she needed time to think, letting the water pour over her, stroking her hair and head and glossing over her eyes. She let the water pull her hair in all directions over her face, until what was in front of her was a blur of water and brown. In the blur, her mind wandered free. Henry had been erratic, and she thought of his visits, the suddenness of them, his trip, and his loyalties to a woman she knew so little about.

Ariella began searching her thoughts for other things she had tried to forget. Her memory lingered at a time when she had been having a drink with Howard at his apartment. Howard was smoking a cigarette. She was worried that night. Earlier that day, she had had a discussion with a coworker on whether she wanted to pursue a life in history, behind the books and inside the museums, giving up a life in the present to live in the past. When she had gone to Henry with these worries, he would speak to her quietly and patiently, listening and absorbing her words. Sometimes, he would challenge her. Most of the time, though, he would just nod and say, "Does it make you feel better?"

Howard, on the other hand, could never give her the sentiment of acceptance and instead always contradicted her. That night had been no different.

"Thing are not fair, and even if you analyzed it all to death – the past I mean – it still won't matter. It's already happened. Get on with it. There's ways to build the future, and think about tomorrow. How childish are you? No, I don't think it's a good idea to pursue your career in this - it's a dead end. There'll be a time when you're tired of trying to fight the thing you know most and just go with it. You're an educated person. Get a real job." Howard inhaled, and the embers at the end of the cigarette crinkled.

"I'm not trying. I'm just doing something that makes me feel less guilty." She held the glass of wine between her fingers and leaned on the railing of the balcony, looking at the apartments below. They were mostly lit, and the flicker of shadows walked around strangers' kitchens and strangers' bedrooms; she had wondered if they were happy people.

"Ariella, I'm not sure how many times we'll need to talk about this same thing over and over again, but I'll repeat it – there's a million inconsistencies and logical fallacies in this unpredictable set of experiences called life," he turned away from her and looked outward toward the evening as if he were reciting some rehearsed play.

"You see it everywhere: why kids suffer when they don't even have the choice of being born." Howard continued, "Like, you see these stories about kids born with deformities or into families with abusive parents who like to throw water on the kids' faces to wake them up, or who throw them against walls and leave them blue or purple. How some really talented person could have been born a thousand miles away and never get the resources to become anything more than a manual laborer, never using his brain and withering away, while I – and I admit this fully and openly – who have no real talents and am pretty mediocre at most things have been born into a life in which I can be making more money than…well, we don't need to go into that. Or how someone could just be walking at the wrong place at the wrong time and suddenly get stabbed or shot or hit or bombed."

Howard snuffed out the end of his cigarette against the balcony railing. Then he turned to Ariella and put his arm around her. She shifted uncomfortably as he said, "I always think about those stories about how suddenly a bomb goes off and just wipes out a block. Who can control that? How random. It makes no sense. No one does *anything to deserve it. You know what they say?"*

Howard looked at Ariella, and she shook her head before he continued, "They say that even drug addicts, the people society thinks are so abominable because they freely choose to use drugs, even they really never asked for it. If you ask an addict, they don't even enjoy the drug or the high. They just watch in horror as they're doing it, filled with self-hate and shame and loathing and hopelessness, like their brains have been invaded by some alien thing that makes their entire conscience and body a sick puppet. Something happens to them that makes them want to turn to it. Some traumatic thing they have no control over. Society blames them and shuns them, and if they're lucky enough they'll be part of some program, but if not, they're on the street until the government disposes of them in the public looney houses. It's not fair. But let me tell you, the one thing that is always consistent and can be the base of every action people have is a rational sense of self preservation, in their own minds. We are beautifully subjectively rational things, and that subjective rationality has built an entire world. I think we're doing a damn good job of it, even if I'm a total hedonist. I have the right to be. I'm living out my selfish gene. Look, Ariella," he sighed as if he were giving up on her with his conversation.

"Look at this world," Howard continued again, mustering up the energy to finish his thought, "Look at those lights, this city, the water. We built this out of sweat and hate and famine and poverty and pure subjectivity. Yes, only a few can enjoy it, but let's enjoy it for the rest of humanity. They were destined to suffer. There's nothing you, me, or anyone else can do about it. So wipe away that self-righteous and ridiculous guilt. It's a waste of energy. Really, it's disrespectful to all those people who lived out or gave their miserably fated lives. Cheers." With that, Howard walked over to the small, glass table on the balcony, where a bottle of Glen Garioch had been sitting and poured himself a glass.

"I do believe that, but I can't live that way." She was twisting the bottom of the wine glass between her fingers, the light off the glass reflecting like water running through her hand. "When you say those things...those things make me so sad. You've become so fatalistic, and you're not as at peace with it all as you believe. I don't believe it."

"So you're going to constantly fight some impossibility? You'll always feel this way.

245

You'll always feel this huge gap between you and the other people who feel they have to fight some fight because they'll always believe they can change the way the Earth is tilted on its axis. You know better, and yet you choose to delude yourself!" His voice grew louder and he finished his drink. Howard walked over to pour himself a second and on his way to a refill, found his energy to convince her again.

Ariella lowered her voice and replied: "No, I don't think they think that. I don't think people are deluding themselves here except for you, Howard. You can't live like some rational machine either. You're a lonely bastard as far as I'm concerned, and you're just trying to lie to yourself so you can excuse everything you've done and not done. Sometimes I'm not sure who's lying to themselves more, you or me." She refused to look at him. In a few swooping sentences, he had made her feel smaller and smaller, as if her relevance in his worldview decreased with each viewpoint she tried to share. With that, Ariella realized as much as they may share in one another's physical company, they could never be truly close.

"Don't you just want a distraction?" Howard was beginning to slur his words, and the whiskey sloshed in the glass along with its clinking ice cubes. He stepped closer to her and lowered his voice, as if he were about to share some great, deep secret. "But you know, Ariella, you can have all the friends in the world, all the lovers, even relationships, and you can still feel utterly alone."

Howard paused, and then he smiled wryly before beginning bitterly saying, "See, some people go off and do stupid shit like killing themselves because they're just too tired to live. It's not even like they're in pain or whatever, but they just get so bored of life, they decide they can't go on with the boredom, the exhaustion, the aloneness. I find that to be the most absurd thing there is. That's what I can't understand. When there's so much chaos and havoc to be done, so much sex, so much absolute ecstasy, it's just absurd. That's what I don't understand. All your worries that you lose sleep over — the horror of man on man, or man on small children and women and old people, war devastations, like how someone can sit there and enjoy torturing someone else by cutting up his organs while he's still alive and stuff, how rape happens — all those things that come out of that little selfish gene we have. We know we are barbaric in our need to survive. No matter how that manifests itself, I get those barbaric things. I can explain them. Why people would actually risk their lives for someone else or kill

246

themselves over some self-proclaimed boredom or pain? I can never understand that. I never will." He spat out those final words and looked around at the lights in the buildings surrounding them.

In the reflections of all the artificial lighting of the city that Howard proclaimed to be the most beautiful thing he had seen, he noticed for the first time that night that she was wearing a dress that made her look like some kind of angel of the artificial lights they were surrounded by. She wore no makeup, her hair fell loosely on her back and shoulders, the tangles talking to the evening. The dress had been white with yellow designs on it, and he could trace out the outlines of her body, the soft and almost clear material clinging onto her legs and moving with the air. The dress was buttoned up in the front from her waist, but she had left the two buttons on top undone. "It's unforgivable," was all he managed to conclude. Looking straight into the building across the street, a cat had hopped onto a desk against the window and began to link its paws. Howard looked at the cat, and as if noticing the attention, the cat stopped its grooming and stared at them. He felt her hand touch his shoulder.

In that moment, Howard felt it immediately. And so it was just like that, two people with the same thread of underlying, unadulterated thing that ran through them. Somehow over the course of time, their axes were tilted to orient themselves as direct opposites, two poles running on a single fire. In short, they were opposite people who ran on the same fuel. He never wanted her more than at that moment, and gently, he touched the hand that rested on his shoulder.

In that moment, Ariella knew that there was no one more wrong for her than him. Henry's touch had kept the darker and deeper parts of her in her own control. But this, this was something that had fought within her. It had been wrong. Every part of it was wrong.

Like that, it had almost been as if he felt her rejection silently, and he smiled. He took another sip of his drink and looked at the night with her. She left his apartment a little later, and they never spoke of that night again.

Ariella rarely visited that memory. In the shower, the water that sprayed from the showerhead was like little fingers that fell all over her body, touching her everywhere and pushing her to thoughts by rubbing itself against her skin. Suddenly, Ariella had the image of herself laughing, and before she could help it, she was really laughing. Smiling, she let the water spray against her teeth and her lips with her eyes closed. The reality of her newfound project unfolded in front of her, and she realized it felt as if she had gained another life. Exhaling, she found herself unable to do anything else but smile...

CHAPTER 5

Testing: "Welcome back"

…Lying on the rock, with half his body floating in the water, Henry's thought before he felt himself slipping into another swamp of subconscious was, "Am I out?"

A distant fog crept along the edges of the dusty, wet road that lay just within sight of the river. It was night; the lights from the little houses emitted a fuzzy gaze that was lost in the thick of the air. The evening was damp, and the fog that settled and nested along the little street with tall lamps made the dark even darker.

A man, begging from door to door along a dusty alleyway, walked along the street and kept going even in the fog and the dark, feeling an odd warmth from the isolated homes, looking into the houses to see what the inhabitants were doing.

* * * * *

It was the next day that Henry was found. Jia Zheng and his eldest son, Jia Mingyan, were fishing along the river that ran three miles south of their home when they saw what looked like a muddied man, his clothing tattered and burnt, sleeping on the rocks. A few steps closer and both father and son saw the bloodied face, the black, dried gash that ran across Henry's forehead caked with dead leaves and dirt, and the limpness of the victim whose only sign of life was a slight movement in his chest.

* * * * *

Inside a large, unmarked building enclosed by a high security fence, Henry was walking quietly in a long, white hallway. His feet made no sounds against the white linoleum floor. On either side of the hallway were white rooms with blue doors. The doors were unmarked, and the rooms were windowless. Henry realized as he was walking that he wearing a black suit. He walked into one of the unmarked rooms, and in the middle of the room was a desk. A small, bald man sat at the desk in an off-white, dirty lab coat, busy writing. The man did not look up at Henry for several minutes, and then suddenly, as if sensing that there was someone in the room, said without looking up, the light dancing off his bald head, "You seem to maintain a calm composure, but you're very agitated inside. Why don't you find a way to let those things out?" With that, he continued with his scribbles and said nothing more. Henry closed the door as quickly as he had opened it and turned to the next door.

Inside this door was another small bald man sitting in another off-white lab coat also busy writing. This man looked up at Henry this time, his black-rimmed glasses covering eyes that blinked curiously, "So you say you've been feeling distant for some time now. How long has this been happening?" Before waiting for a reply, the man looked down at his paper again and continued with his writing.

Henry silently walked out the door in a fluid and quick motion, letting the door close behind him, the clicking of his shoes echoing along the white linoleum floors. He opened the next door to another man sitting at another desk, identical to the two before, in the same off-white, dirty lab coat, also writing in a notebook. The man looked up again and said, "You feel stuck in your own web, don't you? You'd like to stop thinking, wouldn't you?" With that, he looked down again and remained silent. Henry moved from the room as quickly as the others and continued down the hall, entering each room again to a new man sitting at another identical table.

"Something is on your mind. It's been eating away at you when you're not around the others. You feel you're on the outside, looking into two glass rooms. Except, they can see a different you than the you that you know."

"What words do you think of when you hear the word 'love'? How about the word 'fear'?'"

"Why do you think your father died?"

"Did you grow up loving your father?"

"Are you feeling angry about anything?"

"What's your earliest memory? Why can't you remember some things so well anymore? Why do some memories seem to come back, over and over again? What are your feelings about that?"

"Do you sometimes wonder if the world has been turned upside down on its axis? Where do you think you are?"

Each room was the same as the one before it, with a similar bald little man sitting in the same lab coat at the same desk, but Henry knew it wasn't the exact same bald little man sitting in the exact same lab coat at the exact same desk. So each room he went into, he was asked another question, but before he could even stop to answer, the little man would look down at his writing again, forgetting that Henry was even in the room to begin with. Every movement was silent. Every scribble was soundless. The air was hot, dry and unmoving.

Henry reached the last room of the hall. He faced a wall. He turned to his left and walked into the room. A similar little man looked up at him and asked, "Why are you here?" Except this time, the man continued to meet Henry's gaze without looking down at his writing again. Henry looked around the room and hesitated when the little man asked again, "Let me rephrase. Why *do you think* you are here?"

Henry opened his mouth to speak and answered, <Because I came here>. It took him a moment to realize that his speaking was soundless. He was surprised, but as he was trying again, the little man nodded, as if hearing him.

"Ah, yes, the classic non-committal answer. You're not right, you're not wrong, you're not anything. No, your answer doesn't have to be some testable right or wrong. We won't test your hypothesis. We won't do a controlled experiment or even an uncontrolled one. I'm asking you a subjective. A *you think*. Those are glorious questions, aren't they. So, let's try again, why do you think you're here?"

Henry tried again, <Because I am able to be here.>

This answer seemed to amuse the little man. "You mean privilege? Oh, that's funny. I would hardly call it a privilege to be in this little airless, windowless room. You certainly don't feel that way. You're explaining yourself away to be satisfied with something you have no reason to be satisfied with. Let's break it down. Do you believe in fate, Henry?"

<No.>

"What do you believe in?"

<...I'm not sure what I believe in exactly, but I know what I don't believe in.>

"Well, let's begin with that then and work through it. You don't believe in fate, but do you believe in some set of rules that the universe runs by? Say, some set of basic principles or laws?"

<Yes.>

"But if you believed in that, don't you think the initial conditions make a difference? We can solve a number of systems with laws but without the initial conditions the exact trajectory is unknown."

<Maybe, but isn't there more than just a physical measurement?>

"Ah, ok, well now we're getting more serious. What do you mean, Henry?"

<What if I didn't identify with everything that was happening to me? So I start somewhere, with certain environments conditioning me, I'm wired a certain way, but I just plain disagree with it.>

"What do you think will happen to that person - you - who lives as you describe or as how you see yourself?"

<I'm not sure.>

"I would say they'd be easily influenced, wouldn't they, hoping to search for something to grab onto during the storm of everything that's happening to them without their consent. They're just isolated, schismed really, from themselves. It's like a person torn up into little pieces but put together again in flesh. Outside, looks like a person. Inside, all the organs and muscles and thoughts are cut open and up and into little pieces that are trying to find one another. What do you think?"

<I don't know.>

"Well, why don't you look in the mirror." The little man took a mirror that had been lying inside his desk. It was a small hand mirror that couldn't have been bigger than the size of his palm. He walked over to Henry. Suddenly, Henry realized the man was quite short. He only came up to Henry's shoulder. The man looked at Henry intently while Henry turned the mirror around. As he stared at the reflection in the mirror, he wanted to scream. His face was... nothing. There was nothing on his face. It was a blank, pale face with his usual arched eyebrows but without a mouth. Two slits existed for his nose and ears, and his eyes looked hollowed and tired. Everything else was glossed over like a slimy clay mold. Henry kept screaming, but he realized nothing was coming from his screams. He had no mouth.

"Oh, don't be so scared, Henry. You shouldn't be afraid of yourself. Did you think you looked differently?"

<I...I...I just didn't expect. I thought I did. But now I'm not sure.>

"Henry, I'd like to ask you, and I need you to answer very honestly. What are you most afraid of?"

<I admit, I've been thinking about this a lot. The only thing I can come up with is that I'm most afraid of winning.>

"Yes, I know that, Henry. You've known that too, for a long time now. It's sad you have had to keep it inside for so long. Now Henry, can you articulate to me why you're afraid of winning?"

<Because then there's nothing else to do.>

"That's right. And not right. You're right in evaluation of your fear, but you're not right in the fear, and you know that too. But I won't have to tell you anything anymore. Henry, we're all proud that you're even questioning. You didn't have to. Your initial conditions were all set. Just make sure you go back to the right place," then, the man added, "In what year were you born?"

Henry stood still. <Born?>

"Yes, Henry. People are born. They live. Then they die and they

254

disappear. Do you remember when you were born?"

Henry grabbed the mirror the man had held for him from the white desk at which the man sat and looked at it for some time. The two slits of eyes in the mirror looked back at him. <I don't remember...>

"Yes, you do," the man replied matter-of-factly. "Think harder."

<1987> Henry put the mirror down and looked at the bald man.

"No, Henry. You know it's not then. Think again."

<I can't remember>

"Henry, you won't remember. Is that it? Is it so painful, you cannot remember?" Henry put both hands over his face and rubbed where his eyes should have been. The man continued, "Do you remember the year you are in now?"

<2020.> Henry replied.

"Yes, does the year 1946 sound familiar to you? The year 1961?"

Henry shook his head. With that the little man ushered Henry out the door and closed it on him without saying a word. In a flash, Henry opened his eyes. The light forced his eyes closed again, and he began to reopen them, feeling the sting of light like salt water on his pupils.

"One day I'd like to discover a way to turn rocks into dumplings, and no one ever be hungry again," a boy's voice said. Henry opened his eyes again and stared straight into the eyes of a small child he had never seen before...

CHAPTER 6

This Strange Breath

…Nancy Sparrow rarely went to the Our Lady of Mount Carmel church, but recently, she found herself drifting into Sunday mass, thinking quietly during the service. As a child, she was never excited to be sitting in the pews; she wasn't Catholic but she went to a Catholic school. After she left her childhood, she wanted to keep some pattern of the faith she was brought up amongst, although the Catholic Church was hardly the denomination she most identified with. She enjoyed her habits, and the Church was often empty and quiet.

When the service ended and the crowd slowly made its way out toward the door, Nancy Sparrow remained sitting in the pews, her eyes closed behind her narrow glasses. One of the senior priests walked down from the altar, shuffling his way toward her, nodded, and organized himself on a wooden seat in the aisle in front of her where the only other person in the church sat, still as she had been. Until now, she had barely noticed he was there. She couldn't see his face, but his slouched thin shoulders and ruffled red hair made him look young, perhaps still a child even. The two men spoke openly, comfortable in Nancy's presence.

The entire air smelled thick of incense and the Holy Mother stood with somber eyes gazing over them from the altar.

"I have been thinking of what you said about death," the old priest began. He was a small man whose age looked indiscernible, his white hair clinging to his scalp and his voice holding a light crackle as if he were on the brink of laughter. He spoke slowly, the words clung onto his tongue and lips before they escaped into the humid, incensed air, "Anything of value requires shortage. We're somehow inclined to love what we feel is precious, rare, difficult to grasp. I'm not sure why we've felt this way. Take diamonds, for example. It's a beautiful stone, but there are a lot of beautiful things in the world that have far less value. I personally really like maple leaves, but no one would pay that much for a maple leaf as a diamond. It doesn't make any sense to me. Or, maybe your grandmother's last piece of chocolate cake. If there's one piece left you want it more than if there's fifty. Well, maybe that's a bad example. If you knew my grandmother's cake you'd want all fifty just as badly. But let's ignore the bad example. Peter, do you know why the Lord made us this way? Why we suddenly decide we want some random thing and not some other equally random thing?"

The younger man shook his head.

"It's simple," Father Turner continued, "We're meant to love our lives. Our lives here on earth. We came from a heaven, and we will return to that heaven. I was dead before I was alive, and I'm going to be dead again one day. It'll feel like what it felt like eighty-five years ago, the year before I was born. Of course I don't remember any of it. But I seem to be okay that existence extended on so far infinitely before my own birth, so I look forward to it extending on well past my death. Mark what I say, it will end one day. And that's the only reason why we love each day. Why are we clinging, so hard, onto something that is a daily struggle on a land that is the creation of the Lord but is not the Lord's home? Why do we love this life so much when it's transitory? It's the glory of the Lord, Peter, to make this life have a definite, undeniable ending. By giving it an expiration date, we value it more, we know love. Love is the infinite onto death. Life is the knowing that it will end.

"This strange breath. Why me? Why is my particular being to experience such a thing as this little life, out of all the possible people the Lord could have created in my stead? And why this little planet out of all the other planets and all the other universes, the other worlds? The absolute, sheer, meticulous improbability of it *with a known end* gives life value, Peter. Don't ever forget that. This was done on purpose. The Lord knows us better than we know ourselves. Our tendencies, he created. Why we cling onto some things and not others fits into a pattern, a dance, which only the Lord knows. What matters is that every person one day dies. That makes us equal unto one. We hang onto what we know we will lose. The wiser of us will learn to celebrate its transitory state and to love all manners of things which the Lord has touched."

Nancy could hear the rain outside hitting the stained glass windows; she looked up at St. Peter and the crucified Christ. The meaning unto death. The death unto life; this strange breath. The rain hitting the colored windows made them look studded with little lights blinking. Lights were falling from the skies and hitting the glass windows.

"Well, listen to me, getting off track. I just wanted to let you hear it again, Peter, you are gifted. You're an artist. You've said so yourself. Your writing is a gift. I'm just angry at you for writing all these articles under a penname. A penname?! Give this church some glory, come on! You're too young to be stuck here with all us old farts, don't tell Father Randal, he'll get upset with me that I called him old. See the world that has opened itself up to you, Peter. You got this grant. I'll cover for you, but you have to remember to bring me something from out there. I've never gone over to Asia before. But, yes, now that I think of it, do you think you can learn how to cook over there? That would be useful for us here!" Father Turner glanced eagerly over at the young Peter, his eyes blinking.

Peter smiled at his mentor and replied, "Father, I'm scared…of a lot of things. I'm scared what I've been doing these past eight years will be rejected out there once I actually go out there. I'm scared I'll make bad decisions. Or, well, what I guess I'm really scared about is temptation. What if I don't want to come back?"

Nancy remained still, concentrating on her breathing. She couldn't help but listen to their conversation. It intrigued her. To think that young man has spent all this time in a church! Go! She wanted to shout, "See the world now! While you have a chance."

"Then don't come back. We're not holding you hostage here, kid. Neither is God. Remember that."

"But, what made you want to stay here?" Peter looked at Father Turner for the first time since the priest had sat down next to him. Nancy suddenly saw that, as she had predicted, he looked more like a boy than a man. He was the most harmless thing she had ever seen. A pale freckled complexion and soft, brown eyes was far too child-like for the seriousness of his tone.

"Oh, for Christ's sake – and don't tell anyone I said that – we've gone through this story so many times. I just heard God one day, and I knew this was it. Now, do I secretly sometimes wonder about other things? Of course. But I knew it, Peter. I knew it. And I would come on this trip with you, you know that, but I'm just too creaky these days to travel for too long. They'll see an old man like me and turn me right back around and stick me back here before I know it. Then Father Randal will really give it to me." The two men were silent for a minute, Father Turner closing his eyes and resting his hands for a prayer. Then he turned to Peter and said, "Peter, if you decide that's for you, God is always here for you in this home. But if that's not what he made you to do, we'll miss you doing all the chores, but we'll go on. Sorry to tell it to you, kid, we're a dying breed but we can still live without you."

Peter turned his head again and opening his mouth, waiting for the long explanations of gratitude, replied instead shortly, "Thank you."

Nancy Sparrow sat in her pew and looked at the two kneeling priests in front of her. Something settled within her which she could only describe as gratified peacefulness. It was the same feeling she would get when she solved a scientific problem or realized how to set up an experiment to measure something that previously felt impossible, and listening to those words, one by one, two by two, collected and floating out of a stranger, it sounded as if Father Turner had meant to speak to her as well. Whoever Peter was, Nancy felt connected to him. Yes, he was going toward life, something that terrified him through an unknown he had little reason to be terrified of. And she? Perhaps she would embark another adventure, and surely, it would be one that was equally thrilling and mysterious. His words started to sound to her like a challenge. Every word Father Turner uttered swirled in her head until each dizzied sentence rested on the tip of her conscience, *we love life because we die. Could this be happening?* she thought. *Am I dreaming? Have I been dreaming all this time?...*

* * * * *

...Peter stopped speaking and looked up at Father Turner.

"Ah yes, how interesting that it all seems to wrap around itself. You're telling our story now. I do remember this. Or that conversation at least." Father Turner took his glasses off, rubbed his eyes, placed the spectacles back on and blinked. "So, this is when we were speaking quite often before you left, then, was it?"

"Yes," Peter replied. "This is where we enter the story. So I guess it takes us to two-thirds of the way. How late is it now?" Peter yawned.

"It's about 11 pm. Do you want to keep going?"

"This is probably a good time to stop. Should I come back tomorrow during the day?" Peter couldn't imagine that Father Turner had much more in him. He could have finished the story, as he had many nights past in his own mind, turning over the events, but it was better to wait.

261

"Yes, how about 10 am? Or is that too early?"

"No, no, that's a fine time. I'm just, so glad. So glad to be able to speak to you."

Peter quickly slipped his feet into his shoes and stood up from the chair. "I'll see you tomorrow then," he said before walking to the door.

CHAPTER 7

Hand on the Fire, Heart on Fire

The next morning, Peter arrived sharply at 10:00 am to Father Turner's apartment carrying a worn, leather bag. He wore the same clothes as he did the day before and tapped his knuckles lightly twice on the door. Father Turner opened the door to the familiar knocks, and in front of him stood Peter wearing a bright green sweater that was too big for him. "Come in, Peter! Right on time, as usual. Shall we sit where we sat yesterday?" Peter nodded, placed his shoes in the corner, and sat in the armchair in front of the electric fireplace again. He placed his bag at his feet.

"So, did you sleep well last night?" Father Turner asked.

Peter shook his head, "No, no, something troubled me last night. It really troubled me. It kept me up for some time. I managed to sleep, but I wanted to talk to you about it today. I would like to finish the story."

"Have you had breakfast? Or should I make you something here?" Father Turner began, but before he could finish, Peter shook his head. "Well, then how shall we begin? Why don't you start by telling me what you were thinking last night." the priest replied, concerned.

* * * * *

...Jared sat immobilized in his car. He received a large sum of cash for his deal, and he was planning on returning to what he imagined was left of his family: his son and his girlfriend who seemed to drum on without him. The records were fine: the body would never be found, and there had been no word of anything for days now. Nothing was reported. No one questioned anything. An executive takes an impromptu sabbatical was nothing abnormal. Somehow, Jared couldn't move. He didn't have the energy to do it, and something in him had stared at Henry Smith and froze. There were too many other times like this for projects commissioned by those in power he had never met, and he just couldn't quite finish things off like he used to. No matter. As far as he was concerned, the job was *good enough*.

Years and years ago, when he was still a child and to coax him to sleep, Jared's own father would read to him about a story of the fox and the antelope searching for a magical castle in the clouds. With the cash in hand, Jared wondered if the story was still in print. Were books in print anymore even? He had been away for so long that in his return, he kept finding surprising changes. The fox had been drawn with a long, orange tail. Jared remembers the smooth, cool feel of the pages. He remembered the book with its pages worn down and folded until one year, he could no longer find it. Jared wanted to find it for his son; he wanted to read the story as his father had done, and so he began to drive to search for a bookstore that was no longer there. He began driving in the direction where he remembered the last bookstore he had seen, and as he arrived at the old shopping plaza, he realized that it had long been bulldozed down. How long has it been since he had last returned here?

Confused, Jared drove past the empty lot and found himself driving to another old spot again to see if that place was also taken down. He recognized the bridges, and then the old billboards and the highway which split the neighborhood in two. He sighed a breath of relief: at least this had not disappeared on him. Some parts of his past still remained. Those same people gathered around the corners and under the bridges, yet they were different, though he couldn't tell how. Filled with nostalgia and an inexplicable sadness over the missing bookstore, he remained there until three in the morning and refound the same habits, the old physical motion of push and pull, push and pull, all over again. He couldn't even remember how he ended up on the street putting the cash in the envelope and handing it to the man before he was crashing again into that same old self-loathing and shame for what he'd just done.

Jared put his head on the steering wheel, and he wondered whether the best thing for all parties involved was just for him to deliver the cash to Tommy's mother. Then he could take a drive and sit along that old route along the edges of the ocean and watch the sun rise. He saw once on the news that someone had driven off the bridge on that old highway route. It took a team of two helicopters and thirty rescue workers to dig the car up from the ocean. He knew he had enough wonderful "forgetfulness" on him that he could get himself so blitzed that the last moments of his life would just be the most glorious feeling, like watching life fly up into the sky in an array of fireworks. Yes, he had the car, and he had an old highway road that descended straight down into the washed up rocks of the ocean. He had done well in the end, making sure things were settled. Things were in order. Why had he begun this whole journey again in the first place? Why did he get in the car? He could no longer remember.

It was after he came back from his second military tour when he had realized he couldn't sleep again and his usual medication wasn't working that he began just to take a few things to make the mornings easier. He would wake up cold in the mornings, his beard dripping with the sweat that had leaked across his face, his long, shagged hair pulled back in a ponytail. He would wake up like that, finding himself shaking underneath the blankets. The minute he had realized he was awake, he'd feel such a seizure of panic in his body that he was both nauseated and horrified of the idea of getting out of bed.

To Jared, everything about the drugs was loathsome. Some days, it was the smell of it, and the smell of him on it. Some days, the smell was the only reality that didn't make him sick. He couldn't tell when it would change on him. It was like putting his hand over a flame, and even if the fire burned his fingers off and his entire hand and arm and spread to the rest of his body, he couldn't help but watch as he mutilated himself, as he smelled the sweet-sticky stench of a hand on fire.

So as Jared sat there at his steering wheel, he wondered whether he should see his son. A smell woke him from his daydream. He blinked, lit a flame, and held it to his hand again...

* * * * *

"...Do you remember this bag I'm carrying?" Peter suddenly asked, diverting from his story to Father Turner.

"No, Peter. Is this bag significant? I was so enamored by your story about Jared, the tortured soul...burning his hand? Was it real? Or was it something he had been imagining? I just can't get the image...the smell...out of my mind," Father Turner replied.

Peter looked at the small brown bag he had packed and taken for his trip. It was an old bag. It was his grandfather's bag, which was passed down to his father, which was given to Peter when he was six.

"Yes, in this story, he was burning himself. But this bag is very significant, Father, to answer your other question. For my trip, I took it on a bus to the train and the overnight train to the airport," Peter said. He held the bag for Father Turner to examine. The bag was worn, and the edges of the leather had discolored, but there was a feeling of safety with carrying it. "I remembered that my father would carry this bag with him on family trips. He'd put all his emergency medical equipment in it, and the brown bag, ever since then, was known as the "safety" bag...

Somehow, I automatically felt an attachment to worn-down things. I'm not sure what it was about the old smell of library books, or sheets that

266

were washed so many times the threading came loose, or the feel of a yellowed, stiff piano key that would sink down slowly once I pressed my finger onto it, in the old house of course. Part of it was the feeling of safety that came with those things, the knowing, the tradition, the patterns, the history. Yes, I loved history. And I loved history not in the idea of the recorded or retold, the victors' stories or modeled techniques – the regressions or estimations, the beta-hat, so to speak – but the actual, underlying series of events: the real stuff as they could never be retold or fully recaptured. It was the same feeling of vastness of what was before me, unknown but there, hidden and truthful, that drove me to believing in any form of religion. I have faith in the underlying model of history as I do in the theory of god."

Peter finished speaking and breathed in and out. He closed his eyes and opened them again, his long eyelashes batting against his freckled face. "In the springtime of the past, of course meaning before I left, looking out at the lavender garden, I would think about these pieced-together memories. That's what art was to me, what it had always been for me, piecing together moments so that they lasted through spans of time, untouched, unchanged as everything else changed around it...that's what it came down to, single shot memories at some point in my childhood: a leaf floating in the gutter after a hard rain; the steam evaporating off street grates early in the mornings; hummingbirds in the patio gardens in July. Art was the moment that lasted infinitely, and I often wondered, standing there and looking out the window, whether I could write it down – a story – pieced together with just snapshots of memories, little discreet descriptions of singular moments that, strung together like a photographed flip-book, could tell something the normal "and then" story could not.

This bag, then, this bag you see...well this was the bag and only bag I took. I remember staring at it while I clasped the bus tickets tightly. I remember when I made the affirmation to go through with it, the sigh I had made when I had picked up the bag, opened the door to my room not so far from here, closed it and locked it, walked down the narrow staircase and into the empty corridor, out the large main double-doors and onto the street. The rest of it, I never noticed. To this day, I cannot remember whether the sun was shining or whether the clouds had covered it. I just remember the sigh, the bag, and my decision to walk out the door."

CHAPTER 8

Two Extra Keys

July 1, 2020 (Two weeks after Henry's vanishing). Nancy was looking for an elegant solution. That morning she called Reynolds and told him -- without hesitation -- that she had been working too hard, was feeling exhausted and sick and needed a week off. "I'm going to catch an illness not sleeping like this. I need a rest, Doctor. Once whatever this is goes away, I'll be back in usual form next week." Not everything needed to be so complicated. Looking back, if she could change one thing, Nancy would have gone through the script of her life and red-lined all those unnecessary things, the excessive worrying, emotion, the feeling that the only things worthwhile were difficult things. Her desire for simplicity marked a level of confidence that she had matured into over many reflective years. Nancy looked down at her notepad. She reread the scribbles again to herself.

Reynolds had known Nancy Sparrow for years, and during all their time working together, she had never requested time off. He granted it without a question, "Nancy, of course. Please get some rest."

She had rehearsed what she'd say to them, looking at her scribbles again. After her phone call with Reynolds, Nancy Sparrow phoned the main Executive building, "Hello, it's Nancy Sparrow of division III sector five group nine. I'm one of the lead scientists on project nine-point-two. I need to speak with Henry Smith regarding some small scheduling logistics unrelated to the particular project I'm on. We're sharing a few technicians lately. I was told to let Henry know that the IPR project he's aware of won't be finished on time. Can you schedule me a time slot?" The phone call would be recorded, and she had limited time to see him before it reached the directors that she had seen him in person.

"Ah, Doctor Nancy C. Sparrow? Date of birth please? And can you confirm your address, and employee I.D.?" a man asked.

Nancy complied, "May thirty-first year two-thousand and three. Address is thirty-five Elm Avenue Apartment Three-D same city. Employee I.D number is 3986645." At this, Nancy felt twinge of sadness. Her work had always been such a large part of her.

"Great, Doctor Sparrow, we will need to see you in person for a confirmation before having you see Mr. Smith. Oh, wait, I'm getting a message from his assistant. Hold on." There was a silence over the line, and then, "Yes, so Mr. Smith has been away on a private matter. He's been gone for over a week now. His whereabouts are unknown."

Nancy was confused. No, this was not possible. Henry Smith, she knew, had to sign off on the IPR project this week. He did, indeed, have a meeting last week, but he should have been back before then. Nancy shivered, as she felt a slight feeling of anxiousness ripple through her.

"Alright. Thank you," she replied and hung up.

By afternoon, Nancy was thinking of how best to reach Henry's assistant again. She rewrote her script, tossed it out, and began another version frustrated with her own lack of creativity in lying. Sometime mid-way through her re-write, Nancy received two mysterious unknown calls. She ignored both of them. When her phone rang again, for the third time from the same number, she looked at it, picked it up carefully, and spoke into it, "Hello? Nancy Sparrow." She tried to steady her hand as her mind raced across the possible scenarios: had someone found out her

270

plan? Certainly, that would be impossible. She had told no one.

"Hello Nancy, we have not spoken before." A man's voice said to her, it was soft, nearly velvet and heavy with somberness.

"Yes?" She replied to the voice. *He was wrong*, she thought. She was sure she had spoken to this man before, the familiarity of it peeking into the edges of her memory. Where had she met him?

"My name is Larry. I am David Smith's estate lawyer, and I'm calling you based on a few concerns I have for Henry."

Nancy froze, *But how did he know her number? Why her?*

"Yes? Where is this number from?" she said instead.

"I've rerouted it for privacy purposes. But anyway, as you know, we've been in the middle of developing the project nine-point-two, and there have been test runs. A number of them. David had initiated it longer ago than you realize…" Larry began. There was noise behind him. A door shut. Then, "…He developed a key. The key contains select individuals, very select individuals…do you understand, Nancy?"

"Good God," she replied in a whisper, her left hand covering her mouth, her right shaking with the phone. She took a deep breath and then asked, "So it's really been started? Do we know the progress?"

"It works. But what we didn't have finalized was the control. The problem is that there is no selection of time, or periods, or location for that matter."

"So you have no idea where they are right now? Do you know who then?…wait, but how do you know this? You're David Smith's estate lawyer, right?" And then slowly, as she spoke those words, Nancy shuddered. Of course, now she understood. It was an immortality, the

271

bequeathing of time, time over time, and Henry was missing.

There was silence on the phone. "Have you figured it out yet?" Larry asked.

"Yes. How many others?" She asked quickly. This was a business matter, and they had no time.

"One other that we know of. A transporter, a gatekeeper to keep the process open when David Smith died, but he has no vested interest in the results of this. In the beginning, David Smith believed in this, I assure you...but I think somewhere along the way he changed his mind...it had already begun for him and Henry. He had believed in it in the beginning. The other David did not know about, but..." Larry's voice lowered, "...I was able to find out about the transporter from your colleague, Doctor Reynolds."

"Is David Smith really dead?" Nancy was tired of codes and secrets. She decided she needed the facts quickly.

There was a pause on the phone. "He is."

"Is Henry dead?"

"We don't know."

"Who are the others?"

"I cannot speak of it here."

"I thought this line was safe."

"Nothing is fully safe, Nancy. But importantly, do you know how to end the process for those who are in it?" They spoke curtly and quickly to one another.

"Larry, David Smith was the only key that I had known about, and the way to keep the process open, to keep the gate open I should say, was to keep him alive. He died, and we began it again, using the gate keeper...the man whom you and I both know about...he had retired from the military and volunteered himself as a last act of service. I did not know about Henry or this other you allude to. The way to end the process is for the keys to choose it."

"I don't understand that, Nancy."

"They must choose to die."

"...Does that mean David Smith had –"

"Yes," Nancy interrupted, "He killed himself. Larry, who is the third man? Who is the last key?" *It was getting out of control*, Nancy thought. Of course, how could they have ever deluded themselves into believing it could be managed and managed with the integrity they had all spoken of?

"I don't know...Reynolds kept that from me. Who initiated the gatekeeper, the third key?"

"Reynolds did. Right after David Smith died, ending the process for him...I...I believed in it too at the time. I just thought David Smith had had enough. But why did he ever involve Henry? Why Henry?" Nancy could never understand how the man would sacrifice his own son.

"Henry was chosen early before David Smith realized he wanted to exit the process. David wanted to protect his science, and he didn't trust himself...so he put Henry as a personal gatekeeper...but I see...Reynolds clearly didn't understand this since he initiated the other agent after David died." Larry sighed into the phone. "I want to protect that boy. But clearly...the manner that David died, he chose it, he chose to end it for himself...it implies..."

"It's too late, Larry. So you're David Smith's estate lawyer and he bequeathed his son to the science in his own will, didn't he? You thought Henry would be safe in the process, as his father's own guinea pig to the Project?" Nancy was becoming angry. Her voice raised and trembled. She wanted to yell at the man. She decided she could not trust him. *No, the project needed to end.* And who was this man, Larry? Could she trust him? "Larry, who is the third? Is it Duane?" She waited for him to speak, hearing nothing but his breathing. "Is it Duane? I will find out whether you tell me or not. I know the science."

"I don't know," he finally said. "I know he'd like to be in the process, but I don't know if he is one of the keys."

"Are you in danger?" she asked, the facts coming together. She still wasn't sure if she could trust him but had chosen her words carefully. She would continue to choose the words carefully, but she already knew what she wanted out of the Project.

"I'm not sure. I want to protect the boy," he finally said.

"Listen, no one knows what happens in the process." Nancy spoke quickly. "We have no idea what iteration they're on, how long their experiences have been ... folding time is a mystery to those of us who aren't experiencing it. But I do know that once David began the process, he chose to end it...he regained the consciousness to realize the structure of the process, or in other words, he remembered. He remembered it. He *chose to end it.* And Henry?"

"Can you end the Project?"

Nancy thought carefully before answering. "The keys who are alive, including Henry, each need to make that decision. Right now, think of it as three little gates open. We can sway them, influence things modestly, but a reverse process was something that we always struggled with...there were, well, influences against developing the reverse process."

"What if you worked on the reverse process?" Larry asked.

Was he being sent by someone to see where her alliances lay? If so, he was playing a good game. So she answered, "There's been some talk, but again, it's been advised to me that we shouldn't..."

"I'm getting another call. I need to go. I think we're both clear on what needs to be done, Nancy. The boy is innocent." With that, Larry hung up the phone.

Nancy waited for the sound of the phone line to die before she clicked *OFF*. She sat there thinking of the conversation. Had Larry given her an *order*? Part of her hovered on anger and the other part on disbelief. Then she thought of Henry. How had there been three keys without her knowing? She had worked so closely with the Project, and yet this piece of information had always been kept from her. Nancy was never allowed to know the status of the gates, the selection of keys, and now she understood why: no one agreed on it; it was being manipulated. David Smith had elected Henry, and he had changed his mind. Somewhere in between then, he had given Henry enough power to sway the decisions of the Company...*No*, she thought, *Now is the time to end neutrality. I will have to pick sides...*

CHAPTER 9

The Blind Side of the Wall

…"He dropped me off at my parents', and I just haven't been able to reach him since." Dana sat at Ariella's kitchen table with a cup of ginger tea. She let the steam warm her chin. Dana had shown up at Ariella's apartment when the first stars began to cling onto the evening canvas, and the voices of laughter bounced against the streets.

"Come in," was all Ariella had managed.

Ariella sat across from Dana, holding a cup of raspberry tea. She had listened to Dana explain herself thoroughly and repeatedly: *He was distant from her. She was falling in love with him. He never promised her anything, but his actions confused her. She couldn't be alone.*

"I haven't talked to him in a while to be honest," Ariella interrupted. "The last time we spoke was before his trip. Actually, well before his trip. I've been wrapped up with my own travel plans and just didn't reach out to him." It was a lie. She hadn't spoken to Henry because she was afraid to, but now that Dana sat vulnerable in front of her, she couldn't bear to speak the truth.

"Oh, I just thought you two talked all the time." Dana spoke without lifting her head. Her eyes focused on the tea, the steam wetting her long eyelashes. *Perhaps*, Ariella thought, *perhaps Dana was afraid of the answer also.*

Her face tired from crying, her eyelashes wet, her hair knotted, Dana looked far older than Ariella realized. In fact, had Ariella not seen her earlier painted with cosmetic colors, the shiny, light pinks illuminating Dana's otherwise pale face, the darkened mascara hiding her nearly transparent eye lashes, Ariella would have found Dana perfectly average, neither beautiful nor un-beautiful. She was worn, and in between her sobs, her misery had settled deep along the wrinkles of her naked eyes.

In that same moment, Ariella realized whatever wall was constructed between her and Henry, a different wall was constructed between Dana and Henry, and a new wall would be constructed between her and Dana. Ariella wondered if at the end of all the wall constructions, whether there would be any room left for the people who constructed them.

"Are you alright?"

"No," Dana sighed. "No, I'm not alright. I just...no it's not alright. I don't know where he is. I don't want to. I don't want to go to work. I don't want to. I just don't. I'm so tired. I'm so tired."

Ariella was silent, as if waiting to hear an explanation. Then, when none came, "You don't have to. You really don't have to do anything right now. Just take a rest. You don't have to do anything."

"No that's not true. There's too much to do." Dana paused, as if making an invisible list in her mind. "Whenever I think of this, I feel my insides in panic, and my hands began to glaze with sweat, and at once, I want to crawl back into bed and turn the blinds off...Ariella, you're so much younger. I'm getting older. Who am I going to be with? The job is so isolating, my life, everything...I'm all alone—"

"—I think you should go to sleep," Ariella interrupted. "You've been up for a long time, and you're upset. I'm worried about Henry also. I'm really worried. But let's wait until morning to figure out what to do. We can call his office, but all of that has to wait until morning anyway.

You're welcome to stay here. I don't have much space, but the couch pulls out...and I have a clean set of sheets and some new really comfy pillows. What do you think?"

"Alright." Dana's voice was barely audible.

Later that night, Ariella was lying in bed awake as she heard Dana's breathing slow to a deep sleep, inhaling and exhaling. Against the wordless sounds of the breathing and in the darkness, staring at her ceiling, Ariella thought of a conversation she had with Henry years ago. They were walking through the woods near her house in early December when the trees were barren of their leaves. They walked past old stone walls that had fallen down; the only traces of the partitioned-out historic farm lands were the decrepit bunches of rocks that were covered with moss. They both sat down on a fallen oak tree and noticed a little pile of acorns hidden beneath the underbrush.

"Henry," Ariella said, "it looks like someone's forgotten its food." She pointed at the little acorns.

"Oh, that's right. Poor little guy'll be disappointed once it gets colder here." With that, he brushed off the leaves, organizing the little acorns in a visible pile like some sacrificial offering to winter. They got up from the logs and kept walking through the wooded forest. Henry pointed up at the blackbirds that still sat in the trees when they came to a clearing. All of a sudden, the entire field shook with excitement, and a flock of quails with spread tails few into the sky, disturbing the grey, quiet air around them. The blackbirds remained eerily silent. The air was heavy with the coming of snow.

"Oh, I wish I had a camera," Ariella said.

"I wish I had a gun," Henry replied. Ariella glared at him. Then she reached into her pockets with the mittens her mother had knit for her and pulled out two chocolates. She handed one to Henry as if to quiet him. Then she unwrapped the other one clumsily and stuck it into her mouth.   The   chocolate   was   smooth   and   sweet.

* * * * *

Lying on the bed, Henry stirred. It was one of his favorite memories, the taste of the chocolate in his mouth on that cold day while they looked at the quails flying in the meadow clearing. It came to him in a haze, but as he woke up, he ached for that day again. He suddenly realized he had no idea where he was. He was on a bed. His body ached as if it had been hit by an iron rod, the stiffness starting from the top of his head and reverberating down to his toes. He struggled to open his eyes, and when he tried to lift his body up, he realized that nothing was moving except the pain that kept throbbing through him.

* * * * *

July 2, 2020. With the blinds pulled halfway, sunlight crawled underneath Ariella's sheets and sat impatiently like a cat waiting for her to open her eyes. Ariella opened one eye and then the other, and then she shut them both again before rubbing her hands over them and slowly moving her body to find wakefulness. She had heard a shuffling and clicking of metal. It was then, in that very short second, that the fragment of her dream disappeared into that nebulous corner of forgetting and she realized that Dana was still in her apartment. She called out, "Good morning Dana."

The steps and metal clinking inched from the kitchen into Ariella's one bedroom, and Dana appeared holding a steaming mug, and it was then Ariella noticed that the room felt cool for a summer morning. Another moment, and Ariella smelled the coffee. *At least she knows how to drink coffee,* Ariella thought.

"Hey. Sorry, I woke up hours earlier out of habit...well, no, I couldn't really sleep. I just made some coffee since I saw it on the counter. Just couldn't really help myself. Sorry to rummage through your kitchen."

"Oh, come on, don't even worry about that. Are you feeling better this morning?" Every word was an effort, but she wasn't sure how else to respond. It was a pull of feelings, a feeling of pity and understanding. Ariella realized, of all the nine billion people in the world, only Dana could possibly understand exactly what she felt.

"I'm sorry I came here like I did last night. I was scared, and I wasn't sure who to go to. Coming to you just made sense, but I'm sorry to get you involved." There was nothing left. Dana had revealed everything the night before. "I just thought you'd know."

"No, no I'm, well I'm glad you came. Let's look for a way to reach him. Sunday mornings, he doesn't usually go into the office. Not until afternoon at least. But that's a good place to start," Ariella said.

CHAPTER 10

Unlikely Guest and Hosts

…"You went back to sleep," a child's voice called, "I was hoping you'd stay awake when you woke up the first time, but you just closed your eyes right up again." Henry turned his head to see the boy, who blinked his dark brown eyes and continued, "I'm Jia Lan, son of Jia Zheng, my father whom you've already met. My mother, her name is Miaoyu, has been taking good care of you. I've been waiting for you to wake up since I got bored. You've been asleep for so long."

Henry opened his mouth to speak, and he heard his voice mumble, "grummpherresp". How could this child be seven? He sounded so much older.

Jia Lan laughed, "You're funny. Looks like you're still pretty hurt. Do you want something to drink? You don't need to answer. You look like you *need* it." With that the little boy scuttled off and returned a minute later with a cup filled with tea. "This is the best we have in the house. We don't get tea too often, but since you're a guest, you can have some."

Henry slowly extended his throbbing arm and wrapped his fingers around the thick ceramic cup. His headache had also returned, and Henry grimaced as he tried to move. Jia Lan held it with his hand, until both hands managed to put the cup near Henry's mouth. "That's the most...amazing drink I have ever had," was all Henry said before closing his eyes again.

"Well, tea is good, but you're being ridiculous." Jia Lan responded. "So who are you? Where are you from? Are you a foreigner?"

"Who are you? Have you been watching me while I sleep?" Henry asked back.

"I already told you. I'm Jia Lan, son of Jia Zheng. I'm seven, and I live here. You're the stranger. So, who are you?"

"I'm Henry Smith," the words blurted out of him before he could stop himself. "I'm a lot older than you. And a lot sorer. And I have no idea why I'm here."

"How many fingers do you see me holding up?" Jia Lan flashed three fingers up and down again quickly.

"Wait, that was too fast. Do it again. You didn't even give me a chance to look."

"Hm, specimen appears to have some mental faculties missing. Perhaps due to large abrasion to head and face," Jia Lan recited.

"Who are you calling specimen? And I have no faculties missing, kid." Henry was indignant. He remembered very little. He realized he could explain the important things to himself: name, address, place of work, family members, close friends, but he had no idea how he got to his immediate surroundings.

"Keep that attitude up, and you'll get no more green tea," Jia Lan retorted.

"Alright. Sorry. I promise, I'll be nicer," Henry conceded. The tea went down nicely. He searched his mind again. It was as if a rocket had shot itself into his short-term memory and left a crater from the helicopter until his mysterious landing.

"That's what I thought. So, who are you?"

At this, Henry began to slowly articulate the facts: "My name is Henry. I lived and worked in a big city at a biotech company. It's one of the largest companies in the world in the industry. I'm...not really sure how old I am. How odd. I can't remember. I'm almost...how old? My mother's name is Xiaoling, my sister is Erica, my father recently passed away. My head hurts like hell. But yea...I honestly have no idea how I got here or why I'm here or why I'm just sleeping in your house. To be honest, if I can speak what's in my mind, I'm not even sure if I'm awake or not. It could be the dreams. The dreams happen during the daytime, my mind...stretched. Time could be stretched. Or doing cartwheels. I've been having these weird dreams or hallucinations or some combination since who knows if dreams are hallucinations in the first place, and I sometimes can't tell if I'm awake or not. I can't remember. For all I know, this could just be a dream inside a dream. I feel like I've been dreaming without stop the past few months."

"You're wacky, Henry. You also talk a lot. Did the head doctor say you can leave?"

"I'm sure *someone* let me out." Had he seen a doctor?

"Did they check your brain?"

"Are you making fun of me?"

"Maybe. You're funny though. I like you. Hopefully we can keep you for a while. I get scared in the house. At first, they were worried about you, but then my dad realized you were like a vegetable and couldn't even go to the bathroom without someone doing it for you. It'll be a while before you can start walking around normal again. So he wasn't worried. He's working. Don't tell my mom though. She still thinks he's here looking after me."

"You don't sound like you're seven."

"I'm smart." The boy was so sure of himself.

"Are you? What's 9 times 5?" Henry asked, poking.

"That question offends me. Do *you* know what 9 times 5 is? You couldn't even count my fingers. Okay, what year is it?" Jia Lan crossed his arms and stared at Henry, his eyebrows furrowed.

"That's because you tricked me. And the year? It's twenty...twenty-twenty? Or twenty-nineteen? Maybe twenty twenty-one...I can't remember the exact year."

"Are you mad?" Jia Lan put a hand on Henry's forehead. "No, your temperature seems okay."

"Probably, yes, I'm sure there's a chance I've gone crazy. What year do you think it is?"

"It's nineteen-sixty-one."

The child said, "Nineteen-sixty-one," nearly sixty years apart from Henry's memory. Nineteen-sixty-one was the Bay of Pigs, Cuba in exile, Eisenhower warning Americans against the "military-industrial complex", Sputnik, Nelson Mandela acquitted of treason...What other things? Those were the things of history, those things he knew already. No, the child was confused. But the thought of arguing weighted his eyelids, and so he said quickly, "That's definitely not right. But honestly, I can't argue about this right now. Can I have more of that tea?"

Nineteen-sixty-one, and he was already forgetting: Sputnik, Eisenhower...what else? What else? He had just listed it, and now they escaped his mind. Who was the next president after Eisenhower?

"Yup. I'll go get it."

The distant words broke Henry's thought, and the United States of America was a distant drifting into the fog of his memory. He slowly sat upward against the couch. It was then that he noticed his head was feeling heavy. He placed his hand on his head and realized he was touching the crusty exterior of the gauze.

Nineteen-sixty-one and the people were eating bark from the trees, stripping them, planting the roots of harvests deep into the ground, and finding nothing in autumn. The harvests were short, and the rain had not come but left instead the dust and the wind, and of course, the hair of the gone.

* * * * *

"Why did they put the old inherited furniture in the dining room, if no one is allowed to use it?" The woman's voice drifted toward Henry as he lay unmoving in his straw bed.

"I have no idea! But the whole lot of us could barely fit in that kitchen. Chao seemed to get pretty excited over the new inheritance, huh? I'm not even sure that'll go well if others found out that he has it. Things haven't been going well lately, and you know how we've been asked to give up our private belongings. It's probably better here in the city than out there, so they may get away with it for some time. We should probably keep it to ourselves." The man's voice was louder. He chuckled.

"Once they have kids, that'll change things. They should be careful with all this family inheritance. Someone's going to start asking why their families had been so wealthy in the past," the woman replied.

"You worry too much," the man said to her, now quieter and to a whisper, "I think if we're outstanding citizens, things will be just fine. They're hard workers, and they were on the good side of the revolution. No one can say they've exploited the poor or had right-leaning tendencies."

Henry's dream brought him back to the rainy, windy night and the road with the dead man lying. He saw himself and Howard in the car, driving, speeding down the wet streets, the car splashing the water that filled the potholes lining the curb. He hadn't realized just how dark that park driveway was, with the rain and fog clutching and enveloping the black car that flew through it. The car swerved as it flew. Suddenly, he could see, as if he were hovering in the sky above the entire scene, the small figure wrapped up in newspapers, plastic, and what looked like three different tints of brown coats. He couldn't see whether the man was moving or not moving, and the Henry visiting his dreams began shouting at the Henry driving the Aston Martin. Visiting Henry couldn't make a noise; he could only watch, paralyzed, as Dream Henry slammed onto the brakes and hit the body on the ground. It all happened so quickly. When Visiting Henry traced back his memory of what had happened that night, he never realized how quickly the sequence of events actually did happen. It was a few seconds, but that night had dragged on in his mind for what seemed like hours, as if the seconds had inflated and stretched themselves into some space that had inherently expanded just to torture him.

Silently, Visiting Henry saw the figures leave the car – his dream self and the dream Howard. Everything else was exactly how he remembered, the retching, the screaming, the horrified expression he saw on himself and the calculated way in which Howard pulled him away and back into the Aston Martin. The dream faded, and Henry found himself in a limbo between lucidity and sleep. But, grey or black? The question invaded him and tore him toward wakefulness. Grey or black? Henry had remembered the car was cranberry, but here in his dream – which was so real he could almost feel the way the rain matted his hair and soaked his clothes so that they stuck onto his warm skin – it was black. Then he realized it. It came clear to him for the first time since that night. The Company doesn't keep Aston Martins. It never had. Suddenly, Henry jolted awake.

Awake, Henry felt the sudden pain in his head throb down into his neck, and he realized he was paralyzed, lying down on his back. His fingers tingled, almost itching, but he couldn't move them. He suddenly had no idea where he was, and he couldn't hear the sounds of the voices from the distant room anywhere.

Petrified, he screamed. Nothing came out.

* * * * *

Nothing came out, and Jared stared with his eyes open at the ceiling. The paint was cracking. There were pieces of it on his mattress. He never bothered to remove them. He had already memorized the way the white ceiling had cracked down from the light fixture in the middle of the room. There were yellow and grey stains on the corners of the ceiling from where water had leaked through. Jared found that when he stared up sometimes at the cracks, he could see various outlines of continents. Those lines that formed what looked like East Africa when he was looking at it while laying diagonally across the mattress turned into the State of Texas when he shifted his body clockwise by ninety degrees. Jared knew that ceiling very well. He stared up at it often.

With his throat dry and a pain that expanded across the cranium – as if the grey matter in his brain was expanding like bread soaked in water against the hard cavity of his skull – and reached down all the way into his dry throat and settled into the pit of his stomach, Jared tried to scream. He screamed and he screamed and nothing came out.

Jared stayed awake that night. He was used to it. Since returning from his last tour overseas, he rarely slept more than an hour or so at a time.

"Are you still having trouble with your hyper vigilance?" the small, bald man in an off-lab coat had asked him. Jared had visited the test labs, and all he remembered was the long hallway, the unmarked doors, and inside each room, he had been asked a question by what looked like the same bald-headed man.

<Yes.> Jared had answered. He had spoken without really speaking, a kind of speaking with his mind. The bald man had not looked up, scribbled something down in a notebook and then waved him off.

In the next room, the next man had been waiting for Jared, his glasses reflecting the light from the ceiling. "Jared, what memory comes to mind right now?"

<Memory? I have so many...>

"Well, pick one that seems to stand out," the man had replied.

Jared had been silent, the thoughts of the various moments of his life coming toward him in incoherent flashes: playing ball with his dad, being at the hospital, so many hospitals, his son, his dad, dying, birth, the tour, oh the dryness of the desert! Dry oh dry desert, the blood evaporating into the air, the smell of human rot, the things falling through the sky! Yes, the sky!

<In the car, one night> he had begun, <in the car...the lights...the lights were so bright, the red tail lights, and the cars were all around. Yes, they were surrounding me. Everywhere. And the streets on either side of the freeway were lit, like a fire. The whole thing was a fire of lights, and the city in the distance. I drove faster. Faster...I drove through the cars, I drove through them all weaving, until I was so fast. The lights became

streams, streams of color. I was alive! I was alive! I was free, and the lights were shedding off me. I was too fast for them. I was too free.>

At this answer, the bald man had not looked up. Instead, he had put a hand to his chin, picked up a black ballpoint pen, wrote some notes, and waved Jared off.

Jared had entered another room, and it was the same thing, another small, bald man, "We appreciate your services. It was unplanned, to say the least, to have to invoke another person to fill in the role David Smith had left. You will be rewarded, Colonel."

Colonel. Jared was confused. Was the man addressing him? His memory was displaced. He couldn't remember being a Colonel, and yet when the man had spoken to him, Jared knew it was how he had been addressed. *Colonel. Colonel of what?*

* * * * *

"You two should probably be quiet. Our guest has been sleeping. He's a lot less fun to have around than you guys said he would be." Jia Lan stared at his parents.

"Oh, sorry Lan Lan, we'll be quiet," his mother smiled at him. "Did you have a good day though?"

"It was a *stupendously* normal day. Nothing happened today. Nothing at all," Jia Lan responded, his hands resting across his chest.

"Well, son, like they say, you must be boring to be bored!" Jia Zheng added in.

"Father, I never said I was *bored*. I just said that the day was normal. Nothing about normal implies boring. You made that connection unnecessarily." Jia Lan stared and blinked.

291

"Oh, well, same thing. Anyway, when the young man wakes up, call me in." Jia Zheng gave Miaoyu a quick smile and patted Jia Lan on the head. Jia Lan stared back, unflinching and unsmiling. Then he walked out the back door through the unused kitchen.

"Ma," Jia La said to his mother, "last summer, we had more vegetables to put in our congee. Why don't we have any this summer?"

"Oh, son, don't worry about that. It's because we're developing. Developing means sharing the food together now," Miaoyu replied.

"I saw Zhao Zhao licking old popsicle sticks from the garbage. Do we have enough food in the house to last us?" the boy continued.

"Of course we do. We have plenty of ration coupons that'll get us through so many months, and all the way until the next New Year. In fact, we'll get you something special for the New Year." Miaoyu returned to a stack of letters that sat on the corner of their tiled, kitchen counter. She looked at them one by one and brought them over to the table, opening them with a small, dulled knife.

A few moments later, Henry Smith got up from the couch. He instinctively walked over to the voices he had heard. The pain in his head kept him from opening his eyes fully, as if light irritated the throbbing even more.

"Oh, my goodness. He's up!" Miaoyu rushed over to Henry, and put an arm around him, leading him to the chair.

"Well, I've been waiting for you *all* afternoon! Finally!" Jia Lan piped in.

"Lan Lan, why don't you get our guest some tea?" Miaoyu put her hand on Henry's back protectively, as if holding him up as he sat down on the chair.

Henry blinked twice to make sure he was awake, and when his eyes stayed fixated on the same woman and child as a moment earlier, he spoke, "I'm sorry but, I don't know what's happening."

"Oh, of course not. Just sit down, and I'll call my husband in. We'll explain things to you. Oh, I'm so glad you're awake now and seem to be alright. I was so worried." She spoke quickly, and her eyebrows furrowed together as she looked at him. Her eyes fixed on him, or his bruised head (he imagined), or the oddly shaped bloody growth that seemed to emerge from his head (he feared), and for a moment, he was convinced that she was going to begin crying. Immediately, he felt as if he should almost console her, completely taken aback by the emotions on her face, and in particular, the increasingly watery-ness of her eyes. Where was his own mother at this moment? Unable to think of what to say or do, he returned her gestures by patting her on the shoulder and sat down with nothing to say.

CHAPTER 11

Aging is a Vice

July 7, 2020. The neon lights came on one by one at the movement of the footsteps. Division III Sector 5 Group 9 began working again in the morning hours between 6:00 and 7:00. Usually Doctor Nancy Sparrow arrived right at 6:15 and shared a coffee with Doctor Reynolds before they began to check on the instruments and experiments running the night before. Then at 8:00, they usually began their series of meeting calls with various government agencies. This morning, Doctor Nancy Sparrow was gone, sick she had said to him, and Doctor Reynolds walked alone into the empty building with a large cup of coffee in his hand.

It was nearly there. The entire project was suddenly materializing, as if all those years of grant writing, the tedious way he had built this lab as a graduate student in a university and then moved the project from place to place based on funding until finally receiving the golden ticket from a private sponsorship. He never imagined this whole thing would come to fruition the way it has. Doctor Reynolds remembers when he first gathered his advisors during the very early days of beginning the initial research and company that would lead to the Project. He could still vividly remember the feeling of possible failure. Doctor Reynolds remembered clearly the moment he had sat with his wife in the waiting room to hear her radiology report for a cancer screening. The sterile smell of the room had reminded him of his own labs as he had looked at the ornaments hanging around the room. It had been near Christmas time. He had seen in the reflection of the shiny, colorful bulbs a complete failure. Yes, he had failed his project, this life-long affair he had with science and his career. It had been going nowhere. He had been about to run out of funding and unable to help his dying wife who would die six months later, right before he found out he had received David Smith's request to buy his project and employ him as a director on it. This new unexpected luck got him out of bed in the mornings.

Duane met with Doctor Reynolds at exactly 6:30 that morning. He was often the only one wearing a suit, and so his presence was well-known to all the other staff scientists. He walked into Doctor Reynolds' office without knocking and sat in the chair, waiting as Doctor Reynolds finished his coffee.

"Finding a market for this has arrived far sooner than I expected," Duane said with a smile. He sat casually in the leather chair, and his hand extended to the chair's arm, revealing a surprisingly rough hand that had the wear of sixty-one-years, with the grey hairs and brown spots giving away his attempts to preserve youth through the newly re-grown hair on his once balding head and the fit frame he worked on every single evening with his two personal trainers. It was a useless, losing battle. This battle against time was one he was willing to battle until he couldn't battle it anymore. He felt the presence of age in his knees more than anything, but over fifteen years ago, when the first marks of it appeared, he had felt it in his energy levels.

When he was young, Duane felt his energy was boundless, his greatest asset, but now in the evenings when he used to be sharpest, he felt himself growing tired unexpectedly. The mornings were darker and the evenings came earlier. Sitting there in the cold room, he realized he hadn't touched his second wife, Lisa – or rather, she hadn't let him touch her – in six months now.

296

Duane remembered saying to Doctor Reynolds three weeks earlier, "The thing with aging is that it happens slowly and steadily, a non-stop process, which is the whole idea behind the misconception that the young have that they'll be young forever, which is why the mid-life surprises people. It's not like one day, a guy just wakes up being fifty after being twenty the night before. It's just that the guy has ignored that he was aging, slowly inching up to fifty, every single day after twenty. No one really thinks about that until they look into the mirror and see that either half their hair's fallen out or suddenly, it's turned another color, and they don't move around quite as fast, and things seem to feel heavier and sluggish. Then the second half of life is coming to terms with this through oblivion, acceptance and dementia."

"Men, it seems," Doctor Reynolds had replied, "are particularly devastated by the mid-life. As women spend most their younger selves worried about their biological countdown to infertility, either consciously or subconsciously, while trying to lasso the running bull, the young mate, *and* get a career *and* maintain a socially acceptable persona, that very running bull in the first half of life acts like the "rest of their lives" is just some fictitious rumor shown in popular entertainment and happens to other people, like their uncles or dads or bosses. It never happens to them. Until it does…"

Three weeks have passed now, and they were certain this could be brought to market. Duane waited for Doctor Reynolds to drink his coffee and eat his breakfast. "Of course," Duane said as Doctor Reynolds took a bite out of a cinnamon muffin, barely looking at him, his eyes still gazing at the computer screen projected onto his desk, "it'll take the Legal and Special Operations Department a while to handle everything else, and we'll need to coordinate with the Fed team, but the technical aspect…that's all there. That's been in process for years now without any serious malfunctions." At this point he was speaking to himself. His voice drifted.

After a silence, Doctor Reynolds spoke. "One of our departments is having moral qualms about it. Casey spoke to me this morning about whether it's best to be kept as, well, an academic procedure."

"They'll always be having moral qualms about it. Come on, the people sitting there right now couldn't make a decision about left and right if their lives depended on it. It's a circus, a showcase for modern American entertainment. That's what we the private sectors are here for. Pushing them. We give public sector direction. The government exists to appease and comfort the masses."

Doctor Reynolds finished the bite of his muffin, curled the white wax wrapper underneath the remainder of it and replied, "I'm not so sure about that, but it should be a while before we even get to that stage."

Duane inched forward to the desk, "Time moves faster than you think. Start deciding whether you feel this need for moral obligation now that you've completed 99% of something. Let me know when you've thought it through." With that, he got up and left.

* * * * *

As Duane walked out the building, he looked over at the message Lisa had sent him *"Home late tonight. Took dogs to vet today. L"*. When did Lisa surpass him? He had noticed the power shift one evening when he was home alone after leaving work early for the first time in over two months. Lisa had been nowhere to be found. Disappointed and unsure what to do with himself in their ten-thousand square foot empty and well-furnished house, alone, he had sat and watched television on a sofa near the kitchen for hours. He had found he couldn't concentrate, though. Years ago, the roles would have been reversed. Lisa, in a much smaller house, would have been waiting for him, sending messages every thirty minutes.

Duane couldn't say when the little brown specks first appeared on his

298

hands and arms. At first, it was just one, which he attributed to having spent time in the sun. Then, as more appeared, and as his hand looked wrinkled and puffed, he realized that it wasn't a freckle, a sun-mark, or cancer. He realized it was good old *age* – time was invading his body in the form of little light brown moles. Duane saw it as a countdown to death, and immediately, he felt he had a long list of things he was far from accomplishing. All the while, as he was spending evenings and mornings obsessing over his own skin, Lisa seemed to be thriving off the invisible energy given to her during the second half of her life, as if life suddenly provided some nutrients that seemed ineffective for him. Nothing—no list of affairs or evenings alone while she was out drinking and gossiping with her girlfriends – could have made him more resentful toward her.

CHAPTER 12

The Garden

July 7, 2020. The evening I arrived in the city, it was 17:34, and I had had a long conversation with my stomach already. We had conversed from the transfer train station all the way here, the conversation growing loudest about thirty minutes before pulling into the destination.

I reached into my bag and realized I had finished my bag of wheat crackers around lunch time. It was disappointing...the way you think you've got something left, or you imagine the taste of it in your mouth, and you suddenly realize there's nothing. I took out the only cash I had left, a five dollar bill, and walked over to the vending machine in the city train station. A can of coke and peanuts, and there's still so many quarters. After retrieving my meal from the machine, I sat waiting for my bus that would take me to the reception event. It arrived forty-two minutes later...late. I remember watching the passengers that moved from the platforms to the station, rushing in and out with their suitcases, their feet scurrying along.

The cross town M570 came, and there were three stops I had to wait for before the final destination: Parkview Street and Market Avenue. My stomach began talking again, and it took me a moment before I realized this time, it was speaking to me out of absolute terror. This wasn't hunger. I was scared. I didn't know what to expect. The entire time, I had just focused on getting to the right place, make sure I had enough money, all those logistics that become so important until you actually get there, and you realize that none of it is important anymore. And the big task just stares at you. It could have been as if I had floated my way there. None of the details mattered anymore.

I was supposed to meet the other fellowship recipients. Worse, the whole thing was happening at this formal event. I wasn't sure who would show up, or whether I'd have anything interesting to say. I don't know if I've ever felt so out of place in my surroundings before. Nothing else around me stuck out. Just me.

The filled bus bumped its way across the city, lurching at every traffic light. The noise of the cars and the life around me invaded at every street corner. I remember standing in the bus, giving up the free seats for passengers later. And anyway, it didn't matter. I was too nervous to sit. Exactly nineteen minutes later, the bus stopped at Parkview and Market. I grabbed my brown bag and walked to the street, hearing the boom and lurch of the vehicle as it took off again to the next stop. It was a good thing I had a map. Looking at my small map, it would take four blocks east to get to 395 Atlantic Avenue. The foreign nightlife called out to me during the entire walk, the bells of delivery men and bike commuters, the laughter of women at dinner, the sound of music from the restaurants. I stopped at a large events hotel complex decorated with a surrounding iron gate lined with tulips and a grassy courtyard in the middle of the busy city intersection. Who were these people? What lives they had!

I followed a young woman who was headed toward the hotel where the event was. She stopped at the sign outside the hotel doors that read:

Banquet for M.K. Shelling Fellowship and Alumni, Upstairs, 3rd Floor, Ball Room 4.

"Hmm, this is a lot fancier than I imagined. I'm afraid I'm underdressed," she turned and said to me. She wore a simple but neat light blue dress, something I could imagine a fitting well at a picnic. She was wearing a tan suit jacket with it. "Are you coming up as well?"

"Yes. I am. I'm glad I actually found this place. I'm Peter," I replied. I didn't know what else to do so I stuck out my hand.

"Ariella," she grasped my hand and shook it firmly. "Great to meet ya. Let's get up there, and see what they've got for us."

I followed her up the carpeted showcase stairwell that curved from the center of the atrium up to the second and third floors. As we arrived at Ball Room 4, I inhaled quickly and then held my breath: the room seemed to be filled with what looked like sophisticated professionals, and I swear had never seen so many suits in my entire life. The sudden overwhelming noise and clatter of all the voices and conversations hit me, and I stood immobilized, watching as women and men milled around what seemed like a perfectly coordinated socializing dance. No, I wasn't sure how I was supposed to exactly *mingle* in this arena.

"Oh, well, you and I are the severely underdressed ones here! It looks like we'll be sticking together tonight, if that's alright with you, unless you can magically get a cocktail dress for me. My summer dress isn't really cutting it here. And in case you *can* grant wishes, I would like to speak to that tall, handsome-looking gentleman in the corner there." Ariella looked at me with a nod and a smile. Until then, I hadn't noticed the jeans I wore – my only pair – but it was too late.

She moved through the crowd with an ease and confidence I admired and still admire. She held herself with no pretense and a natural wit that was open and comforting. "Where are you from? What did you do before this?" She asked me. I told her the truth. I was leaving a seminary. I had wanted to become a priest, but I had left the vocation. She smiled and offered kindness in that smile. "I hope this next stage of your life is

303

an adventure," she said.

It wasn't just to me though. People came over to speak to her, and before I realized it, I was accompanying the young woman amongst a throng of individuals who were well accomplished and interesting. Far more interesting than me, anyway. She navigated them like they were all old friends. Father Turner, I was fascinated at how open people immediately felt around her. She had put me at ease almost immediately, and then the rest of the night yes, *indeed*, I followed her around as to hide my own shyness.

Hours later, I was exhausted, and it seemed the evening was winding down. "Pete the home awaits me, and you are completely green to this city. I will show you out," Ariella said to me. At this signal, I picked up my brown bag and walked out with Ariella.

"Where, are you...you are going where?" She asked me.

My thought returned to her question. This was a good question. I wasn't even aware that I hadn't looked or asked anyone about the arrangements my own congregation had provided me for the few days I'd stay in the city before flying out. Then I remembered, "I'm staying at St. Francis's on 74th and Watergate. It's not too far from here. I can walk."

Ariella looked at me questioningly. Then, immediately, she called for a taxi cab from the street. She shoved me into the cab before I could even find my voice and said to the driver, "We're making two stops. The Father needs to be dropped off at his church at 74th and Watergate. Then we're going to 26th and East End. Go straight uptown and then take a left." She turned to me and said, "You would have never made it walking."

As I opened my mouth to thank her, she began again, quietly, "I need you to do something for me. I'm not very observant about any kind of religion, but if you talk to God tonight, your God, please do something for me. His name is Henry. He's missing. He's been gone for a week now. We can't find him. No one knows where he is. They all think he died in a helicopter crash off some coast, but they can't find the helicopter, the body or anyone who was supposed to be there with him. I can't do anything about this."

I took out my rosary beads and said quietly and sternly, "Ariella, God welcomes anyone who comes to him. Let us pray." With that, I began my first Hail Mary. After I was dropped off, I said the rest of the Hail Marys on the Rosary for Henry Smith.

* * * * *

That same evening, Jared sat in an empty church. He didn't know where else to go, and he was still floating, blitzed, toasted, miserable. In that moment, he cursed everything around him – the mosaic and broken images of color of the deity, the holy mother, the symbols, fragments. The entire church, it seemed, had become one dumpster that reflected Jared's own pathetic and uncontrollable life in a myriad of color. Where was God in all those panels and colors? Why did God go when Jared most needed the hand that could save him from a spiral into a pit, trapped in the well, that ugly word "addiction", a thing he felt was not himself and not in himself and never identifiable? The image of Christ on the Cross made him nauseated and angry. He was betrayed. Christ had never absolved Jared of his sins, and he felt damned just as Judas was - brother Judas - hanging from the tree. The realization hit him like a stream of light from the painted windows, Mary and the Child, Jesus and the Cross.

Forty fragmented voices wrote the Holy Bible, and yet no voice fully explained how God could so coldly reserve a placeholder spot for betrayal, the position of utmost importance and absolutely damned from the moment of the Immaculate Conception. Jared laughed, and as he continued to sit, his head broken and down, his laughter turned into a slow weep. It began in his back and erupted from him slowly like hiccups. Was he damned to hang himself in Gethsemane along the sweet, sticky smell of lilies and lavender, to rot, hanging? He was like all those other people, whose fates had it such that they were born to die without meaning.

It was then that Jared realized it: he was in hell. Yes, he was Judas, and Judas was in hell, and this was it. Jared and Judas as one. Mary cried at him from her high up window, surrounded by lavender wisteria, which filtered more sunlight from the outside. Then there was only one way to solve this conundrum. He had to get rid of himself and escape.

The last moments were quiet, as if breathing stalled inside the Church. Mary in her swallow blue looked down on Jared, and Jared looked up at her, the fractals of light peeked through her stained glass, which flickered; the clouds were moving fast outside. Were the clouds dancing for him? Jared moved slowly and entered a back door on the opposite side of the altar. In the narrow stairwell, he looked up and found what he expected, a large water pipe amongst a jungle of pipes. Taking out the rope he had carried with him in his backpack, he swung it over the top of the water pipe. Then, he took three steps up on the stairwell, tightened the rope around itself and hooked it onto his own neck, which snuggled it, and leapt.

On the altar, the Virgin Mary cried. Outside in the city, the clouds roamed. Across the tinted windows of color, the light fought through into the otherwise darkened building. In the small stairwell in the very back of the church, Jared died, hanging.

And now it's time that I begin the story of the next stage of the journey...

Part V

CHAPTER 1

The Walk Along the Huang He

There was no more war, and the land hid the bygone revolutionaries and nationalists with new farmland that sprawled like distant dreams between villages. Yet even with the fertility grown on the memory of slaughter, the people could not get their fill. "How much production in this *mu*?" the *gan bu* asked over and over again, and yet every answer they received was unsatisfactory. Every answer needed to be inflated to report to the county, to the province, to Beijing! Every house was searched for grain. Every human was tossed upside down, shuffled, shook, uprooted...for where did the grain go if the land was so fertile? How could they have not fulfilled the promise to the capital to surpass the other nations in grain production? Of course, the only answer was sabotage, and so every person was tossed upside down, shuffled, shook, uprooted for a second time to search for the missing grain. They were shook, shuffled, tossed so much that they began to shrink: their arms first, then their legs, and then the face until there was nothing left but a stomach which extended beyond shape and comfort, protruding loudly. Then they disappeared by way of "three parts natural disaster and seven parts man-made disaster."[5]

Two weeks after Henry's mysterious and unconscious arrival, Jia Zheng

---

[5] Liu Shaoqi, *Seven Thousand Cadres Conference* January 11-February 7, 1962

took Henry back to their meeting place along the cliff side of the water's edge where Henry's body had been washed up along the river. They watched the emaciated people march through the fields. The river crashed into the cliff sides whose sediment stripes carved the land's story along the rock. The backs of men and women rose and fell, like waves on the sea. Their shiny spines glittered in the sun with stretched taught skin.

"I bring you to the edge of the river, the open gap of teeth, rotting, waiting, sucking air from the dry clouds. The soiled water you cannot drink, and the mountain is dry." Jia Zheng extended his hands outwards toward the tumbling river. "You can see the violet cloud rip through the air. See, there, rainless thunder again. We are high up now because the river has retreated." He continued to point. No rain followed as Jia Zheng and Henry walked along the river cliffs.

"Walking alongside you...I sense the presence of another, a third...another presence. Who is the third?" Henry said.

"It is not a surprise to me. People have hallucinations out here. Many people are too desperate, or the air is too hot and dry," Jia Zheng explained.

Henry, unable to think of a response, said instead, "You live in a ghost city."

Jia Zheng turned from the river and stared at the rows of buildings that were covered in a dense fog in the distance. "As I grow older, I see that our lives, my dear friend, are back and forth processes, each a back and forth process...wandering along according to what we believe is the next step. Yes, it is random. We can no longer predict what tomorrow might bring. This is why some forget, or why some turn around and just keep living day to day."

"How do you deal with this and keep your sanity then?" Henry began walking slower, until Jia Zheng was nearly two steps ahead of him.

Jia paused before answering, turned back to face Henry and then said, "I don't know the answer. Some do go insane. For me, I think my mind is the only thing I have left. There were good days. Days when I believed what I was doing was bringing more food onto the table, and not just during harvest time but all year round. I looked at the faces of my family, the warmth glowing from their reddened cheeks, and marveled at the simplicity of life. I try to hold onto that. It's all we have left." Jia Zheng stopped walking and turned to look at the retreating water. He said nothing else.

While the mountain was quiet, there was no peace. The dry air crackled, echoing partial thoughts of spoken conversations. There were rocks everywhere, and the mossy surfaces gleamed on the edge of the brown water. "I'm not sure if anyone will talk about our scattered lives in future generations, if those generations are left. When I began working for the Revolution, as a young revolutionary and now as a high ranking official in the city, I believed...I still do believe...but perhaps I don't understand the bigger plan. Perhaps I'm too simple. Or not intelligent enough," then he lowered his voice to a whisper, "The people starve. I tell you this Henry because I have no hope left. A year ago, I would not have trusted you. They do things to people. Entire families disappear with even the smallest hint of counter-revolutionary tendencies. But I don't care anymore. I have to say it. They starve." Jia Zheng repeated. He looked at Henry, tears in his eyes which slowly gathered and then began to roll down his face, "Isn't it all made from fragments? What will we be to the future in a hundred years? Think about the farmers," he began to weep, the long snail trails of wet dripping down his face. "There have been so many days... so many evenings...after a long field day, toiling in the soils that gave nothing, and the rest of us have sat quietly, hunched, as the daring Huang He shrivels up in hunger, waiting for something. No one to bring them grain." Then, he spoke as if a dark cloud had crossed over him, his eyes to the ground and his voice in a husky and frantic whisper, "We should have saved enough. There is something unnatural happening, and none of us know what it is. But I remember it -- the greenness of the fields and the gold of the harvest that we could keep before giving it all away now to someone else far away. What fate will the wind shake from the skies? Khrushchev? They shout about Khrushchev the capitalist, but what is so important about Khrushchev when there are brothers and sisters hungry at home? I come home, but how will I feed their children, whom are my brother's children, comrade, my brother!? Their empty hands are shaking, the bones from their wrists piercing their soft little skin, worn by the sun. Those little fingers grasping for anything they can find with hungry mouths. We have brought them into this world, Henry, promised them liberation and grain, and we cannot feed them." When Jia Zheng finished, he seemed to sway back and forth, as if the words he just said had ejected out of him a great momentum that his shell body was now reacting to.

Henry swallowed. The man stood before him whimpering and swaying. "Jia Zheng, I'll let you in on a secret that I don't share often. It might sound out of context here, but I feel that I might understand. In my dreams, my day dreams, I am the image of an old man with rotting teeth, and as my hand touches the banister up on an unknown, dark stairwell, I think of the old Huang He...no other river but the Huang He, its mouth open and gaping, and I cannot understand why...And suddenly I am standing at the top of a set of stairs. The twisted, cold, drafty steps lead to a room whose door remained closed. I peer at the door, my memory approaching some distant nightmare, and while I...while I" – his mouth went dry, and he swallowed before continuing – "...while I remain frozen on the stairway, I think of the twisty steps below me. I can't remember any faces, but I remember the dead, rotting, gums and old worn teeth, smiling as they were...just smiling and dying. Clutching the side of the railing, I am afraid, I do nothing, and a shudder runs through me." Henry looked at Jia Zheng.

Jia Zheng wiped the tears from his face with a dirty hand, leaving streaks of brown and grey on his cheeks. He returned Henry's stare with a warm, rough hand on his back, saying, "It is a feeling you have. It's that feeling of dread that you keep thinking of this image even if it does not make sense to you. We have the same dread but with different images. You understand us then. You may not be from here, from a distant village somewhere else, but you can...You understand us."

* * * * *

Later that afternoon, Jia Zheng and Henry returned for a quick lunch of millet soup. "Eat, Henry," Jia Zheng encouraged. "Please, don't be shy. It's our pleasure to host you, and we have plenty of ration coupons for simple grains." They sat at a small wooden table that Jia Zheng and pulled outside to survive the indoor heat.

"Does your mother need help?" Henry motioned to an old woman intently sweeping the concrete front patio with a broom made of twigs.

"My mother enjoys sweeping the floor," Jia Zheng replied. "We once tried to take the task from her, and she objected." He chuckled, took a slurp of his soup, set the bowl down and wiped his face with his arm and said, "Fiery woman. She taught us everything. She wants to keep her dignity. She's nearing sixty now, and it still gives her something to do on the days she can get out of the bed. Otherwise, she's constantly worried she is a burden to us. It's ridiculous, but I can't change her thinking."

Henry could hear a few birds and the sounds of footsteps walking along the alley way of the streets. Other than these noises, it was unexpectedly quiet for a small city. "Where have I landed?" Henry asked aloud and scooped some millet soup into his mouth. His stomach rumbled. He had not realized how hungry he was feeling until he began to eat.

Jia Zheng quickly finished the rest of his soup, picking up the bowl with both hands. After emptying it, he replied, "You mean you really still don't remember any of it?" Jia Zheng frowned. "It was dreadful. I have never seen anything like it...you were just lying there, your body facing the sun on the rock, and your hands...one hand in the water, and the other on

313

the rock. Blood everywhere..."

"No, I don't remember too much, although...," Henry's voice trailed, and he thought about it again. He remembered the man's face, the toothless expression that stared down onto him. The man had twitched, and Henry could swear – by the facial muscles that extended from the man's brow to the upper left corner of his mouth – that it was as if another person was trying to burst out from underneath a human-skinned mask that was sewed far too tight for the face that wore it. Henry remembered getting into the helicopter, the dizzying feeling of flying high up bouncing from thermal to thermal. He remembered the events before getting onto the helicopter...the way he had failed to say goodbye to Dana because the words had glued themselves inside of him; the woman with the glasses, whose name he could not recall; But Ariella, where was Ariella?...those things came back to him, but he couldn't remember them as he lay on the rock thinking he was going to die. Henry wished he could.

Jia Zheng's mother moved from sweeping the doorway to stepping out into the street and began sweeping the street corner where the house stood. *Swish swish swish*, the bottom of the broom made of young sapling twigs scraped against the dust on the steps. Henry said, "During the moments that I must have felt – at the time – were the last few moments of life, I remember nothing, nothing at all. Somehow this brings me an incredible sadness I can't describe." *Swish*, the broom stirred.

The dust cloud became unsettled, *swish*. "But you were so hurt at the time, of course your mind would forget it—"

"—How much," Henry interrupted, grappling at the corners of his mind, pulling with desperate fingers the crevice which had remained shut until he could see a little light peaking through, "How much would anyone want to pay to know what some of those forgotten moments were?" Henry asked. "The critical ones pass by so quickly. I remember nothing, but I would have paid anything to know it." Even at the edge, leaning in with the gun in his mouth, he failed to feel much more than a resignation and imagined – far into the distance – how his disappearance would be an empty press release and nothing more.

What Henry didn't tell Jia Zheng was that he does have one memory he was sure of: he had laughed then as Jared peered down at him, even with the blood flooding his mouth. He needed to find those last minutes, to work through the details and so that perhaps his brain would trigger something new. He wanted to know why he had laughed like that. Every night since waking up and realizing he was in a stranger's home, Henry had mulled over his thoughtless laughter, hoping it would tease out an explanation for why he was here.

"Take your time remembering. You've only been awake for a few days now, and just well enough to leave the house yesterday." Jia Zheng replied and looked outside the doorway. He gave Henry a pat on the shoulder and left him, walking inside.

For the first time since his inexplicable arrival, Henry noticed that the entire house composed of just two rooms: a private bedroom, and a main room where Jia Lan, his grandmother, and Henry slept amongst partitioned portions of the common area. The tea stove was set off in a nook closest to the door. Henry got up from the table and walked into the house. He felt the rough unevenness of the floor underneath his feet. The room had the smell of abandonment, and on his straw mat – in a separate corner sealed off and separated for him and little Jia Lan – was a sheet and a single small pillow. He laid down and closed his eyes, thinking of the return of the man with the coin eyes and of things far away.

* * * * *

CHAPTER 2

Eraser

August 24, 2020 in Henan, China. "Peter, are you still happy you came?" Ariella asked me. I looked down at the fields from where we stood. The boxed rows of farmland spread out ahead of us, and I could hear the sounds of construction workers' voices shouting above the drills. They were like bees in a hive. At this point, silence and noise made no difference to me. It had been two weeks since we had stepped off the plane, the hazed sun welcoming us with the smell of rubber and exhaust. Seeing the faint outline of the mountains surrounding us, I realized it was a clear day outside the city of Luoyang.

It was not what I had expected: the humidity, the stickiness and the oppressive heat in late summer followed us during the day and at night when I slept with the air conditioning on. It rumbled quietly in my room at the local university campus.

"You act like I had no choice." I responded to her without raising my head. Out of sight of the village, we were sitting on large rocks overlooking the sweet potato and turnip fields. My eyes followed the ongoing farming restructuring project which had begun nearly four years ago; it was a drip technology designed to make irrigation in the summers more efficient for farmers, in case a drought ever hit again. It was our second week visiting a small village ten kilometers outside of the city of Luoyang. The more traveled of the two of us, Ariella, was protective of me, and in response, I had gotten into the habit of deflecting her questions on my discomfort. "How were the archives yesterday?" I asked instead.

"Dark. A little dusty. I'm not sure if I've found any of the right newpaper sources yet," she replied.

After our long days exploring the various irrigation projects and looking at the new housing constructions, I would go back to my apartment. I decided I was writing about Li Bai's poetry. At first, I wasn't sure which poet to research and decided to just talk about the Tang Dynasty, but in the end, I went with the most obvious choice: Li Bai would be the easiest for me. The Tang Dynastic poet had married his second wife in Henan. I had accidentally fallen into Eastern Poetry before the seminary and after university, and of course, continued even during my search for priesthood. Even I was surprised at the scholarship I was awarded to study this, and perhaps, publish another book of poetry. My work was well-received at the time. So of course, in Henan, I wrote every day in my diary, and the poetry came easily with my own self-conscious study of Mandarin.

Ariella, on the other hand, would lock herself up in the archives and spend hours – hours! – away looking up material: various newspaper clippings from various propaganda sources, town records, statistics, anything published that was never uploaded electronically. Then she would go from town to town and listen to stories of villagers who passed down the family laid memories of starvation. She had the harder job of the two of us, sifting through state issued misfacts to understand the political climate of the era and then facing the blaring contradictions from what people were willing to discuss. It was interesting, the way people wanted to talk. They were so mistrustful at first, but when she began to get to know them, it was as if they almost yearned to talk, sharing the horrors of what happened nearly sixty years ago.

I often felt, during those days, she was the one doing something *real*, that she was contributing to understanding something bigger, while I...I was merely interpreting.

After peeling an orange, the sticky, sweet yellow residue stuck on her hands, Ariella handed me a slice. I smiled at her and took it without a word. We had spent most the morning taking photographs without speaking much to one another, the hot sun baking us underneath our clothes until our bodies were like little furnaces. The sun threatened to bake all words out of us, and the warm orange slice burst with a cleansing sweetness. In that instance, I wanted to at once capture the contrast with the pen, but instead I winced beneath my straw hat. I could feel the sweat accumulating at the edge where my hat touched my forehead, and I tasted the overwhelming sweet-tart orange in my mouth. I kept it there for a long time, draining the slice of its juice, and then chewed the remains and swallowed.

The vastness of it - the city, the people, the disposability of every single man, woman and child - was impressive and outrageous. The constant work, day and night, kicked up debris which flew into the air and brought with it an overwhelming sense of magic, energy and desire: everyone wanted to make a new living; everyone wanted to make money overnight, and there was the rush of hope and want. There was the overwhelming-ness of life everywhere, and its vastness spread from horror to enlightenment. Where did poetry fit into this? I looked around me, and even talking to her on her research, I often questioned my relevance. But Father, I remember we had discussed this once, and I remember your words, "Perhaps only art can capture the chaos of suffering for our logic will spite itself in its search for understanding." I faltered on the faith of those words in those days. Poetry seemed hardly a comfort, and the world rushed around us, bleeding and loud and screaming horrors, yet I could not tear my face away. I tell you, I cannot not tear my face away. I remember thinking this and focusing on the orange again.

319

"It seems like you're enjoying this so far, though," she said. "There I was, meeting you for the first time at that dinner, thinking the culture shock would be a challenge. But you've proven me wrong." She smiled at me. When I didn't reply she said, "I was mostly kidding." She looked at me again to try to discern an expression.

I wiped the salty, stinging sweat from my eyes. "I often wonder, to be honest...I don't think enjoyment is the right word for it," she continued, "More, like, surviving. But it's definitely more interesting. And different. Like this heat is unbelievable." I wiped my face again with my sleeve, and she said without looking at me or my sweat, "In our other lives before, everything can be really scheduled, and every hour...every minute felt like there was a reason to be there without a really big reason at all. Do you think you miss it?"

Miss it? Those two words echoed inside my head. There were things I had left behind, and here, with the drive of energy surrounding me, I hadn't actually even thought of missing home. Or perhaps "home" is the wrong word. I should say instead, "where I was from". Home had little meaning anymore. There were the inconveniences: my throat itched from the smog and the dust, my stomach was in a constant state of panic, I needed a translator, and I was always sweating...but I didn't have the desire to go back. I was already riding the chaos, and it moved in one direction: forward and not back. So I replied after the echoing stopped, "I appreciate the conveniences more, but I haven't missed it yet."

"Well, that's good. Some people travel and they become obsessed with the differences. Others travel, and they fall in love with those differences. It takes them away from whatever they couldn't overcome in their other lives until they realize all those other things weren't so important or unsolvable in the first place." She looked over at the people drilling and working under the heat.

I looked to where she was gazing. The air quivered in front of her under the sun. The workers were far away, but I could hear the metal against metal breaking through the waving heat. "It's not bad. No, not bad. I mean, bad isn't the word. It's more like…" I paused for a moment. "…it's still an unknown." A tremor of excitement jumped through me. There was a whole unexplored world in from of me, and for so long, I had been locked in my own head. "When did your family immigrate to the US again?"

"Oh long before I was born. But of course, I grew up with stories about a place far away. It held some meaning, some kind of odd longing," she replied. She never shared much about her past with me. Even during our travels, I knew she would have impressions of where we were, that perhaps her memories of her childhood would come back to her. She claimed to have forgotten nearly everything. I did not believe her.

"Would you ever move back?" I asked instead.

"I don't know. There's a curiosity about moving away, of course. Each time I visit the old family home, I think that I would feel something," she shared for the first time. I inched closer, trying to press my ear to her voice to absorb everything she began to tell me. "I'd stand there, at the little creek which ran by our old apartment complex, and I'd wonder if I'd recognize - magically - the old photos that my parents had shown me growing up. Each time I've gone back, I've been disappointed that the nostalgia isn't quite there. It's only in my head when I think about those places from another place. Maybe that's the only thing nostalgia is: missing something from somewhere else and never feeling satisfied. Maybe that's the way you'll feel about home when you're out here a bit longer." Ariella picked up the remnants of her orange peel and threw it into a small plastic bag and put it in her knapsack. "It's as if I've made a big circle," she began again. "Their stories – my parent's – were different than mine. They crossed the 'hero's threshold' when they left. There was no way they could ever return back to here. Yet here I am.

"I feel as if I've just begun to hear the calling…that I've yet to cross the threshold, and that my story is just beginning to materialize. I just have no idea yet on what I'm supposed to do...but I know I have to do it, and that it's important. It sounds a little hokey. It's just like they left so long ago, but now as I'm here alone and searching for the story – the history – that I'm just starting all over on something that I must have known a long time ago, like I've gotten to where I came from and recognize it for the first time." She paused, stood up, and grabbed her knapsack and swung it over her shoulder. Then she lifted her camera from her neck and said, "Ready?" That was it. It was all she was going to share that day. So I nodded, and slightly disappointed as my interest had been piqued by the story she had just begun to share with me, we both began to walk toward the working construction.

* * * * *

Ariella combed through the old newspaper files, her hands screening the dates and names. There was nothing about famine, as she had expected. Those who told stories of it had kept the stories alive generation after generation through spoken memory since the power of the written word had been so twisted, untrustworthy after the calamity of the 1960s until 1976. Most who had enough resources moved out years later, moved across country, moved across the world, moved to another socioeconomic status. Those who moved countries kept their own stories privately, wishing to integrate into the new world with its own history spoken in its own language. With them, these collective memories hid the grave secret: ineffective policy and the zealousness over the eradication of hunger through the collectivization of all property.

And yet, nothing explained the edema. *Death by edema* was the most popular record of the peasants from the neighboring villages. "Of course, as if edema was the root cause," Ariella said to herself. Nothing. It was amazing.

Six to thirty million people wiped out in three years by systemic failures on every level: local, county, province and national, by exploitation,

322

punishment, and covert propaganda. "We've surpassed United States grain levels! We have ended poverty! Hunger is a thing of the past, a rightest thing, and our Great Leader has destroyed it!" Yet, nothing was in the records. It had been completely erased, just like the bones of the figures in the photographs of families Ariella dug up through her old newspapers.

She had been there all day, just like the day before, and the day before that. She had covered three thousand pages, translated them painstakingly from Mandarin. Ariella knew she had special access through her connections she had never explicitly stated in her fellowship application; she had to be careful to protect her sources. Looking at her watch and matching it with the rumbling of her stomach, she placed a guilty hand on her abdomen. "Guilt is a useless sentiment," she said to her stomach. With that, she quickly walked out of the media archive library (restricted access only) and toward her apartment, amazed that the archive had survived the years without being destroyed.

She couldn't remember her walk back. She only remembered the feeling of her stomach as she put her hands across it and the words, "death by edema", until she stood facing her apartment door. Ariella opened it, and stepped inside at which in that moment – quickly and unexpectedly – she was seized by a mounting of feelings which brought her slinking down against her closed door until she was sitting on the ground with her back against the door frame. She was powerless. Everything had been done and could not be changed as the past stayed fixed, happened, occurred, no longer alive. Life happened and disappeared, and she felt that facing the volume of horror, she could do nothing. So she cried, cried and cried and having emptied her heart's contents, she lay on her bed looking at the ceiling, counting the cracks on the paint.

Ariella carried on like this for some weeks, surrendering for the night and beginning again in the morning, feeling somehow that she would be strong enough to go back and dig through the literature and compare it to everything she had compiled, painstakingly: from scholars who had left the country to the testimonials of villagers to the old, hard-copies of newspapers that were no longer in circulation and required restricted access to retrieve. The deeper she dug into the reading and her research, the more she felt she had to put a voice to her findings. Slowly, even the tears were reluctant to come.

One evening during this time, Ariella lay in her bed and listened to the night's sounds with her window open and her air conditioner broken. The dark was like a small orchestra of noises, a few snores, huffing, stirring, insects chirping. Somewhere, she heard a dog howl. She couldn't sleep, and the more she couldn't sleep, the more she noticed the other sounds of sleeping people and the hotter she felt. She kicked off her blanket. Her own restlessness choked her, so she rolled out of bed, put on her day clothes, and walked outside her apartment.

Crawling outside, Ariella stood grateful for the wind that blew across her face and arms. It was so dark that the velvetiness of the night brought all the objects around her closer. Then she looked up and saw what she had missed for all those nights living in a large city; the sky was overflowing with light from the stars. It was kaleidoscope of stars, and it looked like it was moving, as if she were the child turning the lens. Or maybe it was she who was moving. It was hard to tell. In that moment, she stood transfixed at the sight of a night fabric that flowed past and through her, and she realized the miracle of everything she was. She suddenly felt very small: a tiny thing embodying a world of its own, looking at another world; a finite thing trying to understand something infinite; a cup trying to hold a river.

But Ariella's moment was magnificently short. Ariella sat down on the cold ground and looked up at the stars moving across the sky until her eyes dropped slowly, and then she fell asleep.

"My flower--" the voice called out. Ariella felt like she was in a dark corridor, walking with her hands gripping the sides of the walls next to her. Her legs were heavy, and she felt as if she were walking through a thick swamp in the middle of the corridor. "My flower –," the voice called again. Ariella turned to all directions, but could not find where the voice came from. Then, her feet tripped over something. It was the sitting body of an old woman. The woman opened her mouth, a gaping thing empty of teeth, the saliva stretching from the corners, "Have you forgotten me?" she asked Ariella.

Shivering, Ariella bent down and held the hand of the old woman. "Are you all right?" she asked.

"Dear," the old woman said, "child, my beauty, my beauty…remember the rock you lay on as you looked at the stars, and for a moment, you forgot the torture of your body. It was then that you fell in love." and her voice softened to a whisper, and she closed her eyes and stopped breathing. Then her body began to wither and shrink. Ariella gasped and took a step back, releasing her hand from the old woman's. The old woman shrank faster and faster, her skin tightening against a worn body until the skin became so tight that it became to look younger. The woman opened her eyes, and instead of the brown grey of an old lady's, they were bright blue and sharp.

"Ariella," the woman said, now getting up from her seated position. Even standing, she was very small, barely coming up to Ariella's shoulders.

"Yes," Ariella replied. Her eyes fixated on the wispy person in front of her with white hair and blue eyes.

"You will find those holes, slowly, one by one. In that search, you'll find him for the first time. Keep looking."

"Who are you?" Ariella asked, regaining her courage.

"Go to sleep, and dream deeply." With that, the woman began to fade, until her flesh became woven silk, which became tattered bits on the dark ground they stood on, and soon, disappeared into a light dust which was swept away by the black surface of the walls around them.

* * * * *

I noticed a change in her by the end of those weeks of endless research. We saw each other during evenings after we were both too exhausted to type on our laptops. She rarely complained to me during those days. It was as if she had made her decision a lifetime ago, as if her journey was pre-destined and all the sadness she had initially felt was just a mourning of a previous life. I noticed this distinct change in her one day as we were walking along the Huang He to take a break from our respective work, watching the mud tumble itself downriver. "How have you been doing it?" I finally had the courage to ask her.

"Doing what?" she replied, slowing her otherwise fast pace to a near halt.

"I dunno, I'm not sure I could do it, that's all. How do you put yourself deep into this stuff, day after day? Doesn't it get to you? Reading these stories about these people suffering, knowing you can't change a thing?" I was struggling. I was struggling with looking at the beggars and the migrant workers, and I struggled with the bits and pieces she did tell me about her work, and in particular, about the starvation. They were starved from the inside and the out. They were starved and told that they would be saved, but no one came for them, and even as they uttered their last words in their last breath they had uttered his name, the Sun, the Savior, Liberator of the poor. How did she do it, day in and day out, surrounding herself with the hopelessness, the systemic deceit, the ignorance of those in power and then continue to look forward and say, "I will rest tonight and come back to this tomorrow"? As I had suspected, she was braver than me.

"Peter," she replied gently, "I stand between the past, this thing which I can't change and a future which, honestly, I think is indeterminate in many ways and determinant in others. I stand at this intersection, and

326

knowing the past that I do now...after this trip, I stand there screaming. Maybe one person will hear me, but I'm sure practicing my scream. I feel like I'm just building this ammunition around me of how to think of the past and, I guess, look at the present. This is the most beautiful part of it, and I think a lot of it is beautiful because of the uncertainty. The uncertainty is what gives me hope," she said. To me, it sounded like she had rehearsed this to herself over and over again, that somehow she had rehearsed it so much that she believed it. I looked at her and recognized for the second time during our walk just how much she had changed. Somehow tragedy fueled her in a way that was draining me.

"What do you mean the future is indeterminate and determinate?" I asked her. I had never known the answer to that question, and even today, I'm not sure I do.

She smiled when she replied to me. We had both stopped walking and stood facing the river which wrapped itself close to the embankment on which we stood, side by side. The river was active today, so she spoke loudly, "Let me use the simplest example, and maybe it's overly broad." I listened attentively, captivated by her words, hanging onto them. To this day as I repeat this story, I remember the way she said those words, the sounds of the rise and fall of her words, her calm face in the wind, and the background rush of the river: "We will all die. That's certainty. That's the certainty that comes with life, and we forget about it but it's always in us...this known endpoint. What's not certain is how it happens. Now the process of this could make the whole thing worth it or not worth it in my opinion, the difference between a person born into a daily, unmitigating, irrational suffering and a person who is born into love – maybe not every day love, like 'wow my life is so great all the time!', but enough so that life seems worth it. I'm out to try and understand this more. One piece at a time. And I'm doing it my way, by trying to make sense of the past. Naively, maybe slowly, but there's no other way I can imagine it. And I do it because it's uncertain that I couldn't do it...I believe in that chance that makes tomorrow different than today, and I go one step further: I believe that tomorrow can be *better* than today, and one day, I want to understand how." When she finally finished, she seemed to swallow the air as she stopped speaking, like she was taking in the entire moment just as I was. I stood there motionless watching her, and soon I recognized my own paralysis in the awe of the new confidence she emanated.

I had questioned my own faith a number of times. Yes, Father, I have. I have stood in the middle of an otherwise calm afternoon – my heart trembling – offering myself to God and kneeling alone in my own living room, the couch and the table as my witnesses. Faith comes in a number of forms, and I am yet to learn them all. This form, the one Ariella had said to me, facing me as we stood in the intersection of a bloody history and a future neither could determine, shook my core. It still shakes my core. I'm not sure I have an answer to it: do I believe? Do I believe her words? I had met Ariella, thinking that she was the one who had questions of her faith, and yet as I got to know her through our trip, it was I...it was I who was the hollowed one. I searched, I was searching for my master to fill the hollowed clay.

* * * * *

"Did you learn all this about the famine while you were there in Henan with Ariella?" Father Turner asked.

Deep in thought over his story, Peter hesitated, and then nodded, "I learned most of it while I was there. But of course, I had read the books, and I had heard some stories from people I've come across in the past. Being there is very different." Peter looked down at his shoes, and then put his hands on his face and rubbed his eyes vigorously, as if trying to wake himself up. Then he said, "Father, there's an impossibility imbedded in these things we accept every day. Some days, I think it's the devil, and I'm in the desert the way Christ was in the desert. But the devil is so logical! Did they ever teach us this in seminary school? Does the Bible ever touch on the rationality of the devil? Here it is, and I say this quietly because I am afraid to voice it, I'm afraid I will sound like him.

328

Father, you can never take away history. It's happened, gone, destroyed, and even if it's repeated, it's those new souls who will suffer the consequences. Those things – those horrific things – they move in one direction, impossible to be reversed, and I stand at the gateway between that and hope. But where is my hope? Isn't it for a whole new set of souls anyway? The universe exists in a single person, Father, past, present and future. I stand at the gates – and from where I stand – I see the stretches of things that cannot be undone and things that are yet to come. I stand in this Judaean desert, this great, great desert listening to the logic of the devil. 'Dost Thou know that the ages will pass, and humanity will proclaim by the lips of their sages that there is no crime, and therefore no sin; there is only hunger?' the Grand Inquisitor had asked in The Brothers Karamazov."

Father Turner only nodded and sighed. He said nothing else. Then Peter continued. "Like me, what Henry had been missing was the leap of faith that tomorrow will be better than yesterday. It was understandable that any person would have the same struggles as Henry did, especially given his relationship to the Process."

CHAPTER 3

Infinite Loop

...Doctor Reynolds was sitting in his kitchen, cutting open a roast chicken. The empty house was quiet. An orange cat, Salamander, came and rubbed itself on his shin. Salamander looked up and gazed at Doctor Reynolds, arching her back and wandering between his legs. An old syncopated ragtime played lightly on a distant-lit laptop. Hungry, Doctor Reynolds shoved a carved piece of dark meat into his mouth and chewed, his teeth tearing the warm fleshy bits. He swallowed greedily. He tore off a wing, and hastily bit into it, his hunger increasing with the bites he took. The warmth of the meat and the soft texture of the fattened chicken lodged itself in his teeth and on the roof of his mouth. Suddenly, he felt something catch in his throat. He tried to gasp. His jaw opened and a hissing sound passed through him. Salamander purred. As Doctor Reynolds struggled to reach air with his mouth thrashing open and his throat gaping and gurgling, he could still feel the seconds ticking away, drawn out by the sound of an old clock he kept in his dining room. Doctor Reynolds tried to stand up but knocked over his own chair and in his frenzy, nearly fell. Running to the phone, he suddenly felt something ache in his chest. The pain seared from his chest straight to his brain. He still couldn't breathe while his body choked on itself, but he could still remember the smells of the basil oils of the chicken and hear that old ragtime playing in the background. Salamander was looked at him, purring. Then it was dark.

* * * * *

"I want to know the whereabouts of Doctor Sparrow immediately." Duane was sitting in the dark of his dining room and calling the Controller. No one was home again. His wife had disappeared earlier that night without giving him a hint at when she'd be back, and he found that he was indifferent to her absence just as he had been to her presence.

"Doctor Sparrow took a leave for personal reasons and will be back shortly. Her whereabouts are confidential," the voice replied.

"I sit on this goddamn Board!" he screamed into the phone. "I have the right to know where my staff is. There should be a record, where is her record?!"

"As I've said already, Technical Project Leaders for this were given special allowances by David Smith written into their contracts prior to his passing away. This, we can't do anything about. I'm sorry. Doctor Sparrow will be back within the next week. She posted that in her calendar, and our tracker shows that she is still in the country, though...it looks like...like...we're not sure exactly where." The voice was calm.

Duane hung up and threw his phone across the room. It lay there, still in one piece. Just thirty minutes ago, he had received a call confirming the death of Doctor Reynolds. Now, he's missing his other head scientist. David Smith was definitely still dead the last time Duane checked, and Henry was nowhere to be found.

Duane weighed the facts: How could he get access to the controls for the Project when the process operated on genetic coding of two individuals who are now dead and two who are missing? "At least I know now," Duane said aloud. That much he was able to pump out of the good

332

doctor before his death. What did Duane know about the biophysics behind this? It was inconsequential. And he could care even less about the philosophy. "David, I'm not concerned about the novelty of the idea. I want to know whether it can be commercialized, whether this crazy thing can actually be put to use for....*some people*. Is it a valuable – no, it is a feasible – business venture?" he had said when David Smith brought up the hypothetical those years ago.

"You're telling me selling immortality doesn't sound valuable to you? I'd say the entire thing has been the quixotic *Holy Grail* of science. Wouldn't you think?" David Smith had asked. To David Smith, the entire purpose of scientific investigation was for mankind, the actor and the primum movens, to discover the structure of nature and manipulate it. That was what technology had always done, and it was what he believed technology should constantly strive to do. Of course, at the end of the search – the top of the mountain of knowledge – lay immortality. Medicine, both ancient and modern, was constantly working to stand high on the history of disease, genetic disposition, decay, death, petty, *petty* death. Even the poets spoke of it. But was the top of the mountain really a place where one could stand, or was it merely a mirage? David Smith did not truly believe he, or anyone else during his generation on earth for that matter, could actually solve what had eluded scientists for millennia. Instead, he focused on being a magician and in that way, mastered the elaborate use of smoke with a sigh, *"amor fati"*. Duane remembered that smile David had when he answered, the condescending, slow sly smile that inched slowly across his face as if he had figured out everything so far before anyone else did.

"Okay, then, I don't believe you that it's feasible. No one lives forever." He had replied. He had always been tired of David's word games.

"Well, Duane, it's because it's not really forever...it's a loop. An infinite loop..." David Smith had replied and picked up a trade magazine, flipping the pages. "Zarathustra, Schrodinger, Gibbs..."

Suddenly, putting the magazine down and staring at Duane, David Smith had smiled and replied, "I always wondered what the relationship was between entropy and infinite loops would be."

Before he had finished, Duane had grumbled, "That's not why I was put on this project." He crossed his arms, and stamped his foot onto the ground. "I don't need to understand the difference between your infinite loop, the entropic systems or whatever. I was put on it to manage the finances, and that's exactly what I'm doing...and once again, I'm asking you if you think this is feasible." At this, David had only smiled. That had been years ago, back when Duane's head full of hair and color. He had invested his entire career on this, and as he stood in his room looking at the empty ceiling, he felt a frustrating anger rise in him. It was still not complete.

Still, though, looking at the ceiling, Duane had wanted his life back in the stillness of the room as he felt his anger rise and then lower. Was this the only way? Some system, some process he barely understood, the billions invested into it...but, oh, how he wanted to be young again, to feel energized again. The possibilities had inched their ways into his mind and then just as quickly as they came, they had left him as he aged. All of those *first times* had led him into some deluded cave of optimism, every attachment, every sensation that eluded to what *could be* if there were more, gave into something that was endless and always resulted in disappointment: from a kiss to divorce, from an income to fear of losing the income, from experience to aging. Could this solve all those things? For a second, Duane saw his younger self, and in one swift movement, smiled.

It was too late for Doctor Reynolds. "Damn bastard," Duane muttered. "Never thought he'd go so quickly."...

CHAPTER 4

Artifact

…Henry wiped the last bowl dry and set it down. The bowl's patterned design was worn and chipped along the edges. How long had he been here, escaping from the Company and the city itself? He no longer kept track of the days. A part of him was relieved as he assumed the identity of someone else and shed his responsibilities. Another part of him felt guilty: what nightmares did he leave, and what nightmares did those he cared about take on in his absence?

"I'll just be here a few more days or a week at most," Henry reassured himself, "Until I can decide on a plan to return. Then I'll find a way to reach out for help. I'm sure they're looking for me…". Were they? After hearing his own words, he began to question them. He wasn't sure. He wasn't sure he was even safe at the Company for perhaps the lunatic flying the helicopter was no lunatic, and it had all been part of the elaborate plot he was on the precipice of unraveling. Yet looking around him, his new home had an odd yet familiar feeling about it. It was like no other place he had ever been throughout his extensive travels, but he noted the inexplicable familiarity of the place. It was as if the town or city or community was frozen in time, lost as the rest of the world had developed without it and preserving it as a museum of a near past. Henry felt like an artifact, and somehow, he felt safe.

He didn't think of these things until recently, as the fog began to lift from his head. His memories came back to him almost immediately, but it wasn't until a few days ago did he begin to question the nature of his current surroundings. For Henry, questioning was all he could muster to do. He lacked the clarity and energy to go beyond the feeling that something, *perhaps many things*, just weren't right.

It was in this new place without a destination or plan to leave that Henry suddenly wondered where Ariella was. Had she already begun her own travels? Have they begun a search for him and would they ever find this lost land? Has she stopped thinking of him? Suddenly, Henry wanted to talk to her. "Henry, don't think about it so much," he imagined her saying to him and then smiling. The image of her brought a splinter to him, and he swallowed air. As he stood there, with the bowl in his hand, he realized what had kept him from pulling the trigger on his past life – a ghostly thing that had begun to slowly disappear from haunting him even in his sleep – was a hollowness he still felt, which he couldn't locate until he said Ariella's name to himself aloud. "Ariella."

Except, Henry didn't know how he could take Ariella to this life with him. In the end, saying, "Ariella" and imagining the words she would use to speak back to him pitted him with loss. There were days when he thought of how he would describe this life to her. "The destitution," he would say later, "is surreal, but these people have shared everything with me...a stranger, they have welcomed me into their homes, and shared the little they had left...because they...somehow, they too know what suffering is like." He tried to search for the words so that she could experience every single moment he did. In the end, though, she was always far away, and by the time he finished wiping the bowl clean, he realized he had forgotten some distinct features of her face. Desperate, Henry tried to imagine the brown eyes, dark hair, the swift hands, and while he knew those were the colors and mannerisms that set themselves on her, he could not remember exactly how they all fit into place. In a panic, Henry realized that while he was remembering her for the first time, he was also beginning to forget.

336

Henry was laying still on his cot, listening to the footsteps and chatter of people milling around outside his window when he heard Jia Zheng calling him from outside. The sun was bright and waxy. Henry moved slowly, feeling his body ache from helping Jia re-patch his roof the day before, walked to the door, and said, "I'm coming." He left a stain of sweat on the cot behind him as he slowly opened the door.

"Henry," Jia Zheng said, standing at the doorway. "My mother has been really sick. A few weeks ago, she stopped walking like she used to, and in the past two days, she is barely leaving her bed. She is old. Life is hard these days. She will not live for much longer." He turned from Henry, looking at the floor instead.

"Is she in pain?" Henry managed. As he looked out to the nook adjacent the stove, he saw that the rest of the house was still asleep, the little mouths opening and closing, chewing the air, dreaming of food. Their bloated stomachs wedged between skinny arms drifted up and down, up and down. There was enough congee to feed them breakfast, but he wondered when they would actually be given fresh vegetables or meat.

"Yes. She has not gotten out of bed in five days now. She has stopped eating three days ago. She will not live much longer." Jia's mouth tightened as he blinked quickly, trying to hold back tears. "She has been speaking nonsense...nonsense...stories. But of course, she knows, she must know. She wanted to speak to you."

"Me?" Henry had never managed a full conversation with Jia Zheng's mother before. She had always rushed around him quickly, giving him instructions before tending to her chores, but they never had long talks and Henry had always been relieved for that. In fact, Henry never learned her formal name. Now, in the moments before her death, he felt a weight of importance fall on those last few words, and he was unprepared.

"Yes, Henry, she must be aware of her own situation, and I think before she passes, she wants to speak to you as she has spoken to each of us. She believes...it might sound strange...she believes you'll bring prosperity to us. You arrived here unexpectedly, surviving an accident yet looking so strong and healthy. And now as you recover, all your help with the work." Jia stopped speaking and began picking at his hands. He avoided Henry's gaze and instead looked over to his sleeping wife and son.

"Is she awake now?" Henry began running through the parting words he could say. He wanted to part with her to what he imaged as the comforting last things she would take to world of nothingness, calmness, a darkness of unconscious in a deep sleep. He had helped rebuild the house when the wind threatened to blow down the roof. He had spent time resurfacing the walls, and he helped bring in food, even if just a little, enough for an egg during a birthday. Would those things be enough?

"Yes, she has been awake for hours." Jia pointed to the darkened room farthest from the main room in the house, which had the kitchen and sleeping quarters for most the family.

"I'll be happy to speak to her, but is there anything you'd like me to say?" Henry asked again.

"Maybe, maybe she would like to hear the stories of where you are from. Perhaps it would give her hope that that is where she will go." With that, he led Henry to the only private room in the house, where she lay.

She began speaking immediately. "You seem a little stiff. Who are you? I've known you, but from so long ago...and how you have not aged, while I am an old woman." Henry shook his head. Who was she confusing him with?

"Ah...sorry...but... my name is Henry," Henry said slowly, unsure of whether he was better off playing along.

"Come closer to the bed. Hold my hand. Don't the peach blossoms smell wonderful? Smell them." Henry did as he was told and ostensibly sniffed in and smelled only the cold dust of morning. Jia Zheng's mother smiled at him, and holding his hand said, "So, will I be a great-grandmother before I die?"

Henry shook his head.

"What are you waiting for?"

He felt her fingers rubbing themselves against his hand. They were hard, cracked, her nails split and weathered. Henry's mouth was dry. He hadn't expected her to ask him questions, so he replied, "The right time."

She smiled and said, "Oh, right, young people. I forgot. You seem to think you have all the time in the world. Everything is the right or the wrong time. When you're my age, there will be no right or wrong time. There's just time, and it's never enough, and lately, I've been thinking that it's near *that* time. But young people don't like to think of that...the river...is it overflowed? It overflows, it destroys, and then it gives back what it takes. I remember running alongside it in the spring time, early mornings, running to catch the egrets that flew off. Those friends, those friends are gone. At that time, I could never imagine the end of time, and here I am, at the end..."

"Actually" – the words tumbled out of him, as if he had been holding everything in, and it was overflowing now as he sat trying to keep the last of his thoughts together – "I've been thinking a lot of dying."

"Have you? And what do you think about it?" She barely seemed surprised. So he shared.

"I'm not really sure other than, I suppose those last minutes, everything important would be clear. That's what I always thought. That's what I've wanted. I've wanted a peacefulness, a quietness from this. I feel as if I have been living in two worlds, both illogical, and I keep hoping...I keep hoping that in those last moments, I can see those worlds converge, I can understand at least a bit. Is it making sense?"

To his surprise, she replied: "You know, you're not far off. There's a lot of things that peel away when the last moments come clear. You're right about that. Good work. In the end, I think my husband was with me for so long. Years ago...longer than you can remember...he gave me a gift before he died. He told me of a dream he had. He was so sick then, but he told me that he dreamed that he was out for a walk along the pomegranate groves, and suddenly, he ran into the most beautiful meadow. My husband wasn't even walking then. When he told me that, I told that story to my own mother. It was she who said that he was ready to die. Oh, I was so angry at her, child. I wouldn't speak to anyone after that. I told her angrily – which isn't something that you were allowed to do to parents during my time – that the entirety of life as I saw it was making one attachment after another only so they could be ripped away, and we who are left here go mad with loss. And he died. The very next week. Then years later, as she was dying, she told me to stop being angry. Now, when it's my turn, it feels different being on the other end of it. I have a memory...I remember as a child, we ran, collecting the pomegranates that fell to the ground, and during pomegranate harvest season, we would collect basket after basket of them, those red, ripe things bursting onto our clothes and finger nails. They painted our finger nails bright." She paused and looked at him.

"I don't know if I understand," he replied.

"Of course. Well, sometimes, even those who are dying seem to think that they're still part of this world. They're not ready, and they're hanging on. People who are fulfilled don't want to live forever. You wouldn't think that, now would you? I used to think that if I loved my life, I'd want to live forever, but that's not true. I've slowly lost my parents, my sister and brother, my friends. And I'm ready to go," she continued.

"Are you frightened?" he asked.

"This is...this," she said, "is a temporary transition. Think of those stretches of time before you were born. That wasn't so bad, now, was it? Here is the secret. Come closer now. No, no...closer, you're still too far away. Yes, now that's better." She stretched her head from the bed and whispered, "I'm ready to start my real life now." Her grey-brown eyes fixated on him. "There are intuitions that are more real than facts." She gripped his hand. *Memory: the process of encoding, storing, and retrieving information acquired by the five senses from the physical world, processed in the mind through the imagination, connected to other pockets of memory.*

"Can you give me a hint then, on what those are?" Henry asked. *Memory: the piecemeal bits of information strung together through time – moving along in one direction – encoding, Experience.*

She waited a second, closed her eyes, and said, "Turn the key from your own prison and leave yourself by entering the mind of another. I remember," she drifted, "one summer it was so hot. The sun had beat down on us, so that we walked slowly, our skin turned to leather from the summer. We had watermelon down by the water. The water banks were low, and the river moved slowly, like us in the heat. We jumped in after eating our watermelon, the wet stickiness washing off in the cool, yellow water. I can remember the steam rising, and our feet made prints on the shores." *Identity is the analytics of experience vis-à-vis memory through time (Moving backwards - selective; moving forward - inevitable).*

"What a memory," Henry said. "Was it long ago?" The light paled through the house, casting shadows which would play in his mind years later when he could no longer place the feeling to a distinct place in time.

"Yes, so many years ago, I cannot even remember who I was with. Just the sticky watermelon and the cold water against my dried skin," she replied. Her mind searched. It searched along the crevices of horror and madness, pain and grief, and then suddenly seeing the door, her mind walked to the door and turned the knob, opening it slightly. Yes, yes it was there. It had always been there.

"Do you think those things you did in the past...mistakes, any mistakes, those things were forgotten?" he asked. "Surely," Henry found himself saying, "But enough has been done." Yes, he thought, the vast stretches of wasted moments spread out in front of him. He thought of Ariella's voice and realized he had already forgotten its sound. "How do I ask for forgiveness?"

She paused a moment. Then she began with the door fully open, "If you've come this far, my guess is that you've already been forgiven. *But give, do not forget to give.* If you allow yourself to be your environment, to be those things around you, you will understand how those things fit...those millions of things, swarming in its own directions, those tiny pieces of parts of all things move in one way. Of course, of course...you are looking into the past still since that is what you left. Be at peace. The past and the future have no bearing on your own peace." She smiled gently. Of course she knew him. She had known him when he first arrived, and she had kept the secret to herself, hidden in age and the constant maiming of activity: it was all for show of her true consciousness. She could not let them know that she had figured it out.

"I have a lot of work ahead of me, then." He said. His words blurred to her.

Then, she began: "When have you been afraid of work? I remember now. I know you now. You go by Wei. Coming here from that small village of yours, carrying the stories you have. You are brave, don't you see? Do you remember the stories you told in the night to put little Lan Lan asleep? At first, I thought you were making them up, but I think you have just forgotten their truth...the story of how you lay on the rock and you looked at the stars. Control your moving heart. Let it be still. Untie the ropes to the boat and let the water take you back." She closed her eyes, and she weeped. Then she began again with her eyes closed and still weeping, "I have one thing I need you to do for me. Have a great burial for me along the banks of the river. We need a reminder of the life it has cradled, give it some encouragement. I'd like to go home now, Wei An Jing. You'll know the way. Take me there." She opened her eyes and did not speak more. Looking away from him – at some distant place in her mind, some distant laughter, distant running along the river bank chasing the egrets and walking through pomegranate groves – she sighed, the corners of her mouth tugging into a smile with crooked teeth and old brown gums.

Henry did not understand everything she had spoken of, and he was convinced that parts of it were mixed with a past he knew little of. Yet the words struck him deeply. Without fear and softly, Henry whispered to her as she turned from him, pulling the blanket closer to her neck to cover her body and keep her warm: "Though I may not believe in the order of the universe, yet I love the sticky little leaves as they open in spring...I want to live, and I do live, despite logic.[6]" Even he was not ready for what he would say, and as those words left his mouth, he felt as if he had been taken over by a different spirit, a different mind which chose a path for him. In that instance, he knew he had to return.

Jia Zheng's mother died later that evening. Even the great Huang He stood still as the woman exhaled her last breath. Henry passed her wish to Jia Zheng, who, between tears nodded and promised to grant it.

Henry sat there with her body in silence. He thought for a very long time of her words and of his own, and then finally, of his determination to leave his temporary safety.

Henry sat very still. The sat so still the sounds of activity outside the house – the clinking of dishes, the discussion of huddled old women, the shuffling of feet – disappeared into one big monotone of silence. He sat

---

[6] Fyodor Dostoevsky, *The Brothers Karamazov*, quote by Ivan Karamazov

so still he forgot where he was, or what time it was, or what time period he had come from. He forgot about Duane and Howard; his father and Ariella; Coin Eyes and Jia Zheng. Henry sat so still he felt he was beginning to lose himself, first his fingers, then his toes, then his head and neck, until he was nothing but the silence around him. Then, one by one, it was as if all the pieces, all three thousand of them, tossed and scrambled on the floor, came together again from beginning to end. The entire vision of it moved and was still all at once. The streams of color danced, and he could see *time* – wasted, sad, and eroding. The unsaid history, the untold, unheard suffering and passing of hearts and tears danced and sang, liberated and free. Time was just part of that dream, a made up fabric that confirmed a prison, split across two worlds…

CHAPTER 5

Burying Fallen Flowers

...Henry walked past a man who lay on the street and reached out whimpering with long cracked and yellow fingernails, "Help, for the poor..." the man said. Henry searched his bag and found an extra steamed bun, a guilty feeling passing over him for taking Jia Zheng's offering, which Henry then placed on the man's hand and walked away. The stranger would not live, and where his body would be carried, whether it would stay baked in the heat or be hidden away or buried nameless was unknown. All that would be left in a few months' time would be the white of his bones. The man opened and closed his mouth repeated, sucking in the air and chewing invisible clouds as if it were food.

After the first week of mourning ceremonies, Henry Smith had explained to Jia Zheng and his family, "I understand something I did not know before. I know where I came from, and now, I have to go back. I don't even know if I can explain it fully, but I will always be grateful for what I've learned here. You have given me more than I can ever return, and perhaps, somehow, somehow, we'll meet again. Stranger things have happened. I will leave you everything I own, everything in my pockets, and if somewhere on this journey back I can send for help to you, I will. I know it now. I know where I came from. I know where I have to go. I know the place, for the first time."

"Follow the Huang He due west," Jia Zheng had told him, "You will, or you should recognize the village of Red Flowers. It would be two to three days' travel if you moved efficiently." Henry set out along the river quickly, but as the morning passed into afternoon, the heat from the walking settled into his body. He took off his shirt and walked with his trouser legs folded up, letting the sweat run down his back and chest.

Henry stopped to turn around and look down the road. Sighing, he stepped to the river, took off his shoes, and stood there for a long time. Down the road he just came, two people were now dead, Jia Zheng's mother and the nameless man, whose lunch was now dropping from the mouth and into the esophagus and stomach as he slowly died. Who would remember them?

* * * * *

That night, after a long, wearisome walk along the river, Henry decided to sleep beneath a large, dried walnut tree. Within minutes of lying down, he was fast asleep.

Sometime in the middle of the night, when the cicadas lulled into a quieter song and the cool winds swept the tree branches into conversation, Henry awoke in a panic. He looked around him and stumbled into standing. There, next to where had just laid was another man, peacefully curled in fetal position and cloaked in red. The man was small, bald, and had nearly pointed ears. Then as if aware of Henry's wakefulness, the man opened his eyes. "Wei An Jing, ahh, you are returning. It's true." The cicadas stormed loudly around them, as if excited by the new movement.

"Who are you?" Henry asked.

"Oh, you don't remember? Perhaps not. You have been traveling very far, and now you are returning. I'm the monk from the South Western mountains, we've met before...and perhaps more than once, but one

346

stops keeping track of these things. How has your journey been?" The small, bald man asked. Henry cowered. He could not remember so he shook his head. The monk smiled and said, "There is someone who does know, who can explain. But first, sit down and close your eyes, go to sleep, relax, dream and drift…"

Sometime later, Henry heard a voice. "Hello, Henry," a woman said to him.

Henry rubbed his eyes, and opened them. In front of him was a woman he was sure he had seen before, but before he could fully awake, she said, "My name is Nancy Sparrow," she said again, "Do you recognize me?"

"Yes," he replied as he blinked again. There she was, the woman in a grey suit with dark eyes, dark complexion, her hair pulled back in a bun with fierce white streaks. He had seen her around the Company. Yes, she was a scientist. She had worked, worked, does work for his father. "Yes," he repeated, hearing his voice confirmed his wakefulness.

"Where are you going Henry?" She asked. Her voice was calm, as if she had expected to find him all along in this odd place, where he was sure no one from that part of his life could find.

"Back to the village. Wei An Jing's village. It's where he came from, where I'm supposed to be. I need to go there to understand," Henry said.

"You won't find the village," Nancy interrupted. "It's gone, I'm afraid. I'm sorry." She looked down at her feet, as if she was not prepared to be the messenger of the news he had already begun to suspect. He was not where he thought he was. No, *correction*: he was not in the time period he thought he was. Nineteen-Sixty-One. He mouthed the numbers. Then he mouthed them again, slightly differently: *Yi-Jiu-Liu-Yi*. Two different sounds, same meaning. Yes, it made sense.

"I stayed with a true revolutionary, didn't I?" Henry asked. Jia Zheng had been a true believer: he was born into a wealthy family who had owned land, yet his family willingly provided for the farmers who lived on the land. In 1948, as still a boy and barely a man, he had given everything up to follow the Revolution and fight for his motherland. Now, as a retired military man, Jia Zheng settled back with his family, giving up the land they had owned.

"I'm not sure where you were or how you landed, Henry. The others from the village, they died...Henry...I didn't want to be the one to tell you. Starvation. There was the only person, who survived after leaving in 1961. Historically this village disappeared, and from the only records available, now – in the future, there will be one record available – one boy from the village appeared to have left: Wei An Jing. It's not my place to explain everything, so I've brought what you've been searching for." She handed over a soft, brown briefcase that was sealed tightly and locked. "There's a hard drive in there with all the files and recordings."

"Is she real?" Henry asked suddenly, his eyes widening.

"Who is this she?" Nancy appeared uncertain.

"The woman," Henry replied, "the woman whose face I see at night...her name...what is her name... Is she real? Whose world she belong to?"

"Where did you last leave her?" Nancy Sparrow asked.

"I left her after I went into the helicopter with the Company, and then I arrived...no, I saw the man with the coin eyes, the helicopter pilot...Jared. Yes, Jared," Henry mumbled.

"Yes, she is real. That is real, Henry." Nancy Sparrow handed her briefcase to Henry Smith and continued, "Along with the letter which you signed for Jared to fly the helicopter, against the wills of the Board and Duane, are some audio records on the computer I just handed to you that are...well...very valuable. Your father left them for you. I took them before I left the Company."

"You left? How did you get here?"

"I'm a messenger, Henry. I've defected. Well, defected from the Process I helped build and the Company that has supported me as a scientist. It was my choice. Stop looking so confused and horrified. You'll remember again.

"Stranger things have happened. Time is not so different than the distance from one place to another. You know that. But I meant to deliver these records for you, and I was able to transport myself before my defection is on official Company records and I lose access to the Process architecture." Nancy Sparrow looked at Henry, and without a word, took his hand and led him to another place unfamiliar to him. They walked in the woods beside one another with Henry clutching the briefcase, while Nancy gave Henry the information she had acquired over the years, speaking quickly.

"Remember one last thing," she said after explaining the details of the Project and her life's work, "if you choose to end it, and trust me, it's your choice – I've already made mine –it's a two part termination. You need the termination code, and then you need to make sure all the Keys have exited the Process. You'll have access to use the termination code given your status in the Company. How you exit the Process is up to you.

"Henry," Nancy suddenly changed the topic, "I need to leave now. I cannot stay here in this limbo for very long...I don't belong here."

"And this will be the last time I see you?" Henry asked her. He felt safe with her. He felt like she understood him and what was happening to him. Most importantly, she supported him in finding his memory about the Process, a project which was just coming back to his memory after meeting Jia Zheng. Nancy Sparrow had appeared seemingly out of nowhere, and yet it all made sense that she was there, even though he couldn't remember why it made sense. Now she was leaving again, and he was afraid it would all topple over itself as it had done.

"Not the last time, but for a while. It's not safe for me, either. I need to return to the Company." She smiled for the first time. She looked a lot younger than she first appeared, Henry thought. "Henry, I wish you peace." With that, she turned and began walking along the dead leaves in the wooded forest. He stood there and watched as she disappeared amongst the different shades of green and brown. He would return, he said silently to himself. He would return to time which moved forward, and he would search for an ending in this.

* * * * *

Nancy Sparrow wasn't sure how long she walked. As she heard her own footsteps through the woods, she noticed the sounds of another's. Turning, she searched for a person. It was all clear, but she could still sense something else. The Sybil of Cumae appeared through the branches like an apparition and said, "Nancy, this isn't how you imagined everything ending with your work, is it?"

"It feels anticlimactic. He's the last key that's left. I wonder if he knows his own exit from the Process, and this whole thing has driven him to insanity far enough. I hope he does what I've tried to encourage him to do," Nancy and the Sibyl walked together for a long time until they reached a clearing in the woods. There, Nancy spotted a doe eating clovers. The doe glanced up at her, and undisturbed by her presence, continued to its clovers. Everything was quiet. Suddenly, a flock of pheasants flew from the meadow into the wooded patch just north of it. The sounds of their wings beat against the warm air. Nancy looked at their tails, noting the spread of green and red. Then suddenly the fabric of the air itself quivered, and moved, the objects in them distorting like the waves hitting a beach. "Well, I suppose the choice is his. I've made mine. Sybil, are you ready?"

"I have been for longer than you can imagine." The Sybil replied. She and Nancy walked into the meadow, and as they did so, the clouds began to gather and lower. The women found themselves immersed in the clouded fog, and their bodies slowly became shadows. A moment later, they were gone. The clouds parted again, the doe walked slowly into the woods, and from far away, the calling of a blackbird could be heard.

* * * * *

Miles and years away, Ariella looked up suddenly at the sky. She felt drops of rain, but she could see the sun. She stood there in the woods, alone, and suddenly she smelled the musty leaves beneath her. Ariella stood on a bed of old leaves, and as she looked down, she saw small pine trees, breaking through the forest floor, fighting for sun. She crouched down and touched one. Then she looked up and saw that the sun was reflecting fractals off the forest.

* * * * *

<David Smith's recordings part 1>:

<Damaged recording>

<At 120 seconds rolling time>
...It took me many years to find out what it meant to actually have that, and I don't think I actually understood until I was nearing those final moments, for the last time, when I asked my dear friend for it. Yes, Henry, or someone else - whoever has access to these tapes - you may judge me but I did begin the Process. I allowed myself to be regenerated in that way for ten years, and it was the worst decision I had ever made. We had an idea that it would extend life, but how and where the life would go, the consciousness, the little bead of our minds which carries our being from one state to another in one piece of discrete time, we did not know. I did not expect to be here. The heat. The absolute heat.

The devastation, and to be recirculated, from place to place without knowing until now.

To be alive like that, I felt that I was becoming confused with reality and dreams, confused with insanity and reality. Those things are separated by a very thin border, and we often cross into those borders in our real-time life. But that is why we need those transcendental things. Why *it is* so important, in those final moments.

There are gaps which people had forgotten, they were the only places we were able to get to in the Process. Of course, you can imagine that is not always the most pleasant experience. I'm sorry if you have traveled to somewhere unpleasant, Henry. It was not my choice...I had no control over where we would land...

...I'm sorry you were chosen as an experiment, if that's how you felt. Or feel. I imagine it must be...

<Damaged recording>

It took me several iterations to understand and catalogue the full Process. Of course I had a large team behind me, many of whom you would now know. Doctor Reynolds and Sparrow were key personnel whose trust I will always value. True friends. Doctor Reynolds recommended I record myself and save it for you if you were to begin the Process...

<Damaged recording>

...began as a young child. I could not say no to you when you asked me, even though it was against Larry's wishes. Forgive me if I should have stepped in with greater, with greater authority over your own decision.

<End at 600 seconds rolling time>

352

\<David Smith's recordings part 2\>:

Is the tape on? Doctor Reynolds can you alter the microphone a little? It sounds scratched. Yes, yes...that's better. Good. I think the signal looks clear now.

Henry, you are perhaps the greatest love I have ever known. My love for you comes from the small part of me that wishes I were more like you, or maybe in that conceited manner of older people, in the ways I see myself in you. You were always a sensitive boy.

Yes, Doctor Reynolds you are smiling through the glass there.

Henry, I remember you used to cry a lot, and then one day, you stopped crying, and I feared you had become like me. I rerun that memory over and over again, like a mini Process from my own brain.

So my excuse for beginning my Process in the end was that I knew I had wasted Henry's childhood with my own ambitions, and an old man can dream to be close to his son again, can't he? Yes, I wanted to extend those years. Those winters I spent time with him, preparing him to succeed me, I was reaching out to him the only way I knew how. But even though I could extend my life, I couldn't reverse time. No, that's not how it worked. Time had already passed, those moments gone, floating around somewhere in history and transcribed by memory. Oh, and if you had the memories that I did, you'd know why I would want more time to set my lands in order, settle my properties.

I asked Doctor Reynolds to stop it for me after the first two cycles. I returned to unknown lands in an unknown time, and while my life extended itself, I returned to nightmares.

I don't know how much Duane knows. I'm not sure if someone's told him by the time these tapes are ever heard by another human. Duane was my closest business confidant. But as much as I had collaborated

353

with Duane in our business partnerships, since the beginning of the Project and this Process, I knew he viewed it differently. He was an old man, like me. I knew he was full of regrets, like me. If we were given another chance, we'd sail the high seas and discover the mountains and live like we never lived before: we would find our loved ones and hold them close. But we couldn't, and we knew it.

Time seems to dilate in these last moments. Sanity seems temperamental. If you allow yourself to let go of your mental barriers, you'll find all kinds of interesting things...if I were given a second life, I'd try again, as an old man this time.

<David Smith's recordings part 3>:

How could we end this Process for ourselves? This is just a trial run - the few of us, three of us to be exact, the Keys, as I called it. We are given that ultimate choice. To be here or there. To end it and let ourselves go into the oblivion of death or to continue to cheat time. I have begun the process for ten years now, and Doctor Reynolds has measured that my body's internal clock somehow thinks only ten days have gone by. It's measurable, Henry! Do you know what this means for our science?

...I digress. Doctor Reynolds, have you given me the right medication? I cannot sleep. I have not slept. The dreams. Is this a dream? Can you confirm? I'd like you to recite my serial number....I was born on April 9th...Doctor Reynolds? Doctor?

<David Smith's recordings part 9, sections 2-8 are lost or destroyed, their whereabouts unknown>

Henry, if you get this...you must do something very difficult. I understand it now. End this. No one person can inherit it. They must be inherited by an entire generation, the responsibility spread across the conscience of those systems that have made decisions as a group, otherwise as a collective conscious, we are stuck in the same infinite loop. But a single person, my son, a single person cannot bear the burden...if I had the choice to live in the darkest moments over and over again, repeatedly surviving, I would choose to die instead.

Did it matter to the future anymore where the past was hidden? The names would be hidden. The places would be swept clean, and the bones would decompose into the ground. The trees that grew from it would sing songs of flowers in the spring and green shade in the summer, feeding on the death hidden deep beneath the ground for the next finite generation to keep forgetting.

I have begun...they do not know I am recording...they have taken control of this from me. They don't think I am *well* enough to make these decisions, but if you get this make sure it is ended. There are two other keys...find them and make sure they know to destroy this. Doctor Reynolds, I do not know who is heading the Project now. It may have reached someone else. But if the Keys – and this includes you – decide the Process needs to end, it can be done. I'm not sure even how it will all end...where you will be, in one time or another time, or split between both...

CHAPTER 6

Here and Now or There and Later

August 27, 2020. Right after Nancy found Henry in the Process, Ariella and I sat eating lunch together near the construction of a new dam right outside of the village. We had no idea where Henry Smith was, nor had we any idea of what he was going through. Instead, we had picked up a large bag of bao zi from the street vendor outside their empty dormitory, which sat on the east corner of the university. Like the day before, the air was sticky and sun hazed. Ariella requested to be outdoors after a long morning in the stacks of archives. So we climbed to the rocky overview of the irrigation project, looking out on the dusty activity. "Perhaps," I began, "going back is the right thing for you. You haven't stopped thinking of him for a moment. Or at least it seems that way." I felt my own voice tighten when I said it. I'm not sure why. I didn't feel jealous of the man I had never met, but somehow, I couldn't shake his presence off from our trip. I felt as if he was always with us, walking as a shadow behind her, dragging his feet at each step.

"I feel like I had lost him once already, and now, I've lost him again. It's like two deaths," she replied. She looked at me, and I could tell she was hiding something in her expression. Her lips quivered, and her eyes searched me for an answer I didn't have.

"He could be anywhere, and do you think it's your love for him that makes you think he's yours?" I asked pointedly, getting to the point that we had danced around for weeks.

Surprised she said, "I never told you I was in love with him." She turned from me and continued to gaze at the dam.

"Oh, well, it's fairly clear you are, and I'm probably the last person you want when it comes to advice on this. No one thinks this much about a person they're not in love with." I didn't look at her as I finished as I was as afraid of her expression as she was of my observations. I found in the past that people don't always respond well to the truth, and I wasn't very good at lying.

"But I haven't finished my research...I have so much work I haven't even cracked the surface of," Ariella said. I could tell she desperately wanted to change the subject. Explaining to me in minutes the years of complexity that had grown into her ideas of love and companionship was beyond the energy she had, and I understood that. I had not revealed much about myself either and so we both focused carefully on our bao zi, peeling away the outter layers and saving the savory meat inside for last.

Finally, I gave her the advice she had wanted to hear, what I had assumed she wanted from me. It came out of me begrudgingly. I did not want her to leave. "You're allowed to go home for a little for personal matters, especially emergencies. Go home, and see if you can connect with his family. It's understandable. You have a year on this project, and even if you left for a month, you can get a lot done later."

"And how are you so far?" She asked me instead, changing the subject.

It was done for her. Perhaps her mind was already made, or perhaps I hit a sensitivity that she wasn't ready to discuss. So I replied to her, hoping that changing the topic ease the tension I was beginning to feel. "I'm doing exactly what I came here to do." I went quiet. "I'll admit, and you shouldn't let this weigh in too much on your own schedule. I'll miss your company. In fact, it'll be scary to be alone here. I've enjoyed talking to you, and as different as our backgrounds and lifestyles are, we're not so different." I looked at her and grabbed another bao zi from the bag.

It was otherwise an ordinary day. And on that same day only a few generations ago, over five hundred villages from Henan's countryside died without a trace, nearly exactly where we sat. August thirty-first was the day Henry first learned to walk, and coincidentally, many years later, the day he learned he could extend his consciousness – not just his memory – back and forth in a fluid mask of time.

CHAPTER 7

Scientists in Lab Coats

A few days after listening to the recordings Nancy had brought, Henry's minutes had expanded themselves into what felt like hours. He understood, once again, the way the Company had split and spliced time, inserting one life into the pockets of other times, histories, experiences. Soon enough, what was the real time or which one really came first, became blurred. Time had stretched and squeezed itself as his understanding had wrapped logic and coherence into the experience. And just like that – looking at the veneer time – the seconds, minutes or hours meant nothing. In just a blink, he had returned both mentally and physically from some forgotten date in 1961 back to August 30, 2020.

In another blink, Henry woke up from a deep sleep, a sleep he had not had for as long as he could remember. Henry found he had somehow wandered, unconsciously, through the city of his father's Company – of his Company – had managed to crawl into his City bed in his City apartment and wake up to the sound of a car horn while he lay beneath the sheets in his glass apartment. Everything was as if it had always been. The gun remained in the pillowcase on top the safe with his father's medical files.

Walking out onto the busy city streets, Henry's heart leapt: he was back again.

* * * * *

August 30, 2020. The night wandered around him as Henry took off for the main building of the Company. Henry wanted to return to the Company hoping to understand the Process better. But, he wanted to do it alone, without the politics or influence of those who were already too committed to seeing it work.

He melted in with the people who walked briskly with and against his flow in traffic, noting little other than their shared goal: they had places to be, time was moving quickly, and things were always in the way. Closer and closer to the Company he walked. Henry found with each step, his palms began to clam up, his stomach began to dance, and he was forcing from his breath, "One, Two, Three…" to calm his nerves. *One, two, three…three, two, one.* Repeat and over again, stop, look up, yes – it is this way – repeat and step.

Before he knew it and just in this manner, Henry arrived at the entrance of main building. He scanned open the doors, relieved he had remembered his key card and identification.

* * * * *

Deep in one of corridors in the basement of the main building, Henry was lost: the detailed activities in the basement and even its physical locations were always confusing to him. Nancy had clearly said room GB0598, but he found himself wandering between hallways F and E and completely unaware of where GB could be. He knew he didn't have much time. It would only be a matter of minutes before the building cameras would register his face, and then every single person in the Company would know he was back.

Henry took another panicked look at the floor plans and realized that there were two levels in the basement. That made sense, the Process needed to be properly shielded away from other living organisms due to the various exposures. He rushed to the stairwell, afraid of alerting any systems that the elevators would have. Finally, after two flights of stairs, he arrived at the doorway for hallway GB. It was locked – not surprising given the sensitive nature of the experiments. Henry stood in front of the doorway and looked at the lock keypad: he could enter his own code, but there would be a record of his entry; or, he could enter someone else's. Had Nancy forgotten to tell him about this? What could he enter? He deliberated and then suddenly, he punched in: 0108, his father's birthday. Nothing. He would get two more tries before the doors were locked for good on him and the alarms were alerted. He tried again: 5743, the last four digits of his father's social security number. Still, nothing. Henry ran his hand through his hair and thought of all the numbers his father could have possibly have used and felt deflated: it could be anything.

Then, a thought – or rather a memory – passed through Henry. Once when Henry was a child, David had taken him to the bank. The bank and required a security number, and David had said, "These things are so unsafe. You really need two-part authentication. In any case, never use your own personal information. Use someone else's. I always use my kids' birthdays." Of course. Henry typed in: 0411, his birthday. The door's entry light flashed green, and he pushed it open.

It was 4:32 am, and the building was empty other than the security guards.

The temperature dropped by a noticeable thirty degrees. Nancy had warned of this, and Henry put on his warmers in his gloves and turned on his flashlight. It was clear which room 0598 was.

Henry entered the quarantine room outside the actual lab, which was barely labeled to his surprise. Then, walking to the unmarked lab doors, Henry groaned in disappointment: there was a palm scanner to get inside the lab. Of course the Company used biometrics. He could only buy himself a few more minutes in the lab before security would be alerted.

Placing his palm on the scanner, and then swiping his key card, he saw a green light flash. Suddenly, his entire body was surrounded by the light for exactly ten seconds. The lock to the door clicked open. Henry turned the door and entered.

The inside of the lab looked like a mix of what he had seen of the inside of particle detectors in high energy physics projects and a highly sophisticated hospital, with wires connecting the hospital bed-like resting chairs to switchboards, which were connected to the large detectors. There were careful monitors for pulse, electrolyte levels, neuron activity levels, blood pressure and body temperature. Henry marveled at the work: he had no memory of seeing this in person before. Walking around the room, Henry noticed a stepladder in the corner of the lab that led to what looked like another level beneath the basement floors.

At this moment, he heard the door click open. Of course, he expected his own private viewing of the Project would come to end.

"Henry?" a man's voice asked. Henry looked up. It was Duane. "What the hell are you doing here? Can you imagine my surprise when security called me after they noticed someone had activated David Smith's code…and you of all people, you've been gone for weeks!"

"Duane," Henry replied, "I have things I need to clear up here. Why haven't you told me–"

"—No, Henry," Duane interrupted, "You've been dishonest with me. This entire time, you and your Father have failed to tell me…" and then looking at Henry's face Duane cut himself short and said instead, "it doesn't matter now. I know what you've been able to do, and I've made up my mind. The Process Chamber has been prepared, and I intend on seeing it for myself. I have my own technical support, like the way you and David did behind my back." With that, Duane walked over the stepladder and began descending into the Process Chamber.

Nancy's words flooded back to Henry: "There are three Keys". Of course, he had forgotten Duane hadn't been one of them, but if he began the Process...

...In five strides, Henry reached the ladder and grabbed Duane by his right hand, holding onto him. Duane clung onto the ladder with his other hand. It then occurred to Henry that it would take Duane longer undergo the initial stages of Process than it would for him to find the termination code and activate it.

Releasing Duane's hand, Henry fumbled for his pockets. He pulled out a little piece of paper which had the termination code that Nancy had given him.

"Duane," Henry said, "This isn't what you think it is. This isn't what you want."

Duane was exhausted. He had barely been able to hold onto Henry. Between heavy pants he replied: "Henry, you have gotten...everything...you've ever wanted. Don't...don't tell me what I want. You have...no idea...no idea. I know what you...and your father have done. I know what you've...huhhh...been doing the past years...huhhh... I know it...and I did something for him no one else could do. Not even you. Do you remember? Don't... tell me... what the rules are...me...as I'm sitting on the outside of all this conspiracy you've planned." He tightened his grip on the ladder.

"I know you've done a lot for my father. Trust me, this process doesn't work the way you want it to. I just realized we can end this. My father knew it, and he regretted beginning this nightmare..." and looking at Duane's horrified expression, "...hey, just trust me. Move on, Duane. Move on,"

At this, Duane hesitated as if to ask Henry a question. But then like a light that switches off, his face darkened and he continued down the ladder steps without a word.

"I know...what you're trying to do, Henry," Duane shouted with the remainder of his breath. "You're not so clever...Henry. Come back! You child...you're not your father. You're not a deceiving man. Do the right thing."

"It's a two part termination, shit! Shit!" Henry shouted. If Duane succeeded, a new Key would be created, and it would be even harder to have any control over the Process. Nancy had clearly said he – Henry Smith – was the last Key still activated.

Henry had minutes to turn off all sources of energy generation for both levels of the basement to prevent Duane from beginning the Process. *What could he do first?* – Henry thought. He needed time. He needed time to make his decision about the Process, and that would only be possible if he first prevented Duane from succeeding.

Henry recalled the emergency procedures to cut off energy generation from all R&D projects. His father had him repeat and recite. Floor 24 was where the main building switchboards were. There was a remote. Time moved forward, and Henry searched backward. There was a remote located in a place. Inching time, slowly, inched. No, there were two remotes, a main one and a backup. Minutes passed, and he couldn't remember where the main remote safe was located on Floor 24. He could barely remember the layout of Floor 24. *But the backup...the backup...the backup, of course,* Henry thought, *that was on this floor. It was in the basement where all the confidential projects were. There was a remote located in room GB000 in the safe.* Henry began running.

Running down the hall to room GB000, Henry swiped his key card and entered the door. The entire room looked like a library. Henry walked through the bookshelves until he found it. The safe sat at the bottom shelf of a large wooden bookcase in the back of the room. He recognized the books; they were the ones his father had kept at the

366

Company.   Across the top of the safe was a banner: FOR
EMERGENCY USE ONLY. He placed his hand on the palm scanner,
and the safe opened.

Henry retrieved the emergency remote, left the room, ran down the hall,
and found his way to the main basement terminal where he had left
Duane. Henry took the elevators to the 24th Floor. Once there, Henry
entered the switchboard room. He looked at the remote and without
hesitation clicked: "POWER ON/OFF". The building's lights flickered,
and he felt a tremendous tremor throughout his entire body as if he was
being electrically shocked. Then it was dark.

* * * * *

In the darkness, the silence of the building echoed back to Henry on
Floor 24. He realized he had fallen to the ground and fainted. He wasn't
sure how long he was unconscious, but he slowly picked himself up.
Once standing, Henry looked at a reflection of himself in the glass
window that was only illuminated by the lights from the other buildings
the city block. An apparition stared back at him: Henry was no longer the
person he had remembered. Something about him seemed weaker and
older.

Did he succeed in stopping Duane from entering the Process? His mind
weighed in on the possibilities of his failure, but his body was too
exhausted to move. Duane was still deep in the basement.

For a minute, Henry weighed the options in his head and deliberated. He
found it was difficult to focus on Duane. Instead, he thought about the
Process – about 1961, about Jia Zheng and his family, about Wei An Jing
and the famine, and his mind stopped at the meditation that brought him
back to the City to the time he belonged in. Jia Zheng's mother had said
in her last words to him: "Control your moving heart. Let it be still.
Untie the ropes to the boat and let the water take you back." Those
words triggered a memory in him that allowed him to realize the unreal

367

temporal experience he was in; it brought him back to the Process. And that was how Nancy Sparrow found him in 1961, wandering from a small city to a small village in the mind of a man – Wei An Jing – who was no longer alive in 2020. But what now? Now that he's recognized this scientific experience he's been in for years, possibly his entire life? He didn't know. Then he thought of the sacrifice Nancy Sparrow had made in visiting him.

Nancy Sparrow had made a decision to destroy her life's work. At the time, Henry couldn't understand why she was visiting him while he was in the Process, or how she was able to do it. Perhaps she was in the basement room, where he just was. Perhaps she had clambered down the cold chamber stepladder, looked one last time at the thing she had build, and then found a way to deliver a message to him through time through some mechanism she had managed to operate and create for the last time. He admired her for the decision she made.

In that moment Henry's mind wandered from Nancy to his father. His father was never able to do what Nancy had done – he barely took a moral stance on the Project until the very end. "He was too late," Henry said to himself, "The man took action too late. But he was just a man. Like me. Like anyone else."

Without another word, Henry exited the room and took the stairwell to the roof. On the rooftop of the still-darkened building, Henry found his way to the edge and peered over. The protective guardrail was only three feet high. The lights from the buildings around him made him feel small and unimportant, surrounded by a city that was alive and busy. He felt like a child again, staring at the stars, and he was enveloped by the feeling of mystery and excitement all around him. It was a city he loved; it was a life he loved. Yes, he loved it all. Henry never knew how much he loved it until that moment. He loved the warm stickiness the air left on his skin, the soft fabric that clung to him, the brief wind which blew the hair on his arms straight not from its strength but from its beauty: where did the wind come from? What else did the wind touch? Now, it was visiting him, and he was part of it all, the beautiful things that shook him to his core. That was the only thing he felt he knew standing there on the rooftop.

Taking control over his life, it was then that Henry jumped over the edge and into the night.

On his fall down, Henry, grappled with the man he saw with him, as if he were actively grappling another. And looking closely at the other, he saw, horrified, that it was him. Twins. Falling together as they always had. The two were entwined – the man and his twin, like two cavities of the same heart – fighting itself – tearing itself apart – until it realized it was one singular thing. It was then that Henry let go, and he closed his eyes as he fell, feeling that 'yes his moment on the roof was real'. He was alive again. Yes, he was alive. The air flushed by him, and the warm sky embraced him.

Falling down, Henry smiled and found the moon that shined above him. While he saw the blanket of the night sky, he smelled his mother and heard his sister, he thought of his adolescent days with Howard and wondered where his friend was tonight. Then finally, of course, he thought of Ariella. Her face seemed to blur from him, and for an instance, he couldn't remember what she looked like, but he know she would have been proud of him. He heard her voice saying, "You did it. A leap of conviction."

It was dark out, but Henry felt that all the lights of the buildings around him became so clear and bright, giving off an energy that he had never felt before tonight. He opened his arms. What would he have become without this?

* * * * *

Slowly, he picked himself up and descended into the basement laboratory, GA005, past the high security and into the white corridor that had

369

appeared to him in so many rooms. He looked at his watch. It was morning already. There, he entered a room that had a label that he recognized: a serial number for his name. He opened the door, and there at the desk across the room, was a small, bald man in a lab coat. He recognized this man, but he couldn't remember from where or when. The man looked up from his scribbling in a notebook and said nonchalantly, "This is unexpected, Henry. You're not due for an appointment for some time."

"I'm not here for the usual," Henry replied softly with a step forward. Then raising his voice, "I'm here to terminate it. It was written in his will I could come here and choose this. I have the termination code in my pocket." Henry's hands fumbled into his pocket and turned over the piece of paper he had written Nancy's instructions on.

"Is it that time already, Henry? Have you had enough?" The man asked, his voice even and unwavering.

"Do you understand? Did you know we would be taken to those lost places? Did you know where those places were or are?" Henry replied searching for some flicker of expression in the bald man's face.

It was then that the man hesitated and furrowed his eyebrows. He dropped the pen on his desk and put his fingers to the bridge of his nose and rubbed them. Then he looked up at Henry with red eyes, "I would never be able to understand that, Henry," and sighing, "But judging from how your father killed himself and Jared, your bodyguard you tried to set up to kill you, and now how you're coming here in such a rush…well I imagine this did not go how we had planned. With your father and Jared gone, you are the last Key. The decision is yours, as you know."

"Are you disappointed the experience factor was so negative for this iteration of the Project?"

"Oh no, Henry, it's neither disappointing nor assuring. It just is. But perhaps, perhaps...perhaps the human brain is not meant to go through so much experience...we may need to work on a few things. The neuro-pathways may just be reacting in ways we don't understand enough at this point. Well, we've had a lot of loss in our own department, so I imagine the Project will be going through some *reconsiderations*— review of permits, financing discussions, and so on." The man got up from the desk and walked over to Henry. He barely came up to Henry's shoulder. It was then that Henry noticed the wrinkles on the corners of the bald man's eyes. Had they met before?

"But the history, those things that no one remembered...how could they have been so systemically cruel without ever remembering that they had done this?" Henry asked, looking closer at the man, searching for a placement in the familiarity of the bald man's face.

"Who are 'they', Henry?" The man said without moving.

"Entire generations, governments, whoever writes history or erases it," Henry was speaking quickly. He wanted to ask the questions he could ask before they escaped him again as they had in the past. "The history returns, and a single person cannot bear that burden. It has to be shared, collective, out in the open across generations. Collective history has been working on having itself forgotten."

"It sounds like you had the most interesting journey, Henry. It will now come to an end. I just need you to sign this document. You were so close to doing this last time. Don't you remember? But you managed to talk yourself out of it. And yes, please use that termination code next to your signature." The bald man placed one hand in Henry's and shook it, giving Henry a light smile before walking back to his desk, retrieving an electronic notepad.

Henry shook his head and then placed the pen against the screen and signed it. The man motioned for Henry to follow him through a set of closed, glass doors. In the room on the other side was a single hospital bed that was connected to an indistinct computer station. Henry laid down on the hospital bed. Shortly after, the small bald man in the lab coat came over, strapped Henry down onto the table, pushed up his sleeve and injected him with an unmarked syringe.

"It'll only be a pinch, and I'll strap you down on the table. Yes, hold on, just a pinch…".

* * * * *

September 15, 2020. Early morning, Ariella arrived at Gate 32 while it was still dark out and her body still confused about the time. She moved through customs and baggage in a haze, flashed her passport with tired eyes, and found her way to the exit where the blaring taxis rushed her with a greeting: "Welcome back". Looking at the street, she saw a familiar face and held up her arm. Howard drove the Land Rover close and unlocked the doors, "Do you need help?" he asked, leaning toward the passenger window.

"No, it's not heavy," she replied. She hadn't washed her hair that week, and the humidity and dust clung onto her clothes across borders. Ariella paid no time to her own exhaustion and instead, hoisted her belongings into the back seat, stepped into the passenger seat, and gave him a quick hug, "Thanks for picking me up on such short notice," she said. "I got your email on the flight - you've found him?"

"Yes, he's at work. I don't know much else, but we'll head there first. Are you here for long? Before you leave again, I'd like to hear about your trip." His tone was different than she had last remembered. He seemed demurred and worried, and she noticed she was not the only one with bags under her eyes and unwashed hair.

She thought for a moment, and then replied, "Yes, of course. We've got lots to catch up on. I'll be here as long as I need, but I plan on going back…"

Before she could finish, he interrupted, "You should go back. We know he's safe now, and you shouldn't let this hold up what you're doing. It's important. I don't think it'll be good for you to keep dragging things out like this between here and there. It hurts me to see it…to see you so torn." He drove mechanically, looking out at the bridge in front of them leading to the center of the city.

Ariella looked at Howard's face. They had known one another for years, and yet she felt she was sitting across a different person, dragged out from hiding behind humor. As he sat beside her too exhausted to put on the show, she realized she had never truly understood Howard the way she thought she did. "Thank you. I wasn't, well, I wasn't planning on staying for long," She smiled and continued, "I've got the flight back booked already now that I know he's been found. You're right about it, though, I'm looking forward to going back. Strange since the work was so hard, but I'm actually more fulfilled than I've ever been…Anyway, have you got any good stories for me?"

With her words, the car pushed forward across a lit bridge, competing for light against the rising morning.

EPILOGUE

Storytelling

One morning, sometime after Henry's "return", Wei An Jing woke up with a strange feeling, and laying in bed without moving, he recounted a very vivid dream. He had not remembered dreaming for days, so quietly, he retold the scenes of the dream to himself. He feared that moving would chase the dream out of his memory as it often did when he woke up with the sensation of having traveled somewhere far in his sleep, and so finally, after he retold the story to himself twice, he got up, grabbed a pencil and small notebook and scribbled down what he had retold himself. In Wei An Jing's dream, a woman and a man were walking along the broken faces of concrete statues when they arrived at a small gravestone. The woman set her yellow roses down.

* * * * *

"So, in those last moments, did your father say anything? Was it ever recorded?" She asked the man as she straightened her back after bending down to set the roses on the stone.

The man waited a second, searching for those minutes. They came to him vividly, and he replied facing her: "No, he didn't. Not in the hospital during the last few times I saw him. In one of the very last visits, after speaking nonsensically about something, my father began to cry. I had never seen the man cry before, in all my years as his son...and so it was this experience that I felt was...almost this out of body experience. I didn't know what else to do. I couldn't even believe it was really happening. At the time, I didn't...trust my own senses or intuition anymore. So I just held his hand, and he held mine. We held hands like that for a long time. Longer than I can ever remember as a child."

They were silent for a while. Then, the woman said, "It's a deep loss. I can hear the sadness in your voice, but I feel like you shared something together in that last moment. He'll be with you forever."

Without a word, he slipped his hand into her warm hand. She looked at him, surprised for a moment, but without a word the proceeded to walk forward. He realized that he had changed in the past year. Nothing in the past had changed, but in that moment, he felt both that he could understand his past and feel wholly different.

Like this the man and the woman walked through the gravestones and the gardens, looking at the names of people who had lived and gone. Far away, a black bird called, and the clouds gathered to meet. Suddenly, there was a flash of thunder, and it began to rain. They walked slowly, looking at the inscriptions on the cemetery tombstones. The air was thick with the smell of mossy leaves and autumn flowers.

After Wei An Jing wrote this down frantically, he turned the page of his notebook and slowly began recording the next story he could muster to write. He began, stopped, wiped a tear from the corner of his eye and continued again. The piece flowed from the tip of his pen and onto the paper with great and slow agony, as if the thick ink itself did not want the words to be written.

A few hours later, he held the paper up against the light and silently mouthed the words to himself:

6, August, 1963. Qiu Hui - my Qiu Hui - my dearest love, the beauty of wind and

376

sunshine, whom I had promised to marry before I left, died on one winter morning in 1961 when I returned to the village. I had with me gifts from the city which I had saved pennies to buy.

My town lost over one fifth of its members by then. Hunger stole them off in the middle of the night and left us cold in the mornings, returning too late and therefore empty-handed to loved ones who have passed to a different journey, perhaps to a different world altogether. We do not speak of it there or even in the city. I write this timidly but I have no choice. Words on the paper relieve the words in my mind. My chest feels tight with the bounds of wondering what this life is other than growing attachment over years only to have to learn how to say goodbye. One by one, they stole off into the dark.

I often think about Qui Hui, my flower, the most beautiful thing to grace my life, and where she must be now, perhaps far away in the western mountains. I dreamed that I was a bird, and I visited her in the magical mountainside and brought to her each morning dew from the passing night. I will never forget...and I write my dreams in case she visits me in them and in case the morning air invades my mind with the forgetfulness that loses one's dreams at night

* * * * *

"That's the end then. Wei An Jing began to write about his experience during the Great Leap Forward," Peter said, then paused before continuing, "though every once in a while, he'd have vivid and inexplicable dreams about far-away lands and people he's never met. He also wrote those down." He looked Father Turner and said, "So, well, that's the journey's completion." Peter looked at Father Turner, waiting for a response.

Then, "That is quite something, Peter. I'll certainly challenge anyone who tries to convince me that time only moves in one direction from now on!" Father Turner said with a chuckle, rubbing his eyes, and adjusting his glasses again.

Peter shifted in his chair and exhaled. He spoke with his eyes closed: "I'm feeling okay. Hearing myself say it out aloud, it's such a fantastical account of everything...the people, the way they were tied together in this absolute madness is incredible, but it was, it is...so real. And re-telling it for the first time, I'm beginning to see things I hadn't before. I think beginning with the myth makes the most sense when telling this story, though. You know, the first story of the Wu Dang Mountains. Everything was just an iteration after that, like a string which connected all of the stories across time: the flower and the bird from the Land of Illusion; Qiu Hui and Wei An Jing; Henry and Ariella. I'm no scientist, but I think that's the fundamental idea behind the Process."

"I see. Interesting connection. But what do I take away from this story? Are you saying we're always doomed, then? Are we doomed by our history and this string that connects us to the future, where we eternally make the same, basic human mistakes?" Father Turner asked.

"Maybe, or maybe not. Henry Smith was able to finally leave the cycle. He discovered it by living through history and seeing it differently than it was presented – or forgotten – the first time around. And then he willed it from himself; he chose to leave it, and he chose to change himself. I believe Ariella did as well but in a different way, by looking deeply at history and seeing where the cracks were, or rather, where the cracks are. We'll never be able to ignore it. The past is something we have many chances to relive...but the future? I have no idea. I'm not sure we'll ever know where our place is in the larger picture of things – perhaps that's something we'll let the divine keep as a secret, so we have some mystery in our days." With that, Peter closed his eyes and smiled.

THE END

Acknowledgments:

This difficult and rewarding journey would not have been possible without the following:

Mom, Dad, Renda and the Ding family, whose stories helped frame the anchor of the novel.

Daniel, whose behind-the-scenes support kept me pushing through it during the most difficult periods.

Yao, whose art reminds me of our collective history. Thank you for helping the book feel real.

Juli, Morgan and Traci, whose "red pens" helped guide a pile of thoughts into the semblance of a story. I will always be grateful for your brave reads of those early versions.

Nat, who encouraged me to write about China.

George, Maryann, Lucia, Katie, Kate, Evan – whose support, reads, and feedback through various chapters were beacons to keep me honest.

Jeanne, for guiding me to think critically about difficult things.

www.ingramcontent.com/pod-product-compliance
Lightning Source LLC
Chambersburg PA
CBHW022244020726
47496CB00004B/1059